By Bill

By Bill

WILLIAM EDWARD BREEN

To order additional copies of this book, contact:
Xlibris Corporation
1-888-795-4274
www.Xlibris.com
Orders@Xlibris.com
25723

Chapter 1

"Now elected captain of next years football team will be Bill Breen." Said the football coach.

I went up to the mike at the fall sport banquet. I was a bit nervous, but when I heard the applause of the audience, I was calmed. I had said to myself right before I earned this honor, I didn't want to be captain. But for some reason I had controlled myself and I did receive this honor. Daryle was the other captain chosen.

I had started a job at an A & P supermarket a few weeks earlier. I had gone down to this A & P and had applied with all the other people from high school to the new A & P opening in Norwood. This was the A & P grand opening in Norwood. A lot of the guys on the work study – program, from the high school had applied also. This was right before the Thanksgiving break in my junior year of high school.

I had heard all the work-study people were being called down to the new A & P, setting up the store for the grand opening. I was not called, though. I went down the new A & P, with my friend, Timmy. Timmy was dating a girl I had dated, years earlier. We just went right in and blended in with all the other workers setting up shop. There was no order here, because all the shelves were being set up. Everyone had their own hours they kept themselves.

I was working with the manager of the Providence A & P, whom had come up to Norwood to help with the opening. I was moving some duralog firewood. I was carrying three of them. The manager from Providence said.

"Your aggressive. Go take a break."

These were the duralogs we were stacking together. I went on break next door and then came back to work.

Well the opening day was coming up, and the new manager of the store had everyone's name for the schedule for the first week. Timmy and I did not have our names on the opening schedule. I asked the manager.

"Our names are not on the schedule?"

The manager asked. "Who told you to come in here?"

I had been talking to folks whom had been called down. They said that a Charley Smith had called them down the store. Well I recalled this and I said to the manger.

"Charley Smith called me down."

The new manager put our names on the schedule and we were in business.

I can recall there was a girl with a German accent, whom would train the cashiers. As I told you Timmy was dating my ex girl friend. Her name was Paula. She was a cashier there. I still had thoughts for Paula while Timmy was dating her.

Well I can recall one night when I was waiting for a ride home. The Providence manager, whom told me to take a break, was outside also. He said to me.

"Whenever you need a favor, call me at the Providence A & P."

Years later I took this man up on this.

I can recall this time the Vietnam War was ending. All the troops were coming home. I was in an AP Advanced Placement American History course and our assignment each night was to read the front page of the paper. This was when I recall there was always 500 Vietcong killed each week. The Americans had around 250 killed. *AFTER* this we were pulling out and training the South Vietcong to defend themselves.

Well this was now when I received my first connection with the Ivy League College Brown University. I showed a friend of mine Scott, the logo from the letter I had received from Brown University. His sister had gone to Brown. Scott was very smart. We would kid around a lot in the AP History and also the AP Math.

Originally, the Brown University baseball coach looked at me, when I was playing baseball the year before. I received an interview from

Professor Hazelton in the engineering department at Brown. I went there and I had gotten a little nip of vodka before going there. I went by myself to Providence about, a 50 miles ride from my hometown of Norwood.

I went there and met Professor Hazelton and *HE* gave me a tour of the Engineering department. This Professor walked with a distinct curled in feet. I began to think this was one of those really Einstein professors. Also we went to see a car, which the to be engineers were creating from scratch. Making every single part.

I think he smelled the vodka on me. We went to a computer room and he asked me if I wanted to play Russian roulette on the computer. We played a little bit with the computer. I ended the interview by asking him.

"Would this be wise to take AP Chemistry next year?"

He replied. "I think so."

I was on the Math Team, with quite a lot of other to become, Ivy Leaguers. Scott went on to go to Brown. Mike skipped his first year at Harvard. Mark went on to MIT. Fred whom took 6 majors, and also Dave whom had been accepted to Tufts in Pre-Med.

Well I had asked my Math teacher Miss Rekcut this year about questioning the concept of foil. This was part of the math with the example idea of $(5+3)(4+4)$. $8+8=16$ $9+7=16$. $9x7=63$. $8x8=64$. I think she was a bit intrigued with my question. All of my school friends were in this course.

We went to a math meet in the town Walpole one of these days. I had all the boys in my car, which we drove in to the Math Meet. I sometimes think this was like the part in the One Flew Over the Cuckoo's Nest when all the mental patients were on the boat and McMurphy said to all of them as "dr. dr. dr. and dr."

Miss Rekcut had all the girls on the Math Team in her car. Well I had my car and she had her car. We were both the only drivers. This was when I was thinking Miss Rekcut, was a touch interested in me. I was captain of the football team, on the math team, treasurer of the class, and I was working at the A & P. I had seen a movie years later about this can be a bit dangerous, for a teacher to be interested in you.

Miss Rekcut was about 26 years old. She had like medium long dark black hair. She was about 5' 9". Had about a 34 or so inch bust.

Also she had a nice figure. As I say, I had heard this could be dangerous for someone to become interested in a student.

We were at the Math Meet and I was with Fred as we walked around the Walpole school. I saw the Walpole Football captain for the next year. His name was chopper and he was an outstanding football player. I would meet up with chopper years later. He had moved to Conn., this year, so he was not on the Walpole football team the next year. I had met up with chopper years later when I was coming home from college. I did not see any actual action on the Math Team. I was a reserve.

We also had a math meet in Dedham. We would do math problems to do as exercises. Like how you would do physical exercises to warm up for physical activity. We would do this for math problems. I heard that Gen. Bradley would do calculus problems when he was in airplanes. I later took my SATs" in Dedham and I did my best there.

I had gone to the senior semi-formal this year when I was a junior. I went to the formal and had a wonderful time. I was really in pretty good shape. Work, school, and sports were all kicking in. At the formal I saw a lot of my older senior friends, I had when I was younger. Now I was only a junior. I drove in my car as I doubled with my friend Washy.

I had a girlfriend the year before and she told me this particular girl she knew was adopted. I kind of felt sorry for her, so I dated her. At our home, we had a foster girl named Kathy whom was a friend of my sister Maura. If you know anything about the adoption process, you may understand what this is all about. Our family physician lived near this girl. Our family physician, which my family in Norwood had paid for his Medical School, happened to also to be an amphibious landing doctor during the Second World War. I thought years later he might have steered me into dating his neighbor.

My friends outside of school were Robby whom we called Tex. He had come up from Texas the previous year. His dad was in the Navy and he would go around to the different Naval Stations. His dad was in the Navy 20 years. He had been in Texas for a stint of time. So when folks asked Robby where he was from, he said Texas. He then had the nickname Tex ever since. I had also read this is difficult for people to make friends when they come from another school, so I befriended Tex. Tex was 2 ½ years older than me, but one grade higher though.

I can recall the year before we were at someone's house drinking beer and I was with my girlfriend. Well I was under age for driving. But one night I stole Tex car. I drove the night with about 8 beers in me. My date and I drove for about 3 hours in Tex car. I thought this was a little bit like Bonnie and Clyde. I had hit one car when I was backing up. I was worrying about hitting one car lightly and Tex car got a little dent. I had about 8 beers in me. My date I think must have been very scared. We drove for about 3 hours, and then we came to the place where we started with Tex waiting for us. I was worrying about a little dent when we were driving like Bonnie and Clyde.

Then there was Dave Copper, whom was probably just about my best friend then. He was an outstanding football and baseball player. I began to think why did I get along with Dave so well. I began to think the reason why was because he had braces on his teeth for an overbite, and I braces for an under bite. We kind of clashed.

I had gone with my friend Dave to the Junior High School to talk about, the to be football players at the high school next year. We had gotten cards about each player. I would really understand the idea of getting people psyched for things. This seemed I was reading people's minds. I knew what they would react to emotionally. I was beginning to have a personality I loved.

Johnny Cox was another friend. Johnny played good football. He was a real fast halfback. I never knew why Johnny would put out so much in football. I came up with a theory years later. Johnny would always have a girl on his lap at parties. I thought Johnny would think about the girls on his lap during the season and this would motivate him to think about the weekend with the girl on his lap. I really would appreciate Johnny's friendship in the years to come.

Brian Key was another friend of mine. He was to be my friend, which I had in years to come. He stuck by me even when things didn't seem too good. He was also a back on the football team. He turned out to be a Green Beret in the Army.

There was also John Girldy and Jackie Dunarm. I really only hit this off once with John. I was dropping him off one night and we began to talk at an intellectual high. Jackie I would open up to every now and then. Then there was even Chico whom was a really close friend when younger, but I wouldn't see too much in later years.

Baseball season was starting and I was looking towards a great season. I was a starting pitcher and was also the third batter in the line-up. I had all my pitches down straight. I had an overhand fastball and curve. I had directly overhand fastball and drop. I also was working on a side arm fastball and curve.

Also around this time was the Junior Prom. My date was my friend Dave Copper's ex-girlfriend. I was looking towards a wonderful night. I could still remember how I had gone to my first high school function the previous winter at the senior semi-formal. My gal was Kim. I had a great time at the senior semi-formal, even though I was still a junior.

Well this night was to become a nightmare. I wrote a diary after this night a few days later. This is my actual diary.

Please Lord

I am writing these journals so that in the future I will be able to laugh at myself.

The week following the worst night in my life was complete thought. Going from the gamut of nothing bad happening to being ruined. The Sat. following I talked to coach Pete W. He told me the story and kind of laughed. I hadn't think anything bad had happened at that point. I then talked to Coach John D. who was very much surprised. He asked me why did I do it and that I really screwed up. Coach Pete W. said that he would try to squash it quick. He said that he could talk to John P. (vice-principal) good but not dr. M. (principal). Also that he couldn't trust Mike G. (vice-principal). I then went down to dr. M's house where he told me the situation. The way he put it was excellent in the situation he was in. The only good news he had heard all day long was that dr. M. didn't think anything less of me. He told me that my actions were completely noticeable to everyone in the Prom. That part sort of surprised me. I wasn't really aware of the fool I made of myself, and that is the worse kind of fool. What I remember of the night is inaccurate. I was in a cold sweat the whole week after this. End.

I took a meditation course, which was for over 18 years old, but I took this at 17 years old. I began to control myself to sleep at night. This was invented in the lowest point in the United States. I took this with my pal Dave Bird. This was fun.

I pitched in a baseball game against Walpole. Pitching for them was their ace Chuck J. Chuck pitched an outstanding game. He struck out 20 Norwood men. I had pitched this game, and Ivy League Brown University scouts were there. I was thinking what they had thought when they were looking at me. I am thinking now which colleges are named University of, vs. such and such University.

Well this person Chuck J. I thought had put our town down. Like in the Bible when you leave a town, "shake the dust off your feet." This was serious baseball.

Well we won the Title in baseball. I began to know what this was like to be on the bench. This really hurts. I had never been on the bench so much in my baseball career.

Well we played the All-stars in the league, as we won the Title. We played under the lights in Norwood. Well I got to start this game. I was really throwing smoke. I pitched a no-hitter for 5 innings and also struck out 11. I was saying to myself bring on Carl Yestremski. Well after the game, the Boston Red Sox scout gave a card for me to send into the Boston Red Sox Organization to be projected on in the future.

I later looked at this night, as I would keep a lamp on a little bit longer at night. This game was under the lights, which I received the card. I still worried about the Junior Prom.

Well in Legion ball in the summer, I pitched against Westwood and struck out 20 of them. I had given the 20 struck outs from Chuck J. to them. I had like put a town down. I thought years later the reason why I was in the Westwood Lodge was because I had put their town down with 20 struck outs. "Shake the dust off your feet."

The reports were coming in we were getting out of Vietnam and we were training the South Vietcong to fight by themselves. If we weren't getting out of the war, I really thought I would have gone to Nam.

Well I was slowly living down the Junior Prom night. In the summer I applied for a job in a factory. I again had lied on the application. I said

I was 18 when I was 17. You had to be 18 to work at this factory. I really didn't worry about this. I had always thought you could go to confession and your sins would be forgiven. Little I knew.

I began to have captain's practices at 6 o'clock during the week. I got out of the factory at about 5:00. When I would work a second shift about 20 hours I would be really tired. One night when I was like on the 20th hour, I actually slept standing up. I was like asleep for about 5 or 6 seconds. We would pick roofing shingles from a standing position.

I thought one way to overcome a problem like I had with the Junior Prom, was to do boring work. My grandfather whom had come over from Lithuania at the beginning of the century had worked at this factory for 45 years. I can remember all these old folks there would say, "Go to college." There was a quite a lot of WW 2 veterans there.

The first shift would start at 6:30 AM till 5:00 PM. Then the second shift would be from 5:00 PM to 3:00 AM the next morning. I worked with a person whom I hadn't seen in years Steven Brown. He had graduated from UMass Amherst the previous June. He was working here till he could get a better job. He had worked here the previous summers to earn his keep for college. My brother Jack's friend Joey A. worked here in the summers also.

There were some people here whom would smoke dope while they worked. I didn't, because you had all you needed to stay awake, never mind getting tired smoking dope. Steven told me he smoked dope a lot at UMass Amherst throughout his four years there. I would smoke dope on the rides home from the factory at 3:00 in the mornings. I can remember one night when I actually thought I was like in a fog. This seemed I was in a mist. Mostly the good feelings were, because I was so happy the work was over.

One night I can remember while I was taking a shower in our home at 3:30 in the morning. I had the tub full of water also. I had put my head down into the water and I thought I was going to fall asleep under water. But I awoke and pulled my head up out of the water. This tub of water I thought about the next year.

Well I had lied again when I told the people at the factory I was going to go to college. I was really in my last year of high school. I didn't lift weights this year for football. I just ran, ran, and ran. I had been having captain's practices and working. Seager, "working and practicing."

I was sleeping a bit better from the meditation, which I could control myself to go to sleep. I was feeling good about myself again. With the right combination church and meditation I really enjoyed life. I was beginning to love myself. I had given up the little marijuana I would smoke for the football season.

Well the other captain on the team was Daryle. Daryle was no doubt the toughest person on the team. He was the middle linebacker. He wasn't what you would call a scholar, but he had common sense and plenty of this. I had two numbers. I wore 31 for away games and 41 for home games.

When I was dropped off for camp, I thought something later the word, ready. I'll leave this from there.

Our first game was against Waltham at Waltham. I had started the idea of jogging through the uprights and down to the 50 yards line. Then down around again through the uprights and then everybody would be perfectly in place. I thought years later this was like the fox trot.

I can recall in this game I hit Mr. Fred Smerlas head on. He went down for about 20 seconds. I wanted to stop the game. But Fred got back up and went off to the sidelines. Daryle had a very good game also. We lost 15-8. The coach from Waltham said. We had the best two captains 31 and 62. Daryle was #62. I think the fox trot might have captivated them.

Well we were playing Natick. I put in everyone's personal locker then on Thursday statements like, "your no good, you can't play football, you're a sissy." Well Grega the All-scholastic center really got pissed.

He said.

"Who did this? Was this you Billy?"

I like acted as best I could.

"Are you accusing me?"

I began to go at Grega. A few people held me back. If you had ever read the book the Wise Guy, this was like the part when he said that the doctor with the pacemaker really screwed up. When he was really taping someone for surveillance. Well Grega then thought the manager

John Jigger had done this. John Jigger the manager was a bit emotionally retarded.

Well against Natick this day, I put in everyone's locker they were all good. They were all kind now. I later thought I should have put the bad notes in the lockers instead of good to psyche them up at the opposite times.

We played the to become State Champs Natick. We were leading 8-6 with 12 seconds to go on the clock. They tried a long pass, and this was intercepted by our free safety. He then fumbled and they had the ball on our about 10 yards line. All he had to do was just knock it down. But he intercepted and then fumbled. They then kicked a field Goal and won 9-8. Hurt like a knife.

Our All-scholastic center Grega hit one of the key players on Natick and an ambulance had to take him off the field. I heard years later this player was speeding his brains out in this game. Our starting guard Henry whom was the cousin, of Daryle, I asked after the game.

"What happened today Henry?"

He said.

"I think we bothered him too much today."

We would have prayers every time we could on the field during the game. He had just plain common sense.

Well after the Natick game I had a date with a girl named Ann Marie. I picked her up and I asked her mother.

"What time would you like your daughter home tonight?"

I asked her mother this, when I picked her up. I think she said something like.

"She will know what time."

This girl was in my Calculus class and I wanted to have a sophisticated relationship with her. We just went out for the night and I was quite tired and we talked. I think she wanted to kill some time, but I declined.

When I had started school this year, I was asked to give a speech to about 640 sophomores in the auditorium. This speech I gave, I really thought about from speeches on television. I said something like.

"We need you to come to the games to support us."

I was getting a personality, which I was beginning to love. Well in front of the whole class outside, about 2000 teachers and students, I gave another speech. This time I can recall what I said more.

"We think we have a good team and we hope you think so too."

Then was the applause.

I was just having a mediocre year. After the Natick loss I had gone into the coach's room and asked the head coach.

"Why doesn't the fullback run with the football on this team?"

He was a bit tempered and said something like.

"Are you going against my coaching ability?"

I said.

"No, I just think the fullback should run with the football more."

I was the fullback on the team.

Then the head coach said.

"Bob talk to him about this."

Bob was the assistant coach. He said something like.

"We are trying such and such a strategy," or something to this extent.

Well I was thinking maybe my year could be ruined for confronting the head coach so much. I could remember those nights. Would my season be over with running with the football? We were playing, the team in first place in the State then, Walpole.

We played Walpole and I scored three touchdowns, interception, block punt recovery, and 80 yards rushing in 16 carries. The next day I was chosen Boston Globe Player of the Week. With my picture and an article about me in the Boston Paper.

The Globe reporter called and asked me about the game for his article. I was thinking of telling him I had talked to the head coach earlier in the week, and how I said I thought the fullback should run with the football. But I just said.

"We had gone to the run instead of our power the pass."

Well in the papers at the end of 1974, the reports were coming out the North Vietnamese were moving down on the US backed forces in South Vietnam. The assistance of training the South Vietcong to help fight by their own was not working. This seemed just a matter of time till they took over. We were pulling out all personnel.

Our second to last game of the year was against Braintree. We were losing 26-8 at the half. I had taken the opening kick-off the distance for our only score. This looked like we were doomed. Our All-scholastic center Grega was crying at half time. Well, how we did this, baffles me. But we won the game 40-33. I had actually hurdled someone in the game. They had this on film. When we were coming home on the bus, all of footballers were saying out loud.

"Bill Breen, Bill Breen, etc . . ."

I was beginning to think Bill instead of Billy. We had heard the Natick school had been upset by Milton, and we were now tied with Natick in the Bay State League. If we won our last game we would be tied for the Title.

Daryle and I would go out on Friday nights to make sure everyone was in by the curfew. This was like 7:30 on the Friday nights, before the games on Saturdays. My friend Jimbo whom I would pal with did not get along with Daryle. I can't believe we went to Jjmbo's house and Daryle and I asked Jimbo's father where was Jimbo. We were seeing if Jimbo was in on the curfew. Jimbo was quite big, but this wouldn't detour Daryle.

I was looking at colleges to apply to. After the Braintree game I received a letter from Carman Cozza, the football coach at Yale University, asking me if I would consider applying. I can recall he said the credentials for Yale were exceedingly high. Also the Harvard University recruiter was by the school. He introduced himself and said that you just don't go to Harvard by making 80 yards runs. This was the kick-off I had taken all the way back against Braintree. He gave me tickets to the Harvard-Yale game of 1974 the next week before our last game on the next Thursday.

Well I went to the game and I had two tickets. I went by myself. I decided to scalp the other ticket. I tried to get as much money for this as I could. I think I might have asked if anybody was interested in the ticket. A person from Dartmouth University told me that he would give me $2.00 for the ticket. I at first declined, but then I sold this to him for I believe $2.00.When I was at the game I think I felt guilty, about selling the ticket, so I think I gave the Dartmouth person $1.00 back.

Harvard won the game and I tried to see if I knew anybody there to get a ride home. I watched as all the players from Yale were coming off the field. Well I couldn't see anyone I knew, so I went up to the center of Harvard Square. I from there called for a ride to get me home. I saw the Harvard band marching through the square. I *GOT* a ride home and this was a real experience at Harvard.

We had our last game of the season against Dedham. We had our rally in the gym. I awoke in the middle of the night to decide what I was going to speak about at the rally.

I told all the football players when I say, we're in first place in the Bay State League and that's # and then I would point to all the football players on the gym floor and they all would say "1". Well I said exactly this and pointed and said, "#," then pointed and they all said, "1".

Then I went on and said that.

"I hope the hockey, basketball team and wrestling team have as much luck as we had this year."

I can remember walking the corridors after this speech and people were looking at me with respect. I can recall one in particular in Judy. She seemed as if she was interested in me. When I was younger going down town, I would see her. She was, as some people would respect the people whom could party. But now when I gave this speech, she seemed back to reality by thinking about my speech.

Well against Dedham we had a letdown and the game was a tie. We lost our attempt for the Title. Since after the game I spoke to the coach, this turned my year around, and I made All-stars at fullback. Against Dedham I had an about 70 yard run, which I was caught from behind by a Chris T. I thought about this, years later.

Daryle made all-stars also and we went to get our pictures taken for the papers. The man taking the pictures told Daryle to put on a tie. Daryle said, "no". But the real reason was because he didn't know how too. When I said real common sense, I meant really common sense.

Around at the end of the football year, I went to the home of the Harvard recruiter in Brookline Mass. Mr. Don Sorg whom was the father of the triplet girls in our class, drove me and our All-scholastic quarterback Larry, whom went also. Don Sorg had sold a hearing aid to this Harvard Recruiter. Larry was dating one of the triplets. So this was the connection.

We drove there and Larry went to be interviewed first. I was like just in this person's den reading some books. Larry came out and I went in to talk to him. We talked and he would ask questions like.

"What were your SAT scores?"

I told him.

"640 Math and 450 verbal."

I was weak in the Verbal. I told him about the meditation technique I would use. He seemed interested. He then asked me.

"Can you do anything you want?"

I told him.

"Not everything."

He then gave me some Readers Digest to read to study for the verbal SATs. I kind of liked the guy. He told me how he looks forward every year to the Harvard-Yale game. He said he gets hot chocolate to drink at the game when this is quite cold. He bundles up, he says with heavy clothes.

We had our fall sports banquet around the beginning of December. There was more public speaking here also. Speaking to the public this time. Speaking to the parents of the athletes. I can remember when I was looking over my notes for my speech. I had gone to the bar section of the function Hall. I saw Don Sorg there. This was the man whom drove Larry and I to the recruiters'. He was there having a drink. He asked me.

"What are you going to do, get a drink?"

I still was thinking of the Junior Prom when I had been drunk and was thrown out. He was one of the chaperons at the Prom back then. Well when he said this I still thought about the nightmare, which was still lingering in me about the prom. Well I wasn't old enough to drink anyways so I said.

"No, I'm just going over some notes for a speech."

Well I got up on the mike and I think I might have even had some water for speaking next to me. I talked about the coaches. What I thought about them. Then I was introducing Daryle, when I said.

"Now speaking the most respected person on this team Daryle S."

I was thinking I was the most respected.

I was thinking I was the most respected person on this team. That the audience would think, me, whom was now speaking, was the most respected person on the team. I thought this would make them contemplate I in their minds. The speech I would be quite content about years later. I was getting confidence in myself from public speaking.

For the winter I recall I had asked some of the hockey players if I could be the manager of the hockey team. I do not know what became of this.

A girl in my English class Janis, I had asked her, and she said yes, to go to the senior semi-formal. In this English class we were doing impromptus and she acted like when she would say.

"Why don't you come up and see me sometime."

She did this real sexy like. I was a bit aroused. Janis had about 34" bust. She had long dirty brown hair. She had also a very good figure. She had rounded out hips. She was about 5' 8". And she was good looking in a special way.

Well I took her to the semi-formal and I had a wonderful time. I was thinking about how I had the worst time at the junior Prom. I was living down this night. I had bought my tickets to the formal even before I had asked Janis.

I had a wonderful time with Janis after the formal and we killed time in my car. Janis was up there for the best in being intimate with. I had a Russian alarm clock, which went off to tell me this was time to bring her home. I had gotten this from Lithuania.

The next week in school we had another assignment for another impromptu. She was supposed to be pregnant and I was her unwed boyfriend. I don't know where these words came out, but they came out beautiful. After class I was walking with Janis and she said.

"Thank-you Bill."

All my former girlfriends would call me Billy. I felt good being called Bill. Well I would talk to her and she told me how she would take speed sometimes. I brought her to a Meditation class as my quest, and she was enthralled. But her mother told her not to get involved with this.

I got some marijuana one night and took her out. I was thinking this could be some night. We smoked a joint or two and I wanted to be intimate. She told me she wanted to talk. This put me in a tailspin, as I began to get ill at ease. She told me to drive through McDonalds'. This was where anyone of importance would be on Friday and Saturday nights. I reluctantly went through. I thought she wanted to be seen with me. We ran out of gas about one and a half miles from her home. We walked to her house and her brother got some gas and I then went home. In school she walked right by me. She was no longer attracted to me. I figured things didn't turn out, so the next time I saw her I said.

"Thank-you for going to the senior-formal with me."

She didn't say anything to this. She had told me her father had died, when she was younger. Well I meet up with Janis in the years to come.

I was applying to all of the colleges I liked. Harvard, Brown, Tufts, Syracuse, UMass, UNH, and Northeastern. I was going to apply to Yale, but I thought I would play this safe and just stay with them asking me. I had the little bit of money I received at the Harvard-Yale game. I thought instead of applying to Yale and getting an unlikely, I should stay with them asking me. The Ivy League gave Unlikely, Possible, and Likely at the half way mark.

Well I was taking Advanced Placement Calculus and Chemistry. This was equal to one year in college for both. I can recall I was studying the train acceleration in Calculus. I thought about this when I would run with the football. Like "OO, OO, OO," would come out of my mouth as I ran with the football.

In Chemistry the teacher Mr. Fiffy was complained about by quite a few of the students. So the parents had come in to voice their opinions. My grades in both of these, was low 80s". I had my class rank of 41 out of 620 in the class.

My friend Dave Bird and I had received the comeback of the year awards in Calculus. I had taken the Meditation Course with Dave. Dave also followed me in being the Class Treasurer the senior year.

About 6 of us went to the Harvard night at a building at Harvard. We all went there. We heard them talking as this I think was Harvard night. I even met the recruiter there again. At first I did not think Harvard had an engineering Dept. Well the recruiter told me they did. He also introduced me to the President I believe of Harvard. When we were all coming home we began to talk French because all of us had been in accelerated French.

Larry and I went one day to see the football and baseball coaches a the Harvard Gym. We were talking to the baseball coach there. I think Larry had known him. We were in his office and we talked about baseball. I did not seem too thrilled. We then went to the football coach. He told us.

"Did you know the Dallas Cowboys ask to see the game films? The real motive was to study the different in motion plays, which Harvard had. We have all kinds of in motion plays. They were just interested in different audible."

I went to Tufts to be interviewed by the Engineering Dept. there. I said to the professor there.

"You know about the best engineering college in the country, MIT?" He said.

"We think we do here,"

I thought the interview, which you went on, the ones you were the snobbiest at, were the ones you did the best at.

Around this time when I came up to my room in the house, I began to stare at the curtains. I had been smoking marijuana. I could make out a cross. I then thought my eyes were dilating and the only thing I could see was the cross. I then felt my heart and chest jump up. As if I were having electric shock on my heart. I thought I was going to die. Then I heard this voice, which I don't know where, say, "I WANT YOU."

I got up and tried to look at light to get me from seeing the cross. I opened the door and saw then, "I saw the light." No pun intended. Well I began to forget about this ordeal.

Well around this February the ratings for the Ivy League Schools were out. I had gotten possible to Harvard and Brown. My friend Dave Bird had also. My math team friend Scott had gotten early acceptance to Brown. If I recall I'm not so sure, if I had talked to a football scout from Princeton, and he waved the application fee. I am not positive though.

My uncle Joe whom had the nickname "Uncle Sam," was a Probation Officer at the Norfolk County Court. Uncle Sam would say years ago in the military. "I WANT YOU." He with the courts would draft all the boys for Vietnam. I thought I would go to Nam, but the war was ending.

I could remember the pictures of the troops coming home. I can vividly recall a helicopter, which was taking off, and there were Vietnam people whom were trying to get through the gates before this closed. There was this girl whom had this child, and they were both trying to get through as the last people to get out of Vietnam. She was struggling with the marine guard whom was closing the gate. She got through, but her child had to stay. She got through and got on the helicopter.

You could see her dress, which was severing, and the marine guard, whom was closing the gate, but let one in. I also reminisce the helicopters, which they were pushing overboard the decks of the ships.

Well baseball season had come again. We were trying to repeat as champions. We were doing fairly well. Our record was 8-2 and we were playing Braintree whose record was 9-1 in the showdown. I had taken hard drugs in this game. Before the game I had taken two hits of speed. Braintree went ahead 4-0 by the third inning. I came in to relieve Larry, the Harvard friend. I did not give up a run the rest of the game. I was having the rifle action in my arm.

I had heard there were three different types of arms in the pros. The best arm, being a screamer. Then the second is a shotgun. Finally the third is a rifle, which I had. They say if you had an arm, then they could work with you.

The excitement came in the bottom of the sixth. We were down 4-0 and this looked like we were doomed. The bases somehow became loaded and the third hitter was up for us. This person's name was Bill Breen. I think I took the first pitch high for a ball. Then came one of the greatest thrills of my life. The next pitch was down the middle and a little high, but I swung anyways. The ball made contact with the bat and sailed to the centerfield fence. This went over the fence and Norwood tied the score 4-4 by a grand slam homerun by Bill Breen. We then scored another run in the inning, and went on to win the game 5-4. My coach said again, I had thrown as hard as a major leaguer.

In the local papers they called this Billy Breen Day. We went on to win the Title again. I made all-stars in baseball, which went along fine with all-stars in Football. The speed would give me pep and I would have lots of energy. This also made my stomach feel a little bit of good jittering.

While I would take speed I stayed up a whole night sometimes studying. Well I had moved onto harder chemicals. The one being (Tetrahychloric-carbonate.) I knew the chemical breakdown from my College AP Chemistry Course. I also had taken Organic Chemistry. Tetrahychloric-carbonate was the active ingredient in marijuana.

They had discovered years later in Israel, this Tetra-hychloric-carbonate is good for early intervention of head injuries. Too stop the swelling in the brains of head injuries.

I met this girl Elizabeth one night. I knew her from the weekends. I was talking to her about the senior prom, which was coming up. She had plans on going with her old boyfriend. I don't think she wanted to go with him.

I asked her.

"Would you like to go to the senior prom with me?"

She responded with.

"Okay."

I believe she was quite content with these new plans. I liked her a lot. I was taking the tetra-hychloric-carbonate quite a bit. This would give me false confidence in myself. I would not get embarrassed too much, because this I would worry about.

Elizabeth had long black hair. About 36" bust, and she seemed to smile at everything. She smoked a lot of cigarettes, as she would throw out her hand when she went to her mouth with one. She had very soft lips. She had a flat ass and thin legs. I didn't think she was too sophisticated. She usually has her hair over her ears with rounded out hips. She has close to 36-24-36 measurements. Walks slow with one foot in front of the other. She had a smooth complexion. She had soft smooth and a little bit on the light side skin. Breasts are out and a little bit pointed downward. She talks in short sentences.

She came from a very good family in our town. She had a unique personality, which could rise to occasions. She wasn't too smart in the academics, as I had plans on going off to college and meeting an educated woman. I was now on Tetra-hychloric-carbonate practically all the time.

Well the Ivy League acceptances came out, and I did not get into Harvard or Brown. I did get in Syracuse, UMass, and UNH. I had plans on going to UMass Amherst and room with my pal Dave Bird. He was accepted to Tufts in Pre-Med, but opted to room with me in Pre-Med at UMass. I had received a scholarship to UMass to play ball. I was looking forward to playing baseball under the lights with my glasses. Can you imagine what this was for me to play under the lights with no glasses? I would guess with my glove for fly balls to the outfield. I was not thinking of playing football there, because this was very good football. I did not think I would play too much.

Elizabeth would go to my baseball games. I recall her walking over to the grandstands. When we had our class picnic at Rocky Woods I talked to her some. I wasn't going out with her, but I was going to the senior-prom with her. I wasn't thinking of going out with her at this time.

The girl, whom I had dated when I was younger, had showed up at the picnic with her boyfriend. This was the girlfriend of the person whom I went to the A&P with, when we just walked right in and started working. Her name was Paula. Paula was the girl I began to love after I had broken up with her. She was not that tall, but she had a super personality and was very enchanting. When she came to the picnic I began to get ill at ease. The tetra-hychloric-carbonate couldn't overcome the ill at ease I had over Paula. When I saw Paula, while I was with Elizabeth, I felt embarrassed because I thought Paula was a better woman than Elizabeth, and she wasn't my date. I would walk around with a stick.

The day of the prom came and I went with Elizabeth. I had already taken Tetra-Hychloric-carbonate at the baseball game this day. I went over Elizabeth's house, where I met her parents and grandmother, whom had come home from a Nursing Home for the occasion. Elizabeth looked absolutely gorgeous. I can remember seeing the hips on her, which were formed wonderfully. Her breasts would fill out the dress she was wearing. I had forgotten the tickets, so I went back to my house and got them. I was double dating with John Rekab and Donna. Elizabeth and I were in the back seat. I was feeling good I had an attractive date.

We had a case of beer in the back seat. We also had a couple of marijuana joints. When we were at the prom, we went to get our pictures taken. The person taking the pictures said something negative to Elizabeth. I would rise to the occasion, and stand up for her.

I can recall the night at the prom. I had recollected a prom, which was on television out in California years later. I thought of all chemicals, which were supposed to be in California.

I can remember coaxing Elizabeth to slow dance with me, because she wasn't too keen about dancing. I can remember the scent, which she had. This was one of strong and beautiful. She had a scent of strong puffiness. I think I had taken a couple of Tetra-hychloric-Carbonate pills during the prom.

After the prom we went to a party and I felt I was dreaming. I thought I could control people with my mind. My consciousness state was I was actually in a dream sleeping. I cogitated I was in heaven, with imaginary stars in the air. They were flickering in a fluffiness to them. Just being myself, I must have seduced Elizabeth, because she was all over me. I kissed her a few times, deep passionate kisses. We saw the sun rise at about 5:00 the next morning.

I wasn't making any moves towards her, because I wasn't sure if I wanted to go out with her. I didn't think I would use her for the night, because I revered her. I was a little bit more mature than previous years, when I would go out with girls, for the night. Elizabeth was special and I felt a remote attraction to her.

The next day Elizabeth and Donna went down Nantasket Beach to get some sun. I drove down there with John Rekab whom was the person that drove the car to the prom. I can recollect the song on the radio. "Only woman bleed," by Alice Cooper. I was in between liking her and loving her. This was borderline. She told me her parents said to her.

"We like him a real lot," meaning me. I began to see her just about every night and I was feeling hearty and sprightly.

I told her.

"Maybe we will go down New York sometime."

She seemed to be thrilled with the idea.

I became a member of the Knights of Columbus in my hometown. I was 18 years old at the time. I met a lot of older men there. Gerry M. my friend sponsored me. I would bring my friends in the Knights of

Columbus building, because I had a card, which could get us through the electric door. We would play pool and drink beer. The drinking age was 18, so most of us were old enough to consume alcohol beverage. There was a beer machine here at the Knights.

The last month of school, I would cruise at night with my friend Henry. He was the person whom had said. "I think we bothered him too much today," in the football season. We would cruise and drink beer. Henry had gotten into some kind of trouble with the Law and my uncle and the Courts sent Henry to the Marine Corp. We would go cruising and I really felt good. Henry was a beer drinker. He tried some marijuana but he didn't like this.

Well my pal Henry was sundering for the Marine Corp. and there was a party for him. There was rented out a hall, and Henry and his mother went to see everyone at the party. He came to me and just said something to his mother to me. I no longer felt Henry was close to me anymore. We had cruised almost everyday for close to a month together. I thought I was decisive to him. I was going to miss him. They say the marines the first to fight.

We had class Day in the gym at the high school and I sheltered the best baseball player award. Elizabeth and I received our Year Books and then went for a ride in my brother Jack's Studebaker. I was getting to know Elizabeth more and more. We drove to a town about 12 miles away.

We had graduation ceremonies a few days later. I was still taking the tetra-hychloric-carbonate and I was feeling very expedient. I received a scholarship in the class before ours. When I was leaving, I saw my old flame Janis, whom I had taken to the semi-formal. I can recall she had a camera and she was going to graduate the next year. Well here at the graduation I just said.

"Hi."

She just responded with.

"Hi."

Well this was graduation Day. I had our pictures taken with Elizabeth's family and my family. As I was going to my car with Elizabeth, I saw the sport's writer, Frank Curb.

He said something like.

"Who is your girlfriend?"

I said.

"Miss Elizabeth, Sales."

"Sales" was Frank Curb's nickname. He was a great sport's writer in our town.

I was feeling a little better while I was with Elizabeth around certain people. I then dropped her off at her home and I then went to some parties. I went to the house of a girl named Robin. She was a gal of a very good baseball player on the team. I asked to use the phone to make a call. Robin's parents kept on asking me.

"Is your girl friend with you?"

The people at the party were the academic. There was a picture of Rick and I on their refrigerator in baseball uniforms. I was thinking back then, I lusted for Elizabeth to be smart in the books. I didn't want to be seen with her with my scholar friends.

I then went to a party of the triplet girls Maggie, Marie, and Maryanne. All three were going to UNH. These were the children of the man Don Sorg. The person whom had drove me to the Harvard recruiter 's home. Well while I was here, the triplet Marie asked me.

"Billy, my parent's asked me to ask you if you could ask the Prescott gang to leave the party?"

"I'll see what I can do."

I said

The Prescott boys were a tough bunch of guys whom knew what this was like to street fight. I went over to them and addressed them.

"This party is no good. Let's go to another one."

They swallowed this real talk and left the party. The All-scholastic Grega, whom was also in the Prescott gang wasn't there this time though.

When I think of this, if the parents of the triplets called the police, or tried to get the Prescott gang to leave and weren't successful, then this could have been a touchy situation. Well Marie said to me.

"Thank-you for getting the Prescott boys to leave."

I went into the house to take a leak. I had been talking a soft talk with people around my age. I would whisper. While I was waiting for the bathroom, I began to talk with Don Sorg and Mrs Sorg.

Don Sorg said something like.

"Don't start that talk with me."

I was now in the world of grown-ups.

"Billy Breen, your special. Whenever there is applause there is always a louder one for Billy Breen. Wherever you go you make people happy. Billy Breen we like you very much.

Mrs. Sorg said this.

I began to look at Mrs. Sorg and she was rather attractive. I began to think about her then.

She also said.

"This doesn't matter what school you go to."

I had plans on going to UMass Amherst and room with my friend Dave Bird, whom was studying Pre-Med. While I was talking to them, a policeman came to the door and said to Don Sorg.

"There has been a complaint about to much noise."

Don Sorg got up and said something to the policeman.

"There isn't too much noise. Whom complained to you?"

He was confronting the policeman. I began to think not respect policemen as much. Instead of going along with them, try to put up a fight. After these statements I began to feel positive about my personality. This made me feel higher and higher.

We were in the State Baseball Tournament. I had 3 or 4 hits of tetra-hychloric-carbonate in the back pocket. I would take one in the 2, 5, and 7th innings. We were playing North Quincy. Larry, the Harvard recruiter pal, was pitching. I was out in left field. This was the day after graduation.

I can recall when there was a base hit to left field by North Quincy. They were trying to score a runner from second base. I charged the ball and on a run forward, scooped up the ball and threw to home plate. You had to keep your balance when you would go down. They called this play in Boston, the Carl Yestremski play. This was when I thought of Carl again besides the night I had pitched and received the card from the Red Sox scout. Well the runner scored, but I received a round of applause from North Quincy by my attempt.

In football, before going down on the field, from being tackled, I would reach down with my arm and put this on the field and then come back up before going down. I think I only did this very few amounts of time in my football career. You really had to keep your balance.

We were losing 2-0 going into the top of the eighth inning. While I was out in left field, I began to concentrate on hitting a home run. There was no doubt in my mind. I would be up second in the bottom of the eighth. I thought the first person would walk, then, I would hit a home run to tie the game. The day was a rather damp raw day.

The first batter up walked. Everything was going as planned. I took the first pitch high for a ball. The second pitch was also a ball. Then the next pitch I can see coming down the pipe. This was a bit high, but I swung anyways. I made contact and the ball sailed way over the left field fence about 350 to 375 feet. I ran around the bases in a kind of shuffle like jog. I can recall the shuffle as I was approaching third base. I stepped on home plate, and I was so high I began to hurt. When I got to the bench, I was gasping for air. The assistant coach told me to get some water. I was thinking of telling the coach, I was on something, and I knew I was going to hit the home run, before I got to bat. But I decided not too.

The game was now tied, and we had new life. We went into extra innings. I got up in the tenth on a walk. I think I was sacrificed to second. Then there was a single to center, and I came around third trying to score. The catcher got the throw from center field to the right of home plate. Then he dove in front of the plate. I thought at the last split instinct to jump as I was nearing home plate. I jumped over the lying on the ground catcher, and we won 3-2.

They had said if I had slid, I would have been a dead duck. There was a picture of me in midair jumping over the catcher. This was called the picture of the year in the surrounding town newspaper. The coach from North Quincy said Larry and I were the two best players he saw all year long. I thought about the Waltham Football coach, whom said this about me and the other captain in football.

I went to the Spring Banquet, where I received the Most Valuable Player on the baseball team. I also received the Scholar Athlete of School Award. When I received this award, I can recall the people giving me a standing ovation. I was brought back to when I slept standing up at the factory the previous summer. I had stood and now people had stood for me. After the banquet I would see Elizabeth and cruise.

I had gone to a nightclub one night, and Franco, the both ways tackle on the team had gotten into a car accident and a person named David was killed. I went to the wake, and the mother of David said to me.

"He was one of the persons whom was over the house."

I had bought a tap deck off of him. I felt good his mother had said something positive to me. I had heard Franco had a quite rough day. Myself and another player called our football coach, whom was now in California. His name was Bob Lev. Bob had gone back to California at the end of the football season. He had played ball at Yale and he said his roommate was Calvin Hill.

Bob had said to have Franco stay in contact with his friends. I thought this was like the movie with Tom Cruise. When he was a football player in Penn. In the movie a person had gotten in trouble with the Law. As the police were taking him out of the school, he said to the coach.

"Let's see you help me now coach."

This was no longer a sport.

Well I had begun to coach Babe Ruth baseball around this time also. I can recall my first game with my assistant Paul Neirbo. I had begun to crack the bats against the bench screens. I would whistle as much as I could. I was trying to instill confidence in the players. I later thought, this was whistling down to hell, and then whistling up.

The first game I thought I could superintend the outcome of the game by coaching. This seemed I was a public official and you have control over people. I think we won the first game by a landslide. After the game I had all the players run around the bases to stay in shape. This was a level, which I could only wonder about. When all the coaches, which would tell you to run laps, sprints, etc . . . in my sports career. I really enjoyed this. I began to realize you feel better coaching than playing.

Well the second play-off, we routed Lynn Classical about 10-0. I pitched the last three inning of this game. I can remember curling in my shoulders as I pitched. This seemed this was just the catcher and I. I struck out about 6 or 7 in the three innings. I was thinking of being a pitcher than a thrower. I had the arm, but I needed work. After this game, I drove with Elizabeth to the coaching, in my brother Bob's truck. This was a rush.

I would coach and Elizabeth would be in the stands. I remember the 13 years old children I coached. I felt at a grown-up level when I would be with Elizabeth around them.

Our baseball team went to the semi-finals in the State Tournament where we lost to Durfee High 4-2. Elizabeth went to the game. The game was at Brandies University. I was taking tetra-hychloric-carbonate throughout the days. I had tried the purple THC pills, but I did not like them.

Well after graduation, my friends and I rented out a cottage down Cape Cod. Elizabeth and her friends had rented one out a few miles away. The breaks in the car were fixed before we left. My friend Dave Copper was driving my car a 1968 Chrysler Convertible. I was with Tex driving in his car. The person whom supposedly had fixed the breaks, I think knew I would be with Elizabeth down the Cape.

I think Tex and I were smoking marijuana. I could remember the joint burnt my fingers and I thought something very bad was with us. Right around this time Dave signaled for us to pull over. We pulled over in a parking lot. Dave told us.

"The break light went on."

I told him.

"Let me try this."

I got into the car and the break light did go on.

"I think we should leave the car here."

I said.

Then I noticed sparks under the car.

"Get back."

I said to Dave and Tex.

Then the engine caught fire. The fire department came and they totaled the car inside and out, to put the fire out. I called home and told what happened. Then Tex, Dave and I went to the Cape in Tex car. I had the premonition something was wrong. We got to the cottage and we were all high. The breaks were supposedly fixed, but how fixed?

The mechanic's name was Beasa.

Well we were at the Cape and all my friends and I, were high all the time. Elizabeth bought a nickel bag of marijuana. We would play cards together in the kitchen. After a while we would throw the cards at each other. I was really in love. I had a wonderful time the whole week with all of my friends. Probably the best time of my life up until then.

At the end of the time there, Tex and I had breakfast at a restaurant. Tex had ordered, "steak and eggs." The first time I had ever heard of this. The week at the Cape was over and I killed time with Elizabeth quite a lot.

I can remember there was a Babe Ruth game during the week I was down the Cape. I felt bad about this I wasn't amenable to the team. Our assistant coach coached while I was at the Cape.

Elizabeth and I would go for rides in my brother Jack's Studebaker car. I would also use the car, which I helped get a good deal on. I had loaned money for a repossessed car. We saved about 2000 dollars on this car.

Elizabeth would sing along with the song.

"Will you marry me Bill."

She was thinking marriage while I was thinking I would go off to college and I date an educated woman and get married.

I went to the movie "Jaws" with her and I was high. I can remember the part when the two people were wrangling with, to go after the shark first. They were showing each other scars, which they had. The one with the most scars would go down after the shark first. This was one incident in which made me think whom, could suffer the most a few weeks later.

I was taking 4 or 5 hits of THC every day. I played Legion baseball on THC. I actually thought this could make me play better. I pitched a no-hitter on this and this was against Natick under the lights. I was getting back at them for when we lost in football 9-8 with 12 seconds on the clock they kicked a field goal.

I told a person one night I had pitched a no-hitter. This person Jimmy Sivad whom was a Marine in Nam I told this to. He would watch Vietnam War situation at night. I told him I had pitched a no-hitter.

He looked at me and said.

"You pitched a no-hitter?"

This was another case when I thought how much you had suffered. Elizabeth was at the no-hitter game. I would glance every now and then and fire. This reminded me of the pitcher at the beginning of the century Pete Alexander, whom would pitch and look over to his wife in the stands. This would give him confidence in pitching. They had a movie about this man. He might have been a pitcher whom was in the First World War.

After the game I introduced Elizabeth to my brother Jack, whom was watching the game also. I was thrilled I had done well in front of a girlfriend. But I was a little bit abashed by Elizabeth, in public after the game. I still didn't think I had the perfect girlfriend. I had wished she had been smart in the academics.

I was also coaching Babe Ruth baseball these days. I would take the THC and this would give me false confidence. I would be constantly whistling like mad, crack bats, and holler at a fearful loving way at the players. I can remember lucidly the whistling with each player when they did well. I would try to inspire confidence in each player.

Larry was an assistant coach, whom would stop by and help the pitchers on the team. Also was assistant coach Paul Neirbo as I told you earlier. I had plenty of attention, while I felt in control of everyone at the parks. We were in first place in the Babe Ruth League for 13 years older. I liked coaching more than playing.

We had a couple of Legion baseball games, but since I was a coach, my desire to play was over seeded by coaching. I can recall I would drop off the players at their houses, after games. I can recall one player whom I drove home and he confided in me.

"I feel bad about wearing braces on my teeth."

"I used to wear braces."

I was thinking I felt the best I have ever had in my life. The song on the radio, "There is no one on earth I would rather be."

I can recall when I went over my lady friend Elizabeth home one day.

"I went to your uncle's mass when he died, when he was Chief of Police in Norwood. I was the Class Treasurer and I went with all the Class Officers."

I had all of the class officers in my car and we went to the mass and also we went for a cruise after the mass. There were about 6 or 7 of us in my Delta Oldsmobile, which I had paid more than half for when the car was repossessed.

She then said.

"When my cousin Dickie was killed in Vietnam my dad said this was what gave my uncle a heart attack and killed him."

"He was in the marines. Wasn't he?"

"He was on his third 6 month tour of the jungle, when he was shot through the heart. Are you hungry?"

While trying to get on a topic which was not too personal.

"How about a hamburger?"

I asked her.

"Okay, I'll make you a hamburger."

She said.

"I'll show you how I like this."

We went into the kitchen and I showed her how I like to flatten the hamburger first before cooking this.

"I like my hamburger on toast."

I said to her.

"I'll make this your way."

I can remember her cutting the hamburger and I began to feel a remote attraction to her then.

"You like your hamburger this way?"

She asked me.

"Ya."

We both ate and then sat down and viewed our yearbooks.

"What does this stand for?"

I asked her about what she put in her yearbook.

"Ya, I wrote this about Johnny Cox. Remember when I went out with him years ago?"

"Oh ya, I put in Police come to Boston. The song, Remember this song last year?

"Ya, I liked that song."

"Ya, this was why I put this in."

"I think when I have children, I'll have a cesarean section."

"Why do you want that?

"Child birth is supposed to be painful."

I began to think a bit independent. Why have them cut open your stomach, when you can be more autonomous by having the baby straight. Well she then told me.

"I have to go to the store. We'll go in my car."

She rode to the store while I was riding shotgun. I think we got cigarettes. I felt a bit different with her driving and me in the passenger side now. I would usually be driving my car with her. But I felt all right, as if there was a far away enchanting between us.

We drove back to her house and I walked her to her job, where she worked as a nurse's aid in a Nursing Home.

"There are some fresh old men in the Nursing Home."

"At the Nursing Home?"

"Ya, they say to me. Honey, how about a kiss? I just say no to them. But there is this one person whom is really fresh with me."

I got a little chuckle out of this. I was walking with her and I felt this was arbitrary wonderful. I think I loved her then.

I was over her house one night and her brother Neil was there. He was up from North Carolina in the Marines. He supposedly drove 24 straight hours to get home. He was sitting in a rocking chair drinking whiskey. I really surveyed towards him quite a bit. Elizabeth told me.

"Neil is dating one of the Charchis."

I asked.

"Debbie or Diane?"

"Debbie and Diane were two girls in our class.

She said.

"Mrs. Charchi the mother."

I was almost in awe about this. Mrs. Charchi was in her early forties. He really looked like an ugly Marine. He had the ugly smile from physical exertion. I had this type of smile years later when I played rugby.

I applied for the factory job, which I worked the previous summer. I thought I would earn my keep for college by working here. I had been accepted to Syracuse, but I opted not to go there, because they didn't have a baseball team. I thought I could play baseball anywhere. I would go to UMass Amherst and study to become an engineer. I had received a scholarship to UMass. I was going to room with my friend Dave Bird. He had also received the Comeback of the year award in Calculus. He was studying Pre-Med. He had been accepted to Tufts Pre-Med, but wanted to room with me at UMass.

Elizabeth's dad was personnel officer of some type at the factory. I was thinking of maybe asking her dad to see about a job at the factory. But then I thought I would meet an educated girl, and I would no longer be dating his daughter. I wouldn't use her.

At the factory I would pick roofing shingles from an upright position. When I was working at about the 19 ½th hour of a double shift, I fell asleep standing up. I had lied about my age the year before. I thought about the word shingles, as shing-gals. Gals as college girls, while on this job.

Well I couldn't get the factory job, and I was audacious for money. I saw an add in the paper, "College students, door to door salesman."

Well, I was thinking I had my name in the paper for sports, so this would be all right to take an employment ad out of the paper. So I went down and filled out the application. I was popping THC pills the first day. I was putting high school and everything with this behind me. I was to be a "door to door" salesman. I would be selling vacuum cleaners. The head salesman there said I would be on the road the next day.

I can recall the night before, I had gone too a concert at Schaefer Stadium. I had practiced demonstrating the vacuum cleaner at my home. I was looking at practicing demonstrating like I was doing homework at night. I came down this day and I was all dressed up. We had coffee at nine o'clock in the morning. I was bonded with this company. I went with a veteran salesman about 10 or 15 miles away to a residential area in Brockton I recall. He had gone to college and was now a salesman. He told me.

"This is the best job there is. You can make the most money, than any job. You are your own boss."

He had a vacuum cleaner and scrubber in the backseat of his car. This person seemed as if college had done him good. He looked more concrete or polished up. When he told me this, I began to think there could be some important money in this for me. He told me a little of the opening sales statements I would use, when I solicited on doors.

"Say, I'm on a scholarship program with Electrolux, and they are offering me $5.00 just to demonstrate the vacuum cleaner in your home."

I then repeated this to him. This was what I was to say after I solicited at the door and met the house dweller.

"Then give them a card and tell them, you will be right back, to demonstrate the machine. If they tell you they don't want one, tell them I get 5.00 for demonstrating the machine. You don't have to buy one."

This type of talk was new to me. I was a bit tense, but I strife onward. I would repeat this to him and he would put in responses. Then when I said this to him playing the part of a house dweller he said.

"I get 5.00 for demonstrating the machine, you don't have to buy one."

"I already own a vacuum cleaner."

I was brought to a standstill. Words had an onerous time coming out, but I was picking up some.

"Tell them this vacuum cleaner is better than yours. I'll go over a room already cleaned by your vacuum cleaner, and will come up with more dirt."

I had some of the sales responses in my mind. I then met another salesman, whom was getting ready for the soliciting door to door. I was battling with fear of starting, also how will these words come out of me. I was trembling, because I was scared of actually moving towards those first couple of doors. Steve was the person whom was training me. I went all over this again with Steve.

"Just say, I'm with Electrolux. I'm on a scholarship program with them and they are offering me $5.00 to demonstrate the vacuum cleaner in your home. If they say no, then say something like. This is a free demonstration. You don't have to buy anything."

I was extremely nervous, as I wasn't quite sure if I could fight with the words like this. This was a completely new way of talking for me. I frayed through and decided to give this a try.

"Hello, I'm Bill Breen. I'm working with Electrolux, and they are offering me $5.00 to demonstrate the machine in your home."

"We already own a vacuum cleaner."

Steve said acting like a home dweller. I didn't know what to say.

"Say something like. This is a free demonstration. You don't have to buy anything. Or say something like I can pick up more dirt than your vacuum cleaner."

Said Steve.

I battled onward and I was fighting for the words to come out. I would practice these statements in the car, as we would have an impromptu. I went to my first house and this was an experience.

"Hello, I'm Bill Breen. I'm on a scholarship program with Electrolux. They are offering me $5.00 to demonstrate the vacuum cleaner in your home."

"I'm not interested."

She said.

"This cost nothing. I get $5.00 for cleaning a room free of charge."

I said.

This was a pitch I came up with. I will clean a room free of charge. I was being myself now. I felt I was talking to them sincerely and honestly then. I would go to each house and I would start new statements, as I would talk to the house dwellers.

"Hello, I'm Bill Breen. I'm on a scholarship program with Electrolux. They are offering me $5.00 to demonstrate the machine in your home."

I would say.

"I already own an Electrolux."

"Do you need bags?"

I quickly retorted.

"Yes I do."

"Well I'll be right back. I have to go to my car for the bags."

I said to her.

"All right."

She said.

I went to my car and got some bags to sell to her.

"This will be $5.00. Will these be check or cash?"

"Here is $5.00 for the bags."

I said.

I had my first sale ever, and this was a very good feeling, considering I had to go door to door for this sale. This made me feel better for work, as this little felicity gave me confidence in myself. I would go to the next houses with a bit more zest and enthusiasm. I was slowly but surely learning the different pitches to say. I began to think about pitches in baseball as a connection.

"I can get into about 1 out of 30 houses I knock on."

Steve said.

He was about 22 years old and he was going a bit bald already at 22. He was about 6'1" and 180 lbs. He had been doing the sales since he was 18 years old. His dad was the person whom ran the office. Tom was his dad's name.

Well I started and there were no more happy highs on the THC. This couldn't lessen the fear I had looking into the eyes of a person, which didn't like you 9/10 of the time. I became acclimated with these reactions, as I got my courage up for each door I knocked on. I went with this second salesman for the first couple of days. If I had a lead to demonstrate the machine, I would get this other salesman. He would do the demonstrating. He would be on one side of the street, while I would have the other.

Well, while I was with this person soliciting, we went by this lake and Steve said with a quality of confidence to his voice.

"I'm going to pick up those girls."

I was 18 and the other salesman was 22. The two girls were around 20 or 21. I had another weapon besides my good looks, to pick up girls with, my sales talk. Don't give up with the girls in talking. I no longer would think of the girls whom were crazy over you, and wasn't a challenge to talk to them. I still was seeing Elizabeth, but I was beginning to eye a blonde haired girl. I can remember kissing Elizabeth one of these nights, and I thought this was like a kiss of death. This was a really good kiss. Years later I thought she had the nickname lips.

Our head football coach John Fudd started this year a football captain's club. All the captains would get together with this years football team. This was I believe four years since John was coach. I stood up and spoke at the meeting. This was the coach whom I spoke to before the Walpole Game the previous year and I had turned my year around.

At the football club meeting I now thought I liked football more than baseball, even though, I was better in baseball. I hadn't gone to the

Legion baseball game this night, because my heart was really in football. I was captain anyway, with all things considered. The salesman job gave me confidence, to speak up and have conviction in myself.

I no longer was a boy whom wanted to feel good. I was a salesman starting out with the pressures of one. This made me not be afraid of pushing myself. Everything sports, coaching, studying, couldn't be of any solace, in this was time to really grow-up. I had a whole new way of life, which gave me confidence as my persuasive, and assertive way of talking.

I began to train a girl saleswoman, whom was just starting door to door. I drove her to the new site to canvas. This was the idea of site, which I began to not be interested in engineering anymore. I would connect these sites with engineering sites. I began to not be interested in engineering.

I went to lunch with this salesgirl to a restaurant. Steve was training someone else. I saw a waitress, whom was a friend of Elizabeth at the restaurant. I was thinking Elizabeth might have thought I was cheating on her. I knew for a fact I wasn't, because this was a business luncheon. I was feeling more self-assured because I was having a business date. I can remember I was poised and assured of myself. I had gone from scholar-athlete to a "door to door" salesman. I was finding Bill Breen instead OF Billy Breen.

As I was walking the streets these days as a salesman, I said to myself I would get my Masters in Engineering. A day or so later, I said I would play football in college. I was thinking I wouldn't before, because of the level of competition at UMass. Now I thought I would for the experience.

The time came to solicit around my neighborhood. The training salesman told me this was time to do around my neighborhood of where I lived in Norwood. I thought this would be like sacrificing, and I was scared. I would have to sales talk my neighbors to sell them a vacuum cleaner. I was afraid my neighbors wouldn't like me for trying to talk them into letting me demonstrate the machine in their homes.

I can remember walking out of my house all dressed up and I saw my neighbors sitting on their steps. They said.

"Hi."

To me in a more respectful way, than all those days I would go out in my uniforms to play either baseball or football. They didn't have the casual talk this time, as I was all dressed up. I walked out and headed for my first house.

"Hello Ann Carzy, I'm working with Electrolux and they are offering me five dollars to just demonstrate the vacuum cleaner in your home."

"I don't think so."

She responded.

"You don't understand. I receive 5 dollars for a free demonstration."

I came back with.

"All right, when can I have my demonstration?"

She stated

"Would Monday morning at 10:00 be all right?"

"Yes, that will be fine."

She said.

I was actually battling with words. I now had to fight with the English language. Mrs. Carzy did not have that happy smiley face which she would have when I would talk to her about sports, which I played. She now had a stern look about her. This got me to think I now had to picture her as a customer for sales, instead of neighbor. I had to begin to grow up.

I booked some responses to set-up appointments for the equipment. I would notice if the people whom came to the doors were phonies or not. I wasn't quite sure what to make of people, if they were phonies or not. I didn't have a clear definition of the word phony.

I was once talking to my boss in his car and he said to me.

"Maybe you might not want to go to college."

This put a whammy on me. I thought college was supposed to "the thing," *THE* thing to do, to better your-self. The salesman job definitely had the money aspect to this, but was this worth putting up with the abuse of this. I said to myself, whom, would want to knock on doors their whole lives? What kind of person would want to suffer which I thought a "door to door" salesman did the rest of their lives. I thought college was supposed to be the best time of your life. Now to suffer while being a "door to door" salesman, I began to think this was good to suffer. One of these days I said to myself maybe no college, and no sports.

Well back to when I was soliciting around my neighborhood. I received an okay to demonstrate the vacuum cleaner. I remember looking into the eyes of my neighbors and there wouldn't be any of those kidding smiles, as there were when I was in high school.

"I'm on a scholarship program with Electrolux Mrs. Amirault. Would you like me to demonstrate the vacuum in your home?"

"I don't think so. I already own a vacuum cleaner."

"This is a free demonstration. You don't have to buy anything. I get $5.00 for demonstrating the vacuum cleaner."

She finally gave in and said.

"All right then."

I began to demonstrate the vacuum cleaner and I wasn't quite sure how to demonstrate properly. I would put the dirt on the carpet and I was thinking I was embarrassing them. I was a cutthroat. I was going around in circles in distress. I think I began to sweat a bit. I finally gave in and said.

"Sign here."

On the card, which allowed me to get $5.00 for demonstrating the equipment. I had been having a lot of direct eye contact with people when I would meet them at the doors. I left the house where I demonstrated the machine, and I began to talk to my boss. I was talking to him in direct eye contact, and I thought he wasn't blinking his eyes that frequent. I began to not to blink mine, but this was painful. He was telling me.

"You'll get better on demonstrating. You should sell a vacuum cleaner on average of 1 out 3 houses you demonstrate, like me."

I was in a panic. I thought the reason why he wasn't blinking, was because he wanted to suffer. This was where I cracked. I then began to think there was a race to see whom could suffer the most. Now sports, school, and coaching were bad, because they lead to happiness. I called this a day, as the time was around 4:30 and I believe this was a Saturday and the fourth of July was on Monday. The "door to door" salesman worked 6 days per week. I then walked home.

I would now think of looking into people's eyes. I would see which person had suffered the most. I thought the one whom had suffered the most would be in charge of the conversation. I thought about on television and the poor countries of the world like Biafra or India and these people would pull you down from their own suffering, and give you strength to go on.

I can remember going over my grandmothers' for Fourth of July cookout. I had stopped playing baseball. Because sports were enjoyable and you were suppose to suffer. I began to think the good was bad and the bad good. At the cookout I can vividly recollect someone say real loud.

"Jesus Christ."

Which just about put me in a trance, and my uncle Mick said something, but I don't recall exactly what. I heard about the Legion Baseball game against Dedham.

Well my Babe Ruth team was having a playoff game for first place in the league. I had now thought no longer about acting out at the games. So now I had to become bad. I tried to lose instead of win. I had given the coach John Nesnaj of the other team, about a middle-aged man, a forearm to the shoulder. I can recall when he was coaching first base and I heard him say something like.

"Was that a strike Joey? Come on pitcher throw the ball over the plate."

John Nesnaj said.

I came out of the dugout and said to him.

"Are you going against his pitching ability?"

"What do you say to that?"

He said.

I gave him a quick stiff arm to the shoulder. He backed down a bit, and put his shoulder forward then calmed down. I then said to him.

"Don't be nagging my players."

All the men spectators in the park stood up and you could hear this low grown.

"Whooee."

I now thought I was bad and I would think of the song, "Nobody knows what it is like to be the bad man, the sad man inside."

I think this is by the, "Who," the singing group. Well we won the game and I was really trying to lose, but we won 4-2 and won the Title for 13 years older.

Now I was feeling what this is like to be bad after all those successful years. I remember the look on children's faces and they wanted to play baseball so much. I no longer had the hunger and thirst for knowledge, as I thought this was for children.

Well after the game, I took the 13 years old children to get ice cream. I had some whisky or vodka or something, and I tried to get the children to drink. I don't think any of the children wanted any liqueur.

I remember seeing all my high school athletes and scholar friends, which were waiting to go to college. They appeared so innocent, with the hunger and thirst for knowledge. They would want to talk to me, but I actually thought the good was bad, and the bad good, and there was a race to see whom could suffer the most. I thought these people were happy people, and they wouldn't suffer. I tried to hang around people whom were like street fighters. The people whom were going to college, I was only accepted by. This wasn't a challenge to chum around with them.

I can recall when I went to a club, and I was talking to Jimmy Sivad whom had said to me. You pitched a no-hitter. Jimmy had been a Marine in Nam. With the war over I could feel he was one of the ones whom made me feel very strongly now the good was bad and the bad was good.

I broke up with Elizabeth. I had tapped her with my right arm. I thought, "had McMurphy," but was mental." The next thing I noticed was that some friends from my youth came by and we went to the town Medfield, to try and get into a fight. We went there and one of us got into protective custody. When we went to the police station to get him out of jail, one of the policeman, there said.

"That's a Breen."

I felt actually good I was now known for bad things instead of good. I had stopped the salesman job because of a number of things.

Well my friend Tex whom was car salesman, and I did a lot of paling together these days, because he was a salesman also. Tex and I watched one of the legion baseball games from a car and we were drinking beer. I really would look at children these days and I could see the ice cream smile on their faces. All of my friends whom were going off to college seemed like they were so happy about this. I had read years later by a speech by JFK that children hunger and thirst for knowledge.

I recall when I was with Tex and Dave Washy, and we were in a restaurant for fried clams at the Red Wing restaurant. Dave went to hitch hike home about 10 or 15 miles away at about 10:00 at night. I was wondering why would he want to hitch hike home so late at night. After he left, Tex and I went to the counter seats, and wrote on a piece of paper to an about 35 years old waitress. "How would you like to spend some time with two young men?"

She asked a male worker there.

"Who wrote this?"

"These two young men here"

Said the male worker with an astonished look on his face.

Tex and I had the brass to do something like this. The waitress looked at us and I am not sure what she did. I think she gave a little smile uncontrollably.

I began to think about older couples, married or not. And why they would fight while conversing. I would only watch certain shows on television. I thought only shows, which were difficult to watch were good for you. Also I felt the same way about music on the radio. Only music, which you didn't like, was good for you. I was thinking of the elderly people whom had suffered and this was good to be with them.

I can recall when my sister Maura had come home for something another, and I had a rage and threw a cup at her. She had told one of her friends, I had thrown a cup at her, and her friend said something like.

"He must have been just a little angry."

I thought the word, if. If she could have seen something in me then, this could have prevented me from going out that window. If I had told the coach I had taken THC at the baseball game. These were the incidents before I was hospitalized and I would say to myself. Why didn't I do something about this before?

I took for a ride a young man from my neighborhood. I had a stick, which I would hit him with in the car. Domenic was his name and he kept on saying.

"I want to go home."

I thought about sister teachers' in grade schools as using a stick to enforce learning. I also thought about a colonel as having a stick.

I thought about hanging around a street corner. These were the people whom didn't think about studying or sports. They would hang around street corners. This was around my neighborhood where I lived. I usually would go to downtown Norwood to pal around with. I recall the day I tried to be in the gang. I thought someone there said something like, "Sports."

I began to think before you are accepted in a gang you have to fight, someone or somebody so many times. There is no easy way in.

I drove with Jimbo and Johnny Cox up to New Hampshire for a few days. We were at someone's cottage and I remember I threw a drink into Judy's face. This girl I had seen right after I had given a speech in the high school. When I was younger I would hangout with her. I had also hollered at her. After this we went to another person's cottage to sleep. Before I went to sleep, I had been staring people down. I think I was drinking whiskey and I was making people there a fearful of me. The next day I had my demo vacuum cleaner in my car that I knocked on doors with, and I tried to sell vacuum cleaners there.

I was brought up to coach the 13 to 15year old boys baseball team. After one of the games a person whom was coach of the Needham High baseball team was conversing with me and he began to smile a bit. I think we might have been talking about colleges or something. I thought people whom smiled were happy and you were supposed to suffer. So I gave this about 40 year old man a quick right forearm to his left shoulder. He looked at me no longer smiling and with a cringed face he said.

"Billy."

Some of the people in the park noticed me do this. I felt good I was bad. "Nobody knows what it is like to be the bad man the sad man inside."

I can recollect when I went fishing and I had gotten some worms at a bait and tackle store. When I was fishing, I saw two ladies with their son fishing. I remember they were talking.

"I read about acne in the magazine today Joan."
Said one of the ladies.
"Ya, they say young people get this the worst."
The other one said.

I could remember the ladies looked like the housewives I would see on the sales job. I don't think I caught any fish, but I was feeling at a new level of awareness to whom, I would harangue with. Myself I wouldn't worry about any acne anymore.

I went to a social function dance one night. I saw the blonde haired girl there whom I was eyeing. I was ready and waiting to make a move with her. But Tex got to her before I did. I was raging mad. I stormed the building where I saw our 205 lbs. All-scholastic tackle Grega. He was with the Prescott gang sitting on a car, with his friends from Prescott. This was the gang which I had leave the triplet's party.

Grega was the person whom I almost had it out with when I put in everyone's lockers before we lost to Natick in football. Well now I went right up to him and attacked him sitting on the car. I fought off the feeling mentally I could be "jumped" by his friends. I picked him off the car and, "took the bull by the horns," and through him to the ground tar. I was on top of him and I just couldn't hit him. I froze. I then let him go. I wasn't sure exactly why I had done this. He got up and smacked me in the face. I had ripped his shirt in the struggle. I then went home and got another shirt and came back looking for him for an all out fight. I rolled up my sleeves and looked for him, but he was nowhere to be seen. I had held my head high and back, as I looked down at the place all his friends were at the parking lot. I was looking for Grega.

I recall my brother Bob wanted the keys to my car. I declined. I again said to myself in hospital. Why didn't I follow his advice? "If, if, if."

From the Grega showdown I went to a parking lot where my friends and I would pass time. I had learned from the sales job if you embarrass someone, then this person will treat you good. At the parking lot, Tex began to get it on with the blonde. He began to get intimate with her, right in front of us near some automobiles. He was embarrassing everyone. I didn't think my friends knew that they were being embarrassed. Also they will then treat him good. But I did know this and Tex knew this also, because he was a salesman.

Well I began staring at the blonde and Tex and they stopped making out in public. I had begun to smoke a cigarette. I was with Johnny Cox. The blonde and Tex were in Tex car. I was going to start a fight with Tex. Then he said to me.

"Your on your own."

I thought he said this in a deep voice. I thought he said this with a powerful voice. Johnny Cox was laughing and I thought he would side with me if I were to fight Tex. Tex got into his car and I held on to the door handle as he sped away. I had gotten a ride on the tar about 50 feet. After this my close friend Dave Copper said to me.

"What's the matter Bill?"

I had been seeing the smiley happy faces on all the people whom were going off to college to play sports and study. I didn't say anything to him. He told me later he cried this night. I couldn't confide in anyone. I thought the good was bad and the bad good, and this wasn't good to help people. I thought why wouldn't I talk to my friend Dave?

Right around this time, UMass Amherst called, and asked if.

"Are you going to UMass Amherst in September?"

"No, I'm not going to college."

I years later thought of this dragging on the tar connected with UMass Amherst. I had plans to room with my friend Dave there. Dave did go there and studied Pre-Med and got a perfect 4.0 for two years.

One of these nights I was uptown Norwood Center and Elizabeth was cruising with one of her friends. I had about 30 baseballs in the trunk of my car. Franco the person, whom was driving the car when the person was killed, and Johnny Cox and I were throwing baseballs at their car as they drove around. This was a real wild night.

I got a clump of dirt and threw this at the car. I didn't know there was a rock in this. The dirt around the rock hit the windshield, and cracked this. After this, Elizabeth got out of her car and rolled up the sleeves of her jacket. I felt this gesture somewhere inside. She was angry. This was a new quality I saw in her personality anger. I hadn't seen this up until then. I felt a new closeness with Franco and Johnny after this night of hell-razing.

Around this time I had driven with a young friend of mine to East Walpole to look for a fight. I tried to start a fight with two different people there, but they declined. My friend whom didn't have his license drove my car home. I had heard they had a gun in East Walpole. Also I believe I was looking for acid.

I walked to my grandmother's house about two miles from East Walpole in Norwood. My shoulders went up and they stayed up without putting effort in them. I went to the third floor of her house and just contemplated things. I then went to the library and looked up the word charisma. This meant exceedingly high quality for leadership. The word exceedingly I had recollected the letter I received from Yale University had this word in this. The letter said something like exceedingly high standards.

I then walked to my home. My brother Jack wanted his sneakers in my room. I wouldn't give them to him. He told Jack Sr. and he came up to the room to get the sneakers. He then came in. He said.

"Why didn't you give Jackie the sneakers?"

I grabbed a baseball bat and began to check swing him. He backed off a bit. I then went by him and headed for some woods. I went into the woods and got down on my knees, and began to pray on a path. I saw a rabbit come out and walk a little ways from me. I then headed for the Junior high school, where I saw the Queen Brothers' on their bikes. I asked them if I could use his bike to go for a ride.

As I was riding the bike, I thought the police were after me. I think I was headed for Medfield or Natick. I don't recall exactly where I was headed. I thought the police were after me, so I dumped the bike and headed for some more woods. I raced through the woods up by the dump and cemetery. I saw a friend of mine Bobby Molly parked in a parking lot with his girlfriend. I began to talk to him casually like and he got out of his car. I then got in and tried to steal his car with his girlfriend. I was getting the keys when Bobby got a baseball bat. I really thought I could take the car. I really thought I could pull this off. He took a swing at me and I wasn't going to jeopardize a blow to the head, so I got out.

From here I got a ride to Westwood. I got in the back of an abandon house and I got into a yoga position. I was listening to the crickets. I was thinking of going into the house 30 days and 30 nights. I began to listen to a cricket, which came closer and closer. Then I said as the cricket came near me.

"What do you want?"

I stayed there for the night and then at about 6:00 the next morning I walked about 3 miles home. I stayed there until about 10:00 AM and then my dad wanted to talk to me. I got the keys to my car and began to leave. I told my sister to get my wallet. She did and I had about 35 dollars in this. I went for a cruise to the city Taunton Mass. I was having gas put in my car when the man at the pump said.

"It's a beautiful day."

When he said this, I began to think the good was good and the bad is bad correctly once again. I got three donuts, which was the first food I had in three days. I was celebrating good is good and bad is bad once again.

I was driving through Wrentham Mass. When I saw the baseball player Chuck J. whom had struck out 20 against us. He had a six-pack beer while he was hitch hiking. He told me.

"I just got back from Florida. I had been drafted."

He was a pitcher whom could really throw. I pitched against him at the All-star game in which I threw a no-hitter, and struck out 11 in 5 innings of pitching. This was the night I received the card to send into the Red Sox to be projected on in the future. Chuck had graduated the year before from Walpole High. He also told me.

"They really give you a lot of shit down there."

Meaning baseball camp down Florida. I had dropped him off at East Walpole, which was his destination. After this I drove home.

August 1, 1975

My uncle Joe Breen came over to the house and he wanted to talk to me. My parents had asked him to come over because how I had been acting. He was a person whom would never be embarrassed. Things seemed to fall in place for him. He could change an embarrassing situation into constructive for him. He was a Probation Officer, so my parents probably thought he could be a good talker as well as listener.

I talked to him not too serious in the beginning. I wanted to hold in my feelings. I had put on a mask. I was talking to him nonchalant, but I knew he was here for business. I don't know what hit me, but I asked him.

"Is the good bad and is the bad good?"

He replied.

"Ya."

I now was thinking more potently the good was bad and the bad good, and this was true. I could remember reading in the Bible the previous months, while I was having influence from heavy doses of Tetra-hychloric-carbonate in the letters from the apostle Peter. That Christ a good man died for bad men. When I had read this I thought the good was bad and the bad good.

My stomach was feeling the affects of nervousness but not knowing what nervous about. I had fish for supper and while I was eating the fish the day hit me. This wasn't going to be any ordinary night. I don't know the connection between the fish and the night. My grandfather dropped off fish every Friday. He would drop this off with his daughter Lucy, to all his children in Norwood. This would give him something to do during the day.

I then after supper, went up to my room and began to stare at the curtains out of where I heard the voice, "I WANT YOU," six months previous. I was staring at the curtains again. I thought I could make out Jesus or myself on the cross. I tried to concentrate, to give me a better vision of the cross. My eyes were dilating.

I began to stretch in which I would arch my back, back. Then I would just about pass out on the bed. I thought I would pass out by stretching. The scent was like foggy, but no fog. This was a damp odor, like an old age home.

The first stretch and I would descend on the bed, but I was still conscious. Something would go to my head and put me out cold for a few seconds. The second stretch and the odor would get more forceful. Then after the third stretch, I would lie down in bed and stare at the curtains again. I would see more of the cross, which I could make out in the curtains. This was a small figure, which I thought was Jesus Christ on the cross. I just glimpsed at the face. This was when I thought this might be me I perceiving on the cross.

My sister Stephanie knocks on the door and said something like.

"Are you going to watch television?"

I responded with.

"Okay."

Trying not to act inconspicuous as possible.

The fourth stretch and I had just about passed out. I was perspiring. The fifth stretch and I thought I would pass out. I thought I would be out cold. Then I went back to bed where I was staring at the curtains. I thought I would have to stretch 7 times and then I would be all set. As I had a steadying look at the curtains, I don't know what came over me, but I thought I had received a command from God to do whatever came into my mind. The thought of going out the bathroom window came into my mind. I thought I had to do this or I wouldn't be following God's command.

This normal day had an abnormality to this. There was going to be great suffering. I thought of stretching two more times and then I would be all right. But I thought this would be taking the easy way out.

Then I went into the bathroom and took a bath. When I went into the bath, I thought this was a time to be with water. "Sometimes late at night, when I'm bathing the firelight, the who comes a call'n a ghostly white." Seager.

The damp misty odor was there in full scent. I can remember a baptismal of some sorts, with the lukewarm water, as I was fondling this in my hand. I would drop this over me. I remembered the year before, when I had come home late one night from working 20 straight hours in the factory, and I was in this bathroom taking a bath. I had put my head under water, as I was very, very tired. I had just about fell asleep with my head under water, but then I pulled my head back, and out of the water. Now I was feeling I would do anything God wanted me to do, no matter what.

I went back to my room where I had on my bathrobe. I then began to pray as I was lying down in bed. I wrote a note I loved all my family. I wrote each ones names. I must have perspired five pounds as I soaked the bed from head to toe. I then had the urge to eat the note, which I had written to my family. I ate the paper. Looking back at this, I think the paper was like the Holy Eucharist. I was thinking I might not want to go out that window, but the command was still there. The perspiring I was doing smelt sacred. This smelt like a Funeral Home.

I made my way into the bathroom. I was scared so much because I knew I would be going out the window. If I didn't, then things would be worse. Because God knows what is best for you. There would be no demurring.

I opened the window slowly as I felt I was actually going down already. I was in horror. I was petrified. I was thinking I would be falling down head first onto asphalt. I was getting more and more scared. A type of sacredness that would get thicker and thicker. I was onerous and arduous.

My sister Stephanie knocks on the door, as this was the triggering signal to head towards the window. The knock on the door was the start of following through with the command. I began to head towards the window. I think my heart went to hell thinking I was about to go down. I was going over the top.

I struggled through the initial commitment to jump. Then when I was halfway out, looking at the tar, and this seemed I had frozen, but I was still moving. I had to use will power to continue with the course of jumping out the window. I was past will power for most of the leap. As I was going down, my heart felt the depths of hell as I looked down. My eyes dried up with the breeze of going down. I landed with a thud, which was heaven. This was like a crunch that had no pain. I hadn't planned on saying anything, but out of my mouth came, "aaa." There was a hollow feeling as if something was coming out of me, hell. I thought if I suffered on purpose, I would then feel better. I pulled my head towards me as I was going down. So I would land on top of my head instead of face, as I was looking down with my eyes.

Chapter 2

"I have to shave your scalp."

Nurse.

"We have to put a catheter in you."

Said another nurse.

I felt like I was going to have my genitals cut off, as the stretcher was wheeled into the Emergency room. The quickness to get me into where they could work on me after a direct stop. Then the catheter was being put into me was as new to me, as what I had heard of the tubs which the Germans would cut off the genitals of the people they didn't think worthy. While not moving my legs, I felt like they were being held down while the catheter would ooze down the penis. There were the smiles on the nurse's faces, which probably attained from working in Emergency throughout the years. I can remember a broad smile on a Mrs. Connolly's face, which I had known her in my youth.

"He has a deep laceration on his head."

Mrs. Connolly said.

They were shaving my scalp with a manual hair razor. I could remember when I was in 6th grade, and I remember I bought a hair razor, so that I could give myself my own haircuts. I was with my friend Danny as we were practicing using the razor. He had shaved some hair from his legs, and he asked me to shave some off of mine, but I didn't have any on my legs at this age.

He said to me.

"You probably don't have any on your balls."

I had bought the hair razor so I could cut my own hair.

"I have pain in my back."

I said.

This was sharp stinging pain which I could only ally with when I had worked at the factory standing up straight for ten, some times 20 hours picking roofing shingles from a station the previous summer. I would have this burning sensation in my back after standing after hours and hours.

A doctor then said.

"Bring him to the x-ray department."

I was a little bit shocked I didn't have my head cared too. Instead they sent me directly to x-ray. They had shaved my scalp as best they could with the wounded head.

"We are going to move you in various ways for x-rays."

I don't clearly remember, but they could have x-rayed my head then.

"Now, hold your breath."

The technician said.

She would roll my body to sundry degrees, as if she was taking a hook off of a fish she just caught. She breathed of this type of pain, in people coming to her, real physical pain.

"One more time now. Hold your breath."

I would spit out at her statements like.

"You want me to suffer so you can feel good."

Because of my statements a doctor came into the room and said to me.

"We're trying to help you."

His arms and hands went back and head forward as if he was ready to do a broad jump. His mouth opened up like a kissing fish as he hissed.

I responded with.

"Ya, sure."

I was wheeled back to Emergency to get my head stitched up. There were now two doctors working on my head stitching this up.

"I have pain in my back."

I said to them.

I couldn't understand why I wasn't put on a cushion stretcher. I was on a rather hard bed. This was a little bit better than the cold curved bed, which the x-ray bed felt like.

This doctor responded with.

"Be quiet and don't move."

I could feel that numbness sensation of swelling of the Novocain going into my head before they would put in the stitches. The tone of voice of this doctor made me think this was best to keep quiet. This seemed the talking going on between the two doctors would irritate me.

"What are you looking into my eyes for?"

"I'm checking your pupils."

The intensive care nurse said.

I could then see her in a little booth closed in by glass. She seemed to look down the hall while I could see her profile. She seemed at an unrest waiting for her shift to end. She had short black hair and I thought my slightest bit of suffering, which I had done over the past day made me in competition with girls a little bit older now.

"How about a kiss?"

I said to the nurse.

She responded with.

"I'm married."

I was feeling a very mellow feeling when I had faith the nurse might just give me a kiss by the way that I asked her.

My thoughts of nurses whom work in hospitals were controllable were altered, by a rather surprised expression, a little bit, on the face of this nurse.

"Put him on the tilt table."

Said the surgeon dr. Revel.

He said this with a cutting to his voice.

This cutting serious made me staid in I didn't think this was good to be in this situation.

"Now tilt it."

He continued.

"I never expected paralysis."

I said.

I was brought back to the previous year when I had to speak to all the parents and the fall sports people at the Fall Banquet. I was thinking I would program dr. Revel in when he operated on me, he would think, I never expected paralysis, which I had stated.

At the Fall Banquet I had a note pad of what I was going to say as captain of the football team. I was thinking I would program the parents in the audience to think, as I would want them to think.

I said at the banquet.

"Now speaking the most respected person on this team."

The other captain I was introducing him to speak. I was trying to program the people to think, now speaking, meaning me. I wanted them to think I was the most respected person, but I was introducing the other captain to the microphone. All this flashed through my mind, as I said to dr. Lever. I never expected paralysis.

I responded to his command to the x-ray person. His face seemed to comeback to nonchalant, or he didn't seem as serious as he did when I first heard him speak. He seemed to give a very little smile, when I said this to him when he wasn't even talking to me. I was being x-rayed on my back.

"Hi Barzie."

"Hi Bill."

"I brought you a radio."

She had a forced smile on her face. I was thinking I liked Barzie when I was younger, but she was too mature for me then, besides being a grade higher. But now she seemed she liked me truly, to be romantic. She seemed actually to care for me. I had grownup with her. I think people whom you grow up with you have a special kind of bond too, which can't be broken. She sat down on the side of the bed as if she was holding down something. I grew up with her when I was younger.

"I came back from vacation."

Said a nurse whom had medium short black hair. She looked like she was around 25ish. I was thinking she came back to work so she could care for me, Bill Breen whom was pretty well known in town.

I told her.

"I got an erection."

Since I thought there was a race to suffer the most, I thought I would torment by being in a wheelchair, and I could have sex. This organ would work.

"I'm going to get the doctor."

She asserted.

Dr. Stolt whom had assisted on the operation came in and said to the nurse.

"Hold up the penis."

I felt this nurse's fingers, on the prepuce of my penis and this felt like ecstasy. I had feeling.

Dr. Stolt asked me.

"Can you feel this?"

I said.

"I could."

This wasn't a very strong erection but just the same this was a wonderful erection.

. The nurse's face seemed stern while dr. Stolt had a little smirk, on his face as he said.

"That's wonderful."

When he first came in.

"Hi Debbie, What are you in for?"

. "I had my appendix out. How are you?"

Debbie asked.

"I'm pretty drugged up and this makes me tired."

"Hi Patty."

"Hi Bill."

Patty was in to visit Debbie on the recovery floor. I had been eyeing her the previous month. She had long blonde hair and was very attractive. She was the girl whom Tex had picked up at the dance. She seemed concerned as we passed a very small bit of talk. I was thinking to myself I had nothing to be self-conscious about, because there was nothing to fear. My problems now were far greater than a self-conscious manner. She seemed a bit in awe when she saw me in bed, with my head all bandaged up.

I had a distorted image of people. Like their faces were cracked. People seemed to be able to control each other an extreme lot at this point.

"Hi Maura."

"Hi Bill."

This was my sister Maura.

"I'm going to give a gift to Brian in the V.A. Hospital. A car hit him. His foot got injured."

She came in with a very casual look on her face and she seemed more interested in giving the gift to her boyfriend than talking to me. I only had visitors from my immediate family at this stage.

"Hi Jackie."

"Hi Billy."

Jack, my brother seemed very withdrawn. He seemed he was just about spitting the words out of his mouth.

"Jack, could you get me some books on the spinal cord?"

"Ya, I will bring some in. I'll bring the strat-o-matic game also. Is there anything else you want?"

"No, that shall do it."

"Well, I will be seeing you."

"Ya, okay."

The strat-o-matic game was a computerized game I would play when I was younger. Now thinking about this, I feel I was prepared for something like being paralyzed. I had this game to play if I didn't recover.

I had been off the recovery floor and was put on a regular unit with other patients.

"Hi Billy."

Said my second cousin Janet.

'I've been in the hospital for five months now. I broke my leg very badly. They thought they might have to amputate. I broke this in five places, when I was in a bad car accident. I'm getting out pretty soon. How are you?"

"Janet said."

I knew Janet a little before, and I had a liking for her.

She stated again.

"How are you?"

"I'm paralyzed. I can't move my legs."

"Well I'm getting out next week and I can't wait."

I was feeling rather well, because I was medicated quite a bit. I was medicated pretty much so, for the pain I had in my back after the operation. Dr. Stolt had said I would lie in bed the rest of my life, because they can't tell if the swelling will go down in the spinal cord. This just about put me in shock. I thought still things were backwards. This was good to be in the position I was in. I thought I would be in a wheelchair the rest of my life, but to lie in bed I didn't expect to get that bad.

When I heard this news, what came to my mind was, this wasn't good to be in this situation would flash through my mind. Like when I saw the serious of the Neurosurgeon, and also when I saw the very withdrawn look on Jackie's face. They would make me straight in my thinking by their words and actions. My thinking disorder would be made straight from contact with these people.

The next morning and aid came in and said.

"Time to get up in a wheelchair."

I said.

"Okay."

I was thinking this would be helpful. This would be out of bed, and after hearing the news I would be in bed the rest of my life, I thought this would be getting better. This aid's name was John. He put both of his arms under mine and was about to pick me up. He seemed very much in a rush. When he began to pick me up I told him.

"I don't want to get into a wheelchair."

He seemed very sneaky in the way he was going to get me into a wheelchair. So when I told him I wasn't going to get into one he didn't put up any resistance at all. He said while leaving the room.

"You have to get in one sooner or later."

I wondered about how the idea of getting me up in a wheelchair came about. I had heard later I should just be on bed rest for a good while before up in a wheelchair. I also didn't have any back brace on either. Something fishy was happening at this hospital. This seemed John was beginning to become envious in the amount of attention, which I received from the girls working on the unit, and he wanted to be the one helping me. So he could try to overcome his jealousy of me in front of the woman. The aid John, I am pretty sure he was talking to or trying to talk to the surgeon dr. Revel about becoming a doctor. He was just an aid as I think he was just out of high school.

In to come into the room was a person with s strong built and red hair and beard. He came into the room like a Mac truck and introduced himself.

"I'm your physical therapist Billy Kold."

I asked him.

"What is the definition of a man?"

I remember the head "door to door" salesman said one day. "We have another man here now." Meaning me, when I was working with them.

Billy Kold had a full face and a thick tough complexion to his facial skin. He responded to my question with.

"I don't know."

He then later said.

"I will do range of motion exercises with you every day."

"Hi Jackie."

"Hi Billy. I brought you the strat-o-matic game and also some books on the spinal cord. Do you want to play the strat-o-matic game?"

"Alright."

I responded.

"Here are the teams."

"Which teams do you want?"

"I have your teams. Okay, roll the dice."

He said.

We played the game for a short while, and jack would say things like.

"Next batter up and let's go now."

I told jack.

"My arms are getting tired."

I sometimes devise I spit the dice out of my mouth instead of using my arms. Jack seemed to have new life in him. He came in, in a roll of thunder, as he knew I must work to get better. Get active as much as possible. He seemed in new spirits. The forsaken look which he had was now gone. The time was to do something about my ailment.

The next day when I saw Billy the PT, he crouched down on the side of my bed and said to me.

"I was in Vietnam."

I now thought this person had changed over from being a bad person to a good person a physical therapist. I felt good I had someone with his background talking to me. My right knee was twitching a little bit, but wouldn't get any stronger. The lady head PT came by with Billy and he wanted to have a muscle test. The head PT said.

"We won't have a muscle test yet."

"I think we should have one."

Said Billy.

He seemed he was in a racy way begging the head PT to give me a muscle test.

"Not right now."

The head PT said, as they both left the room passing words back to each other.

I got moved to another room with three other beds. I started to think I was dieing. I would stare at objects without blinking, as I would try to concentrate in not to be interrupted by anything.

Ruth Washy whom was the mother of my friend Dave Washy came in to my room. She worked at Hospital.

"Hi Billy. David is thinking about you. How are you doing?"

She commented.

I didn't respond to her as I thought I was seeing my last day. I was petrified. My hands were over my stomach as they are for people at wakes when they are already dead. This was a sacredness, which was the perfect scare, so why be afraid. Everyone dies, so why be excessive if this is the inevitable. I had to stop my ears from hearing anything. I had to be blind to the movements of anybody or anything. When I felt this was okay to close my eyes, I would close them. I would close them when I felt someone had made a move, which wasn't cool or natural.

My football coach John Fudd came in.

"Hi, How are you Billy?"

He said to me.

I still wouldn't talk to him. I was still thinking the good was bad and the bad, was good. I thought John Fudd a football coach was a good person, a football coach. So I wouldn't talk to him. Along with, I thought I was dieing, and I didn't want to have any contact with anyone.

"How are Daryle and Henry?"

He kept on trying to talk to me.

"Ya, it's supposed to be good weather."

He was talking to himself as if I were talking to him. But I didn't respond.

He left after he knew I wasn't going to talk to him.

Right around this time, my right arm rose from off the bed and I hadn't moved this on purpose. The right arm of God was up for me. My right arm when this had first lifted from the bed felt like this was part of me. The right arm was prodigious in stature.

The next day Loretta, an aid came in and said to me.

"Time for breakfast."

"Okay Loretta."

I said.

She showed me some scrambled eggs, which I thought looked like worm drippings. The scrambled eggs reminded me of the worm drippings which worms have.

I talked to another patient there and asked him.

"What happened to your foot?"

"A golf cart ran over my foot."

"Where are you from?"

He said.

"From Franklin."

I recalled my uncle Henry whom was from Franklin and had died Christmas morning 1965.

"Hi Billy."

"Hi Doc Black."

This doctor was the parent of the person, which I had a rivalry with sports and academic while I was in high school. Larry was the pitcher and quarterback.

He asked me.

"Why did you do this?"

He said this with his eyes squinting a bit, and he seemed concerned my career in sports would be just about over. I told him.

"My uncle told me the good was bad and the bad was good."

I think if I remember correctly he didn't respond, and he left the room immediately. I seemed a bit more grown-up as I was talking with Larry's Dad on a direct level, instead of talking about sports or awards I had received at banquets, being congratulated for them. He left the room like he had just down an about face, then would have his shoes skip the floor while he would turn and leave.

"Hi Billy."

"Hi Pete."

This was my baseball coach whom came in to visit me."

"I have some mints which I brought in for you."

"Thanks Pete, How is the team doing?"

"Alright, we won the other day against Wellesley. How could you ever do such a thing?"

He said these words as if he had just spit them out. He was trying to hold back, but the words just came out. I forgot what I said, but I do remember a glow of pride came over me for being in contact with a person like Pete. He was a person whom I thought was bad. Kind of like a hell raiser in a grown-up way. Now I was talking to him with the good bad and the bad good. He was now a good person to me instead of being bad. When Pete smiled you could tell he had suffered. He would have the curvature of the side of his mouth go down. I thought my football coach was good but really bad. I would talk to Pete because I thought he was a bad person. He seemed to be very emotional to me. Not the littlest bit of a smile would come over him. I thought my football coach John Fudd whom came in the night before didn't seem to concerned.

"Good luck Bill."

"Thanks Pete."

And he left.

"What is your name?"

I said to the patient in the bed next to mine.

"I David, I had my appendix out the other day."

"Is this a playboy book you have there?"

"Ya."

"Can I look at this?"

"Sure, here it is."

I thought this person seemed overwhelmed to think of the condition, which I was in, not being able to walk. He seemed to cater to my needs without hesitation. I looked through the playboy book and the pictures of the beautiful nude girls seemed to draw my 100 % attention. I couldn't get an erection from beholding at the pictures but just the same my eyes lit up.

I got a card from my aunt Gertrude. On this card said, Reach up as high as you can, and God will reach down after you. I began to put my arms to my sides and push down with them. I did this for about an hour, as I was trying to drain all strength out of me, so that I could put them over my stomach with about no strength in them. The person from Franklin observed in bewilderment, as he didn't know what to conceive. He would stare at me while I would do this. He seemed in a maze, like he was scared of whatever would happen. I began to not to talk to anyone, as I thought I was explicitly going to die.

The person from Franklin pulls out a Magazine. I began to laugh unbelievably because of the Magazine he was reading. I laughed heroically for about 20 minutes. I thought I would die laughing. A nurse comes in and says.

"What are you laughing about?"

But I wouldn't respond.

"What's so funny?"

No retort by me. I was gasping for air. I was recalling about when my uncle Henry was in the Second World War and he got a bronze medal for directing traffic three straight days without sleeping. I was told back then this was during the Battle of the Bulge but I later heard this was June 6-10 during D-Day. I can remember chunks of laughter. I gradually calmed down and I was completely assuaged.

The doctor whom handled the instruments to the surgeon came in with a small kit.

"Hi, I'm dr. Stolt."

He takes a pin out of a kit and asked me.

"Can you feel this?"

When he touched my stomach with his pin. I gave no response.

"Can you feel this?"

He goes up a little higher with the pin. I still gave no response. He goes up by my heart and presses down harder with the pin on my chest. He seemed in frenzy, as he wondered why wouldn't this person me, talk to him? I thought I was going to die, so I didn't want to talk to anybody. He seemed upset I didn't talk to him. I appealed to think he was under my control. His whole concentration was on me, to try and get me to talk to him. This was difficult not to speak, as this good person, when I thought the good was bad and the bad good was really bad for me to associate with. He takes one last look at me while he walks away from my bed. I could recall he would have revenge for this time I saw him.

My PT Billy Kold comes in and says.

"How are you today?"

I didn't respond to his statement.

"How are you?"

He asked again. But I still did not respond. He seems to realize I am not going to talk to him. So he discourses.

"I'm going to put your legs through range of motion."

While he would be moving my legs in range of motion exercises, he seems to be getting a bit embarrassed or ill at ease, because I am not talking to him. His response to me rattling him is.

"I heard you were laughing. You are a real man."

He seems he is going to go crazy from me not responding to any of his report. He also seemed under my control of giving him the silent treatment. He also seemed, when I say crazy, I mean crazy. I mean almost begging me to talk to him. I was saying to myself, how much actual fighting did he do in Vietnam, because he would have to fight now to try and get me to talk to him. I didn't think then he had a lot of actual combat. He walked away very upset.

This was time for lunch and Loretta came in and said after I wouldn't eat anything when my meal first came in.

"Are you going to eat anything?"

But I wouldn't respond to her. Right around this time a smile comes over my face. This is a smile of peace, serenity, and calmness. I began to talk to the people there, but they knew by their grins after I wouldn't talk to them, I wasn't actually serious, or there was some higher power in me working. Before I began to talk and have this smile, I can remember my family doctor, dr. Yado came by and said to me whatever something like.

"You can really get yourself into some situations. Remember when I talked to you when you were younger and you had your head bruised from the car accident you were in. I told you about how serious you can yourself into trouble."

He said this with an inner upward force, like get mad attitude. He seemed not too concerned about possibly this is just another life. He probably had seen thousands die in his time. He was at the front left of my bed. I didn't say anything to him.

"Hi Billy."

"Hi Billy."

"Hi Stephanie. Hi Maura."

These were my two sisters.

"Are you going to be ready for college in September?"

Maura asked.

"I don't know."

Stephanie seemed a little too young to realize the seriousness of what happened. While Maura seemed I would be all right and there was nothing to worry about.

"We brought in your yearbook. I thought you might want to look through this."

Maura said.

"How are you Billy?"

Stephanie asked.

"All right, Steph."

"Billy when you're at college in September, you might want you to get an apartment."

Maura commented.

"We'll see."

I was just agreeing with her. So they wouldn't worry if I told them what I was really thinking.

"Hi Billy."

Elizabeth said as she came into the room. She had a little smile on her face, as if she couldn't control this.

"Hi Liz."

I said to Elizabeth. But I wouldn't say much more than this, as I just wanted to keep the conversation in the family, because I thought I was going to die.

"What do the doctors say?"

"I haven't talked to any of them."

"Billy my friends miss you."

I didn't respond to her, because I just wanted to keep the conversation in the family.

"How is Brian doing?"

I asked my sister Maura.

"Brian is going to be in the Veteran's Hospital for a while. He broke his foot pretty badly."

"Did you get my card?"

Asked Elizabeth.

"Ya, I got this. Thanks Liz."

I talked to her a very little bit, because I was thinking of the wonderful times we had together the previous months. Right now while writing this, I think she might have known what I was thinking, dieing. She had worked in a Nursing Home.

"Bye Liz."

"Bye Billy."

"Bye Maura, Bye Steph."

"Bye."

"Bye."

Next to come in was, my aunt Lucy and her daughter Patty.

"Hi aunt Lucy, Patty."

"Is this all right to look through your yearbook?"

My aunt Lucy asked me.

"All right."

I said.

She began to go through my yearbook. Lucy seemed rather at ease, and she didn't think anything was wrong.

"This is Franco, the person in the car accident whom was driving the car when a person was killed. And here is Ekyd the person whom was killed in the car accident. Here is Rebbew the person whom had his last rites given to him in the car accident."

I didn't respond to her because she wasn't my immediate family. So I didn't want to have any contact with her when I was dieing. She would make comments about people in the yearbook and kind of hesitated for a little while, while she would browse through the yearbook.

"Bi Billy."

Lucy would say, and her daughter didn't really speak much probably because she was rather young. I believe she was about 12 years old.

"By Billy."

She would articulate, because this was one thing she knew how to say.

I then put the remote control bed down without touching the switch. The man from Franklin put his up when he saw mine go down. He seemed afraid of me because he had instinct something was cooking in the air. He seemed scared for himself, as he was practically in awe of me from watching my actions for those hours. I wasn't talking to any of the help, because I feared death. Just thinking I put the remote control, down without the switch his power in itself. One nurse came into the room and dropped a tray, which she was carrying. This nurse looked in her forties. She looked like she was used to people doing as she said, because they wouldn't have confidence in themselves in the hospital. I didn't bow to her or anyone for this matter. She seemed to blame me for dropping the tray. She held this grudge against me, until finally, she came over to my bed and said.

"Did you ever see the movie Jaws?"

I didn't respond to her, but I got very scared. I became straight in I thought the help at hospital were going to bring me up to the operating table and do some real damage to my back. I thought then these things happen. That there are crooked hospitals when you don't comply to their ways. I didn't respond to her question about the Movie Jaws.

I became very panicky and racy. I think I was losing it. At this point my uncle Joe "Friday" Breen whom I had talked to before I went out the window came into visit me. I felt I could console in my uncle, so I seemed to seek help in him, because I was so scared. I reached out to him and said.

"A nurse came in and began to talk about the movie Jaws."

He said.

"Hold it."

Then he walked to the hallway to the entrance to the room and looked down the hallway. He seemed to be like he wanted to go fast, but he controlled himself to slow down. Then he came over to my bed and grabbed my right wrist and said.

"Oh sacred heart of Jesus."

He seemed quite concerned saying this statement to me. When he said the word Jesus, the word shot through me and I recollected like a blob of some sorts when I was in tenth grade and I pictured the picture of a blob. I also recollected when I ran the hardest I had in my life when I was a sophomore in high school at the basketball tryouts. I then had made up my mind I would show the people of basketball I could run, when we would run sprints in the gym. I had made up my mind I would put out with everything in me then. I ran to the point where something just about comes up from your mouth. There were people I can distinctly recall of Ken and Kevin at the tryouts in awe of my efforts. This seemed you could put them up against the wall and there awe would stick them to the wall. They were in awe so much.

When I heard the word Jesus from my uncle, I recalled the incident in the gym and I now thought I was Jesus and Jesus started this way of fighting for your life. I tried to get up from bed with a busted back. My hands shot to my sides like I had held them there to lose strength in them earlier in the day. I was now thinking I thought marijuana, drugs, and alcohol good. My back seemed as if this was on fire. Excruciating pain which would be burning and burning. I thought I would live in hell a lifetime just so I would live instead of dieing. I would live. This was fighting for my life.

My uncle was continuing the prayer.

"I have asked you for many favors, but I plead for this one, take it."

I was urging forward. I began to sit up. I felt on a new realm of pain thresholds.

"Place it in your open broken heart."

He continued.

I began to fall back, but Joe was now saying.

"And when the eternal father sees it cornered with the mantle."

I again began urging forward, even more pain. I tried to get my uncle from holding onto my wrist, but he had a tight grip on it and he wouldn't give in to my lightly but strongly effort to get out of his grasps of my wrist.

"Of your most precious blood, then he can't refuse it for then it is your prayer not mine."

I was still trying to get up. He now was saying.

"Calm down."

He still wouldn't let go of my wrist. This took about 30 seconds in which this took. I then returned to my original position in bed. I was barely taking in air, when I was trying to get up, if any at all.

I began to think about the eating grapefruits skins and all from this happening. I think the connection might have been about the grapefruit league in Florida for the pre-season tryouts. Also I when I would eat grapefruits skins and all this make you breath better. I thought about this from this ordeal.

Joe Breen gave the person from Franklin a left arm gesture, to try and get him out of the awe of shock he was in, from seeing me try to get up. You could have stuck him to the wall by the lips, because of the craze he was in. I think Franklin just blinked, when my uncle Joe Breen gave him the left arm gesture. He walked over to Franklin's bed and raised his left arm above his head. He seemed rather calm, probably now knowing I would live.

My maternal parents came in entered the room and he walked over to Franklin's bed, and also gave him a left arm gesture. He raised his left arm above his head and the person from Franklin seemed as if he swallowed some saliva. I was calm and I just took a casual look at my dad over by this person from Franklin's bed just to okay the actions by my dad. I was feeling I was just nodding an all right sign, knowing there was more to be done.

"Let's get this all set."

Now there wouldn't be a problem I would live, but to walk.

I ate a hamburger.

I now felt this was okay to eat food, because I no longer was going to die. I was thinking this was the right thing to do, eat. So I ate the hamburger. This hamburger could have been the best food I have ever had. I felt I had suffered for my food. I also felt like a man like my dad. I felt I was a man. I feeling of being grown-up came over me. I was a man.

Something came through me and I thought the time was for me to go out of the bed the back part of the bed. I felt I couldn't use my right arm, because my uncle had held onto this, when he said the family prayer. With just my left arm I began to pull myself up the back part of the bed, which was about at 60'degree angle. I began to "ooo" out air and blow this out in rhythmic fashion, as I was trying to reach God. Trying to make him take heed in me. I was in another world, as I felt I reached him in some magical religious way.

A relative of Franklins' came in to visit him. This relative came over to my bed and asked me.

"Can I help you?"

If I remember correctly I think Franklin told me he was a car dealer.

I felt I was past the point of not paying any attention, and knowing he may be persistent in asking me, so I just said.

"No."

I looked at him with a cringed face as he was leaning to his right in front of my bed. He seemed genuinely concerned, but what could he do for me. I then inched my way over the back part of the bed. I felt I was being on a cross upside down. I was feeling a brown color to things. A rather medium texture of brown came over me, as I was hanging from the bed upside down. I could see the back part of the wall from an upside down view. My arms were to the side like on a cross upside down and I was beginning to pull myself down. I sometime think of Brown University.

A nurse came in and I was feeling I could control some of the nurses there. Or the heaven people which I called them. I was seeing snowflakes in the air, but this wasn't snowing. I thought the snowflakes denoted the heaven people, which worked there. A nurse came in and pulled me back into bed.

"You have to get back into bed."

She looked she was in awe of what I was doing and how I looked doing this. I was hanging upside down over the back of the bed. The smile on her face, she seemed she was a heaven person and I could now control the heaven people. The curvature of the edges was going down a little bit. I felt I could control this person.

"Get me some water."

I would say to her.

She would go running off and cater to my needs as if she were a servant. Another nurse came in and I was once again thinking there was a race to see whom, could suffer the most all the time. She said to me.

"Time to take your temperature."

I let her put the thermometer in my mouth, and while she was there taking the pulse, I bit the thermometer in pieces.

"Crrrach."

She left the room after I began to chew the glass thermometer. Then I was transferred to a private room. My brother Bob came in to visit me in the private room.

"Hi Bob."

"Hi Billy."

"Get me some water over by the sink."

"How much do you want?"

"Just fill the glass."

"All right."

I drank the glass of water straight down.

"Get me another glass."

"Why do you want so much water?"

"I need this right now."

I kept on drinking glass after glass of water as fast as I could. A nurse comes in and says.

"This is the end of visiting hours."

"Can he stay a little longer?"

I said to her.

"No, he has to go."

"He'll just be a short while more. Thank-you."

She seemed she was mad she couldn't have her way. I was thinking about when I would sales talk people and this time I sales talked the nurse into letting my brother to stay longer.

"All right."

She said.

"Give me some more water now, Bob."

Bob seemed like Jackie when he came in this day. He seemed withdrawn. I could see the big arms on him, as he had a short-sleeved shirt on. His arms were big from all the exercising he had done, from the football practices for this year's football team.

"The end of visiting hours"

Said the nurse one more time.

"Thank-you, but he will just be staying a short while longer more."

"No, time to go."

"I have to go."

Said Bob.

"This is all right, you can stay a short while longer."

I said to Bob.

"The nurse said I have to go now."

Bob said.

"Yes, he has to go."

Nurse.

"Just another 5 minutes."

I spitted out."

"I have to go now Billy."

Bob added.

"Bye Billy."

"We'll be seeing you Bob."

I finally said.

Bob left the room, and I began to try to get to the sink over railing on the side of the bed. This seemed this would be easier to lift a car then to get over the side of the bed to the sink for water.

I inched backwards with the bed down flat. I looked at the hand of a nurse and I believe this was her left hand as I was just about out of bed. I gave the last ditch effort and I pulled myself over the metal bar of the back of the bed. I felt my back oozing down ready to land on the bare floor. My back was bending as I curled downward off the bed. I hit the floor and I feel as if a knife going into my back.

"Backkkk."

My breathing went shallow, as I could barely take in any air. I was lying down flat on the floor as straight as an arrow and not moving anything. I was facing with my feet down, toes up, the right side of the bed. My head felt like a blueberry, a little soggy. With all courageous strength in me, I tried to move. I thought my knees were astro-projected out from the flesh by my attempt to move. My arms were vibrating straight, to my sides.

A male nurse comes in and I think he had a mustache and a little bit deep voice.

"Move Bill."

He says looking down at me in the raw.

"I can't move."

I replied.

The catheter must have come out of me when I had gotten out of bed. I thought three female nurses came in crawling on the floor. They looked like snails when they came into the room. One attractive nurse comes over to me in the raw on the floor. I thought to myself, ice cream people, when the nurses came in. They all looked a bright white and their faces reminded me of vanilla ice cream. They had a cutting complexion. People's faces seemed cracked to one side as if their heads were distorted. I liked the attractive nurse in the corner with her face close to mine. I thought sometimes this was like the white piece of white paper, which I had received from Harvard University. I thought this was like a cross body block as if I were diving into *TRENCH* in the First World War. I might even had been dead then. I really loved the nurse close to my face in the corner on the floor. A couple of minutes seemed like years.

I remember next my bent legs, as the four nurses put me back into bed. This felt a coffin to me. Then I recall is trying to get up again.

"Uuuaag."

The attractive nurse grabs hold of my wrist and said.

"Calm down."

I just kept on trying to get up, sitting up this is. I was feeling as if another knife was going into me as I fought onward. I began to go back to the flat bed, but I had the urge in me to try one more time.

"AAUUUghg."

My arms were flat to my side and I urged forward until my head just went down forward. Like you are supposed to bow your head every time you say the word Jesus. I then went back down flat on the bed. The nurses were now standing discerning at me with my courageous attempt to get up. I had fought against the tide and won. I thought this time chocolate ice cream. I thought this was rigormortis.

I was now down flat and I experienced the night, which I don't think too many people have experienced, the night with no air. My lungs must have been affected, because I had very, difficult time breathing. I could barely take in air. The nurse whom passed out the medicine told me to talk to this younger girl nurse whom got next to my bed in a chair. I can recollect the medicine nurse cough as she walked outside the room. She like said something like talk to these other folks before you talk to me.

The nurse next to my bed asked me.

"What did you have planned instead of coming into the hospital?"

I felt straight mentally, as straight on the floor might have meant I was straight mentally. I said to her.

"I had planned on going to UMass Amherst and studying to be an engineer and play baseball."

These were my plans before the salesman job.

"Did you have a girlfriend?"

"I had a girl friend named Elizabeth."

I was having hard time breathing. Tears wouldn't come out of my eyes. My eyes were trying to cry, but the hard time breathing would stop them.

"Did you like her a lot?"

"Yes, I did. We had many of good times together."

I began to see an imaginary clock on the wall ticking from 5:30 to 5:45. I had gone out of bed right after visiting hours and they were over at 9:00. So I don't know where the clock came from. When I saw the clock ticking, I said to myself I wished I were put in an oven, so I could burn to death instead of enduring what I was going through. I remember blinking my eyes once and this was the only satisfaction I had then. Just blinking my eyes was all I could do. My eyes wouldn't close. The nurse was in around her low 20ies and she seemed she wanted to keep me talking. I would force out answers to her. She had her legs crossed and she would wiggle them around a bit as she was a little bit fidgety.

This nurse left after about a ½ hour and a young man came into the room dressed in white.

"Hi my name is Peter."

He sits down in the chair next to my bed.

"Did anything like this happen to you?"

I asked him.

"I had my appendix out."

He said.

I didn't care for this person too keen. I said to myself I remember the pain my sister Maura was in before she was raced to the hospital years before to have her appendix out. But a lot of people have their appendix out, so I then asked him.

"How long were you in the hospital?"

"One week."

He replied.

I was thinking of embarrassing this person in some way, so he would help. I began to whack off in front of this person. This guy just about began to sweat as he moved around like a rabbit that's just been trapped. He was breathing ponderous. He then went outside the room, and got in a rocking chair he got from somewhere. He began to sit in this and let the noise of the wooden chair chafe me. I coughed once a very tough to do cough but with to no avail.

The next thing I remember I was back in the room of four. I began to put my hands behind my head and pull my head down. I would count the stings, which I would get in my back, as this was a reddish white color of pain to me. This felt like arrows of pain I was giving to myself to prepare to go out of bed again. This time I would pull myself down to the end of the bed and then go out of the bed and smash the back of my head on the floor. I was quiet in the bed, as I did not want any of the workers to know what I was up too again.

I began to go out of bed forward. My legs were going out of bed. I noticed they were going right over the side of the bed. I thought they were disappearing going to heaven. I thought there was some kind of force field, which was taking my legs to heaven. I actually thought then my legs were leaving me. I put my scrotum over the side of the bed, and I thought this was going to heaven, disappearing. I thought this would mean I couldn't have children. A male nurse comes in and tells me.

"Get back in bed."

"Go get me a hacksaw."

I said to him.

This put the nurse in frenzy. He seemed he didn't expect me to say anything back to him and on top of this I told him something, which made him cringe. He didn't know what to do. He just ran out of the room. After he left I put my penis over the side of the bed, and I thought this would mean I couldn't have sex. Because my penis was disappearing or going to heaven, which I sincerely thought for a while back then. I was sitting up over the side of the bed then and I truly thought this part of me went to heaven. I have a later than this writings about this in my UMass Amherst diary. I connected this with Yale University like second heaven. Then years later I connected this with Harvard extension.

Donny V. was in the hospital also. I had known him in my youth. He came over to the sink and got some water while I was sitting up. I sometimes think of my penis, as going straight up like an imaginary rocket over by the Ivy pole of the man from Franklin's bed across from me. The male nurse comes back in and the next thing I noticed is my left leg going jerking up and I thought I did have legs, by the nurse whom grabbed this. When I saw my leg I thought I did have legs, but I couldn't feel his hand on my leg. I gave a little.

"AH"

When he jerked my leg upwards, I thought this was my ticket to get straight up from paralysis. This was my opportunity to jump right up from paralysis.

I remember a new male nurse there these times. His name was Claude and I had many experiences with him. Claude was about 6' tall and 180 pounds. He seemed like a monster to me then. He had a tattoo of an eagle on one of his forearms. He seemed to have dark eyes and didn't seem to smile at all. I thought of him as someone whom never yawned. He would hold in his yawns. I thought he was great in this hospital.

When I was in the room of four, I began to read the book "The Winds of War"' backwards. A nurse was creaming my legs when I was reading the book backwards. The nurse was Connie. A short and chubby girl with short black hair and she seemed like an old kid.

"Stop reading."

Connie said.

But I kept on reading aloud. Someone had turned on a radio, which I thought they would drown me out from concentrating reading backwards aloud. I felt if I read the whole book backwards then I would walk. Connie seemed controlled by me, as I read and she would be creaming my legs. I could feel her creaming my legs only when I read backwards.

Sheila Lieno was the sister of my pal Jimbo. Jimbo if you recall I went to see, to be sure, he was in by the curfew on time on Friday nights for the football games in Saturdays. Sheila worked as a nurse at the hospital. She said to me.

"Stop reading aloud."

This seemed to irritate her to hear me reading backwards. So she angrily took the book away from me. I then put my little fingers in my ears and tried to block out all sound. Sheila wheeled my bed down into a private room. I could recall the intercom paging doctors and people all the time. Going down the hallway I felt like I was being damned. I kept my little fingers in my ears. I can remember dr. Black. came into the private room and asks me.

"Can I help you?"

I said.

"I want some food."

"I'll tell one of the nurses to get you some food."

Was the reply from dr. Black.

"I want you to get it."

I was thinking to myself I wanted to tell people what to do, give orders. I felt I wanted to make the most of my time, spent in hospital. This was the parent of the athlete scholar I competed with in high school. Now I was telling his parent what to do. I felt helpless then and I wanted to make the most of this. I was thinking I wanted people to serve me. The reason why I could have the little extra in me to tell a middle-aged person like dr. Black, because I was suffering and this gave me courage. I was thinking to myself I might not walk, but I wasn't going to give up trying and this included telling anyone what to do. I was also thinking I was a "door to door" salesman and this was higher in the disciplines than a doctor. Dr. Black's face had a cringe to this. I thought then, he was thinking I was so sick I didn't know what I was doing.

I would pray the Lord's Prayer with instead of on earth I would say in, "Boeland." When I thought my legs were disappearing, and going to heaven, I called this space, "in Boeland." This was my nickname Boe.

One day, in which I was feeling so bad, I began to just yell out, "Jesus, Jesus, Jesus, etc." I was given a shot of something.

I can recall once when I was piercing one of my ears. I was piercing my right ear with one of the plastic utensils, which they gave me for food. I thought I was the soldier in the group of people whom came to get Christ and had his ear cut off by the apostle Peter.

I can remember one time when Claude the male nurse came in and sat in the chair next to my bed, and I was talking to him.

"Will I be like this the rest of my life?"

He just with a stiff face began to shake his head and also nod at the same time. He wasn't responding to my questions.

"Am I going to walk?"

Then he said.

"You have a lot of work ahead of you."

This would make me turn my head straight up and I would kind of let out a.

"Choe."

Then I asked him.

"Am I going to get any better?"

He would just shake his head at an angle in which I thought he meant no. I looked straight up and began to yell out.

"Jesus, Jesus, Jesus etc."

I then in one quick move grabbed hold of the catheter, which was down my penis and I pulled this out of me. Out of the penis came red white crystallized blood. I think they call this "bled white." Claude spoke up and said.

"You shouldn't have done that."

His tone was louder and he seemed more serious now, probably because he had to clean up the red white crystallized blood. His face was cringed and he looked like he was swallowing something bitter, a lemon or something. Another girl nurse came in and saw the blood, then walked right out. The blood when she looked at this seemed like a force field to her which she could not penetrate coming into the room any further.

The physical therapist Billy told me not to hit any of the nurses. I was thinking opposite. So when two nurses came in to my room on each side of the bed, I punched them both in the face. In the beginning this was just little tap. Then I would with my right fist swing up at the attractive nurse on my right. I smacked her in the face. She seemed a little bit dumbfounded at first, as she didn't do anything in the beginning. Her eyes lit up a bit as she just froze. The other nurse Connie said.

"Now stop this Bill."

This made me hit them in the face even harder.

"Now stop this."

Connie said again.

The very attractive nurse on my right was just frozen. I thought this nurse was a nurse in Vietnam. She seemed like she would do a lot of fooling around with the patients.

When I was attempting another time out of bed, with the bed up at a higher level I was beginning to descend. This attractive nurse came into my room and said to me.

"Are you going?"

She was the nurse I hit in the face and I thought she was trying to get back at me.

I inched a little bit further as I said to myself co-captain Norwood high football.

Then she said.

"Well."

I said to myself tobacco, as well as going both ways, as well as bringing in plays as a sophomore. She then said.

"If your not going."

She then pulled me back into bed.

I sometimes have flashbacks about me being on this nurse's knee and she is pulling my penis, as if to get feeling back. I thought this was what happened during the Revolutionary War. I also thought strawberry ice cream.

"Everything is going to be all right."

Were the words from my sister Judy when she came in to visit me for the first time, coming in from Utah. She didn't seem to break a lip as she spoke. She said this with a stern upper lip. I seemed relieved to see her as I had just about lost hope. The staff there had brought me in a black pillow right around when my sister Judy came in. I think I had reached rock bottom and I thought I was a devil.

"Everything is going to be all right."

She repeated.

I can remember there was a psychiatrist from I think McLean Hospital whom would I think every week come in to see me. I never talked to him. He kept on trying to get me to talk to him. I thought the reason why he was here was because dr. Black was upset with me telling him to get my food. I didn't talk to him, so he couldn't bill me. But I think he was getting paid from McLean. So when he would talk to the help here, these folks didn't even know he was getting paid for talking to them. Myself I didn't talk to him.

They got me up in a wheelchair one of these days, when my sister Judy came in to visit me. I had my arms on a tray, which was on the wheelchair. I would flop my arms around a little bit as the chair was wheeled out to the activity room where there was a television. The Chicago White Sox were playing the Boston Red Sox.

"C'mon White Sox."

Would mumble from my mouth.

"Let's go, c'mon now."

My sister Judy was smiling a bit as I was rooting. There were two nurses there doing some paper work and they asked me.

"Do you want a piece of candy?"

They put a piece on a tray. I was thinking if I took the candy then I would stay at the Norwood Hospital. I wasn't doing that well there.

Years later, I thought this strategy of hoping the other side will win, was used in the Gulf War 1. We were at some kind of standstill, and I thought I gave my strategy of hoping the other side will win. Do you really want to win would be the strategy. Around the Boston area I would cheer for the Red Sox.

"Hi Liz."

"Hi Billy."

"I had some fruit sent in."

"Thanks, How is everybody?"

"They miss you."

"Well I think I'll be going now."

"Before you go, I would like to ask you something."

"What." she asked.

"Can I have a kiss?"

She seemed a little bit caught off guard. Probably because this was the first time I had asked her for a kiss since being in the Norwood Hospital. She looked down on me with a little grin on her face. She then leaned over the side of the bed, and I reached up and held her and went on the moment of ecstasy. I felt a kiss from her could change time, and everything would be like this was before when I would kiss her. She had her mouth opened and we French kissed I believe. I was thinking she might have not kissed me, because I had broken up with her, and she could now get back at me. But she gave me a kiss.

I was thinking to myself I needed her more than she needed me now. She had her head down a bit in a nod type look as she left the room.

"Bye Liz."

"Bye Billy."

I think I said to Elizabeth I was Jesus Christ. She looked at me and I thought she was bewildered.

I was thinking years earlier when I was with a girl named Lisa Fraso. I went for a walk with her one night and at the end of the walk I asked her straight out, "Can I have kiss?"

And she gave me one. I had a lot of faith like this when I kissed Liz."

I think the doctors thought my prognosis was very bad, so sacrifice one for the many. I began to arch my back, back. I was going up on my back. I think they might have called this, "going bananas," in Vietnam. I was like going belly up. I looked out the window here and I thought I had bounced down out of the window and up to another room on different floor in the hospital. I was thinking I could swim in water forever.

Also around this time I thought a machine gun had put me out of my misery. I thought up in the top corner of this room a machine gun put me out of my misery. I thought when I would yell out, Jesus, I was building myself an up, to protect me.

"Hi Aunt Gertrude."

"Hi Billy."

"I brought you in some brownies from Jordan Marsh."

"Thank you. You're the person whom makes me feel the best out of everyone I have seen."

She smiled a bit and I could tell she felt very good about this. She then leaned over and gave me a kiss on the cheek.

"I can remember the card you sent me, with reach up as high as you can and God will reach down after you."

"You liked this card?"

"I reached up when I thought I was dieing."

"God bless you and I have to go now."

"Bye Aunt Gertrude."

"Bye Billy."

I could see a smile on her face, which went down and I thought she had changed.

There was a time when I had again tried to go out of bed. I was saying to myself, All-star Bay State League as fullback. The aid John came in and pulled me down angrily.

Chapter 3

"We have come to take you to University Hospital."

Said the attendant from the ambulance. I could see a better person whom was more understanding from these two attendants from Boston. I felt more at ease with these people than I did with the people whom worked at the Norwood Hospital.

"All right, I'm ready."

I felt relieved I was leaving Norwood Hospital. On the ride there I heard the driver sneeze.

"Archue."

I thought he was acting when he did this. Archue in Lithuanian means thank you. I am half Lithuanian. I would later act sneezing.

I was brought to Robinson 7.

The first person I talked to there was Mel.

"My name is Mel."

"Hi Mel."

"Your from Norwood, right?"

"Yes, I am."

"That's where I was born."

Mel said.

"The first thing we will do is, take the catheter out of you."

Mel seemed very happy and full of life. He would walk in quick steps. He was about 5'8" with medium build.

"Hi I am dr. Train."

"Hi."

"I will be your doctor. The Chief of staff, dr. Kittery will be in charge of your care here. I will be his assistant."

She was an attractive woman with medium long black hair. She had an accent which I could tell English was a second language for her. She was about in her thirties and was a rather sluggish person. She would leisurely strut around the floor.

"Hi I'm dr. Kittery. I am chief of staff here. We will take x-rays of your back after one week, to see if you need an operation."

"Okay this sounds good."

"We will teach you how to catheterize yourself."

"What's this?"

"So you can urinate on your own. I will be seeing you on rounds on Monday and will pass by each day. If you have any questions talk to dr. Train."

"Okay."

This doctor walked to my bedside with a distinct limp. I could tell he had some kind of trouble with his right leg, as this dragged behind him as he walked. He was a middle-aged man with a rough and clean complexion.

I began to catheterize myself. I looked at this as I was doing a Chemistry experiment in my AP Chemistry Course in last year of high school. This was I had passed first year chemistry equal one year of college chemistry.

One day I asked dr. Train.

"Can you give me anything for the pain, I am having pain in my legs."

"We can't give you anything."

She came back with.

I'm suffering. I have pain in my legs."

"Your not suffering that much."

"I'm Jesus Christ."

"They killed Jesus Christ two thousand years ago."

This woman was confronting me with quick rhetoric. I felt she had other patients and she had a good wide view of things. I was trying to get the amount of attention I received at Norwood. But here in Boston, I was probably the best off, compared to all the quadriplegics here. She seemed she cared, but she had about 10 other patients to take care of also. She told me.

"This is Robinson 7."

She came by another day and told me.

"I'm going to test your reflexes."

She would use the little instrument, and hit different parts of my legs, which didn't move.

I have my actual diary of when I was on this floor.

Page 1 Sept. 28

I am right now having trouble to set my mind on one thing. It is sort of BORING. I have been trying to get myself set and write but this is the first time that I have layed down and wrote. The other two times which I have written Junior Prom and Busc incidents turned put good afterwards. I was going to put in alright but I felt was good enough. I am also was thinking if I wrote enough I coulf have some pretty good information for a short story.

I have also been having a lot of trouble programming in on the Breen Ming control. I hope that writing can make the time go by easier. I desire that and that will be so. I have to get back on that Ming control road. I hope that after a while I will be able to look.

Page 2 Page 3

Back and be happy. I have to write some letters to people but I have a little fear in my writing ability. But I desire to reprogram that and enjoy writing all the time. I desire that and that will be so. Some noise was just happened. But I desire that noise shall not have any affect and that will be so. I still have to write something on the time that I missed. I desire that I will b happy and that will be so. I also desire that I will reprogram things that bug me. I will be able to walk again. I desire that and that will be so. I desire that I will want to write every day and that will be so. I desire that I will b happy and that will be so. I will now write about the past to the best of my ability.

Page 4 Mon. Sept. 29,

Today's highlights were dr.Chin said that I will be getting up next week. The dr for the back brace also came to measure me. It was good to hear from him. Marylene was my nurse today, and she was nice, but sometimes she was a little bit mad. I am writing all this so so that in the future I will be able to look at back with a smiling happy face and attitude. I was thinking bout when I went out window and that I was. I am beginning to write a lot more now.

Yesterday Mike, Posk, Wete and Bob came in to visit me. They gave me the game ball. They had won 12-6.

Page 6

I am now going to write to my best effort everything that happened. It all started when I went down for the Salesman job. I got started and it was a completely new way of talking. The first day I was teed but I was still not at a level as the two salesmen whom were training me.

So I continued to be a salesman for a couple of days. Those nights I didn't have any dreams. That was one idea that the Breen Ming Control would be no good. The man I had training me was pretty smart and he looked old for his age. Then I would look people into the eyes to see if I was a phoney or not.

It was sort of who has been on the road longer. This was probably happened sometime before July 4. I quit the baseball team.

Page 7

I was thinking that the object of the game was to lose not to win. And I had won a considerable lot so that had made me quite upset. I went over to grandmother's house on the fourth of July and I would have thought the uncle Mick and grandmother and grandfather and

A big incident that happened was when I was up St. Tims' where I met Cox. I decided I was going to go up New Hampshire with Cox and Jimbo. We went and I cracked a glass in Bart's cottage. I then was feeling aweful because I didn't know what to do. I came home. Wher everything was kind of bad. I went ove to Oldham a couple of times where I was not wanted. Then the incident.

Page 8

Jackie

The man for the brace came this week. He said that he will have it by next Monday. When dr. Kittery looked at my legs, he said that I should be getting up by next week. That would include getting into a wheelchair for a couple of days, than starting the real therapy with my legs.

Elizabeth came into visit me one day.

"Hi Liz."

"Hi Billy."

"Thanks for the card."

"That's okay."

"Good music on the radio."

"Ya."

She said.

I was feeling something different when I told her this. I had reached a new level of mood then. I wanted to show her that I was normal and I viewed things as normal people. She looked down at me and gave a little smile when she was responding with my statement. She gave a caring "ya," to my reply. She then began to talk about what was happening in the town.

"Tex came over to my house and wanted to go out with me. The nerve of him I would never go out with him. He did this after you broke up with me."

"Oh I didn't know this."

She seemed she was blowing out air as she spoke. She would get rather emotional as she made me think I'm the one with the problems and she is telling me hers. I kind of gave a little smile as I heard her speak. I was seeing in her eyes the anger, which was coming out of her in her growing up days of her life. She had confidence in herself which came to blossom when I would see her these days. She was dressed better than when I would see her at nights the previous months before. I would look down the row of beds and see beautiful woman with the men in beds. This seemed like everyone there had a beautiful woman. I felt I could compete for which person had the most beautiful girlfriend or wife. I began to think about the times I was with Elizabeth down the

Cape after graduation. I thought it might be nice to have her in bed with me here. But this wouldn't be allowed. But I still thought of this. Alls I would have to do would be to pull the curtains around the bed and have her hop in.

One day, dr. Train came by the bed and I threw up and at the same time in which I tried to get up I said.

"I'm a Jesus Christ."

Dr. Train went racing to the chief as if she had only one thing on her mind. She got to my left side of the bed after this. The chief came from the opposite direction and came up to the corner of the end of the bed. Put his hands behind his back. He looked like a parrot. He said to me in a casual tone.

"What's the problem now Bill?"

I said.

"I have pain in my legs."

"Give him this."

He said to dr. Train in a deep tone of voice.

"But we can't give him this."

"Give him this."

He echoed in a deeper and stronger voice.

This put dr. Train in frenzy and she didn't say anything after this. She spoke up the first time with a quick remark, we can't give him this, but she gave up the fight after the chief responded the second time.

The chief had come by the bed and sat in the chair to the right side of the bed. He pulled out his pen. He *THEN* touched my stomach with his pen and said.

"Can you feel this?"

"Ya."

He then went on to draw lines on my stomach with his pen.

One of the first days there, I told dr. Train a couple of things. One being I would like to be in one of the only 3 privates rooms, which they had there. These were for girls or folks with special problems. She said no to this.

I also told her I would like to go back to Norwood Hospital. She went and told the chief. He came over to my bed, and just said some thing like.

"How are you today Bill?"

He didn't mention anything about me wanting to go back to Norwood. When I saw him limping over to my bed I just couldn't tell him I wanted to leave his unit. So I just like said.

"All right."

In Norwood I was like a king on a checkerboard, while here in Boston I was like a pawn on a chessboard.

There was a quadriplegic, whom, came in for a checkup and I was talking to him one day.

He said to me.

"If you can feel hot and cold you have a chance of recovering."

"I can feel hot and cold."

"Then you have a chance of recovering."

This person had a beard and long brown hair. He later got a fever and was in one of the separate rooms. I could see him through the hallway and he looked like he was really suffering with the fever.

"Praise the Lord."

I yelled out one day. Doug the quadriplegic in front of me said.

"He's hollering out and he is only waist down."

I got up the courage to do this after much anticipation fear. This was like the salesman job talk along with fear as this was difficult. The secretary to the ward came over to my bed and gave me a pamphlet with how to give your heart to Christ. I was a little amazed about this as I was desperate to try anything to help me.

A big man came over to my bed hopping on crutches. I began to talk to him.

"Why aren't you walking?"

"It took me a year to get my arms back."

He must have been a quadriplegic at one point. This person was a big person from down South and when he spoke you could tell the amount of physical activity he had. He would have the slur talk to the side. He was also in for a check up and he would get up 6 hours per day on long double locked leg braces he told me. He talked to each person in bed. Wherever he went a crowd would gather around him.

One day Elizabeth came in to see me.

I said.

"I don't want to see her."

I was crying profusely. I was like boiling. I was trying to get up out of the bed. The chief came in and got on the end of the bed and looked down at me. I was still trying to get up uncontrollably. I was seeing a little smile on the chief' s face. Like he was saying to himself, I've suffered through worse than this. There was no change in my condition from seeing him. So they then brought on the shrinks.

Elizabeth was waiting out in the waiting lounge and I didn't see her this day. I wondered what she must have been thinking as she sat out in the lounge. She was probably thinking why she couldn't see me today, for what reason? I thought I saw a glimpse of her from my bed in the big room while I was crying.

The first shrink came up and said to me while sitting in the chair.

"What seems to be the problem?"

I didn't respond.

"Is there anything bothering you?"

I still gave no response.

He then got up and left.

I think I was still trying to get up out of bed. A good word to describe how I felt then was I was boiling.

The second shrink comes in and sits down in the same chair as the first shrink and asks me more questions.

"Why are you crying? Why are you trying to get up?"

I still didn't respond to this second shrink. Finally the third shrink came in and sits down in the same chair.

"I'm dr. Pab."

And he says.

"It's a beautiful day."

Then he wrote something down on the folder, which *HE* had. He then asks me.

"What do you think?"

"I would go out that window if I could."

Looking at the window behind my bed.

He then said something like.

"Hmmm."

He asked me some more questions but I didn't respond. I felt a feeling of shame I didn't hold in my feelings. This shrink had big lips and a face like duck. I was thinking this was the Alamo and I had to hold off the three assaults. I actually thought this back then.

My junior high school teacher Dave Powell would come in to visit me. He brought me in some books to read. He would walk with a limp as he had hurt his hip I believe when he was younger. Right before he stopped coming in to visit me he said. "I know this will be all right to not have me coming in here to see you anymore." Looking back with retrospection I really appreciate him coming in to visit me.

I was wheeled out in the activity room once. This was where there was the big table, which everyone whom was up in wheelchairs or walking would eat.

"What is your name?"

"Stephanie."

She stated.

I was a nervous as this was the first time I made contact with some one especially the opposite sex since being here.

"What happened to you?"

I asked her.

"I was run over by a tractor."

She was also on a moving bed, which was called a gurney. She had long blonde frizzy hair and a very good complexion.

"What happened to you?"

She asked me.

"I jumped out a window."

I told her.

My nervousness was decreasing as I would laggardly get to know her more by talking.

"My injury was lower lumbar 2. I had plans on going to Radcliffe instead of coming into hospital."

I felt good I was discoursing to a sophisticated girl. This was one thing, which I had curiosity about Elizabeth about. She wasn't to smart in the books.

"I'm 18 years old."

"I'm 18 also."

I told her.

Stephanie had good amplitude breasts, which would droop down quite a bit. She seemed she might have been a bit diffident when she was physically conformed.

"I am going to get up in a wheelchair pretty soon."

"I hope to also."

I said.

The next day I was out in the activity room again on a gurney, or the staff might have wheeled my bed out there. I was talking with this man whom was on leg braces and crutches. This person had blonde hair and he also had a very attractive girlfriend or wife with blonde hair also. This person seemed to be bewildered quite a bit from thinking he wasn't in very good shape from the waist down. I can remember looking down at him and you would wonder when was the last time he had smiled. I would always be trying to move throughout the days.

"I can move my leg."

I hollered out.

This was just a mediocre effort to move my left knee, and this moved. The people around the table I recall had like no reaction to when I said I could move. I felt the best I have ever felt in my life for this about 5 minutes. I began to just about gasp for air. My eyes felt they were going to come out of their sockets. I wanted to tell someone, but I wanted to be sure I told the right person.

"Jack Dodge, come quickly."

"What is it?"

Jack said.

"I can move my knee, look, look, look."

I showed him how I could move my knee.

"That's wonderful. That's great."

He said.

Joy rushed through me, enormous amounts of joy. There was a smile and a little bit of eyebrow lift up on Jack Dodge's face. Jack Dodge was one of the top workers there. He seemed to be experienced with knowing how to react when some one would now know they would walk. But Jack Dodge even with this good acting aptness couldn't feel the way I did. I had now given physical therapy a try and now I wanted so badly to start the active pt.

My physical therapist Nancy would be moving my legs in range of motion exercises each day. I couldn't move them, but she would move them in inactive pt. I can recall looking forward to this, as Nancy would put my legs up against her breasts each day. I would years later have flashbacks about this.

Nancy was about 27 years old and very attractive. She was about 5'6" and had a very good body. She must have had about close to 36" bust. She had medium long black hair. I really liked her quite a bit for the roll she was playing in my life. She might have been a little bit too old for me then, but this was just the same good to have her as my lady PT.

Jack Dodge if the Chief of staff would be called chief, then Jack Dodge was captain Dodge. When I was first on this unit the name Jack Dodge whom was only an LPN, I thought in the ranks of being a miracle worker. His name I vividly recall had respect.

This time when I first moved, I began to think about things as very seriously. I now had known I would walk. This was unbelievable to me. My whole world was turned right side up. I like looked at me moving and the other people there, as not being able to comprehend how I felt. I now was like in a reality. My world was now back. These people will never move. This was an experience to understand the world where people feel so much despair and leave that world, healthy. This is like getting back to reality. I looked at human beings differently. There actually is a world where very few have come back from. A world, where people, can only read about.

The next day when my PT Nancy had heard of return movement of my left knee she came in for pt.

"Well this is time to move your knee more."

My left leg was hanging over the side of the bed.

"Woo, woo, woo, aaa, a,a woooo."

There was no noise when I began to move the knee. Then I gave the heroic howl. Just like a wolf my head went down and I proceeded to move the knee. I years later had vivid imagination flashes about when the Lord God Jehovah came down to talk to Moses, this was wolf's howling which made him go back up. Nancy was in awe when she saw my expressions moving the knee. I must have moved my knee an inch but this seemed like a mile.

"We will be getting you up in a wheelchair in a couple of weeks." The chief had stopped by and said.

"Great."

I professed.

"But first we have to get you measured for a back brace. A Mr. Rogers will stop by this week and measure you for one."

"This sounds great."

"Hi Liz."

"Hi Billy."

"Everyone is thinking about you."

Liz said.

I seemed to have gotten to know her more now. The situation of me being in bed and her standing next to the bed would bring on an automatic connection between us. On the radio I would hear the song, "If only you believe my darling, my baby, in miracles."

I would look at her when the song was on and she seemed her part in this was she was there. Here next to me lying in bed. Liz was smoking a cigarette.

"Let me try one Liz."

I asked her.

I tried one but I didn't like this.

"Do you like the cigarette Billy?"

"I don't care too much for them."

She then asked me.

"When are you going to start walking Billy?"

"Well I am not sure. I can move my left knee now."

When I said this to her, this seemed she didn't react to this statement. This seemed she had thought like the movies might have programmed society, that everyone walks. I could feel a rather cutting to her voice. As if she was hurting. She would send me a card each week, and on one of the cards was, "I no longer dream about the big pumpkin."

She was thinking maybe I would become a big time baseball player with all sorts of glory and she would share this with me. But now he would not be a great time person. He would have to salvage a life. The last thing on my mind was becoming famous. I just couldn't think this big in the situation I was in then. I had never heard of anyone becoming greatly famous after he had become paralyzed. I was now just thinking of a way to move, not playing sports again. She seemed to cringe a bit when I talked to her.

I believe one of these next days I began to move my left ankle. The chief had stopped by one of these days with Nancy my PT.

"Well Bill, you can move your left leg. I'll just flex this right leg."

He picked up my right leg and flexed this back. I can recall I saw one patient whom picked up his leg on a gurney. I like looked on in amazement at this. I thought something like this seemed impossible.

The next day I believe in the morning I moved my right ankle. I notified Nancy.

"You got return of your right ankle?"

She asked excitedly.

"Yes I moved this a little while ago."

When Nancy heard I had moved my right ankle she said.

"I am going to get dr. Kittery."

She went racing out of the room, like how dr. Train had when I had told her I was Jesus Christ back about a month now. The Chief came over to my bed and a very curious Nancy looked on in a rather interested personally in the next move by me, and the chief.

"You moved your right ankle I heard Bill."

"Ya, this was a little while ago."

"I want you to try and pick your leg up for me."

"Okay."

I said.

"Ahaaha."

"Pull Bill."

Were the words of the Chief.

I could recall in the bed when I had my fingers in my ears, when I was reading the Book the Winds of War backwards. The chief looked back to his left while leaving and said.

"The muscles come back in pairs."

I had set a vow I would put out with everything in me for the physical therapy. This was my vow, which I had to keep. Every bit of strength I would give to the pt. If you set a vow you must keep this.

My bed was moved to the lounge one of these days and a man came over to my bed with the social worker Peggy, and said to me.

"My name is dr. Strange I want to talk to you about your angriness, and why you won't talk to the social worker Peggy."

"I don't want to talk to you."

I spit out.

He was a rather tall chap and he wore glasses. He had a mustache, which I don't really know if this was a necessity for him. He then began to nod his head at me. Just nodding his head up and down.

"He is here to help you."

Said Peggy.

"Don't you nod your head at me?"

But he would just continue to nod his head up and down at me. He reminded me of an ape or something by the rhythm he was in. He was doing this for so long of time I believe his arms began to swing and they did. Peggy was watching very much interested with a concerned look on her face, as dr. Strange would continue with his spectacle. She had her arms folded and looked at the situation rather concerned.

The social worker Peggy I wouldn't talk to when I first came into the hospital. I don't really know why I wouldn't. I just wanted to think physical then. When I would have OT, occupational therapy, by Suzie, Peggy looked on in a rather jealous look. Peggy got me to talk to her in some way.

"Time to get up in to a wheelchair."

Said one of the nurses.

"Great."

I responded.

"We will first have to put on your back brace. I'll show you how to put this on."

"All right."

"Now is time to get you into your wheelchair. You slide down this board from the bed."

Said the OT Suzie.

"If you get dizzy, tell us and you can go back to bed."

Said the nurse Jim.

A couple of hours went by and I said to Jim.

"When am I supposed to get dizzy?"

The OT Suzie seemed very happy from all the days she must have been through the procedure before with other patients. The staff, nurses, and therapist seemed very happy and were always joking and smiling. My PT Nancy seemed under control and she would put a pout of a look on her face, with mouth closed tight when she would be with me.

I can recall when I would go out in public in the wheelchair. We would wheel around the hospital outside. I am thinking the emotion I felt then. You would be wheeling the wheelchair. I can recall going over curbs with some of my friends watching. I felt so embarrassed that this would make me put out so much harder on the exercises. For me out in public was my motivation to get better. My head seemed as if this would go on fire when I would see people outside looking at me. I would try so hard to get better then. A wheelchair is very hard to wheel at first. I really look at the marathoners in wheelchairs as really something.

One day when I was having pt out in the activity room, I began to throw a ten-pound weight, like I would do before the oncoming baseball seasons.

"What are you doing Bill?"

Nancy asked me.

"I m going to play baseball again."

I retorted.

"This is very absurd to think this now. You can barely move. To think you are going to play baseball is far fetched."

"Well I am going too. I used to workout this way before the season to strengthen my arm."

I can recollect something just came over me. I had a real lot of faith. Like how I had when I tried to get out of bed at Norwood Hospital. This seemed to me I was germinating. I seemed I was on my knees throwing the ten-pound weight. But I must have been just crawling. Something like a fire came over me.

"Do you want to go to the cafe, Liz?

"All right."

She said.

I got into my wheelchair and I wheeled down to the café with her, with her walking.

"The doctors say I will be getting up on the parallel bars soon."

I can remember wheeling by the crossway above the roads and people were walking by while I was with Elizabeth. She was walking by me. When I saw a particular person walk by I don't know whom, but I can remember looking down to the left side while Liz was on my right. I was now going down to the café where all the personnel would eat. I was now going to have to visage all those people there now with a woman. There was danger ahead.

She carried her and my meals on a tray. We sat down on one of the small tables and talked and ate.

"See how much I can move?"

I showed her as I wiggled my legs a bit. She just gave a little smile and said.

"When are you going to walk on your own?"

"I don't know."

I said.

She pulled out a cigarette and instituted to smoke this.

"Dave went off to college down in Florida."

She said.

This was Dave Copper one of my best friends before I began to have problems. She would have on a constant smile, which seemed to be on here face whenever I met her eyes. When she spoke their seemed something was caught in her throat, as if she had some kind of static to her speech.

"We're going to get you up on parallel bars in two weeks."

Said dr.Train when she came by one day.

"Will this mean walking?"

"We'll take this slowly."

She said this with a tone of voice like I'm just doing my job.

She wouldn't be elated for me, but she seemed she would just be waiting for the day to cessation. I can remember one day and this was daybreak, and she was walking sluggishly to the staff room. She had a strand of hair hanging down from her forehead, as she would just call this, another days pay.

The chief would come in on Saturday mornings and do a little opus. I was out on a gurney and he mentioned to me. Not talking directly to me, but wanted me to hear his statement.

I can recall when I was very sad. Then two nurses came next to me and began to just talk. I was so bewildered I felt much better. I was thinking why don't they talk to me. I'm the one feeling bad. But I was so astonished I stopped feeling sad.

"It' fun."

What came over me was, he meant the exercises are fun. I had been having pt in my bed this first week when I began to move and I had been giving so much effort I had not even felt any strain.

"We are going to get you up on this tilt table. We will strap down your stomach and legs."

"Sounds good."

I said.

"This first day we will just let you stand and let you get down before you get dizzy. Do you feel dizzy?"

"No."

This was my first time standing in months and this seemed like the Intensive Care Unit at Norwood Hospital. I seemed to be out of my body and picturing myself lying down flat on the tilt table, when I was standing up straight. Now I remember, there was a mirror at the end of the parallel bars, which I looked at myself standing. I felt the PT's were there and dr. Train might have been there. They were looking at me as if they were studying me.

"Your taller than I thought."

Nancy asked me.

"I am almost 6 feet."

I responded.

I was sensing my smile on my face. My lips and smile was what I was thinking about. All the blood would now be circulating in a different fashion now. I seem to recollect the chief had passed by and said something to him self. Now let's see what he is made out of. His head would look up to the left, then go back straight down looking at the floor.

"Well we will get you down flat now."

Nancy said as a PT cranked down the tilt table.

"Today I want you to put on long leg braces and we will walk."
Said Nancy.

"How far will I walk?"

"Just down the end of the bars and back."
She said with solicitude.

I got up from the wheelchair and onto the parallel bars. My orthopedic shoes weren't in yet, so I had to put on my own shoes. These didn't have the steel notch at the bottom of the shoes. So this was a little gauche looking. I moved my left arm on the bar and then my right leg. I continued this process with my right arm and then left leg. I was actuating very slow and I couldn't believe I was walking this laggard. My mind said to me I can walk normally, but my legs didn't respond to me telling them to go faster. I proceeded down the end of the bars and then went back into the wheelchair. I actually thought this would be impossible to get back into shape walking normally.

After one week with long leg braces and parallel bars, I was put on short leg braces.

"We are going to try you on crutches today."

"Outside the bars?" I said quickly.

"First in between the bars and then outside them, if everything goes all right."

The therapist was Robby.

This girl was 27 years old about and she had the most beautiful eyes I have ever seen.

"Move your right crutch then left foot, then left crutch, left foot. That's good."

She said with absolute certainty.

I walked about ten feet to the hallway and I could feel my legs quavering, with a halo of some sort around them. I smelt the air and this smelt fresh. The air in between the parallel bars seemed stagnant. But the air outside the bars smelt recent.

"This is wonderful."

I said happily.

"Back into the wheelchair now."

The wheelchair was following me as I walked to the hallway, just a bit from the PT station. The wheelchair I had chosen was from a person whom walked after he got through with this wheelchair. I figured this would be a lucky wheelchair.

I had begun to talk to a chaplain once per week. I can remember asking him about Jesus.

I asked him.

"Do you believe Jesus was God?"

"Jesus was a tricky person."

He asserted.

I had wheeled down to the chapel for Mass on Sunday. The head chaplain was there, serving the mass. I wheeled up to the altar, and received the communion. This head chaplain asked me one day, I had a choice to see him or the other chaplain. I had been seeing this other chaplain for a couple of weeks for about a half an hour a day.

My opinion was the head chaplain, whom saw me at the Mass, seemed to think my problems were outstanding and he would like to talk to me, because of this. He butted in and told the other chaplain whom I had been descrying with I could see him instead of the regular one.

I told him.

"I would like to see you instead of the head chaplain."

This chaplain's eyes lit up and he seemed very anxious to talk to me. He had held off the assault of the head chaplain butting in and trying to see me. I thought he really tried to help me much more after this. I just looked at this so natural seeing him.

I had begun to breakdown once when I was seeing Nancy.

"Why are you crying? You have feeling and movement in your legs. Why are you crying?"

"Mine wasn't an accident like the others. Mine wasn't a car accident or diving. Mine was on purpose."

She was startled. She didn't give any rejoinder to my statement.

"Doesn't this always seem to be raining out?"

I said to Stephanie, while we were talking out by the parallel bars one night.

"Ya, it does. I'm still going to Radcliffe. I'm going over there to check for wheelchair adaptability."

I hate the mornings getting up and going out for breakfast."
I said to her.

"Ya, me too. I feel like putting the covers over me and going back to sleep."

"That Mrs. Valent. She really is something."

Mrs. Valent was the head nurse and she had a very commanding way about her, when she would get the able bodied people in wheelchairs up for breakfast. She had worked in the hospital 40 years and had been with the chief when he opened up shop in 1957. She was about 60 years old and she was a very vibrant woman. Someone had given her a name she was a marine drill sergeant.

"I'm doing good on the parallel bars, but this is awfully difficult."
She said to me friendly.

"Ya, I see you on them."

Stephanie didn't get any return. She would have to like hop with the crutches.

I can recall there was a blonde haired PT girl whom would put up resistance against my legs in between the parallel bars one day. I tried so hard. She kept on putting up more and more resistance with my legs. She would be down low against like my knees as I tried to move more and more.

I began to be crazy over chocolate candy bars. I would look towards walking to the gifts shop to get candy bars. This was my reward of walking to the gifts shop or even wheeling to the gift shop.

"Hi Aunt Gertrude."

"Hi Billy."

"It's good to see you."
I declared.

"You look like you are moving your legs better?"
She said caringly.

I was getting into the wheelchair from bed and this picked up my spirits incredibly.

"Let's go into the activity room."

"Hi Doug."

"Hi Bill."

"What happened to you Doug?"

I asked him.

I wasn't quite sure what happened to Doug. Doug was a quadriplegic. He had his upper arms, which he could move, but no lower parts and fingers. I could see and hear Doug's long fingernails rasping on the table, as he would pick them up and droop them down making noise on the table.

"I was going 100 mph and I hit a tree. They thought I was dead. They put a blanket over me until I moved my right arm, and they could tell I was still alive. I'm from Michigan and I've been to 5 different hospitals trying to be rehabilitated."

"Wow what a story."

My aunt Gertrude said.

I was happy to see my aunt Gertrude. She was a very religious person, but she knew there was a time and place for religion. She knew her place and time.

"Doug's wife would come in everyday and see him each night. I was thinking this was a very dedicated wife. There were other wives whom left their men when they were injured.

"Hi Liz."

"Hi Billy."

"Let's go into the activity room and I can lift my weights.

"Okay."

She said.

"Are you going to play baseball again Billy?"

She asked me.

I could recall, when she was walking next to me, she wasn't a short girl. She was about 5'7" and she had on red pants, and she seemed different in she looked more grown up than when I would know her before. She still had the soft naïve voice. I remember looking down at my braces on my legs while walking with her. I felt progress from going with her in a wheelchair and all the times talking to her on bed rest.

"Are you going to go to college in January?"

She asked me while we were next to each other sitting down. She was sitting next to me while I was lifting the weights with my legs.

"I don't know." Je ne sais pas.

I was sitting directly next to her and I would look at the red pants she had on over her legs. I could make out the size of her thighs and her crotch. They seemed so beautiful. How much I wanted to be healthy then and with her like this was before. I recall her looking down at my right leg, as I was lifting the weights. I can remember trying to lift as much as I could with my legs. She seemed a bit livened up. I was actually showing her how I was getting stronger. This was the real thing. She would no longer have a companion in a wheelchair. She would no longer have this embarrassment to combat against. I was upright.

"Well this is all I have to do."

I said.

"Let's go back to the bed."

I said enthusiastic.

This seemed like sex therapy looking at her thighs and crotch next to me. She had her jacket opened and I could make out the little bit slanted downward breasts.

I can recall I would play sports and my girlfriends would see me play. I would look at them and this would inspire me to try harder. But this wasn't a sport. This was much serious.

"I'm not going to be working tomorrow, so you can increase the weights when you feel you can do more."

Nancy my PT said.

"By the way how much are you lifting?"

"Thirty pounds."

I said proudly.

The next day the chief was out in the corridor and he asked me.

"How much are you lifting, Bill?"

"Thirty-five pounds."

I exclaimed.

I sometime think this was an act by Nancy and the chief to see how I would do on the third floor, which was the psychiatric unit. I can recall back when I was a "door to door" salesman and I thought one of the houses which I knocked on, and the people wanted to buy my product. I thought this was a setup by the company to get up my confidence.

The chief would put his head back a bit, then downward. I had increased automatically, because I wanted to be the strongest possible as soon as possible.

"On the weekends I want you to walk down to the entrance to the hospital three times."

Nancy said to me.

"Can I do more?"

"I don't think you will be able to."

She said

"I'm going over to the candy store."

I said to Mrs. Valent on the weekend.

"You can walk this far?"

Mrs. Valent said curiously.

"Ya, I've been doing this for a while now."

Her eyes lit up a bit because she was startled, I could walk this far on braces and crutches.

A new patient came in and he was an awfully angry young man.

"I'd give anything to be on crutches like you."

He said.

I said to him.

"Once you get this far you want more and more."

"I thought I could take anything from being in the Army. I was in the Army three years. They are going to have to knock me down from these parallel bars when I get up on them. I'm going to walk out of here, even if I have to walk on my hands."

He was banging his fist on the back of the bed and moving his hands and head as much as possible. He seemed to almost go cross-eyed because he was so mad.

"Tell that doctor I want to leave."

He was talking about the chief. He left after about one week and went back to the hospital he was in before. His attorney came in and tried to tell him to stay here. He wanted to go where his wife didn't have to travel so far. I believe he was from Vermont.

"I could move my right leg before I came here, and now I can't."

He also said.

When they asked him to catheterize himself, he said.

"Don't they have a pill I can take for this, to urinate again?"

I began to think I did do my own catheterizing myself. There were only about 16 people in the AP Chemistry course I passed in high school. I had passed one year of College Chemistry in high school. I looked at the catheterizing myself as doing an experiment.

A patient came in whom, walked into hospital but was never to walk out. His name was Nick and he was a Greek. He had two children and a beautiful wife, which came in to see him every night.

"What did you get for dinner, Nick?"

I asked Nick one night.

"I got a bacon burger. I ought to give it to the Bruins to use as a hockey puck."

"Ha, ha, ha, ha."

I laughed.

Nick would always be watching the Bruins on television each night. One day Nick was going to x-ray department.

He yelled out.

"I'm going the morgue for an autopsy."

"Ha, ha, ha, ha."

I laughed again. This was a laughter, which would make me get pain in my back, which had the back brace on.

Another day Nick was in his bed and he got an erection. He yelled out this time.

"Nurse, nurse, nurse, muscle test, muscle test."

What laughter I would get from these farcical but serious comments. Nick was all out serious about these statements, which he made. He was an electrician before he got ill. This seemed like he was chewing food while these statements would come out. His wife would bring him in fish each night to eat because Nick didn't like the hospital food. He never seemed to smile, not at all ever.

"Nurse, nurse, nurse."

I said loudly.

"Roland."

I said when a nurse came in.

Across from me was Roland whom had a trachea in his throat. He needed to be cleaned out by suction tubes. The nurse would work on

Roland for a short while. He couldn't talk. He could only gargle. This was the trigger to call someone for him. After a week or so he could talk and I asked him.

"Where are you from, Roland?"

"New York."

He responded.

"See the picture of the car I was in?"

"Jesus Roland, that's a wreck."

He had a lovely wife and one child. Roland had his head scalped from the neck traction screws.

Another person whom happened to be my age at 18 was in one corner of the big room. His name was Bruce.

"Where are you from Bruce?"

"I'm from New Jersey. I'm from New Jersey. I was driving a small car when I got into an accident. That's the last time I am going to be driving a small car."

That was probably a factual true statement.

"Where are the two girls I see you with?"

"Oh they are up from Jersey. There staying in a hotel in town."

These two girls came up to take care of Bruce. They were very attractive girls whom were a little short, about 5'4". They seemed to allure my attention.

"See you around Bruce."

"All right Bill."

Bruce was a quad whom got back the use of his arms a little bit, but they needed a lot of physical therapy.

A priest came in and asks me.

"What happened to you?"

"I broke my back."

"Would you like to receive Holy Communion?"

I nodded my head.

"Body of Christ."

"Amen."

This priest seemed rather bored. In that I don't conceive he enjoyed what he was doing. He had to probably put up with all the people saying they didn't want to receive Holy Communion. This was the situation, which you were in. You to even question you don't want to receive Holy Communion. You didn't even think God could help you, or your faith. There were no casket clothes here.

Page 10 of my actual diary.

I also was doing a lot of fishing during this time. I remember one lady and mother wathcing two boys fish while reading about acne. Maybe a little with Cox and Jimmy.

The tex incident was pretty big, when tex was with Al's girl and they were getting it on in front of everyone at Sparks. By making everyone else kind of be embarrassed. They would then come closer to the people who embarrassed them. So I just talked with him for a while where the talk became more serious. Until finally he came out of his car and said in a real low voice, your on your own now.

He then got into his car and I held on to the door of the car and got a ride on the tar. Then after that I went to Cox's house where I slept over and cracked a glass. I wasn't working then. Oldham and Edmo incidents and also when I went down Daceys' that night and the hunter scare.

I went to the top floor of grandma's house where I stayed one afternoon. After fasting and not eating. I then went home in my car and came baxk down that night. Next page.

Maura incident yelling at her.

Coached a Babe Ruth baseball team prep league and slugged old man Jansen when thought trying to lose baseball games.

Went after Greg ripped shirt.

Dropped glass when saw darly.

To Grammas' slept in the room upstairs. Woke up the next morning. Drink just liquids during the day. Then went back to the house with shoulders high and proud. Went to Liabrary first where looked up the word Charisma-meant exceedingly high for leadership.

Went home where Jackie wanted his sneakers. I didn't give them to him because I still thought you were supposed to make people suffer. Dad came up and broke the door down, but I ran out the door and went into the woods where I knelt down and began to pray for about a half hour too an hour. While I am writing this I am thinking about how I will be able to look back at this being happy, just like the other times.

Page 13

Went into woods for about a ½ hour praying. I heard all kinds of crickets real loud.

I then was going to decide weather to go home or take-off and come tomorrow. I wasn't sure what to do. I desire that I will be able to walk again. I desire that and that will be so. I took off to Fr.Macs 'where I met the Queen brothers. I took one of there bikes and didn't come back with it. Where I would have sworn the [police were chasing me. I dropped the bike off at the end of Winter St. and took off for the woods.

I had also taken one of the shirts off of one of the Queen boys'. I must have been running for close to an hour. When I finally came to the Willet school and I saw Bob Molly with his girlfriend. I ended up having a fight with him, with him having a club or something. He finally had the final say, when he took off with car.

Page 14

When he left. I saw (chuck something) he gave me a ride to the Westwood Junior high where I got off. I headed down the street until I came to this old house which looked like no one was living in it. I went to the back of the house in which I had to open a gate which was a creaky door-hinge entrance. It was like the gate of heaven would look like.

I stayed in there from about 12-4 Just praying and thinking I needed to stay in there for 30 days and 30 nights. I was lying on the ground which smelt like an old age home. I was alsos arching my back back. After a while I went up to the barnlike structure. I opened th door slowly then went back to me step spot, and just laid there

Page 15 While I was laying there, coming from the door was a cricket and it started coming towards me. When it was about a yard away from me. I said it in a low voice which I decided later was a voice from God. "What do you want?"I then got into a yoga position in the middle of the backyard and just wondering about things. I then went home where I slept for about 5 hours. My dad came up and wanted me. I then ran out he door, and took the car. I proceeded to drive about 40 miles when I came back I had just about decided that everything was alright. My mother said their will be fish for supper. I ate the fish and sat down for a while. I went up to my room where I tried to arch my back back. I had to do it seven times.

Page 16

I could make out a crucifix on the window direction. The thought of going out the window then came into my mind. I went into the bathroom after that and was just in there. (Opened up window and then my sister knocked on door I then went out the window.

I was down the Norwood Hospital and while I was down their

I had a lot of bad experiences down at Norwood Hospital. (with Cluade – main character. I will write a section on the Norwood Hospital Expedition.

Page 17 Oct. 7

I took a shower today. Washed my hiar and it feels a lot better.

I got into a wheelchair te 5th of October. Stayed up for about 4 hours. felt pretty good. played strato-matic with th old man. I had some pretty good games. played Strat yesterday and didn't play that long because of all the other people talking etc. at the table. I have a little bit of doubt if I can really play that 4 or 5 hours a day.But I desire I will play strat an enjoy it to the outmost beauty. I desire that and that will be so. I desire that I shall have faith of faith that I shall be hapy extremely happy. Just like I felt sfter the senior prom an during it with no drugs at all. Also how I felt after

Page 18

I hit the homerun against North Quincy.

While I was here I have the idea that I am not being helped to the 100 % ability. I feel real good now while writing. So I desire that I will write a lot. I desire that and that will be so. A girl just walked by scratching or just rubbing her back to the sink. She just went back to the second to last bed where she is feeding a person. I desire that anyone trying to embarrass me and the using that energy or spirit or something to help someone. I desire that person will feel better and better. He will she will feel better and better.

Page 19

I am confused right now a very lot. I was playing strat-o matic with the oldman for a while, until he left.

I remembered that I had played it this afternoon beside that girl spinal cord. I left first night before pops left together.

When I came back to play some more strat she was up the other end. I played for a while. Then it was just me the girl an Koko. Koko left after a little while. I then played with one of the girls that. I had a great time playing with her. I don't feel any different. She was smoking and drinking coke. I didn't feel any different, and I remembered back when I whenthe SS was smoking. I felt better.

Page 20

I keep on bringing myself back when I rea after the stitches were out it was all down hill then easy goings. Also bringing myself baxk to when I jumped out the window and I was searching for my god. An also when I was quite happy when I thought I was going to die and what gave me that attitude was reach up as high as you can and God will reach down after you. I desire that that girl with the spinal contractions will feel better and better. I desire that Koko will get better. I think that I should stay to myself now. .

Back to real.

Koko was about 30 years old. I can remember him tell me once. "I have two boys. I am neck down. You are only waist down."

Koko was like on bed rest for about 7 months. He got back use of his right arm so he could feed himself. He was in an electric wheelchair.

Then there was Walter whom I took liken to. He I believe was a diving accident. He had his arms but no fingers. They call this a C-6 break. I thought this would be worse than a higher break where you lost your arms a bit. Walter had to use a manual grip wheelchair. I thought this was worse than electric wheelchair. I can recall talking to Walter and he told me he flew planes.

Walter had told me he was in the process of a divorce. He said the injury to him put the icing on the cake with his divorce. When I was transferred to the psychiatric unit a little later and Elizabeth left me, then I was in the same boat as Walter. As his wife left him.

This was the famous 1975 World Series with the Boston Red Sox verses the Cincinnati Reds. I had the year earlier gotten the card from the Boston Red Sox scout for them to project on me in the future. Well all of the patients would be watching the games at night. When Boston had the big hits all of the 10 or so beds, you could hear the roars from the beds. To tell you the truth I had fallen asleep at the late innings. Then when I heard the roars I awoke. This was really like medicine to me. This automatically forced me to awake. Then I would fall back asleep. Only to be awaken again, by the roars from the beds. As in you had to use a lot of energy in the mornings to get up, here I was like rising when I heard the cheers as if I were being controllably getting up at night, when the World Series was happening here especially in Boston. I did get the card to send into the Red Sox organization to be projected on in the future. I heard anyone in the Red Sox organization they take care of.

I received my first pass to leave hospital since Aug. 1, 1975. There was only one way to go which was up. I had made a lot of progress and I was looking forward to seeing my friends. I wanted very badly to get back into the swing of life with them. I really enjoyed being with them very much.

Walking down the narrow hallway with leg braces and crutches, I saw my brother Jack's Studebaker parked in front of the hospital entrance. This hallway was to become a familiar place for learning how to walk again. This was Thanksgiving and Jack was home from college. The thought of leaving the security of hospital and going out in public on braces was scary, like running a gamut.

I was angry I needed supports, but content I wasn't still in bed. I got into the backseat of Jack's car. He was driving. I saw the spot where I had climbed the step for the first time without my PT Nancy. Now I could go up and down steps without railings, which picked up my spirits. This seemed like a little thing, but this was one thing I could do which a wheelchair couldn't.

During the ride home I began to get emotional. I was leaving hospital where I had seen some days. I was trying to fight back the tears, but they kept coming. This was a regular autumn day. This was on the cool side and a little raw. We went by the Chateaux De'Ville, where our senior prom was held. I had taken Elizabeth and had a wonderful time. I thought I wouldn't see opportune times like those again. I would say to myself if I hadn't taken the tetra-hychloric-carbonate I wouldn't have to have gone through this agony. I wondered if I would be all right physically. At least I was leaving Hospital. But what did this mean?

When I got home I could see my neighbors sitting on their front steps. I remembered them sitting there after I came home from playing sports. I had felt haughty of myself knowing I was a good athlete and I was always getting my picture in the local newspaper. I can remember coming home from football games and practices, sometimes hitting my legs saying. "These legs are going to take me to heaven."

I also could recall seeing my neighbors when I would go off to the "door to door" salesman job. I would be dressed up in suit and tie. I thought I was no longer a jock but a man, a professional salesman. They would look fortuitously at me while they would be sitting on their steps, I would say a calm confident, "Hello." They wouldn't ask any questions, but would respond to my hello with just a "Hi Bill," and a look of respect. I didn't feel young and cocky talking to them anymore. I was a man and this came out in the way I spoke. I was supercilious of myself neatly dressed up.

Now I was going into my home with leg braces and crutches. They said hello in a way, which seemed apologetic. They seemed just about in reverence of me when they looked at me. I felt ashamed of myself for having jumped out the window and for needing supports to get around. I was a cripple and I was feeling what this feels like for cripples to be out in public. I thought my neighbors didn't like me as much as they did before. All pride in myself was gone. The quote in the Bible, "Pride cometh before the fall," was correct in my case. I was feeling the full force of abashment.

I went to the Thanksgiving Day football game at Dedham. Walking to the park with my supports I thought I was walking equivalent with my braces. I was making an entrance. I bought my ticket with my brother Jack and two sisters. I heard from dr. Black.

"You got the sticks."

He seemed to be on the same plane as me. This made me feel well someone discerned where I came from. I said.

"Ya."

I went over to my high school friend Okey and talked to him a little bit. I could tell he felt a little ill at ease. He was looking around to see if anyone could see him, with a handicap. When he left I felt a quick jab of pain. I had gotten respect from Okey in the aforesaid years. Now he was ashamed of me. But I had learned from the salesman job there would be more doors, try your luck elsewhere. If one house doesn't let you in try another. You have to figure on rejection.

I moved down a small hill and headed for a group of scholar friends, whom were standing in the corner of the end zone. I was feeling out the territories. These people were back from college on the Thanksgiving break.

Steve "Spock," commented.

"Are your legs getting stronger?"

And I said.

"Ya."

I said Ya, so he wouldn't think, I would need supports the rest of my life and I was okay. At this time I wasn't sure how much strength I would get back. I was feeling a little bit more at ease with these classmates. I put my crutches up against the wire and I just stood there with them. I began to talk to my friend Hal. Hal was going to Harvard in Pre-Med, and was quite a guy.

There wasn't much gaucheness when we conversed about the game. He would hold his head high and speak in a distinguished way. This didn't seem going to Harvard had gone to his head, like this had to other people whom were going to Ivy League Universities. Hal was an abase person.

While I was there Jack Sr. came by and put some cardboard on the ground for me to stand on. Maybe he wanted to keep my feet warm. But I really don't know why he did this.

Later Elizabeth came by and said.

"You're walking without crutches?"

She couldn't see them up against the wire. Wanting so badly to say yes I said.

"No."

Her voice was comforting. I could count on her not to feel embarrassed about me. She knew where I came from. She had seen the slow progress I had made. From being flat on my back, to wheelchair, to parallel bars, and now braces and crutches. When I heard her voice, I embraced her with my mind, because I had someone whom could understand. She seemed to be saying, we're together for this one. She had a lot of faith I would be okay again.

We went for a coffee and I was feeling lucky to have someone whom liked me despite my physical handicaps. She carried the coffees and we went over by my pals, out of school. Elizabeth appealed sparked up and her hair was pushed back behind her ears. She had a type of bowlegged to her walk and she had a confidence in herself I had never descried before. She was the only person whom stayed by my side. I would call on her and this seemed she would come a running. She would talk to me without self-conscience, and had liveliness, to her voice. She took the lead of the conversation with my buddies. This was a new characteristic for her, which was blossoming.

Then my friend Tex tried out being seen in public with me. He suggested we go for a coffee. At first he didn't seem ashamed to be with me. He was a car salesman, which made him have conviction with people. As we were coming back from the coffee stand, I noticed him get a little self-conscience. His head started to rock from side to side when you are really embarrassed. He did try though.

After the game I had Thanksgiving dinner with my family and then went back to the hospital. I remember sitting in the chair at the table and this seemed I was treated as if nothing had happened. I was a bit bewildered. I went back to the hospital at night.

I had gotten a pair of army pants, which I am not sure but they may have come from the Veteran's Hospital. I had tried to get into the V.A. before going to Robby 7.

"Today, dr. Kittery's assistant is going to watch you walk, to see if you need the short leg braces anymore."

Nancy said to me.

"Hi, my name is dr. Honorato and you've seen me around. Could you walk up and down the parallel bars for me?"

I walked up the parallel bars and he says consulting with Nancy.

"He looks good."

"What do you think?"

Nancy says to the doctor.

"Ya what?"

I say.

This doctor had his jowls down a bit as he watched me walk. My legs below the knee were a little bit wobbly but not a great deal.

"This will be all right to walk without your braces. Your balance seems good."

"This great."

I said to them excitedly.

I began to talk to a psychiatrist when I was on Robinson 7. His name was dr. Blue. I would talk to him for a while during the day. One night he came in and I had gotten undressed and was in bed. He came by and said.

"Do you want to come to my office on the third floor?"

"I just got undressed. I am in bed now and I am not going anywhere."

"Would this be too much to get undressed and come down to my office?"

"I am not going anywhere."

So he sat in a chair next to my bed and we talked. I pictured myself seeing him in a chair in a black suit with his shoulders curled inward a bit, and he seemed like a checker on a chessboard.

A few days later he asks me.

"Do you want to come to the third floor?"

Dr. Blue asked me.

"I don't know."

I replied.

This was the psychiatric unit Robinson 3. I was very hesitant, and I didn't have any time to think about this. He brought me down on the elevator to the third floor and got off. I didn't want to make a harsh decision. But anything was better than staying on Robinson 7. I was pretty depressed.

"Well you have to make up your mind now."

He said.

I was like in a maze. I was just about in shock thinking I was making a major decision.

"Well all right."

"We will make out a schedule for you. You can go up to Robby 7 for pt and then come down here for groups. You will have the morning group at 8:30, 9:00 and 10:00 o'clock is then the community meeting, then discussion group. You will then go upstairs for your pt. Then come down for lunch on the third floor. In the afternoons you will have your ot here. Then go upstairs for your afternoon pt. This is your schedule."

Said one of the nurses on Robby 3.

They had started me out with a full time schedule. I was a little in shock thinking I was going to have to get regimented to this new schedule while I had all my steel on.

"Why did you jump out the window?"

Dr. Blue asked me.

"I GOT a command from God."

"Well we will have to find the real reason why you jumped out the window."

"Did you hear any voices?"

"I heard a voice back in February, I WANT YOU, when I was looking at the curtains in my room."

"That was an hallucination."

"I thought the good was bad and the bad good."

"That's psychotic."

"My uncle told me this before I jumped."

"That's all for today."

This doctor had black hair and he would sometimes have one strand of hair hanging down over his forehead. Like how dr. Train would on the seventh floor. Dr. Blue talked like a computer, with that choppiness to his speech. He also seemed to be embarrassed easily. I can remember once when I began to laugh and he turned red.

One day when I was in a group, the doctor leading the group whom also happened to be the shrink I talked to on Robinson 7. This was when I didn't talk to Elizabeth this day. I also happened to be breaking down then. In this particular group this doctor would constantly be saying.

"And that could be a problem."

He was a doctor whom looked like a duck, in which he had black hair, which he parted back very neatly. When he said this once, a person in the group Dorsy said.

"You could come in here and see me hanging, and alls you would say, and that could be a problem."

I laughed and laughed and laughed. This person Dorsy was taking the place of Nick, whom made me laugh on Robinson 7.

When we were having a community Meeting in which all the people on the unit would be together, Dorsy started to say.

"And that could be a problem."

He also would say.

"Time to make fun of the psychiatrist time. And that could be a problem."

I kept on laughing and laughing. This doctor there began to get embarrassed. He looked sick. His face looked like he was pouting. He didn't know what to do. He began to have dyskenesia of his facial muscles. He looked like he was almost going to start crying. He needed help.

"Lose those things."

Jack Dodge said about my Canadian crutches.

"I hope so."

Jack Dodge said this with a cutting to his speech. Jack's nickname on the unit was Belly Bean. He wore glasses and he would put his glasses up over his eyes instead of downward when he wanted to move them.

"Hi Bill, I'm Peter Sewob's mother. How are you?"

"I'm getting better. How's Peter doing?"

I asked her as I was walking to church one weekend.

"He's doing fine."

She said with concern.

I felt a little bit of confidence, because I looked back how I was captain of the football team and Peter was one of the players. I felt not too much ill at ease about the one crutch I was now on. I would holler at her son when I was captain of the football team and this brought back very good memories.

"We are going to go swimming. Stephanie is going to come also."

Nancy my PT said.

"Dr. Kittery does Bill have to wear his back brace to go swimming?"

Asked Nancy to dr. Kittery.

"Yes, he should still wear this."

Dr. Kittery said.

Dr. Kittery seemed he didn't want to take any chances with me, and my back. He said this with a little bit of commanding but he got his point across. I had pushed Stephanie's wheelchair down to Nancy's car. I really felt close to her then. We all tried to help each other.

We went swimming at the University pool and this was a change. I can remember when Stephanie was getting undressed in the changing area. I seemed interested in seeing her with no clothes on. Whatcha do.

"Do you want to go to a movie?"

Tex asked me one weekend.

"Ya, what's playing?"

"The Groove Tube."

He responded.

"I have some pot. We can smoke it if you want."

Tex said.

"Here Billy, do you want a hit?"

"Ya, I'll try one."

I was smoking pot. I was saying to myself the condition I was in and I'm smoking pot. I want to act as if I am normal and if my friends were smoking pot, I will too. This seemed I was taking a risk, like how the psychiatrist would say to take a risk for things. Maybe not pot is the right risk in their book. I just got tired at the movie from the pot, and I had to fight laziness.

A person whom was also a patient on the Psychiatric unit was Wally. He was a big person whom played ball at Northeastern University

Football team. Wally had gotten into a depression. Wally would smoke pot in the shower.

I asked him one day.

"Can you get me some pot, Wally?"

"Okay for five dollars I'll get you a nickel bag. Be sure you just smoke this in the shower."

"Right."

Wally had a big belly and probably ate to assuage his depression. I smoked some pot in the shower and when I came out I was feeling rather high. Thinking about this now, I smoked pot and I still had a back brace on. I must have thought I had pretty good balance.

I was talking to this worker there and she had blonde hair and was very attractive. I tried to score with her earlier, but she didn't respond to any of my words. She was a little bit older than me about 22 or 23. I think I recall her name was Linda. She was sitting in a chair next to my bed and I was lying down. I would usually lye down when I didn't have anything to do. I was talking to her and out of my mouth came while being stoned.

"Your beautiful."

She looked at me for a few seconds and then got up and left the room. I said this with as much perturbation I could muster. I could have been talking to a Mac Truck by the way she reacted towards this. I think she must have been a schizophrenic with no feelings or more than likely she must have thought she was better than me. I could see her the next day with high boots on running around to the different rooms to get people to get their medicine. I didn't make any headway with this girl at all. She wouldn't even give me the least bit of compassion. Good riddance to the goody. This was one reason why I really despised the psychiatric units, because the opposite gender staff, in my case the females wouldn't ever give you any bit of compassion.

"May I speak with Liz?"

"Hello."

"Liz, this is Billy. Do you want to go for a ride on Saturday?"

"All right."

"I'll pick you up at 11:00."

I walked up to the steps of the house without my cane.

"Is Liz home?"

"Yes she is. I'll get her for you."

Her mother had come to the door.

"Hi Liz."

"Hi Billy."

"Let's just go for a ride. All right?"

"Okay."

We proceeded to go for a ride and I was sparked up a bit. I loved going riding with a woman.

"Let's go to John Rekab's house."

He was the person whom we doubled dated with to the senior prom.

"All right."

She responded.

We pulled up to John's house and I began to toot the horn.

"Toot, toot, toot."

"Why don't you walk up to the door?"

She said this with some anger, as I think she was rectifying my laziness. She said this with a bit of cutting which caught me off guard.

"Okay."

I said to her as she had just about knocked me out with her outburst. We had our first fight. I walked up to the doorway, and there was no answer at the door.

"Do you want to go to a donut shop to meet my brother Jack and his friend?"

"Ya, All right."

We went to the donut shop and I put my arm around her as we walked into the donut shop. I didn't use my cane. Instead I held onto her. We went in and my brother Jack was there with his pal Ken having coffees. Jack looked like he was in good spirits, and probably thinking in the back of his mind, this could be something if I could play sports again. He knew physically I had lost all my supports, and this was comforting to know.

"I'm going to have a donut and a coffee. What would you like Liz?"

"I'll just have a coffee."

She said.

We had drove through Dedham while we cruised. I dropped her off at home and got a quick kiss from her over the bucket seats. I was thinking back when I kissed her at Norwood Hospital. I remembered the caresses I had gotten off of her when I would drop her off at night after graduation. I would try and tease her all the time then.

"Will you come in to visit me?"

"Ya, sure I will."

"I had a nice time Liz."

"Me too."

"Bye."

"Bye."

At a family meeting, dr. Blue said to me.

"We have questions if you should be driving or not. We don't think you should be driving."

The psychiatrist dr. Blue would look down towards the table with his hands clasped together as he would look downward at an angle and speak. He had just about perfect memory. Straight from the book, would come all the knowledge. "You feel a little worried. Were you a little anxious first?" He had a very austere outlook on things.

"Hi Maura, Anne Marie, Liz"

"Hi."

"Hi."

"Hi."

This was my sister Maura and her friend Anne Marie, and Elizabeth.

"I can't drive for now, Liz."

She would smile at me and look down at me and say.

"Okay."

"I thought we could go for rides when I came home on the weekends. I had a nice time driving with you last week."

"I did too."

"How is your brother Neil doing? Liz."

"He's out of the Marines and he is going back to high school. You getting out soon Billy?"

"I'm not sure right now."

She seemed to make me smile a bit, as she would be thinking of the future all the time.

"Well we might as well be getting along now, Billy."

Said Maura.

Liz was kind of quiet when I would be talking to my sister Maura and her friend. I was testing her if she could join in conversation with my sister whom was a year older than Liz. She would just have a little smile on her face and she would look down at me.

I thought years later, Elizabeth was like hysterical about all, which was happening. Then if she were to visit me on the psychiatric unit she would lose some of this hysterics. I thought this was something great, and she didn't want to lose this, by visiting me on the psych ward. I guess she didn't like me this much.

When I was on a cane I was talking to dr. Blue in his office. I got my cane and smashed this on his desk. Then I threw the cane at him. Dr. Blue in one motion threw his hands out, and the cane came exactly back to me. I thought this was when he made a stand in Gulf War I.

"Hi David."

"Hi Bill. What are you doing?"

"I'm trying to run."

I was trying to run in between the parallel bars. David was in his wheelchair and would have that big eyes, eyebrows down look and said to me.

"If you keep that up you will be playing for the Green Bay Packers."

I was lifted up in spirit and continued to try and run.

"We are going to try and skip today."

Nancy said to me at the beginning of the PT session.

"I'll try too."

I said

I began to shuffle down the corridor with the best I could skip like action.

"Look he is running."

David said from the entrance.

"Look at him."

Bruce spurted out.

Then came this roar from the beds.

"Yeh, yeh, Yeh, etc . . . ."

Bruce would muster up the strength to talk when he said his comment. He seemed he was really interested in what was going on, on the floor. While David would have maybe the tinge of jealousy possibly probably because he was waist down while Bruce was neck down.

The people in bed, I seemed startled they could still have hope and joy that someone else was making it. I wondered to myself what this might be like not to move anything for years and years. I had my head down a bit looking at the floor, as I skipped as best I could down the hallway. I wondered to myself maybe the reason why these people didn't walk was because they wanted too, too much.

When I was going into church one Saturday evening, one of the priests commented to me.

"You don't have the crutches anymore?"

"No I don't need them anymore."

"That's great."

"I have a cane now."

This priest seemed a little incited when he said this.

"Have you been smoking pot?"

One of the nurses asked me.

"I smell this in the bathroom. We will have to talk about this."

"We can't treat you if you continue to smoke pot."

"Where did you get the pot?"

Dr. Blue asked me.

"I got this from a patient."

"Who was this?"

"I am not going to tell this person's name."

I usually would smoke this in the shower. I became very serious when they said they couldn't treat me if I continued to smoke pot. I said to myself, the little I knew about psychiatry, maybe they could help me here. So I like set a vow I wouldn't smoke the dope. I hoped they could help me.

"You never talk to any of the staff on your free time. All the other patients talk to us when they can, but you don't."

"I don't know. I have nothing to talk about."

Since I had supposedly mental and physical problems, I couldn't think of anything to say, because I had been comforted by these problems.

"You will be discharged on Feb 20."

"Wonderful."

I said to dr. Blue.

"Nancy I'm going home on Feb. 20 which just happens to be my birthday."

"Great, I think you can have pt down the Norwood Hospital with Billy Kold."

I still didn't have bladder control back yet, so I was wearing a condom and leg bag. I went home on Feb. 20 and this was a good feeling. I was still like in a maze, because I knew and I thought, I wouldn't feel much congruous. I was still down in the dumps and I had stelazine to take care for this, but this didn't seem to help any at all. When I got home I went directly up to my room to lye down.

"Hi Henry."

"Hi Bill, Ha, ha, ha."

"I got out of the Marines last week."

Henry said.

"I just got out of the hospital Hank."

"Franco."

"Boe, let's go down to Fall River and we can get laid by this girl I know down there."

My nickname was Boe.

"Sounds good."

Henry said.

"Why not."

I said.

"I went to school down there, when I was kicked out of the Norwood School system in tenth grade."

Franco said.

"Let's get some beer."

Henry said.

Franco was the person whom was driving the car when a person was killed right after high school. I was with my old friends now and this felt good. But something was missing. I wasn't in good health physically and this was always nagging me. I felt a little bit wearisome in I still had my leg bag. I wondered what the girl would think about someone with a leg bag. Franco was in the back seat while I was up front with Henry driving.

"I'll see if she is home."

Franco says when we got there.

"She is not home."

I gave a sigh of relief when I heard this, because I was self-conscience about my leg bag.

"Let's look at the boats."

Henry said.

Henry was drinking beer constantly and he might have been not to smart in the academics, but he had common sense and plenty of this. Henry was always trying to be funny and was rather comical. He drove me to his car and I went home.

I went to a nightclub one night. I met a girl I hadn't seen in years. Her name was Judy Quat. I was a sitting with her at a table and I had a drink. I didn't have my leg bag on. I just had the little like condom on my penis. Well I went into the bathroom there and the condom fell off and this full with urine came out on the floor. I didn't get any on my pants, which I really can't believe I didn't get my pants wet. I walked out of the club and I was going to walk about 2 miles to my car. But I knew I could never walk this far with my legs buckling. So I asked my friend to give me a ride to my car, before my urine would continue to flow with no condom on this as well as no leg bag.

"Hi Bill."

"Hi Billy."

I was down the Norwood Hospital for pt and mt. My PT was Billy Kold. He seemed very anxious to get started with the pt. He was a rather racy person whom wanted to get enjoyment while giving pt. By the look on his face I wondered, who was helping whom.

"I didn't think you were going to make it."

"Well I'm here for pt."

"Let's see here now. I'm looking over your records. You've been having ½ hour pt sessions in Boston."

"Ya, that's right."

"We can do Monday, Wednesdays and Fridays, and one of these days we can take a whirlpool."

I wondered how could a whirlpool work. The little bit of biology I had I thought the spinal nerve had to be strengthened not the individual muscles.

"Today we will just have a muscle test and see just how strong you are."

"My knees buckle on me when I walk about 100 yards."

I said to him.

"You can try walking one telephone pole one day then increase to another when you feel ready."

We went into a PT room and I had a muscle test.

"Push, push, Push, Pull, Pull, Pull, etc . . . that's good your strong. What's this?"

"That's my leg bag. I still don't have bladder control back yet."

His face cringed as if he came across one of those gory hospital secrets about some people, which have some type of not so attractive contraptions. He wasn't cut out for the dirty work.

"You have gained a little bit of weight."

"Ya, I suppose so."

"Drinking a lot beer?"

"No I don't drink."

"Well that's all for now. I'll see you on Wednesday and we will try to get down, in a three point stance."

I left there and I was remembering what Billy said about, a three point stance. I could barely walk and he was telling me I was going to get down into a football three point stance. He was so racy he would take the fun out of thinking what was possible at what time, away from me. I was thinking if I could just walk upstairs and into a car I might be able to salvage a life.

I can remember when I walked up to the variety store about 200 yards from hospital. I can recall I saw the person Jansen, whom I had given a forearm to when I was coaching Babe Ruth baseball. He looked on in amazement, and I think I just said to him.

"Hi, I'm sorry about when I hit you at the Babe Ruth game last year."

"Ya, we all kind of get angry."

I then proceeded to walk back to the hospital like a night crawler, as my knees were buckling and this was quite awkward looking. I can remember seeing people whom worked in hospital walk by, as they were on their breaks. I can't explain the embarrassment I felt as I was walking back to hospital.

On Wednesday I came down *TO* hospital for more pt.

"Today we will get up on the Elgin table and do some exercises."

"All right."

I said to the PT.

"Pull, pull, pull, etc . . ."

Billy would say holding onto my foot.

"I'm getting a workout also."

He said.

I was putting out with every bit of strength I had. My head would go back and then look towards the left as he was holding onto my right heel.

"Now some hip exercises on the parallel bars. Turn, turn, and turn. We will finish this off with some stomach exercises."

I believe sweat was coming down from his forehead, when he was giving me the exercises. Sweat was coming down from my forehead as well as sweat was coming out of my eyes.

Now was Friday and the last session of the week.

"Hi Billy."

"Hi Billy."

"We'll get down in a three point stance today. Like this."

He showed me the stance. Then, I got down in a three-point stance, like I had in football. My legs began to bend, and I was wondering could they stay at this position. Could they hold me there? My knees felt the impact of what this is like with weak knees, the buckling in them. My back would feel I was almost a hunchback. There was no emotion involved in this for me at all. I was just thinking of the uncomfortable in doing this. My right foot would shoot forward, as I had to make sure I had the correct balance for getting back up standing. My back would wobble upwards as I would stand up straight. This was the last exercise for the day. Then I walked right out of the PT department.

"I was urinating blood and debris throughout the night at 15 minute intervals."

I don't know how I put up with these nights. I would get pain in my penis and bladder when I would be urinating.

Talking to dr. Kittery's secretary. Dr. Kittery wanted me to come in on the first Tuesday of the month to the spinal cord outpatient. I had to wait till next Tuesday.

I don't know actually what to make of this. I was so used to feeling down in the dumps I had been accustomed to this way of feeling. What is waiting another week? I've been through worse. I just had faith I felt better and had overcome some despair and depression and now I had this new problem. I can recall I looked down one of these days and I thought I'm going to hell and there is no doubt about this.

I went into the outpatient clinic and I saw a dr. Slesh.

"Let me feel your bladder?"

"Okay."

"Feels a little tough here. Sounds like bladder stones. Come into the hospital on Sunday."

I felt like the people whom had their scrotums cut off by the Germans in the experiments they did to people. I was lying down flat on the bed, and I was at the disposal of the doctors. Dr. Slesh was a very good surgeon and he gave me this impression when, I was checked by him. Dr. Slesh had a good reputation and I thought spinal cord patients always had the best doctors. I thought he was one of the best.

"I'm here to see dr. Slesh."

I said to the receptionist of hospital.

"He wants you to be admitted to L Building."

She said.

"Admitted again?"

"Yes, he wants you to come into hospital."

I couldn't believe what I was hearing. I still had to endure more.

"This is your room. My name is Rene."

She was a tall nurse, in her about mid twenties. She was attractive but maybe a little to old for me. I would try to score but without any success with Rene. I was thinking of the song, which had the name Rene in this and I thought of the song when I saw her. To tell you the truth I thought of whistling the songs, with the name of the girls in them. They would always be thrilled to hear their names in songs.

"Make yourself comfortable."

This statement "Make yourself comfortable," like appeared on my computer one day. I was debating to put in this part about the bladder stones hospital stay, because this is a bit too much on the hospitals. But I put this in and I'll think about to have more control over myself.

On Monday dr. Slesh after the x-rays were taken said to me.

"We will try the crusher on you tomorrow. This is the device which goes up the penis as we will try to pull the stones out."

I was diagnosed as having bladder stones. I was very, very weak these days. This seemed just coming into the hospital made me weak. When I had gone to x-ray, I felt alls I could do was take one step onto the x-ray table.

"We couldn't grip the stones. We will have to cut open your bladder."

They had now put a catheter in me. I was now going to be under the knife again. I had confidence in this dr. Slesh and I enjoyed seeing him when he would stop by. He would stand at the end of the bed and have his chart there, while I would be talking to him.

"You will be under anesthesia and this will be the same procedure as when we tried the crusher on you."

Well they operated this time and they said.

"You can have one of the stones which we took out. We had to send the other one to the lab to see what the make up on this."

"I feel a little weak."

"You'll will be a little uncomfortable a day or so."

I thought I would have to just about start the pt all over again. I was very weak. I slept for three straight days and I also came down with a fever. The catheter in me was very irritating.

Dr. Slesh came by one of these days and asked me.

"How do you feel?"

I said to him.

"I wish the stones were never taken out."

I said with a rather accent of uncomfortable. Dr. Slesh didn't say anything to this statement. He seemed bewildered. His face kind of cringed a bit and he was speechless.

"Hi dr. Train."

"Hi Bill, I've come to check your muscle reflex. Okay?"

"All right. How is everyone doing on Robinson 7?"

"There doing fine."

She was checking my muscle reflex.

"Your muscles seem all intact."

She checked my reflexes with her little kit, which held her instruments. She came here with a little strand of hair coming down on her forehead and she looked attractive. She was about 30 or so, but I liked her just the same. She seemed to be interested in me a little bit, or maybe this was just an act. I always liked dr. Train.

"Hi Bill. How are you?"

"Not so good. I feel weak and I don't have any energy left."

"Put out with all strength in you."

This was my psychiatrist dr. Blue. I didn't think he had the backbone to say something like this. I thought he was saying this just for the sake of saying this, and to seem strong. This just went into one ear and out the other. I didn't think he had thought about the statement, which he said to me. He was over close to my ear when he said this. I could recall when I would talk to him about how hard the pt was. He would say he played football in ninth grade and he knew what hard physical exercise was.

As I am writing this now I am thinking I have a lot of anger towards psychiatrists. I was putting them down quite a bit. I think this is one thing they like is for people to get angry towards them. This is one of the other ways they are paid besides money. I think I put them down quite a bit. This will change.

I was again so weak and I didn't think I would get any better. I was thinking about the bladder stone, which I had in me. They knew I had limited mobility and I should have been watched for bladder stones. I had called the lab to see what they found out was in these stones. My sister Jessica wrote an essay about the stones. She was only 8 years old then.

"Hi Nancy."

"Hi Bill."

This was my PT Nancy from Robinson 7.

"Maybe you will want to go up to Robby 7 in a wheelchair?"

"I don't know about this."

"They would be happy to see you there. Bruce, Walter, and David are still there."

I was very weak and I thought a trip to Robinson 7 would be like I was a patient there again, and I didn't want this. Nancy seemed a little bit peppy in she wasn't thinking what condition I thought I was in then. I thought I would just about have to start the Physical therapy all over again.

"I really don't know Nancy."

"All right Bill. If you have second thoughts, I would be glad to see you up there. Bye Bill."

"By Nancy."

"Joe, are you in hospital here?"

"Ya, I am being treated for bedsores. What are you in for?"

"Bladder stones."

"I passed a stone once."

Joe said.

"Really?"

"Ya, this hit the urinal with a thud. I would like to introduce you to my girlfriend Sophie."

"Hello."

I said.

"Hi", Sophie replied.

Joe was from South Boston and had got shot in the back. He had been in a wheelchair for a while. I was joyful he had found himself a girlfriend while being in a wheelchair. I thought this would be hard to do while being in a wheelchair.

Elizabeth had only visited me once when I was on the psychiatric unit. I thought the psych doctors were saying they wanted to see Elizabeth and her family. So she didn't visit me, because her family didn't want to have anything to do with psych doctors and their diagnosis. Also with her visiting me, there might have been the outside chance she wouldn't be strong enough to be around mental patients.

"What's your name?"

"I'm Harry. What's yours?"

"Bill."

This was the patient whom was in the bed next to mine.

"I work in Boston and I am from New Hampshire."

A doctor arrives and says to Harry.

"I'm going to have to take some blood."

He takes some blood. He must have defaulted the vein, as blood was coming out of his arm and this was all swelled up.

"Wow, that is something. Doesn't he know how to draw blood?" I said.

This doctor looked young and a little bit nervous, probably because this was an internship for him.

"I hope this will be all right."

Harry said to me.

"My name is Sara. I have come to give you pt."

"Are you dr. Kittery's secretary?"

"No, I'm from the PT department."

"She came down here to give you a workout and you thought she was a secretary?"

Harry said with a little indignant voice.

"Uh, Uh, Uh, etc . . ."

Laughter began to come out of me. One in which you couldn't stop. The Pt began to smile, as if I were in a different world. Harry became serious, as he might have thought I was laughing at him. But the PT must have known about this type of laughter and where this comes from. She kept on smiling as I was guffawing. This PT looked very much like dr. Kittery's secretary. I thought she would be sent on very serious situations from Robinson 7.

"Today we will do a muscle test."

Sara said.

"All right good."

I stated.

She went through the different exercises and gauges their strength.

"Your muscles are the same strength as when Nancy gave you your last muscles test."

"They feel weaker."

"No there about the same. I'll see you tomorrow for exercises."

For some reason I always liked the muscles tests. I would probably do the same amount of physical activity, but psychologically these tests felt better than the regular exercises.

She had given me the muscle test and I don't know where I got the strength to do even this. Maybe the laughter had given me strength.

"Today we are going to walk."

"Ah. Uh, uh."

I groaned a little bit, as I stood for the first time with the stitches in my bladder.

"You hold onto me and the Ivy Pole."

"All right."

We walked about ten feet and I didn't even think I could do this, but I did.

"This is all for today. We will do more tomorrow. See you tomorrow."

"Try to walk on the balls of your feet."

"Ya, like this?"

"Ya that's it."

I then went back down on my heels. I really gave a little breakthrough strife then. This seemed I had begun the Pt all over again and I wasn't going to stop at any cost. I was becoming a real man. I like gave all strength like the psychiatrist told me to.

"You can go home this Saturday. We are going to take the catheter out today."

There was one night here when I awoke at about 3:00 o'clock in the morning and not feeling too well. I think I took a walk with the Ivy pole or whatever. This particular night I sat down and I said to myself, I feel fine, I feel good, I feel fine. I had instantly controlled myself to feel good. Instantly feel well.

Dr. Slesh said to me one day.

"I don't have to wait another week?"

"I feel as if the bladder is healed expedient enough."

"That sounds good."

I was supposed to stay there two and a half weeks, but I stayed there a little under two.

The doctor had told me I had to stay two and a half weeks but this was less than two. The doctors are good about this in making people feel better this way.

Chapter 4

"I'm going out."

This was what I did when I first got home.

"Hi Hank."

"Hi Bill. I heard you had to go back in?"

"Ya, I had a little operation on my bladder."

"Let's get some beer."

Henry said.

"Ya, All right."

We began to drive and I told Hank.

"Stop here Hank. I have to take a leak."

"Ya sure."

"Wow that was a close one."

I had gotten back bladder control when I was in hospital. My aunt Mary had gotten me a frappe, when she visited me one day. The muscle was still weak, and I had to strengthen my sphincter muscle. I let the urine out just when I got my *FLY* down. Believe me, I had just about let this go, but I held out a little longer and this went on the ground.

We drove to Natick where we had lost to the to become State Champs Natick 9-8 with 12 seconds left on the clock. They kicked a field goal. Back then I can remember asking Henry. What happened today Henry? This was in the bus ride back. Henry had replied. I think we bothered him too much today. This was when we would say the Lord's Prayer on the field.

I could recall years later when I was at a half way house and a person there said that one of the valuable players for Natick had been taking speed during the game. I had taken speed in a baseball game against Braintree, in which I was just about the whole team. I was thinking if we could trade in the baseball title for the football title to protest the game under grounds that we had taken enhancers. The football title we would have instead of baseball. I would take this.

"Let's get rid of these empties."

Henry had dropped them on the side of the road. I said to myself this night does Henry still think about jocks and sports, and why would he still litter. We drove back to Norwood and I got into my car and went home. I didn't think too much for the drinking, as I would when I was younger, but I forced them down just the same.

Elizabeth came to my house one day.

"Hi Billy."

"Hi Liz."

"You lost all your braces Billy?"

"Ya."

"What are you smiling about?"

I asked her.

"I'm smiling because your are."

We were uncontrollably smiling at each other. We might have been saying to each other hospital gone, real bad days are gone, and we made it through.

"You look good Liz."

She had on a very nice pants and jacket combination. I thought a little bit of making time with her there, but I felt uncomfortable at my home. I also thought I wasn't too desirable a person physically and mentally. As she was smiling she nonchalantly said.

"Can you Billy?"

My head felt on fire as I shook my head a bit. I felt all blown up. I still had problems. She said.

"Bye."

And I also said.

"Bye."

I can remember her going out the door sideways and she really looked good. She walked right out and I thought to myself she was going and she was leaving me. I didn't or couldn't feel anything when she left. I wouldn't be embarrassed about myself if we were to get intimate again. I didn't really feel to manly of a person.

I couldn't really walk that far because my knees would buckle on me, and this was very uncomfortable. This would happen if I walked about 100 yards. My spirits weren't good. I thought I would have an arduous time getting around the rest of my life. I was I guess depressed. I went to a nightclub in April, and I met the girl whom I took to the senior semi-formal. Her name was Janis and she was walking by while I was at one of the tables. She stood erect and had her feet apart quite a bit. She stopped and began to stare at me then walked out. I was feeling the flow of fresh blood to the head. I was self-conscience about having jumped out a window and also just meeting an old girlfriend. I said to myself, there I am out of the hospital and drinking in a nightclub 7 months later. I said to myself. Where are you? I'm out in public again. I'm back to normal.

When I went to the spinal cord outpatient on the first Tuesday of the month, dr. Train whispered to me.

"You must walk."

She got close to my head on the left side of me and said this. This had reminded me when she had come to check my reflexes when I had the bladder stone operation. I was lying down on one of the examining tables and I was saying to myself, more. I was feeling like I had my scrotum cut off, like how the Germans would do to people they deemed unfit. She had the curtains closed when she said this. I gave no reaction from her statement. I was saying to myself how can I walk with the knees buckling. Also the chief asked me.

"Bill let's see you walk on your heels."

I walked across the room on my heels. I was saying to myself what am I going to do for a life now? I decided to try and hang around a street corner with the low. I knew from my experience before when I tried to hang around the corner, these people just think of people, which you have to fight, to get in the gang. This was the language of the street. I can recall driving down to the corner, and I was scared they wouldn't accept me, as they didn't before I was in the hospital. The night is when I made my move, to try and make contact with these people. There was a small convenient store across from the corner, where they hanged out. I pulled up carefully and said something like.

"Tommy."

"It's Bill Breen."

Said Als.

He came running over to the car window passenger side and said.

"How are you Bill?"

"Good Als, good."

Als was my age and should have been in my grade, but he was attracted to the low of the street corner. He was tall about 6'3" and 200 lbs. I would be thinking they had accepted me, because I had fought and no longer was the good person. As I believe sports, school, and coaching, which in most people's mind would be heeded good.

"Als do you want to go up Bubbling Brooke?"

This was a restaurant which about 5 miles away.

"Okay sure."

He replied.

As we drove there I could tell he still thought of me as the big dude of high school. Now wasn't to long since I had graduated. As we drove there it began to rain, and I called this racooning.

"Look like it's racooning out Als?"

"Ya, sure is racooning out."

I don't know why but I called raining racooning. We had hamburgers and French fries. Als face reminded me of the look I would get from people the aforesaid year. Like Bill Breen is hanging around with me. The look was one of I'll do anything for you.

I asked Als.

"How did you stay back in high school?"

"I was absent too much. Everyone and I would go over Edmos' in the mornings instead of school."

Edmo was an older person about 22 and he was out of high school and would work in a factory or someplace at night. He lived with his mother and she would go off to work in the morning. So Edmo would have the house to himself. These people were the street fighters. They didn't think about school or sports, but street fighting.

My old friends I just couldn't keep up with. I was so much out of shape that this was just too much to be with them. I had all kinds of problems. I would try to every now and then, to be with my old friends, but I was caught in the street gang now. I just had so many problems.

Well Als and I had a jolly time talking about racooning. Then there was the hunter, whom was the toughest in the gang, so he was the leader. This was the reason why he got the nickname the hunter. The hunter had joined the Marines his senior year in high school. I recalled back when I had come down to the street level, before I was in hospital and the hunter gave me the most trouble, about hanging around the street corner then after being a goody.

Well I got back at the hunter these days. We were parked in a parking lot and the hunter was biting his bottle of beer. I said to the hunter.

"Hunter is trying to embarrass me by biting his bottle."

And I began to laugh and laugh. I believe this had embarrassed the hunter quite a bit, by my laughter. The hunter didn't know what to do. He just moved to the side quite a bit and looked quite gauche. In the years to come most of or all these people joined the Army or Marines. Als got stationed over Germany in the Army. The hunter was found with some syringes in his apartment where he was having a fight. He was run out of town and sent back to the Marines in San Diego, California. Als was in the fight and he got bitten in the face and required about 40 stitches.

My two friends Ed and Brian and I, decided to go cross-country. We got a cooler and all the essentials. We had tetra-hychloric-carbonate and beer in the cooler. Ed and Brian were to be in the Army when we got back. They both had already signed up.

I was seeing a psychologist once per week in my hometown of Norwood. I was seeing him when I went back to taking the tetra-hychloric-carbonate again.

I began to take two hits of THC per day. We shoved off the beginning of June and Ed had just graduated on the first of June. I can recall we were on the Mass Pike heading for Brian's uncle in Syracuse NY. I was usually lying down in the back seat with the cooler, which we would have the beer.

We made this to Syracuse at about 10:30 at night and we called for directions to their home. I slept on a cot. I would usually sleep late, because I wasn't in 100 % health. But here I did not want people to think there was something wrong with me. This was the idea you would put out for only people whom you respected. We had turkey and Brian said to his uncle.

"Billy was captain of the football team."

Is that so?"

"Ya."

I said.

I was now connecting with all the people the year before, and I was anxious to be with them. I had just come out of the hospital and I thought I was away from my friends for centuries.

I was worried about my knees, which would buckle on me if I walked more than 100 yards. The THC would pick up my spirits for the short term. We went to the Syracuse Airport with Brian's cousin. I walked into and around the terminal, and I felt a bit better in my knees. But the backseat of the car was like how the bed would be to me months before.

We drove to Niagara Falls the next day and we went to the Canadian side. I couldn't figure this, as we had to go by customs. We had tetra-hychloric-carbonate. At the border the person there said something like.

"If you have any illegal contraband tell me right now."

He checked the trunk of the car. I really couldn't realize what we were doing. We could have all been arrested going through customs if they found the THC. I think if we were arrested, I wouldn't have been that scared, because this took quite a lot to scare me now. We gave the customs a little marijuana, which we had. We went through Customs but we had to also comeback to America after being on the Canadian side of Niagara Falls.

We were parked and we were going to take a walk around Niagara Falls, and take pictures. I told Brian and Ed, I would wait in the car, because I thought my knees would buckle on me and I would just about have to crawl back. My friends coaxed me to walk. So I under intrepidity I decided to give this a try.

We walked about a mile and I had new life in me. I sold some THC to a person from Canada about 3 or so hits. I began to have new in born strength to get better. One thing I did this time was to roll my fingers. I would do this with girls when I would be intimate with them. This night in the hotel I said to myself this would have been nice if I had gone cross-country with Elizabeth. I think I even thought of driving back home and to see if she would want to go cross-country with me. I thought I could have some happy attention with her by taking her cross-country. I imagine I thought this, by all the folks whom had gone for honeymoons to Niagara Falls. On the way back to America we went through customs without any distress.

We would split the driving between ourselves. I with new inborn strength in my legs thought I could, "go anywhere," Stevie Nicks. I began to get motivated to get strength, as I began to have confidence to get better. I would take two hits of THC per day and I really enjoyed this. I think I was also taking what the doctors recommended stelazine also.

I began to carry things, suitcases, cooler, etc . . . into the hotel rooms and I was beginning to have a base. Ed's older brother had moved to Denver Colorado, the year earlier, and this was our next relative stop by. I knew Ed's older brother Ken from playing cards when I was younger.

When we were at Ken's apartment I talked to Ed. Ed's dad had died a few months earlier. I began to talk about how I was in agony in hospital. Ed said he would be paralyzed from neck down just to see his dad back with his mother. I said something to him like.

"You don't realize what this would be like."

"If I could just see my mom and dad together again, then I would be paralyzed from neck down to have this happen."

We went to the tour of the Coors plant and other landmarks, Hoover Dam, Grand Canyon, Hollywood, etc . . . I can recall we drove by some baseball players in Arizona and I recollected old memories of playing baseball. I recalled they played lots of baseball in Arizona. Also that lots of Arizona players make the pros.

We drove to Los Vegas. Here for some reason I felt comfortable but I couldn't tell why. I began to play cards at quarter anti. There was a house dealer. These card players really knew their stuff. I was taking

THC during the day. I can recall I had a drink at a card table and I spilt this. I lost about 12 or 15 dollars and then I came to my senses and said to myself. These guys are really good, don't waste your time.

From here I went to a little stage area with a girl singing. I saw this person in a wheelchair watching enthusiastically. I went over to him and said.

"I was paralyzed once."

"Ya, I've been in a wheelchair for three years."

He said.

"What level, were you injured?"

I asked him.

"T-5 and T-6 on the back."

He blurted out.

This had been the same spot I had been injured on the back T-6. He was watching a band play. He seemed somber watching sitting in the wheelchair watching the band. When he told me he had been injured thorasic 6 on the back I got excited.

"That was the same spot I was injured."

I began to get charged. I pulled up my shirt and showed him the scar on my back. I was furious. He told me.

"I jumped two stories onto a side walk."

When I heard this I exploded. I told him.

"I jumped out a window two stories."

He began to get panicky. His head began to shake. I told him.

I had been taking THC before I went out the window."

"THC."

I think he must have thought there was some kind of healing affects from THC. The average person without medical terminology thinks there is a pill for something like paralysis.

He asked me.

"Do you have any?"

I told him.

"Ya."

And I gave him a hit of THC. He was in frenzy. He couldn't wait to get the hit. When I gave it to him, he gobbled this down without hesitation. He told me.

"My jump was a nervous breakdown."

We exchanged words somewhat. He told me.

"I've been in a wheelchair three years now."

I told him.

"I had recovered from being hurt one year now."

He told me.

"I want you to meet someone whom I have been going around the country with."

He wheeled across the casino and I met the about 5'8" 160 lbs middle-aged man. He asked me calmly.

"Where on the back were you injured?"

"T-6."

His tongue would come out of his mouth frequently. He reminded me of the mental patients on Robby 3. He talked slow but I answered him fast but slow. I wanted to talk fast, but I realized I should talk slow.

This person in the wheelchair and I went back to the stage where the band was playing. My friends Brian and Ed came over to us. I think I gave this person another round of THC and myself. We sat down in some chairs and we began to talk. He sat in a regular chair and I sat in his wheelchair. He was talking to my friends when I began to think again people could purloin movement from you, like I thought on the spinal cord unit. His legs were wiggling, as he would use his hands to move them. I began to get scared he could steal movement in my legs. I was a little bit scared.

I told him.

"I had gone out of bed after jumping out window."

This was when I had gone out of bed at the Norwood Hospital with the busted back.

He said something like.

"The follow through."

He looked like he realized why I had recovered and he hadn't.

"Oh this was this."

He said.

His legs were wiggling. He got some spasms, which were fresh in my mind when I would get them this unmitigated. There was a band there and an attractive singer. I asked her.

"Would you like to dance?"

Her reply was like.

"Not now."

Or some thing like, But I kept on trying to coax her.

"Come on just one dance?"

I said.

"No thank you."

"Can I buy you a drink?"

"No thanks."

She responded.

I had new inborn confidence in me, which would make me pushy. He and I went into the bathroom and he emptied his leg bag. We came back to the stage area and we talked some more.

He told me.

"I'm from Bethlehem, Penn. Out of all the places to be from Bethlehem. I'm not going back there unless I'm walking. I got my stomach back after three years."

He moved his stomach like how a wave in the water would move. He reminded me of the Southerner in the hospital whom would walk around six hours per day on long locked leg braces. The rebel had gotten back his arms after one year. I thought these were the men whom would keep on fighting, after the medical time limit of one year for return was over. They were the fuzz of wheelchairs. They would still be fighting this instead of accepting they would never get anymore return. These people would never quit.

He also mentioned to me.

"I heard of an Indian whom just jumped right up from paralysis."

This was surely some coincident which I didn't forget for some time.

I can recall we passed a restaurant, which they said they had steak and eggs at 5-9 in the mornings. I could recall I would think about having steak and eggs after I would feel very good. Like to celebrate.

I can recall once when we were passing this tractor-trailer truck and there was one in front of us also. I said.

"We are being sandwiched."

Brian got excited also and said.

"We are being sandwiched. What are we to do?"

This was a mostly comical statement, but we got a lot of mileage out of this.

We made it to the West Coast. We were on Ventura Highway and I put on the tape with the song Ventura Highway by the singing group America. I went into the Pacific Ocean and I only thought for a second this was cold water but this was warm, warm. I got sunburned quite a bit.

We went to my cousin Lorna whom was my uncle's daughter in Pasadena California. I took for granted we could stay there with her two children. I now look at this she was very nice to my friends and I to stay there at her home. I look at this now we might have been encroaching. I could remember I had an attraction to the name Lorna.

After leaving Lornas,' we went to San Francisco. Here we got lost walking and I walked about three miles in San Francisco. The word got back from San Francisco.

"Billy walked three miles in San Francisco."

My spirits were definitely improving. I could recall when I was on the THC I could not feel uncomfortable. An example of this would be when we slept in the car one night in a park. I slept on the hood of the car. The next morning in a hotel, when Ed wanted one of the beds, Brian gave Ed a smack in the face, because Brian was rather touched I had slept on the hood of the car, and wanted me to have one of the whole beds.

I can recall we were in Philadelphia on July 4, 1976 celebrations. This was the 200th anniversary of America. We were on the docks of New York, and I now think of my grandmother whom came over from the old country, Lithuania. This was my first time in New York, and I could recall all the tall skyscrapers. I remembered when I had been seeing Elizabeth before I was in hospital. We talked about going down to New York together sometime.

I was thinking back then, of taking Elizabeth to Nova Scotia on the Blue Nose Ferry in Bar Harbor Maine. I thought of being intimate with her on the Ferry as well as getting a hotel there in Canada. I could recall I would call her Elizabeth Taylor.

We were in Connecticut when we had trouble with the car. The mechanic said he wouldn't be able to fix the car till the next day. This happened to be at a truck stop also. So we drank coffee the whole night until the mechanic could fix the axle the next morning. We then drove about the last leg of 200 miles home.

The trip was very good for me. Whatever the depression which was in me was now gone. I could recall when I had gotten home my aunt had died. This was my uncle Sunny's wife. When I was at the reception after the funeral, at my grandmothers', I said I would lose weight. I weighed about 225 lbs.

I can recall when I saw Stevie Nicks at Foxboro stadium this month. I thought she saw me there and she knew how I looked, and very good to her.

I can recall before I decided to lose weigh I would go with these corner people and we would go to another town and get hot fudge sundaes. I began to be friends with a person named Wally. Wally had gotten a Mohegan haircut.

I now in the summer began to jog a bit at a track. I would be very slow legged, as I had to strengthen my pull up strength in my quadriceps. I think the only things which kept me going these days was I had felt so down in the dumps in the hospital anything would be better.

I can reminisce I moved furniture with my friend Tex into his apartment. The doctors said not to lift anything for two years, but I was lifting heavy things after about 14 months. I thought my friend Tex, whom was a car salesman, would question the doctors. I really struggled then though carrying the furniture.

I could recall I didn't wear my back brace going to the shower one day when I was on Robby 3. Thinking of this now, this gives me the willies. I wanted to take a shower without the back brace, so I could have the hot water on my bare back.

I had stopped taking THC once I had gotten back from cross-country. I saw one day two of the baseball players I had coached in Babe Ruth right after high school. I had gotten a pizza with them and then we went into Robby 7. I was sitting down with the two boys when the chief came out of his office and sniffed the air in through his nose. He then went into his office and closed the door, really slammed the door. I thought he was mad at me. Possibly he might have been able to smell the marijuana on me, or my clothes. "Close the door." Clothes the door. The chief was my best friend these days.

I can recall when Wally and I drove through a Jewish cemetery. This was my new Wally. The old Wally I knew was on Robinson 3 with depression. With these corner people I felt I had gone down a level of friends. I began to think people have the same names but they are in different parts of your life.

My friend Johnny Cox and Charley Hoppy and I went into the Combat zone in Boston. I was in the back of the van in a bed. I was listening to the tape of the greatest hits by the singing group America. We went into the Combat Zone and Johnny and charley got head from a hooker there. One of the hookers there said.

"*Hello*, What about him?"

Johnny said.

"He had a back problem. He needs sex therapy."

Johnny said after.

"Oh, I like the way she put it down her throat."

I think they both paid 10 dollars for this.

I can remember before we went to the Combat Zone, we went to a party for the people from Prescott. I met my friend Grega, whom I had attacked after high school. He was the 215 pounds, All-scholastic tackle. I was at this party and they asked me to leave. I went into the van and Grega said to me.

"I was going to kill you then. I felt very bad down on the bottom with all my friends." This was when I attacked him in the parking lot after high school. I began to think about how you become accepted by gangs in new neighborhoods. The only way is you have to fight. I think of the word accepted as accepted in colleges. Another way is to be accepted. Grega also said.

"I had just gotten back from the practice to the Harry Agganis Bowl earlier in the day before you attacked me."

I began to think I made him fight. Really fight, and this could be used for things like football or studying in the future. After you have fought you bring back memories of fighting, and this will get you through difficult times in the future. I can recall years later at my 20th high school reunion Grega said to me.

"I thought you were crazy. You told me you had blood coming from your nipple once. I thought you were crazy. Until one day I was running and I must have rubbed my shirt against my nipple and blood came from this"

Well I had plans on going to UMass Amherst in September. I really felt bad Mass Rehab would only reimburse you to State Colleges. I began to think I lost something. Mass Rehab would reimburse you just partially to Private schools.

Well Hunter had an apartment in South Norwood. I was dropping off someone there when our gang was going to fight South Norwood. The South Norwood gang was coming to Hunter's apartment. Hunter said.

"Into the apartment."

I was with Als in my car, and I began to chuckle a little bit at hunter. Als got out of my car and I left. Well the South Norwood gang the Southies, came into the apartment and someone bit Als in the face and he required about 40 stitches. The police came and they found syringes in the apartment. Als got quite a big scar on his face for life. The hunter was sent to San Diego in the Marines.

My friend Tex, whom I would meet up with every now and then, said that some one wanted to fight him. I said to Tex I thought fighting was rather childish. I would bump into my old friends every now and then.

My brother Bob had gotten into a car accident and broke his femur bone, which was the big bone in the leg. When I visited him once in hospital he told me Billy my old PT, wanted to see if he could drive me to a Universal to lift weights. I still had thought sports were for children, which I thought from the "door to door" sales job. So I declined. I think my brother Bob thought I should have done this.

My brother Bob had a pin put in his leg. I didn't think this was too serious, until I saw Bob walking up the street on crutches. He I think was on crutches for three months and then he used my cane. I saw Bob hopping up the street on crutches.

As one of my friends would say about people going off to college, and being "hoopy." My Mass Rehab Counselor was asking me if I was watching television to help me concentrate. She said I could take classes to help you learn to study better.

When I would look into the mirror I saw ugly. I had thought ugly was beautiful before hospital and now I looked ugly with about 40 lbs over weight. "What would happen if God was a slob like one of us?" The song. I didn't think about being intimate with the opposite sex. I didn't think beautiful girls were interested in me.

My Mass Rehab Counselor was named Patricia and she was rather attractive at about 26 years old. I was thinking of going to college. I asked her how much Mass Rehab would pay for a private school.

"They will pay $1500 for private schools per semester and they will pay all the tuition for State Schools."

This was where I thought the US system was not as good as other systems. I was in no condition to work 50 or 60 hours per week, to earn my keep for college. Alls I could do was to get an education at a State School. This was where I thought I really lost something when I had played by the rules. This was like losing a part of me. If I hadn't had felt so bad in hospital I don't know if I would have been able to cope with this loss.

I signed all the papers to go to UMass Amherst. I had put on 50 lbs. and I was too young and too heavy to realize girls, I would call beautiful before the sales job, weren't interested in me with so much girth.

My brother Jack had ½ a semester left to finish at UMass Amherst before he graduated. My sister Maura was in her third year at UMass Amherst. They both had apartments off campus. I think under schools rules you had to stay on campus the first two years.

I was given a room in the campus Center Hotel before they assigned me to a dorm. While I was in this hotel room I really liked watching Television. I enjoyed this more then usual. I had registered for my classes there. I was in the College of Engineering. After a few days they allotted me a dorm Central-Brown. I missed privacy of the hotel campus.

I saw a girl there whom was a little big but had a very good smile. She was from England. I had remembered I read the Germans had paralyzed England in WW 2. She looked at me and I could see a little light in her eyes. I can recall the rooms were called suites. There was one room, which had a television, and was the lounge. I first began to be interested in the show Mash.

My roommate was person called Spin. He was from the town Sharon, about 7 miles from my hometown. There were bunk beds there and Spin took the lower bunk. I began to think about gangs again. This was the level of people here in the dorms. Spin had a small refrigerator. I used this for cottage cheese, which I bought. I also brought some chicken broth. I had begun to stretch on the suite floor in my room. I looked like what people would call a slob.

There was a girl on the opposite suites, and I was a little interested in her. I bought some books off of her. I think she was interested in me, because I would go to the football field. I can recall I went into her suite one day. She was a girl whom I think was a little bit interested in me. I was big but I think she was thinking I would go to the football field.

I was having an onerous time getting up in the mornings for classes. My study habits really didn't come back. I at first began to think of the adrenalin of being a student. I would be carrying the books and walking to classes. I began around this time to think I could write a book. I kept a diary of my time here in the dorm. I began to write as much as I could.

I can recall one of the persons there whom had the only single room. He was very disciplined as I could tell he concentrated on studying 2 or 3 hours per day. I met my friend Dave whom I had planned on rooming with the foregoing year. He had been in Pre-Med and was doing very well. He had straight A's. He was also a vegetarian. I also saw a lot of other friends whom were going here.

I was beginning to think of my personality by the way I walked. I thought my personality was denoted by how I walked. I must have walked about 4 or 5 miles every day. If you remember when you were young and you would think about how you walked. The only time in which I felt good was when I walked. I can recall this was September, and this was still halter season for the feminine gender.

I would come home for the weekends and see the corner folks. I recall one of these nights I controlled myself to turn red or flush on purpose. I had controlled the blood flow to the head.

I can recall I was at my brother Jack's apartment one night. We were playing Kitty Whist. My brother Jack and I were leading 20-14. My brother's friend Whitey said to us.

"Hey snake, I think this is going to be a close game 20-20 and then we are going to win it."

My brother Jack's nickname was snake and the game is over once someone reaches 21. We were playing for a dollar per person. My brother Jack said to Whitey.

"If you are so sure, how about raising the stakes to 2 dollars per person?"

Then Whitey said.

"Well I talk big, but I don't back it up with money."

Whitey said when he would live in the dorms with Jackie they would call him "Floor Stepo," Because Jack was so tough. I was getting acclimated to the very physical world once again.

There was one day when I was driving home one weekend and I thought of using my other arm for things. So I would eat lefty, brush teeth lefty, comb hair lefty, etc . . .

I went to the Math Department at University about skipping the first semester Calculus, because I had credit on high school Calculus. I spoke with a lady in the Department and she said this would be all right for me to skip first semester Calculus. I felt very good about this.

I can recall when I would walk up the stair to the incongruous floors. I had begun to enjoy walking, up and down stairs, and to and from classes. I began to feel the feeling of being a student again.

I can recall one of the tactics was to squeeze scissors in the dorms. When I would go to Jack's apartment we would go by a cornfield. I can recall this vividly.

I recall I went down by a field adjacent to the baseball field, where the players were having fall baseball practice. I thought you made the team if you threw-up while doing sprints. Well I began to run sprints in the field adjacent to the player's field. I ran and ran like there was no tomorrow. My speed was good, but I had trouble turning, or running then turning. After about 20 minutes of running sprints, something came up from my mouth. I thought that someone was shooting down at me from the High risers at UMass. But I think this was a little fictitious.

After baseball I went to Football practices. I went into the locker room and watched the players being taped up. I was thinking a little of having my legs taped, but my lower back needed lots of therapy. I went out to the playing field for the freshmen and sophomores. I talked to a Yale educated doctor there.

Well I played Frisbee with one of the assistant trainers there. I recall an injured player began to say a few words to the players on the field. I might have said something, by just yelling right out loud. Well I talked to the doctor for a little while. Then one of the players on the field hurt his knee. He had to be sustained off the field. The doctor gave me a look like this was my fault the player hurt his knee. I went with the player and in the doctor's car, to where the doctor dropped me off. The player must have gone to the hospital.

Another day I can recall after the end of practice our team had run sprints. I was thinking of the old strategy of whom, would be the last person into the locker room. There was one person whom was a straggler at the end of the day. There was also a person whom drove his motorcycle back to the dorms.

Whenever I saw policemen I felt a connection with. I was about 220 lbs. Police looked at me as if I were a police partner. I was thinking now when I would come home for the weekends, I would hold the chain for the first down markers at the high school football games.

The first high school football game was in Waltham. No there was a scrimmage at Boston College High. I can remember the players in the bus and the coaches and trainers in the cars driving there. Then at Waltham I was standing next to a policeman. I then moved away. Then the police officer I thought said something in my head like, I could help you.

I went to a football game against Needham around this time with my friend Tex. Tex began to talk to a police officer there and I began to really think this was good to talk to police officers. I went to another game against Walpole. While I was there I cleared my throat loud, and there was fumble on the field. Cough it up. I saw my College AP chemistry teacher there and he looked at me as if he was looking me over. I also saw dr. Black there and he was spitting a bit, because he had a cigar. I began to think people could be denoted by their spit or saliva.

I was praying to myself constantly. I would be trying to say four things all at once in my head. Then all of a sudden I began to say this prayer. "This is a prayer for the creator of all God that he shall be happy that he created me and he shall keep me from being unhappy." Then what would pass through my mind would be the words, "Bless us and save us."

My car was towed because I left this parked in after hours parking lot or something another. I was beginning to think of the Mafia, CIA, and Russian spies. I thought there was a Russian spy whom was paralyzed from the neck down and learned Karate. I was thinking about all these people throughout the days. This was a little bit bigger than the people whom I would hang out with at the corner.

I can recall one of these nights there was someone whom came to the door at night. I then heard someone say, "Is that shorter?"

I thought before you go into a mental institution, someone comes to your door. I thought the person whom came to the door of people's houses was whom, had the most Jesus in them. I had been a "door to door" salesman. I thought Jesus went around the country and decided whom, goes into mental institutions.

When I had my car towed I had been walking through the campus center at UMass. I saw a person whom I thought was "Leuger." He put his hand to his head. Like jostling his hair to one side. I thought this person was a CIA agent. I thought he had come down from above. Like the song, "Dust in the Wind." I thought about when I had dragged onto Tex car the previous year before I was in hospital. When I saw this person whom I thought was a CIA man, I connected him walking with me dragging on the tar of Tex car.

Around these days I had wrote Elizabeth a letter. I was beginning to get interested in girls again. I think I wrote her a letter when I was in the campus hotel.

Mark whom was a friend of Jacks' came up to see Jack here at his apartment. When I told him I saw a CIA agent he and Jackie would like make some kind of sound, which they would say together. We were driving home and I thought some lesser agent was following us home. I could remember looking at the driver and he smiled a bit. I thought I had a little bit of Elizabeth in me.

There was one weekend I was riding a bike and I went to the corner store. I saw a couple of girls from my class whom had very good bodies. These two girls wouldn't usually be at the corner. Donna and Cheryl were the two girls and they had beautiful bodies. I talked to them as they were drinking. I began to see the breasts on them and they looked so gorgeous.

I pedaled to the Bowling alley in Norwood after this. The aforesaid day I thought I saw the CIA agent. I had years earlier gotten a job at the A&P which used to be next to the Bowling alley. I had started a job at the A&P by just walking right in and start to work. They were hiring people from the work-study program at the high school. They were just setting up the new store. I heard from people whom had gotten hired for work-study. This was when I was in eleventh grade.

"Who called you up?"

I said to one of the work-study person George V.

"Charley Smith. He said to come in at 3:00."

I had been with my friend Timmy. He was dating the girl I liked quite a bit Paula. We started working there by just blending in with everybody as they were just setting up the new store. When the store opened we saw our names weren't on the opening schedule. Before the store opened you just wrote down your hours by yourself. I told Timmy.

"Let me do the talking."

"We aren't on the schedule Mr. Mays."

I said to the manager.

"Who told you to come in here?"

"Charley Smith told me over the phone."

I said.

I made sure I knew what to say before I said anything. I had done my homework.

"All right, you come in on Tuesday 3-11, Friday 2-6 and Monday and Wednesday 2-7."

"All right."

I said.

At this store there was a manager from the Providence Rhode Island store to help set up the new store. I had carried extra fire logs then and he said to me.

"Your aggressive. You can go take a break."

I was waiting at the end of the night for a ride when the manager from the Providence store said to me.

"Whenever you need a favor, call me up."

"All right."

I didn't think I needed any favor from him in high school.

There was the head lady from Germany whom trained the cashiers. There was a person on work-study whom wore glasses. I called him, "Secret Squirrel." I would say this to the other people working there as we would be bagging or getting carriages. This girl from Germany I began to like. I began to think how she spoke English and how I took five years of French. I had bumped into her when I was on a cane in the Dedham Mall.

UMass Amherst diary.
Sept. 13.

It has been two days now since I have been thinking like it was in hospital. That is there are all kinds of signals in the world. Signals which regulate your life and an example would be if someone is doing some kind of work means you should work in your thoughts. This kind of reminds me of how I have put in problems before and they have come though. How I projected on them in the future. One of the main ideas is of cough which in harshness determines how long you have been on the road. I desire that will not bother me and that will be so. I desire that I will be back to how I was before I went out the window. One point is how I was watching television that is superman, and one person my roommate spin said that Mash was on. That kind of meant Mash my problem that I had. I remember back in the hospital when I thought I had to drink water to get better. Thinking that was going to heal me. Right now I was talking with spin and I asked him about the doctorate, and he wasn't sure. While I was talking to him I kind of brought back the idea about how he once said that the people on the show were good actors. He just got up and put something down. My mind right now is kind of negative. I just coughed again which might mean that I am still suffering. I would like to think that I got all the suffering out of me before, but I don't know. It kind of seems I am bringing back the idea that people can read my mind. But I would like to get rid of that thought forever. I desire that and that will be so. I haven't been doing any studdiing lately. I am kind of bringing back when I was little and who was the actual leaders of the groups. There was one in Cox – and Cox just might have been the toughest in the gang. Another one was John Don and he was definitely the toughest in the gang, when I was little. Spin just looked in the mirror which might mean that he is the mirror of myself. I desire that I shall be happy and that will be so. That kind of brings me back my memory of the dream But if we are all children of God that we are all children of God. This is still a problem that I have and wish to solve. It brings back how I once thought I wonder if I would be happy or not. I desire I will not suffer anymore. For the simple reason that that I believe I that I will be happy as I am and I desire I will be able to solve any problem ever. I desire that I will be happy at all times. I desire that and that will be so. I have in my mind that people can read my mind.

I would like to get rid of that if I possibly could. But I would like to make these people very happy for what they gave me the idea of. I desire that I will not be unhappy like I was these last couple of days. I desire that I will not worry about the signals anymore or how I might suffer again. I desire that I will get rid of that thought and that will be so. I desire that I will continue t write whenever I have a problem and that will be so.

The idea of breaking the natural signals is in the possibility. Because I have done it before and I would like to think I could do it again, but I have some doubts which I would like to get rid of. One doubt is that possibly I know that I am doing it but I desire that there will be some day in the near future that it will change that is it will turn around all of the signals will have nothing to do with me. I desire that and that will be so. Everything will be like it will be like it was when I was as senior in High school. Feeling that I am pretty smart, athletic, that I will have a good job. Have a nice girlfriend It kind of seems it will be a hard thing to do but I desire that I shall that I shall do it, and that will be so. I desire that I shall try to get back to how I was when I was a senior in high school. I thank you Lord for letting me feel a little bit better today. It is progress and I know that it will take time but I desire that I shall do it Lord. I desire that and that will be so, everything shall get better and better. I desire that and that will be so. I shall be able to solve any problem. This brings to mind the other problems which I have written about and I have solved. It could be good if I could remember everything that happened and understand it. I would not mind if I could look at the positive side of a lot of things. Be happy most of the time. I am definitely getting better the last three days. I desire that I shall feel better and better and that will be so. I thank you God for letting me feel a little bit better the last few days. I desire God that you will make it fun and that will be so. I desire that I will not suffer on purpose anymore and that will be so. I leave it in your hands God. You can do what you wish with me, because you created me. I am not studding right now God but I desire that I shall study. I remember when I was in B.U. Hospital, I thought of dr. Kittery as someone whom came back from just about the impossible back to a man by just holding your leg would make them feel better. That kind of brings back to me the idea that I had when I thought that my legs were in heaven when I pushed them out of in the Norwood Hospital. I have the idea that the people can read my mind but I desire that they can not. I desire that and that will be so. I still have the idea that God came and Jesus Christ came from God but I desire that I shall not worry about that and that will be so. I desire that that idea shall be completely erased from my mind. I am feeling to feel a lot better now that I have begun to start my exercises, but I still want to improve. I desire that I shall make it and that will be so. I am getting better God and I thank you very much for that and that will be so. I believe that I will get even better and better. I desire that and that will be so. I still have in my mind that people around here can read my mind, but I desire that they will not be able to and that will be so. Christ did once say that whatever you pray for you can get whatever you want if you pray hard enough. I desire that I shall pray for being able to change the situation which is in my mind right now. I desire that and that will be so. I desire that I shall pray so that I shall pray so that I shall change th situation which I have created. I desire that and that will be so. I desire that I shall get back to how i was before the accident but as dr. Kittery said better though. I am hearing noises outside my window which are kind of disturbing me a little bit but I desire that they will go away. I desire that and that will be so. I desire that I shall have a positive attitude at all times and I shall get better and better. Oh God you want me to be happy I thought that when I heard that. I am hearing whistles outside my door but I desire thata they will have no affects on me whatsoever, these people in these suite. I think that they can not read my mind but I desire that will be so. I desire that will be so. I think I have a worried imagination right now. But I desire I will not and that will be so. I desire that I will get to the point where the people will be as if they were really just not acting. I desire that and that will be so. I desire that I shall believe that I am just creating this problem in my mind. It is just a feeling which I will be able to control. I desire that and that will be so. I desire that I will be able to solve this problem and that will be so. I desire that and that will be so. I desire that nothing is impossible. But I want to switch the situation that I have in this world that is me changing the idea as me being happy as I was before. Christ said that you shall pray for anything in my name and it shall be granted you. I am not as happy as I think I can be. I just went down a little bit but I desire that I shall come back up. I desire that and that will be so. I desire that I shall be able to solve that problem and that will be so. I was feeling good for a while then but I desire I shall solve that problem and that will be so. I was just worring about the change that spin had in his change. I desire that that will not bother me and that will be so. I desire that and that will be so. I believe that you have in your mind the ability to solve any problem that ever was, ever is, or ever will be. I reallyn only came down once tonight and this is an improvement. And I thank you Lord for letting me be a little happier than I was the last few days. I desire that I shall get better and better. I desire that and that will be so. I desire that. I have a problem here in which there are people who have suffered more than me and people whom haven't suffered more than me. So I do believe that I'm pretty close.

The other night I cleaned a fire chimney with my cousin Paul. While were cleaning I took my job as if it were an operation and the signals one that I tell uncle Joe who Santa Claus with red nose to meet to meet him. A Cop came by and checked area with chech mark what progress I made. Last night I thought Jesus was calling when heard knock after reading small pamphlet had given me. Right around here I began to write with my left hand. I had steadily making progress. I thank you Lord for having me Lord have this progress. My goal is to get to a point in which you mostly go up instead of down. Last night I thought there was a crow who cawed three times which meant if I disobeyed Jesus three times then he said that I would deny him three times but I don't know if I did or not. This life is getting better and better. I thank you very much for that Lord. I think that I could write a boook about this. The idea of ice-cream Kelly. The idea of a chessboard that. I had a thought today that I possibly could. I desire that I shall run and run hard, I desire that will be so. I have a chemistry quiz tomorrow and I desire that I will do good in it. I desire that and that will be so. I desire that and that will be so. I would like to think I will do good in this quiz and that will be so. I would, I have doubts that I will do good in this quiz but I would like to get rid of this doubt on this quiz. Thank-you Lord for letting me do this.I would like to do good on this quiz. My math is having some problems too, but I desire I shall solve that problem also. The last couple of days I've been wondering if I will be able to get it up or not. I have the idea that all humans have one thing in common in that the God or Gods are reallyn playing with us in bringing us up and down. The last couple of days I've been wondering if I will be able to get it up. I desire that I will be able to get it up and that will be so. I desire that I shall be protected at all times. All the accidents I thought were on purpose in the paper before I went out the window. I desire that all the problems. The most important thing that I've noticed is the change or the jingling noise. All the people whom have to be the lowest form of life and that is to do something which they do not want to resort too. I desire that whenever I feel to start to feel a little bad I shall reemeber I am protected at all times. All the humans have to give signals to feel better. I am definetely getting better and that is what is good, but all people should be equally happy throughout their lives. There should not be any injuries that make people unhappy. Someone just making us feel good and bad at all times. I am having a signal from a person in this room. I'll make a deal with you God if I can get it up and wrote a book that will make me real happy, and you must want us very happy. The people you created you would want to be as happy as you. That is you will love us at we love you. Just as a parent loves his children. The idea that people whom are trying to find cures for diseases. The wars that people start. Who created a person who wants to destroy other people. The idea that I might be a bad person, which is making me feel a little bad, which is giving me a little scared. Thd door that is shutting upstairs. Who are telling me to stop. But I don't believe that I should. I desire that I shall write as very lot. The people whom might have to read to be happy. The machines which are just going up and down. The idea that people have to move when they hear something else move. The noise from nothing which makes you movingless. The criminals, the slums. The idea that I might be hanged or drowned is scaring me. I would like to get rid of the idea that I had to run t just to throw-up. The idea that I might burn in hell for 100 years is scaring me. The idea about the colors which control me. The idea that I might have to resort to queerdom which I would like to get out of my system, but I will always remember these writings. The riots in Harlem and the Watts. I will always be protected when I am standing sitting or the blacks in Africa. The idea of the smooth signals.The blacks and whites and chineese which do not get along. The idea that a person might go blind or the handi-capped. The quads, the amputees, but thank-you God for healing me, but the pain I had going down. I would like to never had have. The idea that we draft and Army like to told to fight or do anything that you will tell us if it is good or bad.

If I could kill two birds with one stone by making myself happy and a lot of people happy by working real hard and playing baseball and showing people what they can do, what is possible. I could make myself very happy and I would think that it would make other people happy a:lso and what would be good for me an for other people. What actually controls us to do things. We ate all in this together and it is our job all of us to do something about this. The idea that I might not be able to walk again scared me considerably. I just wonder I do not even can consider what it would be like to be paralyzed from neck down. It scares me just to think of it. All the murders wars and everything. If I write a lot I will have a security of which I think would be a pretty good thing. All of the injuries around. When I was in the 7 floor of Robby 7 that was one scary thing. The signals about left and right, the colors which mean yellow for slow green and blue for slow also, red for nbad and white for real good. A matter when someone is horney the stars when they come out flash of and on. The real reason when people go to dances now when I chewed the ice it meant that I was horny and someone else was horny. The police siganl when he went into the bathroom with nhis left hand which meant that I should go with left, leave the left hand which meant that I should leave the bathroom. I desire that I shall be able to solve any problem at all times. Th idea that nobody would serve me at the bar because I was probably not liked should change the idea that a person just said thank-you when I do not really think that he meant it. The wonderful thought that I shall be happy most of the time and instead of having none like me. That I shall sit here for a very long time and just study a lot of people. Th idea about smooth that is real gently which means that whoever I am talking to shall mean that it is real smooth. The idea of coughing which will siganl against someone to suffer a little bit, but I desire I shall not make people suffer. The idea of hair growing shall make you stronger. The idea that the left leg will remove something from another person. The idea that when you watch tv you you can become up or down just by watching it and also that If you want something bad enough you can get anything you want. The idea that when you are working you can control how you feel. The idea of going to a place with a lot of people can get you up by watching the musicians in their movements. The idea that whenever you have a real problem you can go to a game and just watch them play. It was about this time when I ran sprints next to the baseball players so they could see me working. I ran to th point that something comes up from your mouth, and also I went down to the football field and just threw a Frisbee with the trainer while the football players were working out. The idea of saying thank-you and see you later which will really mean it. The idea if you have. A car went nby which meant to go fast.

Which might mean that nothing had problems too. The idea that when you see a truck go by I tmakes me atleast me feel a little down because it denotes that he the truck driver has been on the road longer than I have ad that he deserves to control me or make me feel as if he is in my control. The idea of the cafetaria people when they clang the dishes makes you work a little bit. That is to go down a little bit. The idea about the colors and that they mean something to you especially when you see an ambulance go by or a fire engine that something is really going to happen to you. The idea that when the wind blows means to you that you are tired or winded. Why do people really have to get old or have the fear of dieing. The idea that if you grow hair you can actually get stronger. The idea that people joining together to solve any problem that is any problem never dieing just living in a place where you can be very happy atleast most of the time. Maybe this could happen to me again. Life I would like to think it couldn't. The ideas that if you project your feelings into someone you can make them feel how you want to. The idea that if you embarrass someone a little bit than they will make you feel a little better. I definetely feel myself getting stronger by coughing. The idea of a horn which actually means to blow your own horn that is brag about yourself. The idea of loud music which means loud and clear. That is you understand what the person is saying and also how you walk with your feet can determine. How RM got into his accident. Ho if I keep on writing I will be able to have a rock chest. I desire how I will sit up and write all night. I desire that I will try to and thata will be so. How RM has flebitis. The big thing. The idea that if yuo do everything the opposite you will be happier. Right now while I am listening to my mother sister, and Liz who has polio and it should be healed. The reaspon why I am writing this. That I could have a good book to write if I could. The idea of the epidemics. The reason why I am writing this that I a programmed not to write this, by things which I have no control over that is that every human being gives signals to each other right before they do something which means that they know that they are all in this together. The idea that people have to sacrifice things just to be happy. Why people have so many problems, but are programmed to do things be things, doore wind, window colors esspecially which make then happy and sad. The idea that children might havve a time in life at one time to suffer, because they think it is a good thing to do. The idea that people have to have the fright of death. The idea that birds make you feel good only to come back down. The idea that people have to go to old age homes which might give them a scare. The idea that we are programmed to do bad thinhgs which might make other people unhappy. The idea that people cough. The scare I had being impotent, spinal cord injuries, cancer, motorcycle accidents, diabetes. The idea that we are contacted by Gods which just play with us.

The idea that when we came home today with Liz the idea that possibly I could put how my legs were in heaven to her to heal them because my legs had innumerable astrength to heal hers. (This Liz a was my sister's friend from college, not the Liz whom I had as a girlfriend) The idea that when someone coughs or hu hu's means that how long that they have been on the road of how hard that they have worked. The idea that when I went into the woods I shit on the leaves or trees which kind of meant that I hope that I had shit on the bad parts in life. The idea that you just have healing powers on earth. The idea of jingling a bell which might mean natural. How I decided now that I should maybe do something or atleast try to do something abouy everything. I can kind of look at it that when I was in a wheelchair I would have wanted anybody in the world to do something about it. And that would be to try the impossible if possible. I would like to put in that when am airplane goes by means fly or move. I used to try to want to take orders from that is who could I really trust. I thought that if I could trust my own penis by asking questions and seeing which way the urine went out as if I was right or wrong. Left standing for wrong and right standing for right. The other thing that I remember is the idea of a shower which means unter or the devil. The idea that some day I might get old and how my dad helped me get better and that I should repay him some way. I even think that the animals are in this together with us also. The idea that all people should share an equal amount of suffering should be equal for all no matter what. I remember how I was in the hospital and Bill the therapist used to tell me to work. That is I had to try t pull myself out of bed with him there pulling. How I thought that people could rea my mind and get me to do something as if they knew what I was going to do before I did it. I thought that the only reason why I was not happuy before because I thought that I couldn't get it up but I don't actually believe this is so now. That I possibly could have healing powers in my waist down because I really thought they were in heaven. And if they were in heaven then I possibly could do something about someone's legs because mine were in heaven. When I bring back to the hospital I can remember after I went down for the first time I was back in the hospital where I went up for the second time and that the third time when I fell off the bed and I thought I had no feelings in my legs from the waist down. Then I went up for the fourth time and I lot of other times after that numberal little times but there is one time I remember vividly. After I went u for the fourth time I had the feeling to push myself off the bed and my legs would be in heaven. The first feeling that I had was kind of a tough feeling, in that when I fucked it would be a fuck that had a little bit more to it then an ordinary fuck, one that was a little bit tougher or more sensation or a force field around my prick. And I remember the fourth fifth time going down how it was passed tough and back t good with even more sensation then before. If my legs were actually in heaven than I could actually heal other people that is have healing powers. The idea that I could actually be a Jesus Christ or a person with healing powers. I don't know about the Jesus Christ but someone with healing powers like him. When I just about healing powers Liz downstairs said she wanted an ice cube. Which might have meant she was horny for what that I was thinking. The idea that humans give signals right before they do something which means if you should do something about it or not. That is if yoyu should do something or not. I do not actually believe that if I got married that than would actually make me have these healing powers. One mjor point was the idea was whenever you have somebody say something right before you think of something then you will know whether to say something or not. The idea that my parents would possibly want to be young again, would be a nice feeling to have. The night when I was watching tv in the campus center was like the television show was better than actual tv show to the point that it might possibly be happening that the people would actually die on T.V. That there is a mutual attraction between humans like magnets. The idea that people can control each other. The main idea that if I was disabled I would want someone to do something about it. I could possibly have been one of the luckiest persons that ever lived. The idea that I might be in a wheelchair the rest of my life, scared me considerably so much that I feel I should do anything in my realm of possibility to help someone disabled. I desire that I shall try to do something and that will be so. I would like to think that I do and that will be so. While I am writing with my opposite hand my hands are getting bigger. Which I like considerably. I would like to become a therapist to help people get healed. A Physical therapist who works with the handi-capped, because I believe they are the worst off. They got what might be called the shaft in life. I would like to be a physical therapist whom works with spinal cord patients especially. The idea that I could possibly a very good therapist had really got me a very good idea in life in what I should do. I like the idea that my hands are getting bigger has brought me to the idea that dr. Kittery just put his hands on me and I felt better. And the therapist Billy D. who put his hands on me and they felt better also. Te thought that I am one of the luckiest people in the world to be able to walk again, talk without getting tired, stand up or sit down without having no pain, is really should make me feel real good that is good enough to do a lot of things. When I heard a plane go by it reminded me of Walter in the hospital how he used to fly. I can remember David in the hospital who could have been one tough person.

The southerner in the hospital especially the Georgian, Bruce who was in the Fiat accident, Nick who, could have been one funny person. Stephanie the blonde. I think that I could become a pretty good therapist has really made me feel happy. I have been trying to see just how tough I am, if I could see if I could try to get myself to go down on purpose. I have to try to get myself to try to where when I was going down out the window. Before I was praying arching my back back praying knowing that I was going to go out the wind going into the bathroom praying the when Stephanie knocked on the door the window was open and when I went down as if something was coming out of me, going down as if you were actually losing something from yourself, screaming but I kind of wish that I didn't scram. Going down hitting the bottom with a kind of thud. How about the second time going up which wasn't really that bad just going up and coming down. If I was paralyzed I would like people to do something for me and that is anything. If I was disabled I would want people to spend a lifetime if possible. If I was disabled I would want people to spend even a month or year of their time just so that I will be able to do something with my legs again, and that is anything even spend a long of a time possible to be able to do something with my legs, because I would never have wAnted to spend a lifetime in a wheelchair. The people in the hospital would not spend that much time with me but they kind of did but if I was in that position I would try to have my body do anything possible spend a week exactly with me just to get me out of that disability. That I had that is anything.

Because when you are disabled or in a chair you ind of lose hope in yourself. You feel as if you were like a worm or something having to dress yourself all day long, move you legs with your hands or if the quads have been confined for life for some unknown reason. What etc . . . that reason maybe being in pain, just in a wheelchair, having to move your whole body with your hands, thinking that you will never walk again, never have sex again, and not knowing if yoyu will. Esspecially sex which is the wonders of life, thinking that you will be confined to a wheelchair, having to wear a condom, having to pull your shit out of your asshole, sleeping at night thinking that you don't want to wake up in the morning, thinking that you ca do nothing to get out of that Godamn chair. Who decides who is going to be in a chair and who isn't. having to cry just to be happy. Thinking that people want to see you suffer just to make themselves happy. Thinking that you will never walk again never have sex again. I was in that situation once and I would want people to do anything in their power to do something. Thinking that people would like to see you suffer.

Thinking that somebody might possibly throw you into a window when you are in bed, thinking that you will never come again. Nnever have sex again, thinking that people are trying to take your strength, switch it over to theirs'. Living with people whose only happiness is sleeping which they do not know what they are doing, having some dreams in which you can not walk, like some people having to be pushed around. People having to make you cough just by pushing your stomack. Thinking that some body might steal your arms but hoping that they never will. crying at times wishing you that you could jump out a window just to get it over with. Having people dig in your ass taking apart your asshole. Thinkinhg that people want to make you suffer doing things even a second time thinking that it is the right thing to do. Just thinking that you will never walk again. I was in that position and I would do anything in my power to get people out of that situation. Having to dress yourself two times per day, take your clothes off and on by yourself. Having to reach down thinking that yours was not an accident but it was your will just because you thought it was good to sacrifice. Knowing that if you make it your situation make people happy. Having to wake-up in the morning when you don't really want to get up in pain just using around. having people make you happy by giving you a back rub. I was in that position once and I would have people do anything in their power to get me out of that god damn chair. Just thinking that their is nothing people can do to help you. Having to lie in bed for months thinking that then only time you will be happy is when you eat. Having people come in and stick needles up your arms 5 or 6 times at a time. Having someone cut you open. Thinkig you might live in hell 100 years or possibly eternity. I was in that situation and I would and I would anybody do anything in their power to do something about it. I had an idea today that whenever you feel down you ca move your left leg which will mean leave alone. Your right foot will mean good, and it should be very good because of te condition my feet were in. It should mean a definite meaning. A very convincing meaning. When I just flick my knee it could mean the same thing.There are signals that humans and dogs give to each other. The policemen aren't ordinary men they are the men whom have very good control over their mental faculties. The idea about the night in the campus center about some people came by at night and projected into my mind the idea of shorty which they would try to make me feel down but if I met person later, because he might have made you feel down a little bit you would later on make him feel good. I desire that if God me rebelling against you is going to make my hand rebel against me then I do not think I should hurt you because I would be actually be hurting myself.

As I believe the idea do unto others as you would have them do unto you. Last night Saturday night I had a dream that I thought that I was going to die. I was a little scared ut not as much as I thought that I might be. I also had another dream with tex in it which was about how I should use Breen Ming Control with my left hand and left index finger. Then he said something about his little baby finger. That kind of makes me think maybe about the children or that I maybe a baby. But I kind of doubt that I am a baby. it kind of brings me back to one situation in the hospital but I do believe I was not happy. I kkind of think that it was a possibly maybe a different kind of world. One in which people are in a world which possibly there is not for for how happy they are. They were kind of like a living dead. They were as white as ghosts. If I could make people happy with leg problems that would make me happy and them also. But if I can do it I would like to be able and I desire, that if I do have this power I would like to and desire to be protected at all times. I do not want to think that I am better than other people but I would like to think that I was one lucky person. And I should do anything in my power to make people happy to the highest extremes. The idea that God's sperm was Jesus Christ and him dieing was like the pain of coming out. I sort of believe that I might have been God's sperm also with the powers of a real Jesus Christ. I kind of know for a fact that I did not disobey Jesus three times. I would like to think that I was the apostle Paul. That would make me happy like as if I were a real apostle. I believe that I am tempted by some evil forces at times but I would like to get rid of that evil force. All that I desire is that I make people as happy as I can and myslef happy too. I thought that I was programmed to forget about how there is things programming you to think about things that you want to think about. Things that are programming you to think about things that you really want to think about things that are making you change your way of thinking. I almost lost it when I went to Terry's house but that was a flash of time when terry gave a right hand movement which kind of made the idea that there is still a common thing about people have and that is they know inconciously that we are all in this together and it is someone's job to get us all out of it. I got that idea from my brother Jackie when he said unconciously that he had to make a computer program to Mrs. Terry and that was unconciously telling her, that he did not want to be a computer program. My brother Jackie jut put up his left hand with his left fist which made me kind sign t fight it. Was not strong fist a kkind of weak one barely closed which meant that I had lost a little bit but I did not loose it and that denotes that he said one one and mark just said Dutch.

Which might have meant that people can get into Dutch which might have meant that people can get into Dutch. Which is counted by something. Cars are just passing me in my car which just might mena unconsciously to you. Cars are still passing me to go. Mark just lit a match with one he just it up another match. But if it went out twice but he just might have meant that he did not light the match on purpose. My brother Jackie just dropped a ash which just might have meant that we are just matches. They just changes a tape but it seems they didn't really change it but meant not to change it. Jackie just put down the washers and wipers gut have meant to wash the water. Jackie just went faster jus then I bit my fingernails which might have meant to keep on biting. Mark is looking at the paper and he just might be hinting to us that we are all paper and he writing a red paper in red on a sheet of paper. Which might mean that we are all paper. And he just for a second opened the glove compartment that maybe he hinted to fix the paper. Which might have meant that he did not want to be paper. Even though Mark just should the Volkswagon which meant Paul to me the apostle which had healing powers. Even thought that it is getting tougher I would just like t look to the future when I could see myself healing people. I wrote before to solve problems and they were solved and I think that it is my duty to be a healer if I possibly could. I have not been praying while I have been writing. I been just. I have just been thinking that people have been telling me to hit the ball which I have been telling me to hit the ball. That I have been having just to think about being able to grow new legs is something or just thinking about changing my power in my legs to someone elses. Mark just said that if I have any clues in her which might bring back to me how I thought that I was an old timer. I just saw Mark try that move his U.S. coat which means that we are just the clothes. That something unconscious are passing me which means that they are not passing because I am a slow car. But that we might be a paper and we would burn the paper. My brother Jackie just moved his right hand that meant that we are just actually right. Mark just went to his reefer which meant lick. Lick it maybe. Jackie is moving his voice which might be this is a recording, one which is one which is broken and it is not doing what it is programmed to do. because he doesn't want to be a recording. Jackie is keeping on turning off and on the windshield wipers. That might mean this is a broken recording. Mark is keeping on reaching for the ash tray. I desire God that I will keep on praying forever. Mark is urching which us might mean to me that I should keep on reaching.

There are cars passing me which even though they are passing me they just might mean to go along with your thinking. We are passing a rental truck which just might mean that we do not want to be rental material. Cars are still passing me which might mean. It reminds me to fit nothing something which controls everybody. It reminds me of when I went to California and I felt like a low form of life. One that doesn't have that much strength. It is not even raining and Jackie has the windshield wipers on which is the opposite of what your suppose to do. A yellow car just went by which reminds me of Washy and Washy was a fighter against Paul R. for a girlfriend. And I though I might not be able to have a girlfriend ever again. Mark is just rolling the paper which brings to mind how I should roll the paper which we have. The idea about how it is going to be bumpy. Jackie kind of gave a breath which meant to me that maybe he missed. He also began to bow that maybe it meant to bow to Jesus Christ. But if he is my God I will bow to you. But if I can be higher in the Kingdom of heaven if I thime I think that it would be to my best advantage to fight because in the end it will be all North. If it's I could lick nothing than I could be very happy after that and be able to create miracles, on earth just if I could think that like I think at times that maybe I could have died on the cross that if I had not been paralyzed. If you knew all the time that you were going to die on the cross then I will bow to you. But not I could be higher in the kingdom of in the heaven by praying then I will be able to fit nothing which would be better too. Then I could be eagle to a child in heaven because we are all children to God. And we just looked at a cementary and it must really scare people to have the fear of death. But I just look at the days I would give anything to be dead. Mark just shook his hat which meant that I should shake it. If I could do the four things all the time or three that would mean that I would be the father, then son the Holy Ghost or a God. Then I would be able to create miracles on earth like maybe bringing yout back to people. I ask you God to give me strength to do it. I remember I talked to my uncle the other day and he leads to God the cancer, and he would. I have asked God if you have the supreme power and the supreme power and the last say. This could remind me of Tex which I thought that I could change something in the eyes of everybody's eyes. I desire that I will be able to stay up all night. I desire that and that will be so. I desire that I will stay up all night and that will be so. I desire that and that will be so. I desire that I will be able to listen to the signals and that will be so. Tonight I feel that it is like the night Sunday that I should stay up the whole night to pray like the garden of Gethsemane, which the apostles fell asleep instead of praying. I just read that Jesus said that blessed are the single hearted for they shall see God. Maybe their the ones whom do not give their heart to Jesus, because they might want to be single hearted in the Kingdom of heaven. That maybe the apostles told everyone that they should give their heart to Jesus because they are afraid of suffering. Which in the long run it would be much to their advantage if they go through with it and become very strong for eternity in the Kingdom of heaven. I kind of accidently clsed the Bible which I was reading which means that I shouldn't pick-up again tonight. Last night September 25 or so I had a dream that I possibly.

I am in Math right now and one of the main problems has been pussy and in Math the teacher is drawing a function of derivative which looks like a pussy. The Math is g kind of like a little bit of getting into a pussy. He just used his two fingers into the pussy. The idea that it is not possibly the idea that it is the pussy sucking the (cream) out. The idea of a tit and that might be the point at which it erects. The idea that it might be x squared as good. The tip of a tit. The teacher keeps on putting his middle finger out which just might mean suck. The teacher keeps on putting his left hand in a hile sign and he said, "Y" which might mean why did Hitler go on when he could have been quite happy as like he was. But what actually made him go on ebecause he wanted to be number 1 possibly. The idea of negative infinity. The idea that he wanted to be 1 ovee e. which might mean 1 over equal the teacher just wrote A2, that maybe I have 2a's. H is kind of putting the peace sign. He said ey which is equal why. maybe who says. The idea that my mark does not matter but actually how much I am getting out of it. Maybe equal/2 the father. The idea that Hitler wanted to go back to his mother. He might have wanted to suck on his mother again. He might have wanted to suck on his mother again. The idea that you might should get away from prayer a little bit. He just had underlined A (x) dx. The hile is going down a little bit. I do remember that Hitler loved his mother very much. All humans have the ability to solve any problem at all times, such is ppie squared for infinity. O to h nothing go to hell or heaven. I am now in my History class with the idea of

Napoleon. I would like to think that I could make as much progress. The man is very. The looks of a fish. A girl tuna. It is not really what the person is saying but what he is unconsciously saying in his knowledge. THE FRENCH REVOLUTION, understanding a Napoleon would be a very good thing to have in my background. The only thing that actually matters is what you actually think. If I make it up to playing baseball I could possibly write a book in which to make money. I have to write a lot so that I could have a good book to write long enough. So that it will sell and all the people I am talking to will be in it. My happiness is all that really counts. If I could make other people happy too then that will be all the better. The History teacher is now pointing to his hair which means to me the idea of Lee how he is balled and maybe General Lee a real fighter. Walpole rebels the idea of General Lee has the player rebel maybe. To rebels they do very good. I desire that I will write a lot and that will be so. I do believe that Jesus is God and that he does not lie but some people peotitilizi.END.

This word peotitilizi was the last word I wrote before I went to get help at the University. I went to a counselor there at the School. I was worrying quite a bit and I knew that something was wrong. When I went to talk to a lady, I don't recall whom but she walked me to a psychiatrist's office where I spoke to a school psychiatrist. This psychiatrist gave me a prescription for stelazine and also told me I could only continue at the University if I were in therapy. I went to the infirmary and filled the stelazine prescription. I would have this on me and you could always here the pills in the bottle in my pocket.

One time when I was up Amherst I saw I thought was a CIA man. I was quite scared so I went out of the student center and it happened to be on a Friday. My brother and Mark were in my brother's car. We went to get our other car, which was towed and we got this car and went back home. While I was home I was riding my sister's bike downtown Norwood and I saw what I thought was a mafia man signaling me to get into a Lincoln Continental with is arm. Like, get in," get into the car. I got very scared. I thought the mafia person and a very lot of cars had come down from above. I looked at a girl whom was inside the Lincoln, and I thought she was a girl whom was made. I could remember I had read in a Reader's Digest in the 60's the mafia was fighting the A&P.

When I saw the Mafia person with his arm, I went into the bowling alley and called my friend Paul Cup's dad whom was chief of the State police in Massachusetts. I called him up and said.

"Mr.Cup, you don't know me. I am a friend of your son Paul. I think the CIA is after me."

"How can you tell?"

"I just think this."

I replied.

"Write me a letter and tell me all about it"

"Alright."

I responded. I wrote him a letter but I don't think I ever mailed this.

The next day I went down the recreational Hall and I was playing pool, then a man whom, I thought was a Russian spy came into the room. I was saying to myself could this be the, and his right leg went up just about as when I was going to say Russian spy. I then recognized him as the wrestler and football player from the next town over from us Walpole. But this person had moved down Connecticut his junior year. I then said to him.

"I think I've see you before."

He said.

"I think you have."

He then left and he was about 5'9" and weighed about 170 lbs. He had on a short sleeve shirt and he had two big veins coming out of the opposite sides of his elbows. There seemed to be complete coordination between his whole-body. His arms had the look of doing a lot of push-ups and pull-ups not weight lifters arms. His name was Chopper and he looked like he was in top shape. He left the room and went to the benches in the recreation hall. I saw him sitting there and then I left and took a walk around town. I was heading back to the recreation hall when I saw this frame heading up the sidewalk. I headed for the park in front of the Post Office. I thought he was paralyzed from neck down and then learned Karate. This is all I remember after going to the park.

I could recall back to when I was in high school and I was on the Math team in my junior year. I had driven all the Math team players in my car. I went into the gym with the Math Team player Fred Cleveland. I saw this person named Chopper bouncing a basketball. I could tell this was the football player well respected in the league. I then went into the Math Meet. This person chopper had moved to Conn. his junior year. We had beaten Walpole 26-6 my senior year and I had gotten the "Player of the Week," in the Boston Globe. I even think he would have been Walpole's captain also.

Chapter 5

I could only go to UMass Amherst if I were in therapy. So I stopped going to school there. I also tried to take 6 majors at UMass because I wanted to catch up with my school buddies whom were one year ahead of me. When I was home there was definitely some thing wrong with me. My uncle Joe Breen came over to our house and came up to my room and he made some kind of motion with one of his eyes. I then thought I could trust him. We went to the Westwood Lodge. While I was waiting in the waiting room there was a person whom moved one of his eyes. My uncle also moved one of his eyes again. My uncle told the admitting doctor there.

"He was one of two to walk out of University Hospital in 6 months."

Then he came outside and said to me.

"We pooled these guys."

My uncle had been a probation Officer at the District Court. The admitting doctor thought I should be admitted to the open ward. I was a bit apprehensive so I declined. From here I went to Joe's home and had dinner.

The next day I had an option rather to sign myself into Westwood Lodge, or I could have gone to McLean Hospital. I had my first thoughts of McLean Hospital. I thought this place was bad. This wasn't good. I began to get very agitated about being in the Lodge. I was thinking of running head first to the steel door and smashing into this. I thought about the lion in the movie the Wizard of Oz, when he ran out the window after seeing the all and powerful Oz.

The doctor there put me on stelazine. I wouldn't swallow this. I would go back to my room and take this out of my mouth. I was on the unit there where I could come and go as I pleased on the grounds. I escaped and I went to the Norwood Library. There I looked up the movie producer Cecile M. De'Mille. I then walked from there to my house. The Lodge had called to see where I was. I then got a ride from there, back to the Lodge from my cousin Chris.

I was going on passes out of the Hospital. I could go home for short periods of time. When I got home I would put the stelazine pills in my desk draw. The shrink couldn't tell if I were taking the stelazine or not. I think he thought there was some kind of reaction because I was using my left arm. When my mom went into my room she noticed the pills in the draw there. She called the doctor and when he found out I wasn't taking the pills, he put me on an injection of prolixin. He thought I was taking the pills. I would go on passes out of the hospital. The left hand was the reaction he was seeing. Each week I would get an injection of prolixin.

I met a person there whom was in WW 2 and the Korean War and was from Hingham Mass. This person said.

"I see a doctor for guidance. I was in the military 20 years and I have to adjust to outside life."

I went with him to a package store where he bought a bottle of whiskey for the chef at the Lodge.

I also recall talking to one of the first persons to have anesthesia back in the thirties in Boston. He had a leg cut off. I recall I thought about people growing new legs. Someone said.

"Only lobsters can grow new legs."

I told my brother jack this. He was agreeing with me a little bit but I am not sure if he was trying to allay me. Some other folks would say you are a little off.

I was in the Lodge for about 6 weeks. I began to do volunteer work at the Veteran's Hospital in Boston. I felt more myself there. I was escort service there. I would escort the patients around the hospital in beds, gurneys, wheelchairs etc . . . I remember I would try to act as professional as I could, by moving the feet legs of the wheelchairs. The food was good also.

I called up Elizabeth and asked her.

"Would you want to go out together?"

She replied.

"I'm seeing someone else now."

I said to her.

"Okay."

I then hung up. I thought of putting up a salesman pitch, and try and talk her into possibly going out a little bit. I also thought that I didn't look good enough for a woman the stature of Elizabeth. I called up another girl whom I had known in high school. I had gone out with her after we had lost to the State Champs Natick in football. Her name was Anne Marie. I said to her.

"Would you like to go to a movie or something?"

She responded with.

"Sure. Call me before the weekend."

I called her up and said.

"Would you like to go to the movies?"

She said.

"My mother doesn't think I should go out with you."

I was put in frenzy. I thought the reason why she didn't want her daughter to see me was because I had jumped out a window. I responded with.

"All right."

I wasn't about to declaim my way about what her mother had said. I was thinking to myself I ought to tell her don't let your mother make your decisions. I had my hopes up too high. I thought this was a sure date. I had gone out with her in high school and I didn't kill time with her because I wanted to have an intellectual relationship with her. I began to get awfully self-conscience about having jumped out a window.

I can recall I put up a fence around our home. I would use my left arm for digging and nailing. I was really feeling a lot of energy from using my left arm then. I began to think a fence is like your own force field around your home.

At the V.A. I exchanged jokes with one of the patients there. I said to him when I was pushing his bed to x-ray.

"*Your* on your way to the morgue for an autopsy."

He began to laugh and he said to me.

"They ought to put paraplegics into outer space."

Because of the bedsores, they were always susceptible to. I had begun to think about what important this is to know your place with words. If I had said this to ordinary person they would possibly say something like, that's inappropriate, which is the most favorite line for people in the mental health field to say to patients. Possibly a person would call this morbid also.

I could recall years later when I was on a psychiatric unit and we were in a community meeting. There was one person whom was in very, very deep despair. I said to him.

"I heard years ago in Russia, in the time of Catherine the Great, there was a person named Orloff. He was going to have his head cut off, at one of the daily executions. He got up on the plank and there was already a head cut off, on the level. So Orloff gets up and kicks the head off the level and says."

""Make room for me.""

Because Orloff was so casual he got off and didn't have his head cut off. Orloff later married into Catherine the Greats family. This person in deep despair began to chuckle. All the nurse and doctors began to say something like, that's inappropriate. Before I said this I knew the doctors and MHW workers wouldn't understand what this is like to be really very, very, low. This person whom was chuckling was in Harvard Medical School before he came into hospital.

I really enjoyed the job at the V.A. of going to the different floors with the patients. I can recall I saw the head spinal cord doctor, whom happened to be in a wheelchair himself. I said to him.

"I was a spinal cord patient."

He said very quickly.

"C-vertebrae?"

"No, T-6."

I can also remember when I was on an elevator with him and he said to someone on the elevator.

"The blood is circulating"

Months later I thought the new addition, which they were building, they were using blood for oil. I began to have thoughts about the people whom would hit the beach. I thought these soldiers would have their chinstraps on tight, so they couldn't take in any air through their mouths.

I thought they would go over the side of the boat and go down to the bottom of the ocean. They didn't have any air to breath. I thought they would eat oranges for air, which was in the oranges. The people, whom had already done this, could help people whom had fell down to the bottom of the ocean.

I thought my uncle George Augusta had done this. After WW 2 he studied art for ten years. I thought his helmet was like a temple. The soldiers would have to walk on the bottom of the ocean under water till they got to shore. I thought these people had gained strength and they didn't even need air to breath even though they were under water. They could walk around without air. I thought my uncle Henry could be doing this. He had died as I said Christmas morning 1965. My imagination would get very excited every now and then. I recall reading. "An imaginary worry may be unreal, but a worried imagination is very real." I thought my uncle Henry was directing traffic up the cemetery since he died in Christmas Morning 1965. He had gotten the bronze medal for directing traffic three straight days June 6-10 1944.

I can also recall when I spoke with my pal Dave Bird. I was going to room with him in college after high school, but I never made this there then. He was studying pre-med and got straight A's for two years there. I told him I read in wartime people disappearing. He said. That's crazy. But I stuck to my guns.

I went to have my license renewal, as this had been five years since I last began to drive. I walked into the registry and took the eye test.

"We have to examine your eyes to see if you need to wear glasses." The registry officer said.

"I would like to take the test without the glasses."

I could recall when I was in tenth grade. I had gone to the registry in Boston to get my learner's permit for driving. I was captain of the football team my sophomore year. I went with my pal Dave Copper. When I had gotten my learner's permit for driving a motorcycle I had to wear glasses, because my eyes were not strong enough. My pal Dave Copper was about an inch taller than me, and about the same weight, with a little lighter hair. I told him to take the eye test and for him to say he were me. He went through the eye test and took the manual test also. Then he went off to the side. When they called for the person Bill Breen to come up and sign for your permit, I went up and signed the Learner's permit. You followed orders perfectly Dave. Thank-you.

"All right, go ahead."

This registry officer said to my question here to see if I could pass the eye test.

"Good."

I replied.

I looked into the eye machine and tried to adjust my eyes as best I could.

"Read the top letters please."

He said.

"E, B. A, G, F."

I repeated.

On the last two I squinted and hesitated a little.

"Good, your eyes are all right. Go and get your picture taken. He's all right not to wear glasses."

He told the picture taker.

I was ever so grateful my eyes had improved. I never really wore my glasses, before when I drove. Now if I got stopped I wouldn't have to wear the glasses. I wasn't quite sure what got my eyes better, left hand, med, doctors, meditation, etc . . .

I was talking to another patient there and as I was waiting she said to me.

"He laughs at me every now and then."

I said

"Ya, I noticed he laughs at me also."

When I told this to the psychiatrist he said.

"I laugh along with you, not at you."

I can recall a while after when I had been working at a job and he asked me.

"How much do you make?"

I said something like.

"Minimum wage 3.23 an hour."

He began to laugh.

I then said to him.

"I'm going to play professional baseball and then pay the spinal cord unit for the money which they accepted for insurance."

I would also say to him.

"You can't help me. I've suffered more than you."

You can't blame the guy. He had a Mercedes payments and nice home in Wellesley mortgage to pay. He would have me cooperate with him. I liked him a little because he was a regular doctor for five years before becoming a psychiatrist. But our relationship was because of fear and I had to cooperate with him. I think he was really on a control high. I think my uncle whom worked at the District Court was really overseeing everything.

My friend Brian had joined the Army and made the Green Berets. I was out of shape quite a bit. I don't think I was too attractive of a figure to girls. As I say I was like in limbo.

I began to go to UMass Boston and I took English 101 and a Calculus course. I finished the English 101 course and I received a C.

I got a job as reading electricity meters in my hometown. I did this for about 6 weeks. I was really having a hard time in the mornings with the shot which I was on. The injection was a muscle relaxant. I with my weak muscles, the injection might have been good for your mind, but on the body very bad for weak muscles. I don't believe there was anything else I could have gotten, because the pills I didn't swallow were one of the other options I had. I think the doctor was waiting for an ideal time to get back at me for when I didn't swallow the pills and he thought I was taking them.

On the corner hanging out, this looked like I really lost something by going down to the street corner level. But one day I thought of giving all of them names like in the Bible. Frankie I called Jesus. Then my pal Mark whom was Wally's real name, I called apostle Mark. But Mark or Wally said he didn't want to be a follower. He kept on saying this joking around like.

Then I called Paul or Dunsy something or other and he would say.

"I don't want to be a follower."

Everyone would kind of laugh.

John Bulb came up and said I'm John the Baptist."

Tommy said.

"I'll be doubting Thomas."

His brother Marty I would call Mathew.

Tommy Ally I called Thadeaus. Bobby D. I called Barthalameu. Als or Bobby whom was bitten in the face and received 40 stitches I called Barnabas. Peter or Bird I was Peter. Johnny W. I named John Zebedee. Greg whom was named Lebeau I changed to Rommel and then to Andrew. There was James son of John, Son of David. There was Paul whom I stayed at Paul. This was the cornerstone.

Paul whom reminded me of myself I told to get into a fight. He was captain of this year's high school football team. He did get into a fight and I think this really helped him in the future to get through things. He said to me after the fight.

"I got in to the fight like you told me."

His face was all swollen from punches.

Tommy or doubting Thomas would say let me put my hand in the side of Jesus then I would believe. We all would laugh over this.

I recall I tried my old strategy of jumping right over a player when we were playing a pick-up game of football. I got up high, but I toppled over the player trying to tackle me. I was playing quarterback and I would try to shake people off of me, with my legs. In August I began to jog and run sprints.

I had stopped seeing the psychiatrist when I worked the electricity meter job.

I went back to UMass Boston in Sept, and I took another Calculus course and also English 102. One of these nights I took a hit of acid. I later heard acid was LSD. The next day I went to the Math Class. I took the "Kool acid test," The book by Ken Kesey. I took an aspirin because I got a headache from the acid.

My godmother Carol came out from Utah. She was about 35 years old. I was intimate with her. I really felt she took care of me really. I didn't realize till later when I was a godparent the responsibilities of them. We spent a few nights together. Carol kissed very well. I thought girls whom smoked cigarettes kissed better than girls whom didn't, as Elizabeth smoked cigarettes also.

Carol had a hysterectomy. I thought if I touched her with my right leg in this area then I could heal her to be able to still have children. I began to ball her with my right foot. "Football."

I was finishing up English 102 and also the Math Course at UMass Boston. In the English class I began to write papers lefty. The professor had me up in her office for conferences. I had written a paper why did the Germans attack France in 1870 in the Franco-Prussian War. The reason was because of our Civil War. I also thought World War 1 and World War 2 was the broken recording.

Later than this, I had talked to my friend Dave R. about how I would touch girls on the shoulder. I was talking to this woman professor one day outside the classroom. I put my hand on her shoulder. I was about 20 years old and the professor was about 40 years old. I now can recall I would get so excited talking to girls I would bend over as if I were taking a leak and touch their shoulder.

I told the professor I received possible acceptances to Harvard and Brown. I was like embarrassed going to these State Schools. I wasn't in any shape to work a lot and make money to go to a good school. This was always on my mind I was paralyzed. I would always feel my body not in shape big time.

I was wondering why she had me in her office about 3 or 4 times. I think now she was upset about how I would tell her I got possible to Harvard and Brown. I don't think she took this to cool at UMass Boston. I thought she might try to confuse me because of me talking about Harvard and Brown.

I would go to the wheelchair people where they go during the day at this school. There was one girl whom was in a wheelchair and she was acting in a wheelchair. I told her I don't think this was a good idea. I was thinking that acting in a wheelchair, would be very upsetting to folks whom actually needed them.

I was doing a paper about something of people in wheelchairs. I was interviewing a girl in a wheelchair and I asked her.

"How is your hearing affected?"

"I hear acute sounds. My hearing is acute."

Well I did some research on ^ and v which denotes feeling and no feeling in English corrections. I could tell I wasn't really in good shape not just physically now but also mentally. When I had these conferences with the professor I also around this time was intimate with Carol my godmother. The professor would have me in her office and I thought of possibly killing time with her there also. But I know this was really out of the question. I thought the professor was upset I was intimate with someone and I didn't have to pay anything to the professor. Mass Rehab paid my tuition for this school. I thought the professor was upset I didn't really pay anything myself, and she thought I was seeing her for free. Also I think she liked my Harvard and Brown connection. Maybe she could also get some of this.

The last day of class there was a person whom was in the back of the room whom was observing. I thought he was there under orders of the professor to observe me. I was writing papers lefty. I was slowly losing it. I think the professor was a bit jealous about the Harvard and Brown I would talk about also. I think we had cake the last day, and I do believe I passed English 102 also.

On Robby 3 I was diagnosed a schizophrenic. In this English course we were reading about schizophrenics in a story we were reading about. I thought the professor tried to get me to open up about how she might have thought I was called a schizophrenic. I thought she was unsuccessful in having me be an example, for a schizophrenic. She I think thought about this. I think with the person whom observed the class from the back of the classroom, I don't think this helped me any at all.

I asked my friend Johnny Cox if he wanted to join the Marines in the buddy system. He denied though. I was jogging quite a bit. One day I went down to the Marine Corps recruiting. I was thinking of joining the Corps. The sergeant Boxer introduced himself and a girl marine did also.

"I'm sergeant Boxer. This is corporal Arc."

"My name is Bill Breen."

"Your interested in joining the Marines?"

"Yes."

I said.

"Would you like to look at some slides we have of the Marine Corps?"

"All right."

We sit down with him on the right and me on the left. This man seemed very enthusiastic to talk to someone whom was interested in joining the Corps. To the point he was very much interested in me.

"We have two different options here in the Marine Corps. You can go down to Paris Island in North Carolina or you can learn to be a flyer by studying air at MIT."

He was telling me all this as the slides would go by.

"Are you any relation to Joe Breen over the Court House?"

"He's my uncle."

I thought my uncle must have sent recruits from the courts to be Marines from the Probation Office.

"I looked into Cal Tec., in California, in high school."

I felt good in myself now, because I knew I was smart in the books and he would think of me as tough in the books.

"How are your eyes?"

He asked me.

I told him.

I used to wear glasses but I passed the eye test without my glasses the last time at my license renewal."

I thought this was a common thing for people to have their eyesight improve. I thought this because I recalled talking to my aunt Gertrude one day, and she asked me if I wore corrective lenses. I told her I did. She then said. "Have they corrected your eyes yet?" I then thought that anyone with corrective lenses, then your eyes could be corrected.

He was expounding to me the different slides. I could remember one slide of marines jogging in unison and this really picked up my attention. I thought I could hear their feet, hitting the ground there in the Marine recruiting office. I don't remember any audio sounds so where was the noise coming from then.

I knew this person would have to know what kind of contour I was in. I saw him look down at my legs and I picked up my left leg from off the ground about a foot. I could tell he thought this one was all right. He then looked at my right leg, and I moved this a little bit. This day I wiggled my right leg and his eyes and head lit up. I could tell this meant something singular to him. He gave me some pamphlets to look over and think about.

I remember thinking if I joined and they got hold of my psychiatric records. Then this would be very mortifying especially the psychiatric records which I had. I wouldn't want to take the physical and flunk because of the doctor thinking about my psychiatric records. I wouldn't want to be known as being turned down for the Marines for psychiatric problems.

I was stretching in the side room at my home one night. I had helped build this room when I was about 13 years old. Here I began to talk to whom, I thought was my uncle Henry. I recall I had lost 50 lbs. I had on pants, which I had worn in high school. I was sewing the pants when I began to talk to my uncle Henry.

"Give me some food?"

I thought he was saying to me at first. My uncle Henry had died Christmas morning in 1965 of a head wound. When I thought he said, give me some food. I got some grapefruits and also ham pieces. I cut this up and I ate this. I was thinking about when I fought for my life and I thought about eating grapefruits skins and all. I began to think of myself with a stiff neck. I began to think I was an eagle. I began to stretch in this room and I had thoughts first after I stretched.

"This is Yale University. Now we are asking."

This was what I received from Yale when they asked me to apply in high school. They said the credentials for Yale are exceedingly high.

Then I stretched again and I thought of Harvard University. I thought of the color white and this was still possible. I stretched again and I thought of Brown University. I thought of possible here also. I think I had thoughts of going to Brown University and taking pictures at the campus there. Then I stretched again and I thought of Tufts University. I can't recall what I actually thought, but I recall the sound "beep, beep."

I can recall this time, a person was hit by a train and he had his penis amputated. There was supposed to be a special doctor at Boston University whom would try and help him. I had stretched and had thoughts of Boston University. I now thought this was like the five times I stretched when before I went out the window on Aug. 1, 1975.

I began to think I could talk to my uncle Henry. This was like Nov. or Dec. 1977. I had heard back then he got a bronze medal for directing traffic in the Battle of the Bulge. This was really June 6-10 1944. I thought my uncle Henry was directing traffic up the cemetery all these years. I could recall back when I worked at the factory and I had been on my 20 hour of standing up and I fell asleep for about 5 seconds standing up.

I went to see my urologist one day in Dedham. They told me to fill out the insurance form to see the doctor there. This was the dr. Slesh, whom took the bladder stones out of me. He had operated on my bladder and I had told him after, I wished the stones were never taken out. At his office I threw the clipboard over the counter. I then got up in the hallway and began to direct traffic of the people going by. I could remember I would say.

"Tank."

And I would motion for a person to go by. I had heard the chief at the spinal cord unit had been a tank commander during the Battle of the Bulge and he had lost his right leg. He lost his right leg to a hand grenade. I had at this time thought my uncle Henry had received the bronze medal in the Battle of the Bulge. But I later heard this was June 6-10 1944 D-Day. He also was in the Battle of the Bulge.

I could recall when the Chief's assistant dr. Train had told me in 1976. "You must walk."

I thought I had to walk to University Hospital, which was about 30 miles away. I took Neponset St. in Norwood for about 2 miles, then route 95 for about 6 miles, and then Route 128 for about 8 miles. I was coming to Blue Hills in Milton when I thought I would climb Blue Hills for on the side. This was the winter of 1977.

Around this time I got a charley horse in my right leg. I thought the Chief had done this with the limp, which he had. When I was on the Milton exit my left leg also began to get a charley horse. I then saw a helicopter up in the sky. I thought if I walked to University Hospital this would have made some news.

I actually crawled the last half mile to the Howard Johnson's restaurant. There I called my brother Jackie whom came and got me, and I went to my grandmother's house. I soaked my feet in a pot of hot water there. I had been talking to my uncle Henry as I walked.

One day I went over V.A. Hospital for what I do not remember. Something was driving me to go there. I left my car running in the back of the hospital. I walked right in at about 7:00 at night. I was headed for the 50 million dollar addition for the new spinal cord unit, which they were building. When I was walking in there I saw a good-sized man with big belly, whom was working with tubes of blood. I said to him.

"Are you Valpe?"

He said.

"Yes."

This was Valpe construction, which was putting up the new building. I sat down in a chair as I watched him with a machine with tubes of blood. I thought they were using blood for oil for the new addition they were constructing. I said to him.

"I'm just a sweeper."

He responded with.

"Is that so?"

I saw a janitor walk by with his mop and bucket. I took the mop and cleaned up some on the floor. The next thing I notice is a security guard came down the hall. He was a middle-aged man. He asked me.

"What are you doing here?"

I began to panic a little. I thought I could get a job by walking right in without filing application. Just start working like I did at the A&P job. The next thing, which I descried, was a young man came wheeling down the hall in a wheelchair. He said something to the security guard.

"He's all right."

This person must have known me when I did volunteer work there. The security guard then asked me again.

"What are you doing here?"

"I am applying for a job."

"Come back tomorrow and tell them Flaherty sent you."

Well I came back the next day and a different security guard asked me.

"What are you doing here?"

I said.

"Flaherty sent me in to file application."

We went to personnel and they checked out where Flaherty was on duty the night before. A girl there said.

"He was in section 5."

Two security men then escorted me out of the hospital. As they were walking me to my car, I saw Ken whom had worked as an OT in the Spinal unit at University Hospital I was at. He now was working at the V.A. hospital. I said to him as the two security guards were next to me.

"Hi Ken."

"Hi Bill."

I was thinking the commotion I caused might have kept a few minds in wheelchairs inhabited for a few minutes. I could think this would be a little excitement for them. But when I said hi to Ken, I got the impression I was a bad person being escorted out of the hospital. I can reminisce the expression on Ken's face when I saw him. This was not good to be escorted by security guards.

Around this time was the Blizzard of "78". I had gone out for a ride when my car got stuck in snow. I walked about 2 miles home in the Blizzard. My face was frozen with frozen sweat. My hair was like icicles from frozen sweat.

I went to the Norwood Hospital some way or other and the next thing I knew I was in the Westwood Lodge again. I was in the Lodge this time for 2 and ½ months. I was put on haldold, which was the last resort medicine for my condition. I began to run sprints andI got into fairly good shape. I would feel negative thinking the 2 and ½ months I was in the Lodge, I could have gone to Paris Island in the Marines.

When I left the Lodge I went to a half way house in Brighton. I did not think you could recover from mental problems, so I tried not to talk to anyone whom would outright admit this. This was in June and I began to play baseball in the Boston Park League. My coach was Red. We would drink beer after games in the Boston Parks. I heard Red would get everything deducted from his taxes. I didn't play too much as my arm wasn't in too good of shape. I would usually keep score or I would also go up into the stands, and bring around the pan or hat for the fans to donate to the game.

The first game I dressed for was in Casey Town Field in Dorchester. I pitched in this game and I struck out one person on a curveball. I had my second balk ever in baseball. I would pitch batting practice for the games. I would sometimes play right field.

After one of the games, a person whom went to UMass Amherst and played baseball there asked me.

"What was this like to be paralyzed?"

The coach mumbled something to himself after this. I felt now I had really done something good. This player's eyes lit up and he began to look at me very pryingly. I could recall I had plans on going to UMass Amherst and playing baseball there. Seeing this person here, made me feel this was right what I did by going out the window. I thought for a very long time this was wrong or a mistake. I thought to myself I would earn my respect back by playing baseball.

I saw a girl Denise whom called me her dancing partner on her high school picture. She was dating one of the players on the team. I would say to Red.

"Red could you put me in? My girl is here."

"This is a big game. We can't take any chances."

Red would say.

I would look into the stands at the girl Denise. I would try to get a hit or score with her. This was a little bit like when I would look at Elizabeth in the stands. I asked Denise.

"Is this something serious with you and your boyfriend?"

She said something like.

"Ya quite a bit."

She told me her family was moving to Kentucky. While I was around her I began to think about how I went out the window. My body was pulsating negatively. I dreamt years later about the disease schizophrenia. I began to think I had like leprosy, malaria, ect . . . People didn't want to be around me.

When I pitched in one game I got the save. I would hear the fans in Boston cheering and I felt good about the applause. I can recall when I got to bat once when we were under the lights in Fallon Field in Roslindale. I dug in with my cleats at the plate. I felt a bit tight and I adjusted to playing under the lights. I hit the third pitch in between second and first base. I got my traction down and I pulled out of the box and began to pick-up steam as I ran down the line. The second baseman made a good play and I was thrown out at first.

I would also play outfield sometimes. I wouldn't wear my glasses. When the ball would be hit to me, I would guess as I stabbed at the ball to catch this. The ball club won the Boston Park League Title, which the playoff games were played in Brookline Mass. Here in this game there was a fight at third base, when one of our players slid into third base. Our whole team got off the benches and both benches erupted. Red and I were the only two whom didn't go to the ruckus.

I was on the bench most of the time. I really began to feel for the folks on the bench whom didn't play too much. As I said I would usually keep score and bring the hat around into the stands for donations. My high school player friend Rick had gotten out of college to pitch a game in the playoffs. I saw this person's mother in the stands after we had won the Title. I tried to meet this person's mother, because I wanted this to be like how this was in high school. I didn't feel I contributed enough in the game to earn her respect. We smoked cigars after the ball club won.

I took one Economics Course at the satellite college in Norwood. I think this was like two nights per week. I met the man there whom had been my history teacher in high school. In my second semester of the history course, I questioned my grade. I said to him I checked my tests results and I should have gotten two points higher at least. He did the math for my grades and said he would change the grade from 83 to 85 on my transcript. I had said the person whom had sat next to me in this history class, I would check his grades with mine each test, and I should have gotten about 10 or 12 points higher than him. This teacher said the reason why, was because of class participation. I didn't go off to college right after high school immediately. So when I got my transcript I noticed he hadn't changed the grade, which I should have gotten at least an 85.

He also had begun to date the guidance counselor, which I had, after high school. This was the counselor whom had come down to the Norwood Hospital and told me about the doctor whom paid off the teachers and coaches to help his son. This Guidance counselor had come to the Norwood Hospital when I was there, and told me this particular doctor had paid off the teachers and coaches, for them to help his son. She was also in the convent. I think when I was yelling out

Jesus back then, she was affected. I think they call this in Boston, "Spilt the beans."

The person in this History class, whom I said, I would compare grades with, also happened to be, the person of this doctor's son. Now this teacher was moonlighting at this college campus, where I was taking this Economics class. I think changing the transcript is a very serious offense. Two points, one Russia, and two China want.

I went back to doing volunteer work at the V.A. Hospital. I also got a job assisting the PTs at the Mass Hospital School in Canton Mass. I had also got an apartment with my pal Wally. Wally had gotten into a car accident and died. He had broken his neck. He had moved back home when he was in the crash. I heard this was the second time this person had killed someone while drunk driving. I was seeing the shrink at the Lodge. I was thinking before I became ill, I was the one with the mind. Now I was the one without the mind. I thought psychiatrists were smart people. I would ask this shrink.

"What are they working on in the future?

He said.

"They are trying to have pictures of someone while you are talking to them over the phone"

I would roll my own tobacco cigarettes. I thought I was rolling a joint. I would roll the Dedham Courthouse as if this were a joint.

I played baseball under the lights in Roslindale. I would think the lights were on. Dedham was in between Norwood and Roslindale. I would think we put the squeeze on Dedham by lights in Norwood and Roslindale. Or even West Roxbury, which was also on the other side of Dedham. Meaning the lights in the V.A. in the West Roxbury parking lot.

My friend Wally had died as I told you. He broke his neck in a car accident. This was a rather shock to me. I started the job at the Mass Hospital School. I would walk about ten miles everyday escorting the children in wheelchairs. I would talk to myself as I walked. I thought if I talked to myself on the left side of my mouth was God and the right side was Jesus. This was when I started talking to my uncle Henry whom had been dead for 13 years.

I went into the spinal cord unit and the Chief said to me.

"I don't think Bill needs to be coming in here anymore."

The only person whom I could trust was now gone. Alls I had was deliberating out of the sides of my mouth to my uncle Henry.

I was thinking of taking karate lessons, and also working out with the pro-ball players, and the high school team, for the preseason. I was being cutback on the haldold, which I was now on. I believe I was on no pills and I was just talking to the shrink about once every two weeks. He told me I only had to see him about 2 more months. Well I wanted to be the one to decide when to conclude. So I did at February. When I told the shrink this was over, he took off his glasses for the first time I could recall, as I walked out of his office.

I went to my apartment and then I wasn't sleeping. I saw my aunt over my grandmothers' and she said maybe I should take some of the haldold, the medicine, which I had been on. I had some old pills. I was thinking of taking some of them but I thought I don't know what my reaction would be after I took them, because I wasn't seeing the shrink anymore.

I went to my apartment and began to do push-ups as if I were going to entertain football. I began to imagine the Chief as up in the left side of my television set. He was like at a desk as if he was judging, whom would go to hell and whom goes up, as he would put his left fist up for someone whom would go up. I began to think I would imagine wolf's howling. I thought this was the wolf's howling, which made the almighty go back up during Moses time on Mount Sinai. I was also counting deer instead of sheep in my mind. I think now I was under the care of my family physician dr. Jack Yado instead of the psychiatrist. I wasn't sleeping for the second day and I can recall I went into the conference room of the OTs and PTs at the Hospital school. They were rather studious of me. I wasn't sleeping at all.

I recall the show, The Russians are coming was on, and I had seen this show at an ex-girlfriend Paula's home, when I was young. So I was bringing back memories of this. I also began to conjecture in my mind a person whom would put people into ovens, like they would in World War 2. I thought if I didn't flinch while being in the oven then you can make it by. I think of, flick your head of hair, with the word flinch.

I thought you would be in the middle of the sun when you would be in the oven. I thought the middle of the sun was pure THC or Tetrahychloric-carbonate. I thought you are blind in the middle of the sun. This was like I was dreaming now.

I went into Boston and almost crashed my car at the expressway exit. I had come very, very close. I went into the outpatient at University Hospital. This was the same hospital of the spinal cord unit. I went in there and said very loud.

"Give me valium."

Then said louder.

"Give me valium. I want valium."

Valium I wanted to get to sleep. As I was leaving I put up one person's chin. Like chin up. I thought also Chief was known as, "Chin," Chinese nickname.

After leaving here I ran around the building, and I thought I was playing for the Boston Red Sox. I felt in extraordinary shape. I then got into my car and drove to Boston City Hospital. This was just like dreaming. I can still remember driving there. I was like stop start, stop start all the time.

I went into a backside door and I thought I would just start working. I thought the Chief had done this. Just without filing application or college just start working. The Chief had started the spinal unit in 1957. I "decided the desire," to get some attention. So I dropped a flask glass and this just split on the floor. The personnel came into the room and I said.

"This was an accident."

They then continued on with what they were doing. I went up to the front desk and as if I were at a bar I said strongly audibly.

"Give me some valium."

One of the workers there said something like.

"He's in trauma."

I answered the paperwork for the insurance, which I had. They put me in a room on a bed. I began to think of the Chief as getting up everyday with one leg. I thought the Chief really looked after his patients. I wasn't getting any circumspection, so I thought I had to say something, which would get me help.

"I was Boston Globe Player of the Week in Football."

Then a person came in and said something, but still no care.

"I got a card from a Red Sox scout."

Still there was no care.

"I was spinal cord patient."

I said with inborn confidence. A person came in and looked at the scar on my back where they had operated. He seemed a bit angry as he pulled the shirt up and then down. I was saying here.

"I'm a Jesus Christ, I'm a Jesus Christ, etc . . .

A person came in and took my wallet. A woman doctor then came in and said.

"We called your psychiatrist and he wants us to give you this 40 mg. injection of haldold."

They must have found an old prescription in my wallet. The doctor then gave me the injection. I said to her.

"I thought I was going to be blind for eternity."

She looked at me with her mouth curved pleasantly upward. I thought she liked me. She really liked me. What I figured was, my psychiatrist at my home for him in Wellesley, and this was downtown Boston. The woman doctor I think liked me because I had psych problems. From here I was sent to a Boston Hospital. I can recall the despair I had in the ambulance going to the hospital. I was saying to myself, when is this going to end. I'm getting sicker and sicker and the shrink is taking the grocery money. How can I ever get over this?

I was at this hospital and I saw a dr. Friday. I can recall he was using intimidation tactic, so I cooperated with him. I had to say something, which he would like.

"I thought I was going to be blind for eternity. I was paralyzed."

When I told him I was paralyzed he said to me.

"What does the statement, don't cry over spilt milk mean to you?"

"Don't feel sorry for yourself."

I responded with.

I began to think dr. Train whom was the doctor on Robinson 7 was being used as a sexual liaison for this dr. Friday. I would picture dr. Friday putting his hands behind his head and like mentioning to dr. Train. Like come on baby turn me on.

I can recall I wouldn't eat food here. I would have food brought in.

Dr. Friday said.

"Eat the food here."

I would get a dry mop and clean the floors here. I was thinking when I was in tenth grade and I had a job cleaning for the retarded. After a week or so here I went to the Lodge.

I told my psychiatrist.

"I was in spinal shock."

He said something then I said.

"I had trauma."

He said.

"Trauma is after you have an injury."

I wasn't cooperating with him. I can recall a person came in with a tape measure. I thought they were trying to intimidate me with shock treatments. I was outdoors one day and I began to holler out loud, "I'm a Jesus Christ, I'm a Jesus Christ, etc . . .

They escorted me into a psych unit. I hadn't had anything to eat. I thought my psychiatrist was saying in my head, no food. I thought this spell or whatever came over me was because of no food.

They were thinking about shocking me. I called up the Chief and talked to him, but he was only listening. I said.

"They want to shock me. I remember after I went out of bed for the second time at Norwood Hospital, I thought I had no legs. I thought they went to heaven."

He didn't say anything. The word from the Chief was.

"The back might not be able to hold the shock."

My brother Jackie also came in and said to me.

"Cooperate with them. They'll shock you and then have you sign the papers after."

I also called up the person whom told me in high school, when I was working at the A&P years before. He said to me then, whenever you need a favor, call me up.

This was the person from the Providence, Rhode Island A&P. I called him up and left a message about the situation. The next thing, which happened a day later or so, a person from Rhode Island came in as a patient. This person would also holler out things like I did. I thought I would follow my brother's advice and cooperate with the shrink. I said to him.

"I saw this outline of a figure walk down the steps of my old home and then out the door. I had opened the door of this figure to go out of the house."

I could tell he gave me no perturbation and I was cooperating with him. Years later when I was salesman again, I would walk out of the house and repeat the steps of this figure, I saw walk out. I would do this and snap my fingers. I reminisced when I had gone to my uncle's office at the Dedham Courthouse, as Probation Officer, and he would snap his four fingers there.

My friend Dave Bird came in to visit me. I would pal around with Dave now these days. He was the person whom turned down Tufts Pre-med to room with me, but I never made this to the UMass then. There was a ramp outside the window and he said.

"Just walk right out."

I said.

"You just don't walk right out of these places."

He asked me.

"Why are you here?"

"I hadn't slept in three nights, and I went into Boston City Hospital."

Dave had a band on his head. I thought he was a person whom experimented with chemicals and with no consequences. After he left I began to get a bit anxiety. I began to stretch in my room over and over about 30 times every hour or so. I talked with a dr. Baldy. They wanted to prescribe me on 100 mgs. haldold per day.

"Hi Bill Breen. I'm dr. Baldy."

"Hi."

"We want to try to put you on 100 mgs. haldold per day. I am consulting to see if this will be all right for you."

"Were you a World War 2 veteran?"

"Yes, I was."

I thought I could trust him. He also stated.

"I know you can get straight any time you want, but we would like to try the 100 mgs. haldold just the same."

Since I thought he was a World War 2 veteran, I thought I could trust him. I later hearkened him being a World War 2 veteran was a fib. I began to think about when I fought for my life and I tried to get straight up from paralysis. I thought I could tap into this power any time I wanted if the situation deemed serious enough to get straight.

I was going into the bathroom stretching constantly. I began to think of Judy Garland whom was a patient there years ago. I was being built up to 100 mg. a day. I thought the head of the Lodge was saying in my head something to the expanse I was now under my own insurance. I was now over 22 years old.

I remember I would go into the bathroom and then stretch and then go up on my feet, tip toes. I told one of the nurses there, one day.

"Do you want to see me fly?"

"Ya, All right."

I then did my usage and then she replied.

"I didn't see you fly, but saw you land."

I remember I was purloining a bath, when I would have one of these spells. I would go under water. I brought back memories when I almost fell asleep under water after working 20 hours at the factory. If I could get to sleep I would be all right.

"Scream a lullaby." Carly Simon.

I can recall I received a card from the people at work and I was rather moved. I had gotten this position through the CETA program. The person whom was with the CETA program, said I needed a note to get back to work. This person at CETA said I had to follow the procedure here at CETA.

I had plans before this hospital time, I was going to work an extra hour at work in the mornings by getting up, the very disabled. I had plans on leaving the shrink, taking karate lessons, and working out for very serious baseball. Now I was back on pills.

I was discharged from the Lodge and then went back to work. The person whom I told I would work the extra hour with, she like cursed me for not notifying her. When I got back, she like cursed me under her breath.

Around this time I would go to a restaurant, and I would smoke a cigarette and have a cup of coffee. I always felt I would be welcomed because I was paralyzed. This particular day the manager at this restaurant like, shut me off. I was now thinking I couldn't go on thinking nothing was wrong. I recall the manager put a glass upside down on a table. This meant I was shut off. I really wasn't to have anything at this restaurant. I think I began to put my head down now.

I went to the pre-season tryouts for the semi-pro team in the Boston Park League. This was just like this was when I was younger. "Don't make it easy." Stevie Nicks.

All the baseball players on the team would use aluminum bats. I would use a wooden bat, because I knew in the pros, aluminum was outlawed. We would practice at high school fields, and the Park in Roslindale, Mass named Fallon field.

I can remember I hit a pitch at batting practice, and I pulled this quite a bit. I thought I hit this up tight of the bat like swafe'd the ball. I was thinking of signing a contract with the coach Red. I believe a few people on the team had contracts.

I felt bad about no karate lessons, which happened to be free also. I was now on 100 mgs. haldold per day. I could notice a kind of felicity on the face of the shrink probably knowing he would be getting paid for at least another year. I was going to be on the 100 mgs. for one year. He asked me one day.

"How much do you make?"

I replied.

"3.23 per hour."

He began to laugh.

"I'm going to play for the Boston Red Sox and pay the spinal unit the pay, from the insurance company, whom paid for me on the spinal unit."

I didn't understand the shrinks then. I years later thought they were aggravators. He got serious and didn't say anything. I had fought back against his laughter. I couldn't trust him. I had a relationship with him built on fear. I couldn't trust him and he kept right on taking the money.

I said earlier there was a girl patient there also, whom said to me.

"He like laughs at me every now and then."

I said.

"He laughs at me also."

So I asked him about this one day and he said.

"I try to laugh along with you, not at you."

I now think he was just waiting for a time to get back at me, when he thought I was taking the pills, when I wasn't, when I first began to see him. I had fooled him and I think he was rather upset about this. I also told him if I ever come off my pills again, to call my uncle at the Dedham Court. I said to him one day.

"Call my uncle."

"No."

He would say, and his head would move a little. He would even smile a bit. Talking of the word even. When I would leave the hospital each day I would say to the OTs and the PTs there.

"Have a good even."

I had read in the Bible the word for evening was even.

My uncle Joe Breen would say to me to get a real big stomach like Luis Tiant on the Red Sox. I was now rather spruced, as I weighed about 175 lbs. I was thinking I would rehearse the children at the Hospital School, about the games each night. I would tell them about how my team did and me also.

I enjoyed walking the best I have ever had these days. I would talk to myself walking. I must have walked about 8 miles every day. I would jog at the high school in Norwood and also practice sliding. If I sprinted the last couple of hundreds of yards I would run myself into anxiety.

There was about 4 or 5 players on the team whom played in the minors in pro-ball. I was thinking I would play ball in the parks of Boston. I thought about when Harvard would play Tufts in football years ago, they would travel to Harvard by wagon train. I was thinking I would be like Christ in which people would come from miles around to see me play. Everything was inception to get rather easy. I repeat the song by Stevie Nicks, "Don't make it easy."

I can recall being in the outfield after one of the practices. I had been shagging balls in the outfield and I really enjoyed chasing balls at batting practices. I left this practice and I really felt the great feeling of adrenalin.

The first game this year was on May 21, 1979. I would think of my uncle Joe Breen, whom would think of all my classmates, whom would be graduating college in June, as Junior. They would be graduating in June. This was May though for the first game.

I had been working out with my uncle Joe Mink. I had my high kick a little bit less than when I was younger. I felt my arm wasn't quite as flexible as this was years earlier. I wasn't sure if my arm would be back to 100&. I thought years later the 2 ½ years I had off was like when the World War 2 baseball players would come back from overseas.

My best thought was I would do better under the lights games. I now was wearing my glasses for night games. Most of all when I would play under the lights I like would guess. I thought because I couldn't see 100& under the lights without my glasses, then other people couldn't see 100&, especially the hitters when I would pitch to them.

The years before, I was thinking I might have possibly flustered myself, because I wasn't in 100& health. I had a little trouble with pop flies. I would look straight up, but my lower back was a bit wobbly.

I saw the movie about the person whom played basketball for the West Coast San Francisco. This was about a person whom went from Sand Lot basketball to the San Francisco Warriors I believe. He supposedly had an operation on his hip and then played pro-basketball. I would wake up in the mornings and look forward to the day very much so.

I was addicted to fall asleep at night by the television. So when I would be in a hospital I couldn't get to sleep. So you could figure, when you are in a hospital and not sleeping, they would give you something to get to sleep. They would give you their medicine to get to sleep.

I was beginning to be interested in a nurse at work. I was feeling a bit ambivalent about this, as I thought I was attracted to her over fear of the psychiatrist. The psychiatrist I couldn't trust, and to tell you the truth, I had a bit of consternation, because he would threat to give me shock treatments. If I didn't do as he pleased he would always use the threat of shock treatments. I thought he tried to give people scare tactics, as much as the courts. I think my uncle at the local court would be thinking, this is gravy compared to jails. So the shrink wanted to try to fear, as much as the courts.

My boss at the Hospital school whom would give pt to the students never had any schooling. I also heard he never filed application there. He had a pace maker put in around this time also. He would ask me.

"Do you take any medicine?"

I would fib and say.

"No."

I told my friend Dave R. whom I would see every now and then.

"I wonder what this would be like to be paralyzed twice?"

Dave had stopped Pre-Med at UMass Amherst. He did go back there three years, to try and complete, but he stopped. I was thinking of having Dave moving in with me at the apartment. My friend Wally, whom had died, had lived in the other bedroom, when he was living.

I recall I was going to run at 6:00 AM in the morning with my friend Dave. The first day I think I showed up, but he didn't. The next time we were going to go jogging at 6:00 AM and he showed up and I didn't. I would talk with my friend Dave. He made me deliberate about what this is to compete against people. He said to me.

"Compete against each other."

When we would see whom, could get up at 6:00 AM to jog. I didn't really feel what this was like to feel the rewards of work. I can recall I would try like sliding into a base after jogging and I would say to myself, I did it. I slid.

I told my friend Dave about having new legs.

He would say.

"This is crazy."

I remember when I would get into one of theses spells, I would think about when I had wished I had gone out of bed completely, the second time when I had fought for my life at Norwood Hospital.

I can remember when I had lunch with my immediate supervisor Lorna one day.

"Ya, I was paralyzed once."

"How were you injured?"

She questioned me.

"I was coming down off of roof when I was sun tanning and I slipped and fell."

I was still feeling bad about having jumped out a window. This was something, which I couldn't talk about. I felt very bad about this.

Lorna had just taken over the head PT position there. She would call herself a physiotherapist. The other assistant PT there besides me was Charley. His wife was a nurse there.

I would talk out of the sides of my mouth as I walked throughout the days. I think this was why I came down with Tardive Dyskinesia of the jaw months later. A while later my jaw would rock from side to side. I thought Jesus was talking out of the right side of my mouth and God on the left side of my mouth. When I had a mediocre problem, I would discourse with Jesus. When I had a difficult problem I would talk to God because I thought he was tougher than Jesus. I would like say things like.

"Listen to me. Listen up, Listen up."

By doing this I would motivate myself to go jogging. I can recall I would get through the process of putting on the sneakers.

"All right, All right, listen up."

The word listen, I thought very seriously, my uncle would say this to whom he called his customers, at the Dedham Court as Probation Officer. My uncle Henry whom had died Christmas morning 1965 had erected Joe's house. He built his own home also. I heard he was going to put up a street.

Chapter 6

May 21, 1979.

I went to work expecting to play my first semi-pro baseball game this night in the Boston Park League. I was on my habitual routine of assisting the PTs escorting the children in wheelchairs to different parts of the hospital. I began to be a lefty instead of a right again. I also was striving to be as independent as possible, by reading the paper standing up. I had spaghetti for lunch and I was talking to this middle aged man. I asked him.

"Were you in World War 2?"

"Yes."

He replied.

"Did you see action?"

He didn't even respond to this. I think he just mumbled something. Well I began to get nervous after this. This person's ear had a growth to one of his ears. This was like a pointed ear.

I asked Lorna the head PT.

"Could I leave work? I'm a littler bit nervous about the game tonight." She said.

"Okay."

Whatever happened to me came out of the blue. I was a bit nervous. I drove home to my parent's house, where I drank glass after glass of water. I drove to a restaurant about 4 miles away. I was thinking this was a little bit more than a bit upset.

I came back to my parent's house and went upstairs, and looked out the window to my brother Bob in his truck. I thought of going out the window then and I would be the father in the trinity. This was my first chance to go out the window.

I then went downstairs and back upstairs. I thought this would have been my second chance or Jesus in the trinity. But I still didn't go out.

I then went downstairs and came back up, where I got this shrill while I was going up the steps. As I neared the window I heard someone say downstairs.

"He's going I tell you."

Then out of the side of my mouth I said something like, go or jump and then I went out.

I had already planned what I would say when I went out. I spit and also said.

"M."

Because when I went out the first time I said "AAA," when I was in mid-air. Now M would be the second letter in spelling out America.

I went over the top of the windowsill and went down. As I was looking down my heart felt the depths of hell as I looked down at the slate with my eyes. I spit and said, "M", as I landed on my face. I could picture a white line flash across my mind.

"I can move my legs."

I squirmed my legs. I tried to move my legs forward, as I looked up at the sun in the sky. I urged my head forward a little, and then let this drop back down. I recall the ambulance men came and they put a neck apparatus around my neck.

What I was wearing on my feet blew off me. Like when someone is going 100 miles per hour and hits something, and their footwear blows off them.

When I got to Hospital a doctor said.

"Send him to x-ray."

"Hold your breath. Okay now exhale."

The x-ray tech said.

I was going through the procedure of transferring as if I couldn't move. They stitched up my face, which had a little laceration there. I was acting that I couldn't move my right leg. My uncle Joe Breen comes in and says.

"Let me see you move your leg."

I was made straight in I thought this was pretty serious not moving a limb. He said this with a bit of hesitation. I picked up my leg and moved this. He then said.

"How to go. I'm going to punch you in he face."

"Nothing seems to be broken, but we will keep you over night in hospital for observation."

One of the doctors said.

My psychiatrist arrives on the scene and asks me.

"Why did you do this Bill?"

"I was nervous about my baseball game."

He wrote this in my chart there. I would say to him.

"Are you doing better, are you doing better?"

I said to this shrink.

He wouldn't reply.

Then he said.

"We will get you out of here."

He said while trying to control me. I think he thought I didn't want to stay at the Norwood Hospital. I wanted to get out all of my anger of him in public. My relationship with him was built out of fear.

I saw my family doctor across from the room I was in, laughing with another person. I stayed the night at the hospital. I met a person whom was a colonel in Vietnam the next day. He was in for burns.

"I was a colonel in Vietnam."

I met this person in hospital while I was there overnight in the morning.

"More toast nurse."

"Okay, You are eating a lot of toast?"

"Ya, I am pretty hungry."

"I would smoke marijuana in the jungles of Cambodia in the jungles."

The colonel said.

"Weren't you scared a lot?"

"No, this wasn't to bad. I got used to this."

This person wore glasses. He was about 5'9" and medium built. He just stood at the door to his room.

I began to get a bit tense, because my old girlfriend Elizabeth worked at Hospital. My aunt Jenny came in to see me in the morning with dr. Stolt. I told Jenny to hold on to my foot.

"How is my lovey-dovey doing?"

Jenny would ask me.

Jenny was a nurse for practically 40 years at hospital.

"Grab hold of my foot and I will pull my leg with my head back."

I proceeded to do this also with my other leg.

"Ah, Ah, Ah."

When I pulled up my legs.

Dr. Stolt had read my records from the previous night. He was the doctor whom had handed the instruments to dr. Revel the surgeon on my back.

"You were nervous about your first baseball game. This is supposedly the reason why you went out the window yesterday."

"Ya, this is right."

I stated.

"When you play baseball again. I would like to watch you play."

"Good, I'll tell you if I do again."

"Can you be my psychiatrist?"

I asked him.

"I can't be a psychiatrist."

With preferable a chuckle he said.

"I thought that surgeons could be psychiatrists."

"What's wrong with your psychiatrist?"

"He would start laughing giving someone a physical."

He began to chuckle again.

I told him.

"The reason why I didn't talk to you when you tried me with the feeling pin, was because I thought I was dieing."

I also asked him.

"I heard you adopted six children"

I said to him.

"No, seven."

He said.

"How about a kiss Aunt Jenny?"

"Anything for my lovey-dovey."

She gives me a kiss on the cheek.

"What about me?"

Dr. Stolt asks.

She then kisses him on the cheek also.

I could recollect this floor when I was a patient with the back problem years before. I thought I like bounced out the window back then, and I then bounced up to this floor. The window would be opened wide, while I would be there, back then.

"There will be an ambulance to take you to this Boston Hospital."

One of the nurses says.

"We have a psycho over here."

This nurse was treating me nicely until she heard I was transferring to a psychiatric facility. She had her hair down to her neckline and was rather attractive. She would mosey on around the hallway. Now she would have a cutting to her voice, when she would say anything to me. A rather active pout I would describe this. They put me on a stretcher and I was wheeled out. While I was being wheeled out, I went by the outpatient room, and I said out of the sides of my mouth.

"This is God here now. This person can talk to me because he was a miracle recovering from paralysis."

I would say this rather loud and the people would look at me and discern at me as if I was half crazy and half sane. I was wheeled back out through Emergency.

I was brought to this Boston Psych unit and this wasn't quite a wonderful place. There was a little hallway with a television, and the barn like door, to force socialization. There were about 6 beds per 20 foot by 20 rooms. As I was brought there, a doctor very indignantly asked me.

"Why did you go out the window?"

"I wanted my name in the paper."

I was thinking I could get my name in the paper being paralyzed again.

"Send him to C-3."

This doctor replied.

The only person there whom I recall in the beginning was a person named Arnold.

"I have in my wallet a ticket stub from the 1946 World Series against the St. Louis Cardinals.

"Whom won the game?"

I asked him.

"The Red Sox 5-3."

He said.

"I also have a stub to Babe Ruth's last game when he played with Boston."

"Wow."

I said.

I recall there was a girl whom would sleep on a mat in the activity room. Someone had said she was insane. I was rather tense these first days there. I can recall there was a white female, whom got into bed with a black male one night. I decided the desire to memorize part of the Bible. The saying, which I remembered was, "Remembering without ceasing, your work of faith, labor of love, and the hope of the coming of our Lord Jesus Christ in the sight of God our father."

I would also stretch throughout the days. I remember these nights in Jamaica Plain, Boston. I would study the nights. I can recall about Frankie Boston, which was hot dogs and beans on Saturday nights. Electricity seemed to have nostalgia here. This might have been because at this hospital they gave shock treatments.

I would recall when I would go to baseball games at Fenway Park. I deduce when someone would think of Boston around the world, they would think of Boston Hospitals. In the hospitals what would come to the minds of patients would be, "night shift."

I can recall when I was here the last time I would eat my skin on my legs and feet. I thought the Chief had done this to his right leg, which he lost.

I had about 7 stitches in my face from when I landed on the slate from the leap of faith. A nurse said to me.

"There will be a doctor to take out the stitches in your face."

I wanted to be independent of the doctor to take out the stitches. So I went into the bathroom and began to crow bar out the stitches out of my face with my watch. I could recall I had stitches in my head after the first leap. I thought that once the thorns were out or the stitches, which I would analogize with Christ's thorns. That once they were out then there was the easy going or all downhill. I pulled the stitches out of my head the first time. Now I thought I had to do this again.

I can remember in the bathroom and the type of pounding pain, which I thought I had while crow barring the stitches out. I thought I was really feeling Christ then. They decided the desire to shackle me down after I tried to take the stitches out.

My uncle Henry whom had died on Christmas Morning 1965 had thrown a crow bar at some type of machinery and the crow bar came down and hit him in the head. There was ice on some type of machinery. He then died three days later of the head injury.

From here I began to think of the Boston Red Sox. I thought Tip O'Neil was the director of this hospital. I heard Tip said we are all Red Sox fans till we are 10 or 11 years old. I believe the reason why I thought of Tip O'Neil, was because a little while later I received a personal letter from Tip telling me to stay in close contact with our congressman Joe Moakley. I would get signatures for Joe's re-nomination door to door.

When I was shackled down I began to yell out.

"Boston Red Sox, Boston Red Sox, etc . . ."

When I would say this, I began to think about what this would be like to be a professional ball player. I would be in my own world when I would say this. I would think I was better than people. I thought I was a really serious ball player. I would just concentrate and concentrate on this. I would also say.

"I'm a Jesus Christ, I'm a Jesus Christ, etc . . ."

I began to think of the wall right next to my room. I thought I would have to go right through this wall to play pro ball. While I would yell this out, I thought years later when my uncle Henry was pinned down on the beach during D-Day, he would be saying Boston Red Sox, Boston Red Sox to himself, while pinned down. He probably would say this because when he grew-up he thought about the Red Sox, and if he were to get any help on the beach maybe the Red Sox.

Also he might have been saying real quiet like to himself on the beach, "I'm a Jesus Christ, I'm a Jesus Christ, etc . . ." while he was pinned down on the beach. I was actually hollering this out, but he could have been just saying this to himself quietly, on the beach.

I can recall when this particular mental Health worker came into the room. I began to whistle the tune.

"I've been working on the railroad all the old long days, can't you hear the whistle blowing Dinah blow your horn."

Well this worker began to say.

"Get some juice up here right away."

The juice would be what at this hospital means shock treatments or electricity. I also began to say out loud.

"Under below dive, under below dive, etc . . ."

I thought I was saying what people would say in the First World War for protection. They would dive into a trench for protection. I can recall when I was saying this one night then two mental health workers sat in chairs next to my bed and began to talk to each other. Them talking to each other seemed to chafe me. I had a flashback about when I began to cry at University Hospital on the spinal unit and two nurses were like talking to each other. I was so baffled back then I stopped crying

"I brought you in a submarine sandwich."

My *SISTER* Maura said one day.

She fed me the submarine sandwich because my arms were shackled down.

"I feel terrible. I haven't slept in three nights. They say I have hollered a whole night straight through."

I don't recall eating anything in three days. Because I was hollering so much, I wasn't responding to any of the meds they were giving me. They were thinking of calling my parents to have them legally amenable if I were to die. I think of the expression, stop. This would mean I would just control myself to die. Just stop. I could recall when I had heard the statement, "step alive."

This I thought meant the alive or the living would be stepped on as if God was stepping on them and they would be buried or stepped into their graves.

They said I hollered a whole night straight through. I can recall an injection they gave me of thorazine into my leg. This injection felt like a rock into my leg. After I had gotten out of being shackled down one of the patients there said.

"When I heard you yelling, I thought this was Judgement Day. When you were yelling under below dive, I thought this was a submarine submerging."

I think around this time the CIA Director Casey was to be indicted for something. This looked like an embarrassing situation for him. Then the next thing you know he dies. I think all of a sudden he had a brain tumor. Well I didn't die this time, but I was accepted to McLean Hospital. I thought maybe he stopped his life and I in return, was accepted to McLean Hospital. My way of paying back was Casey all of a sudden dieing.

I had been thinking about if I hadn't had the "door to door" salesman job and just went to study to become an engineer. Well I was subsided a bit when one patient came in. He was an engineer, which the Boston Police had picked up.

"They said I was a baby, so they brought me into the Hospital." This person said to me.

I had been thinking if, if, if, I had done this if I had done that. Well when I saw this engineer whom the Boston Police had brought in, I had begun to not think, if.

I could remember an idea, which came to me, if you had just hit the beach, and you were stranded on the beach. Would you want someone next to you on the beach whom looked beautiful or ugly?"

I can recall to play for the Boston Red Sox you had to change time. When I got the card from the Sox scout while pitching. I was saying to myself bring on Carl Yestremski. Now here at this hospital I thought of the Carl Yestremski play. This was when a person was trying to score from second base by a hit to left field. The left fielder scoops the ball up. I saw myself making a backhanded play against the Green Monster in Fenway Park in unreality. I had been on the field when I was about 9 years old and got a baseball.

I thought Jesus Christ was the earth, and everyone buried in the earth, goes to Jesus Christ. I can remember the announcement in the Lord's Prayer, "On earth." I thought this would be my land when I had thought my legs had gone to heaven. "On earth as it is heaven." "In boeland." I would say instead. My nickname was Boe.

I can also allay with the statement in the Lord Prayer, Thy Kingdom come. I thought about coming or reaching orgasm as kingdom come.

"Hi, I'm Gerry. I went to the school Notre Dame. Would you like a cigarette?"

"Ya."

I said.

I smoked the cigarette and my throat felt like a raspy chimney. The cigarette tasted very good.

"Do you like the cigarette?"

"Ya, this tastes good."

I smoked the cigarettes and this felt like furtherance. I was now waiting for a bed at McLean Hospital. I can recall there was a nurse whom took care of my stitches on my chin, from when I tried to crow bar out the stitches. This nurse was in hospital whites. I had asked her.

"Are you a regular nurse?"

She said.

"I'm both."

I had sentiment for what this is like to get real care and what you have to do to get that care. I was thinking all the hollering I had done to enable me to see a nurse in whites.

I can recall there was this really gorgeous looking girl working there. One day there, a girl patient, grabbed her necklace. This girl whom worked there, I would think when someone would be appareled in blue, I thought this girl whom was dressed in blue thought pink. I would think some girls like to be circumspect in pink, but this girl whom worked there liked the color blue.

There came a person on the unit whom was told to take his medication. He was standing next to the metal door. The psychiatrist asked him to come onto the unit.

"Open this door or I will put my fist right through this."

He also said.

"I was in the Green berets."

I thought about my pal Brian whom was a green beret around this time. I said out loud when this person was on the unit.

"Marines."

My friend Jimmy Sivad, whom was a marine in Vietnam, had told me the marines would fight the green berets. Jimmy was the person whom said back then. "You pitched a no-hitter?" Jim had told me the marines would street fight the green berets in Nam to get ready to fight the Vietcong.

I went to the café one day with my sister Judy whom was in to visit me. I really thought time had changed. I think now when I went out the window again this was like time repeating itself. I thought I had to be like perfect to get out of this hospital.

When I had been hollering out at night, a patient came in to talk to me. He thought they the staff there were really doing something to me, because I was hollering so long. Well he said to the staff.

"I have friends, I have big friends. You are going to hear from my friends."

After a few weeks I got into an ambulance and went to McLean Hospital. I felt I was like blinded. This would be like the hot sun after running sprints. When I got there I met two doctors whom were doing the interviewing. They had asked me a few questions. I told them.

"I will show you how I talk out of the sides of my mouth."

"This person can talk to me because he was a miracle for recovering from paralysis."

I stated.

One doctor couldn't control himself and he began to laugh. The other doctor looked at him and kind of like said in his head stop the laughing.

I was brought to the Bowditch Cottage and into my room. I can recall I had wrangled with this doctor whom projected to the other doctor to control himself. I might have said something about Harvard and Yale. I talked to this doctor also about the card I received from the Boston Red Sox scout.

I can remember the first few weeks here I would do exercises out back of the Hall. I also began to do an outline of my life as if I were writing a book. I would exercise about 20 minutes three times per day. I would go to the Café each meal. I was put on lithium at the Boston Hospital because they had cogitated I was a manic-depressive. I was also on haldlold I believe. They just put me on the lithium only and I was supposedly psychotic because I didn't make sense. They could tell I wasn't a manic-depressive then. I could recall the only thing I remembered on the lithium here, was my administrator dr.Tray South said to me.

"You think you are making sense."

Also I can recall when one of the nurses there said to me.

"Think about what you are going to say before you say this."

One day I asked the head nurse if I could give a speech. She said okay. Her name was Shelly. I thought about the statement I had made up, "decided the desire." There were a few patients here whom went to Ivy League schools. I thought of giving a speech.

I gave the speech as I would spell out the letters D then e then c then I as I was spelling out "Decided the Desire" in the air. Then I said.

"Decided the desire whom is the most prettiest girl of them all?"

Then I would say.

"Betty has worked in nightclubs."

This was one of the girl Mental Health workers. She had sung in nightclubs before she worked here. I would play Kitty Whist on the weekends with her. I remember one of the younger girl nurses there left the lecture area when I spoke. She left when I talked about Betty as the prettiest girl. I think looking back at this I was doing fairly well here by giving lectures.

This statement, "decided the desire," I had written in my journal on Robby 7. I can remember when I thought of whistling. Meaning how high a pitch you can have. I really enjoyed playing Kitty Whist on the weekends.

I thought I would do my college here at McLean. I later thought of the song, "The way I do." by the singing group Breath.

I would go jogging around the hospital, and also I began to lift weights. There was an MHW whom skipped his senior year in high school and went to Brown University. He went to Brown early. I went running with him around the hospital and when I sprinted the last 100 yards, I went into one of these spells. I went into my room and I began to do sit-ups. One thing about these spells I would do a lot of work with my stomach.

This person from Brown told me he did research of how pills can be annexed to people's brains. I thought possibly the only hit of acid I did, years before, might have affixed to my brain. And this was what was causing these spells. When I would be in these spells I would have energy for doing exercises like sit-ups. When I was in the spell after jogging, the Brown man came to check on my room, and I made contact with this person and the spell went away.

There was a lady named Linda Axel whom came into the hall and asked me some questions.

"Why did you come into the hospital?"

There was a questionnaire, which she was filling out.

"What goals do you have?"

"I would like to be able to study again."

I then asked her.

"Can I have a kiss?"

"No."

She said.

I was thinking how I was on the Intensive care unit at Norwood. I had asked the nurse back then for a kiss. The nurse said no then also. I was beginning to have flashbacks about the physical and mental conditions.

One time I was coming back from the café and I got into one of these spells again. I went into the hall and took five mgs. prolixin PRN. Medicine taken as needed. I walked to the Admissions building and I began to hear the squirrels and birds and also I would look at the patients. I thought I would pick up the characteristics right there on the spot from these people. I was at the portal of the Admission building when I went back down and hit my head on the stone ground. I felt like the soldiers whom had come to take Jesus to jail, and the soldiers supposedly fell backwards.

I then went to the hall and rang the doorbell. One of the MHWs came to the door and I fell backwards again. One person held onto my right hand and another on my left and I got up. I went into the hall and I got into bed. I tried to go down and bang my head on the floor. I wished I had done this when I went partially out of bed, the second time, at the Norwood Hospital. When they saw me doing this they brought me to the room where they shackled you down.

While I was shackled down I thought I had to go through what I went through when I was paralyzed in fright years ago. I thought I was on the parallel line in the Korean War. I was like hearing whistling sounds as if shells were a coming. I began to try and go up on my neck. I would do this when I was on the wrestling team. This was like trying to get out of a pin. My eyes began to scan up into my head. I would try to sit up and say like I did on the spinal unit on Robinson 7. "I'm a Jesus Christ."

When I would go back up on my neck, my eyes were going up into my head. I would arch my neck back and my eyes would begin to go down, as I would just about try to go up on my neck. Thinking of this now this reminds me of when I was at Norwood and I began to pull myself up out of bed and I was just about going down when the nurse came in and pulled me down. Then I was thinking of Brown University. Now I had the person from Brown University here. Maybe connection.

I began to think of all the people whom might have been in this room shackled down throughout the years. I thought McLean Hospital had some kind of pact with Bridgewater State Hospital, which real bad cases went there. I would also keep on saying also.

"Boston Red Sox, Boston Red Sox, etc . . ."

There was a Lithuanian worker from South Boston whom also had been a medic in Vietnam. His name I believe was Joe. He was there helping me then, since I was half Lithuanian. I can recall one MHW named John came into the room and I told him.

"Loosen one of the straps, I want to scratch my nose."

John loosened one of the straps and I slapped him across the face. He then got my right hand and shackled this back down.

The pain was coming from my eyes, as I was tied down. I believe this was about 5:00 AM the next morning when I finally fell asleep. I slept for about 2 hours. When I was awake at about 7:00 AM, I had the feeling I thought I got, when I banged my head on the ground the day before. This was like a hollow sensation in my head. I thought all the suffering I had done the night before, was worth this, for this sensibility I experienced in my head, for the about 6 or 7 seconds upon awakening in the morning.

In the morning I had two dropped eggs. I think I went back to my room later in the day. There I continued to write. After a few days I began to look up into the corner of my room. I was thinking about when I was at Norwood Hospital in August 1975. I thought then an imaginary machine gun had put me out of my misery, up from the corner of the room back then. I began to yell out.

"Maggie, Maggie, Maggie, etc . . ."

This was the name of the machine gun I wanted to put me out of my misery again. I recollected when I was at the Norwood Hospital and I thought about a machine gun putting me out of my misery. I think this was part of an up I had created for myself by yelling out Biblical names.

I asked for artane, which they gave me. I also tried to hypo-ventilate. Well they shackled me down again and the spell left me. I felt secure being tied down. I can recall the next morning I began to sing the song, "Please Come to Boston." I then again went back to my room a day or so later.

Another few days later I got into another spell again. My sisters came into visit me and they told me my grandfather had passed away. I then yelled out.

"Glory to you oh God, Glory to you oh God, etc . . ."

This time I was shackled down again and I tried to break the straps. This time I thought the straps were Billy Kold's arms. The PT I had at Norwood. I also this time began to yell out.

"God, God, God, God, etc . . .

Then after a while I yell out.

"Help, Help, Help, etc . . ."

Supposedly McLean didn't believe in medicating people. I think because I said help, help, help, this made them think I had something very serious. A person came in and gave me some medicine. When I got the medicine I sat up like I did on Robby 7 when I said then. "I'm a Jesus Christ."

Then dr. Train had given me something, after the Chief had told her too. Now I was put on a shot of prolixin and this stabled me. Into come to see me was a dr. Eloc. He came in chuckling while he spoke. I had come down with Tardive Dyskenesia, which my jaw would rock from side to side.

"Hi, I'm dr. Eloc."

"Hi."

I said.

"Why did you go out the window?"

"I was trying to paralyze myself."

He said something like.

"You got to be serious."

I think he wanted to have something in the psychiatric field because this was his specialty.

I also told him.

"I was a paraplegic."

He said.

"I thought they don't recover."

I said.

"Some do."

He was like chuckling and this first time I saw him I also began to chuckle along with him in jest.

"They asked me to come here because they noticed movements in your jaw."

"I don't notice anything."

"I'll be bye to see you later in the week."

He was a big jolly person with a big belly. He would try constantly to get me to laugh. A week later he comes by again.

"How are you?"

"All right."

"How is the dyskenesia?"

He asks me.

"This seems to be bad right now. I didn't notice this before but I do now."

"Well the suggestion of this can bring this on."

"We will begin to videotape you. My research assistant Patty Van will be bye to see you. She'll be in to see you in a few days."

When I saw Patty I told her my orthodontist whom was in World War 2, I will see about my jaw. I thought I could only trust people whom were in some kind of war.

The first time I saw dr. Eloc I did chuckle along with him. The second time I didn't when I spoke with him. Then when I saw him he talked about the research drug he would like to try on me. I asked him.

"Were you ever in the service?"

He said.

"I was in World War 2 in the infantry for a few months. Then I was called back for the Korean War where I was a psychiatrist there."

I was saying to myself he must have been able to handle the crazies in the Korean War. I thought I did like the guy.

"We are going to transfer you to the Intensive Care unit East House and I would like to try a research drug on you."

Dr. Eloc said one of the next days.

I said.

"Bye Shelly."

I said this to the head nurse of the old unit as I left. I had quite a bit of emotion when I said this. I thought I had scored with her. I thought the pain of going out he window was represented in the way I had said "Bye Shelly". A reason why I think I was transferred to Intensive Care was because I was giving speeches at this Hall, which I left.

"Good night."

Shelly replied.

I was relegated to the Intensive Care unit of the hospital called East House. Here, as I was coming onto the unit I saw about 6'4" 250 lbs. man coming towards me. He said as he held out his hand.

"I'm with the welcoming committee."

I then shook his hand. He later introduced himself as Julio Somoza, the son of the Nicaraguan dictator. Well I shook hands with him, before I even knew whom, he was. I had thought in the past I wouldn't shake hands with people because I didn't want to talk to mental patients. So I was glad I had responded to his handshake.

I began to use my left hand instead of my right, which I had started to again. I began to get acclimated with the littlest of pain.

I was in the room with just a mattress and blanket and dr. Eloc came in and sat down on the bare floor.

"I would like to try this research drug on you named Inderal. I'll give you the papers on this."

He told me.

"I thought I would see action in the Korean War, but I was a psychiatrist in Japan."

He thought he might have been a surgeon like on Mash.

I said to him.

"That's like action talking to mental people during the war."

"I don't know."

This person was very jolly and had a big belly and he would begin to chuckle on his closing statements.

"There will be my research assistant Patty Van whom will see you the first two weeks every day. Then periodically after this."

"Where was the Inderal first researched?"

"Over in Israel and then England. I'll see you in a week or so."

I was started out with 80 mgs. Inderal my first day. His research assistant Patty Van came in and asked me.

"How much inderal are you on?"

"80 mgs."

"How do you feel?"

"I feel really no difference."

"Well they will check your blood pressure and pulse twice per day and possibly increase by another 80 mgs."

"That sounds good."

I replied.

"I'll see you tomorrow."

And she left.

I was beginning to feel different here at McLean. I thought there might be hope. I could possibly over come this problem. The next day Patty came in again.

We exchanged greetings.

"Did your physician increase your propanolol?"

Propanalol was the chemical name for inderal.

"Ya, another 80 mgs."

"How do you feel with the increase?"

"Maybe a little better. My jaw isn't rocking as much."

We were sitting down on a couch and she seemed calm and cozy. I was feeling good that Patty liked me a bit, and she would come close to me. I always felt people in the mental health field, especially girls, wouldn't get close to me. But she was different. Maybe she was getting big bucks.

My physician was dr. Tray South whom had come from the old hall to do a resident here on East House. I had asked him on the old unit." When you would study at Harvard did some people begin to yell in the dorms? He said then. Some did.

Patty came in one day and said.

"Ya, I noticed your jaw not rocking as much. The propanalol is supposed to be good for the dyskenesia."

Into come into the room next was Dave whom was in charge of the jogging group and the weights.

"Bill would you like to join the jogging group?"

"Ya, sure."

"We have a track behind the gym for jogging on Mondays and Wednesday and then on Thursdays I will drive you to a track in the van. There is a little track behind the gym."

There was a little track out back of the gym, which I believe seven times around was a mile. I had initially started the weights before I was transferred to East House. I had to stop, because I had the shackled down problems on this unit. Never mind lifting weights but getting off the unit was the problem.

Dave had said I had stopped lifting weights. I thought I had a good enough excuse of I couldn't leave the unit. I thought at times when I would yell out, and Billy Pt and Claude would respond at Norwood, then Dave would come when I would yell here at McLean.

Dave said.

"You will have to sign a contract you will be punctual for the jogging group in the mornings at 8:00 AM."

"All right."

I said.

Dave was bitter about how I had stopped lifting the weights before. I thought he felt the weights and the jogging were more important than the psychiatric.

"When you jog, you should feel your body as you jog. Take down your pulse after you jog. Then mark this down in your jogging notebook."

"Okay Dave."

Dave was a Vietnam Veteran from Boston College. I was thinking the way I felt when I had Billy at Norwood PT. I would put out. I would be on time in the mornings no matter how tired I felt. I wouldn't let the side-affects of the meds from being tired use as an excuse for not being on time in the mornings. I wouldn't want Dave to think I wasn't tough. I had told Dave before I signed the contract for why I was late before.

"If they gave you strychnine, how would you feel?"

But now signing the contract there were no excuses.

"Hi, what's your name?"

I asked a dark haired girl.

"Carla Somoza. Yours?"

"Bill Breen."

"I'm in the jogging group."

"Me too."

She said.

"I took myself off of an anti-depressant by myself."

"Good for you."

I was thinking these Somoza's were political prisoners here at this Hospital. They I think were paying cash. I heard they had billions in Swiss Banks. I thought I was going to be in this hospital a long time. I began to think this would be a community for me. As if this was a small town here.

I didn't care too much for the jogging in the mornings, as I would have a very obscure time getting up. I would drink enormous amounts of water every day. I thought water was created for some special reason and I did not mind consuming large quantities of this.

"Barry."

I said to this about 6'2" 220 lbs. man.

"Mr. Breen."

Barry had grown-up in my hometown and had joined the Marines during the Vietnam War. He told me he wanted to go to Nam in the jungles. But they told him. "You want to go, you don't go."

"What brings you in Barry?"

"I was in the Quincy Shipyard chemical explosion. I went down after one person and he was just like rubber. I went into the hospital after this and lost 30 lbs. I was going to kill the doctor for not letting me stay out of work, when he said I had to go back. I said to myself I better get some help before I kill someone and end up in Walpole State Prison."

"I think this was a wise move you made Barry."

"Ya I hope so."

"Where are you living now?"

"I own a house in Plainville. You going over the café?"

"I don't have the privileges yet."

"I'll see you after dinner."

He *SAID* and went to the café.

There was one night on the unit, which I remember distinctly. Barry and Julio were in the television room with a few of the other patients. There was some music on and I started the show. I began to walk lifting my right leg up and down, and as I walked my head going back and forth. Julio did his West Point walk about facing. Barry went into the bathroom with both knees together as if he really had to take a mean leak. I then did another walk and this really got Julio charged. The patients and staff were laughing, as the show had to go on. Julio began to walk a rather slow way and I couldn't detect what type of walk this was. So I asked him.

"What type of walk is this Julio?"

"Eagle."

He said.

"I couldn't tell this."

I replied.

"Ya, this is a casual walk with a little swing to the arms, with a stiffed neck"

"Oh."

I said.

In Christmas time I wanted to go to all the units and sing Christmas carols. But they wouldn't allow this.

Julio was a big person about 6'4" and 240 lbs. He once told me he was a strapped down to a bed and he got up and walked with the mattress strapped to his back. He was what I would call a master of words. He had gone to West Point in America for a few years.

They were slowly but surely accruing the propanalol. I would have my blood pressure taken twice per day, before I received the propanalol. One nurse there Debra, I could recall she would put my arm up against her breasts when she would take the blood pressure. I was having a flashback of when Nancy my PT would put my legs up against her breasts. Now the nurses here would put my arms up against their breasts. This was something I would look forward to in both circumstances.

Debra was about 5'7" and had long black hair. She was about 27 years old and had a rather nice body.

I didn't think about giving speeches here as I did the other unit. I thought this was one reason why I was being transferred. The old doctor I had on the other unit I think felt bad about how I wasn't helped there, so he was now doing a residency on this unit. He was the reason why the propanalol was being increased without hesitation. I can recall when I was coming back from jogging and this was raining out. This doctor saw me in the hall tunnel all soaking wet.

"Your soaked."

He said.

"Ya, I wanted to get the jogging in but I was caught in the downpour."

"I'll unlock the door for you."

"All right."

Said I.

I saw a smile on this doctor's face, which reminded me of the song by Stevie Nicks. "When the rain washes you free you will know." He had a smile, which was one of prolonging helping on his face. As I said earlier I had asked this doctor do they begin to holler in the dorms at Harvard while studying? He said. Some do. He like most of the doctors here went to the Ivy League schools. My pals whom went to the Ivy League from high school I missed very much.

I began to do more while the propanalol was being amplified. I began to lift weights. I can recall one day when I had lifted weights and my legs felt like rocks. I began to punch them. Usually my legs would be painful if I hit them, but this time they seemed like rocks. I thought of the show the Hulk, when the Hulk was paralyzed and he slowly got back strength and he began to punch his legs.

I can recall one night when the movie One Flew Over the Cuckoo's Nest was on. When the part of the show, when they were acting cheering, came on for the World Series, I began to cheer also.

"Come on Tommy lets get a hit."

I said kind of out loud.

"Ya come on Tommy, you can do it."

Dean the patient there said.

"Ya, let's get a hit."

Another patient said.

"Give them the heat pitcher."

I said.

"Ya, let's go now."

Dean responded again.

"Come on Tommy."

I can recall this attention I was getting interfered with one of the MHWs there. I was getting quite a lot of attention now, and the MHWs didn't like this. I thought they tried to get me to stop getting the attention of the patients. This type of attention was interfering with these MHWs. I thought maybe the Red Sox might have called the hospital to see how I was doing.

I had begun to play the guitar here. I once played for one of the nurses. I sang a song for her as I played the guitar. I thought I did very well with this girl. I think I might have even scored with her. This was the first time I ever played or sang for a girl. Even if you have something wrong with you, you still can score with girls by playing an instrument and singing along. I was thinking of getting a big book of songs at Harvard Square to play from. I was that much advanced.

There was a girl whom one day gave a lecture about composers. We were in the dining room and she began to speak. I began to whistle like I would when I coached baseball, as to get a lot of attention. This girl tried to ignore me when I was whistling. These people have really big egos.

I had stopped playing the guitar when I got a job at a Nursing Home in Medford. I was a Rehabilitation Aid. I would give physical therapy. The job was going all right. I had stopped the guitar and lifting the weights, because I was commuting to the job during the day. I came off the shot of prolixin and I was just on 1440 mgs. propanalol per day. I wasn't on any psychiatric meds at all. I started this job part time then I increased to full time after about one month.

This girl whom tried to give the lecture, I continued with to learn the guitar more. She completely had me learn a new way of strumming. I didn't like this. I thought she was trying to get back at me for when I whistled in the dining room, during her lecture. I didn't care too much for the new way, so I stopped playing the guitar.

When I would need things, which had to be unlocked from the MHWs, I would say things like, "Hey checks, hey checks here." This was what they called the MHW's workers. I would say this as if I were the concessions at the ballparks. They would say at the parks, "Hey ice-cream, hey coke here, hey peanuts." I begin to think anybody connected with the Red Sox organization they take care of you. The Red Sox were helping this way here in the hospital.

I had started smoking cigarettes around the time I began to see dr. Jon Elec. He would smoke like long tipirillos with an extension to the cigarette. At the Nursing Home I was trying to stop smoking. I would smoke about a pack per day. The people at the Nursing Home, I had told, I lived in Norwood in my apartment, instead of the hospital.

I recall I went to a restaurant after work one day. I saw one of the MHWs' there while I was eating. He gave me a look when he saw me eating there sitting down. This was where a lot of the workers would get food while on break. I don't think he liked looking at me now here, as both of us were customers.

I began to drink water as I was coming off the butts. My mind began to get watery. I had told the administrator at the Nursing Home I had sought professional help. I had gone over my immediate authority. I was under the Nursing Home's insurance. I was let go from the Nursing Home.

My immediate supervisor told me the reason why I was let go was because they couldn't take any chances on law suits and also I didn't help one of the nurses when a patient had fallen. When I had an appointment with my psychiatrist this evening, I was out the door after the session, and I told him I lost my job, and he shut the door in my face.

I began to get a milky mind. I thought from all the water I was drinking from trying to stop smoking cigarettes. I hadn't told anyone I was let go from my job. The next day I finished out the job. I had their insurance at the Nursing Home, but I didn't use this. This last day I was giving the pt I began to say to myself, Physical therapy wasn't sequential. I began to be no longer interested in Physical therapy.

When I went to my vocational counselor after work, I had begun to put my bottom teeth out. I had an under bite when I was younger. The counselor had escorted me back to the hall and I was put on prolixin pill form. Dr. Eloc also increased the propanolol by 40 mgs. "So he won't go psychotic."

When I was coming back from this setback I had gotten my football helmet out of the trunk of my car, and I would go out jogging with this. As I was leaving the hall one day to go jogging I would put the helmet on. I can remember when a staff member looked at me with the helmet on, and he looked like he just saw a ghost. He would have a cracked awe about his face. As I was relinquishing the hall I saw another patient there. He asked me.

"Are you going jogging Bill?"

"Ya Will."

Will didn't have any expression on his face at all. He was a person whom had been going to Harvard Medical School and had gotten pretty down in the dumps from something, which shock treatments and meds didn't help. I heard they were giving him meds, which would make him feel worse, so when he came off of them, he would feel better. The staff was the patients and the patients were the staff as I had on my football equipment. I was bringing equipment in.

There was a patient there named Earl Lincoln. He was about 55 years old and had been a patient on East House for 15 years. He was a millionaire and he paid cash for hospital. He every so often would get into a rage and would attack one of the nurses, as he would attempt to strangle them. He wasn't actually a perfect physical specimen, but the nurses would need a male staff to calm Earl down. I can recall one day talking to Earl in the entrance lounge.

"How long have you been here Earl?"

"15 years, I'm a turnip."

Earl I muse was a lifer. He was someone whom would be in the hospital the rest of his life. He began to get out and take walks when I was there. He might have been like someone paralyzed whom began to get out after a very, very long time. Years later I would meet up with a person named Booth. This was Lincoln and Booth during the Lincoln assassination. They were still fighting here by names.

There was one patient there whom wanted to talk to me. I told her she could for a dollar. She gave me a dollar and I spoke to her for a short time. After this the staff cut back on my privileges, until I gave the money back. I told them I wouldn't give the money back. I think the staff was jealous someone would pay to talk to me, and cash on top of this.

My $150,000 of insurance was running out and I went to a General Hospital in Somerville, Mass. I remember there I ran into hard times and I would yell out.

"Christ, Christ, Christ, etc . . ."

I had antecedently yelled out Jesus, Jesus, Jesus, then God, God, God, Now this time was for Christ, Christ, Christ, etc . . . I had read in the Bible anyone whom calls on the name of Christ shall be saved.

I was doing quite a lot of reading here at this General Hospital. I would walk downtown Somerville during the days.

I had grown a beard after getting out of the hospital. I would recall back when I grew a beard after I got out of the Boston Hospital for the back problems. Now this was time to grow another beard. I thought then, you grow a beard after you get over hard times. One day I drove home once and the tears began to come down again, just like they had when I came home for the Thanksgiving game in 1975 from Boston spinal.

Chapter 7

Rehabilitation two

When I got out of the hospital I called up an old girlfriend Paula.
"Hello."
Said her mother.
"May I please speak to Paula?"
"Paula was married three months ago. Whose is this?"
Her mother asked.
"Bill Breen."
I replied.
"Your one of Paula's old friends. How are you?"
"Fine."
I came back with.
"I will tell her you called."
"Bye."
"Bye."
After this I tried another girlfriend whom I had.
"Hello, May I speak with Janis?"
"She is not here right now."
Said her mother.
"Whose is this?"
She asked.
"This is Bill Breen."
I responded.

I felt rather awkward, because I was self-conscience about being in a mental institution. I said Bill Breen with not too much confidence. I was rather ashamed.

There is this old saying which I remember writing down years ago. This is by Phillip Brooks. "Sinning Clandestinely," is the name of this. This goes like this. "To do nothing, which one might do at noontime at the Boston Common: To keep clear of concealment, it's an awful day when there are eyes which should be avoided, subject to be feared to be talked about. The bloom of life is gone when this happens. Keep that day off forever if you can."

This quote is how I felt exactly. I was embarrassed about having gone out a window. I couldn't talk about this to anyone. I was deeply ashamed of this. Just embroider this feeling and this is the way I can explain how I felt when I said Bill Breen to Janis's mother.

I went to my fifth year reunion. I can recall a girl there named Mary whom I will never forget the way she treated me this night. I can recall when she gave me a couple of kisses. And I will forever be beholden for the way she treated me this evening. She mentioned to me not many of the people there had changed. She was a Rhode's Scholar from Dartmouth University. I met a person I give the nickname of "Boston." He said he was in Medical School and he was studying hard.

I was living in a halfway house in Brighton, Mass. I was here for 6 months. I took out a six months membership to a YMCA there in Brighton. My old apartment I had given to my sister Judy and then my brother Jackie also moved in there. Jack was going to Boston University for his Masters in Physical therapy. Judy was getting her degree at UMass Boston.

I had been hearing about my older brother Jacks escapades playing rugby. I didn't think rugby was like other sports. There was no equipment like in football. My brother Jack had visited me once at McLean back then, when there was a MHW there, whom Jack knew from rugby. I could recall at McLean in the café when I was declaiming with another patient there, and I said about the rugby MHW.

"That person is really tough."

I saw this MHW look at me and like say in his head, this person thinks I'm tough.

I had been out of hospital quite a while and I thought I would give rugby a try. This was August 1981 I recall. My brother Jack's friend Tom N. was on the team. I got a ride to my first practice with him. He I believe was a little hesitant about driving me there. As we were driving there Tommy began to say.

"What kind of meds do you take?"

"I take pills which they call prolixin."

Then he said.

"Those pills you were on before were just getting you sicker and sicker."

When he said this I could detect he might not want to be seen with me at the practice. We got to the practice and the first thing we did was stretch. Then we went for a jog. I began to think the jogging was like in football when you would, "jog it to the fence and back."

I can recall the next drill we did was tackling. The player in front of YOU would be carrying the football when the person behind him would tackle him. We would practice laterals, as we would march down the field. I can recall the scrum. This is when both sides are pushing each other while they are crooking over. They would be competing to get bridle of football. I could recall my legs were feeling like security mushy feeling, like they had stress. I was really putting out. The name of my position in rugby was fullback. I had made all-stars in football as fullback. Now I was a fullback, fullback. I was having a little trouble with the laterals as you had to lead the player on each side.

At the end of the practice we began to run sprints. We did about 50, 50 yards dashes. I recall I read in the Bible the psalms, of the apostles before going there. I thought this was like food or drink. I was being nourished spiritually.

I can remember running the sprints and I was thinking of the piece of paper, which I received from Harvard University with the possible acceptances to this school when I applied there. I thought maybe still possible. After practice I was talking with my brother Jack, his friend Tom, as well as another friend Joey A. A feeling of embarrassment came over me. I was still playing sports. This was a feeling of self-conscience, which I had to combat while playing rugby.

I can recall in the scrum when my legs were pass the point of pushing, and I still had to do more. They were pass the point of no feeling and still had to do more. I can also remember after running sprints when I put my arm behind my lower back and arched my head back. My brother Jack when Tommy told him about how many sprints we ran he said.

"50, 50."

I thought that my chances of recovering were maybe 50, 50.

The second practice there I drove myself. I had gotten an orange freezes with Tommy after the first practice. This second practice I recall I had to kick the football like in a punt while running down the field. This was like football when I played when younger. After this practice I could recall driving by the Veterans Hospital and I said to myself I loved myself. This was only the second time I said this to myself in my lifetime. I can remember I looked like an ugly Marine. My face had an ugly look about this, from so much physical exertion. I was thinking of going in the hospital the night before the first game. But the folks I was talking to professionally said this is an indicator not to continue to play rugby. I could recall a dream I had around this time. I dreamt the Norwood High hockey team was skating sprints on the river down South Norwood. I dreamt the river was frozen and the team was skating there. I had in high school asked to be the Manager of the hockey team, but the coach I think said no. I'm not sure though.

I also recall then, I would write over the words I wrote, in another pen, of my diary I had of on Robinson 7. I would write over the words in another pen.

I saw dr. Eloc after playing rugby. He talked to me quite seriously and said.

"Do you like running?"

He said this with a lot of feeling as if this wasn't good to run. I felt I was in contact with him then.

"I feel better after I run."

I replied.

"Ya, this can be helpful at times."

He said.

He had his eyes closed a bit as he spoke. He had an incongruous tone of voice as if he were a controlling person.

I got a job at the William Carter Co. in Needham Heights, Mass. I was storekeeper in the storeroom there. My job entailed filing requisitions, mail, power jacks and other duties of the storekeeper. This was an assiduous job, as the challenge was there everyday. On the interview I told a person named Roger. "I'm hungry Roger." My boss was Roger whom had worked at the mill 40 years. He came down with arthritis after I had worked there about 4 years. I once said to him.

"Roger, did you ever hear of alfalfa?"

"You mean the little rascals?"

He said.

"No, Roger, alfalfa sprouts for arthritis."

I said.

"Oh no I haven't."

He had thought about when the little rascals were on and there was the character alfalfa. I had given him an article on alfalfa for arthritis, which my aunt Mary had given me.

This was every morning getting up for work, while taking all of these medicines. I can recall I thought of the time I did rigormortis and this kept me carrying on. I had to make sure I was on time. I thought dr. Eloc whom was a psychiatrist in the Korean War had me like rushing. I think folks in the military knows what this means. All the meds I was on and this wasn't so easy.

I began to go to a satellite college in my hometown. I was thinking realistically I would get my associates in Engineering. I was in my third semester and I had a lot of momentum for getting my associates and then a girl I was seeing at Mass Rehab changed locations from the Norwood Office and left. I had said to her I wanted to go to a good school. She had told me the school I was going too, was the school she went to. So I thought she was quite upset and then decides to change locations. I began to feel different at this school and I decided to stop college. I deep down inside thought I would be back to sales. But I was saying to myself a salesman doesn't need college, but I thought I would get the degree anyways. But the girl I was seeing left and I fell apart a little. I even think dr. Eloc increased one of my meds a little bit.

Dr. Eloc was monitoring all of my medicines. I was seeing a psychiatrist also. I was talking to this psychiatrist one day and I said to him.

"Your beautiful."

He said.

"Thank-you."

I would always talk about how this was good to look bad, or ugly. This psychiatrist said thank-you. I think he went suicidal after this. Would you believe this, he even would drink beer while he was giving therapy. He must have gone suicidal. I'm thinking now that the reason why this is in this book. There was one time when I was late seeing him and he had left. I was about 20 minutes late and he had left this night. When I asked him the next time I was here 20 minutes late, he said he had waited. Then was the time when he had shut the door on my face when I lost my job. I went on the psychotropic medicine after this. I did ask him if he could monitor my medicines and he said no. He I was paying straight money to just to talk to. He would charge me for his walking time to the unit. Whom else could I talk too? I overly trust people.

I started a second job on Saturdays with an arborist. Most of the work was done in Brookline, Mass. This I did with my pals Jimmy Sivad and Joe. I needed the money. I can recall one night when we were coming home in the bucket truck and Jimmy said.

"I stayed up till 1:00 drinking last night."

"Gee Jimmy, those days are gone for me. I have to be in the crib by 9:00."

Said Joe.

Joe was about 6'2" and about 220 lbs. He was quite a big person and hardy robust. Jimmy was the Marine in Nam and was one tough dude. He had two children from his wife. He drank quite a bit and when he would be a feeling it, he would talk about the war. He was the person whom I wrote about in the beginning when he said. "You pitched a no-hitter?"

I would go to my aunt Lucy's house to eat English Muffins and have a cup of tea every Saturday, before I was picked up for the tree job. I would look forward to this very much so. I would begin to talk about what happened to myself with my aunt Lucy. I think she was one of the first people whom I talked about what happened to me outside of the doctors.

I had started seeing a new psychiatrist dr. Negirl. When I saw him I came up with the idea of standing guard outside dr. Eloc's office before I saw him. This was like a guard would stand outside of wartime doctors when they are seeing a psychiatric military person. I think this is for, if the person really has trouble, to help the military psychiatrist.

One day when I was at Carters' I was talking to Ralph and Tom. These men were about 50 and 55 years old respectively.

"I saw a Christmas tree walking up the street the other day. A person was carrying this. You couldn't see him behind the tree."

"What color was it?"

Said Tom.

"It was green."

I stated.

Ralph had a hard time controlling himself. He was chuckling away.

"Did it have presents under this?"

Tom asked again.

"It was dark. I couldn't tell."

I said as I was already prepared to say that it was dark out.

Ha, ha, ha, etc . . ."

Ralph was still trying to repress himself.

The tree job on Saturdays was manual labor. I can still feel my lower back pushing those tree trunks up in the truck. Wow, was I strong. "I was as strong as I could be." I picked up one tree trunk and this must have weighed 300 lbs. When I was walking with this, Joe said there were people around there, watching whom said.

"Look at that person."

Joe then picked up one of those tree trunks and tried to walk as far as I did, but he couldn't. My legs were vibrating when I was walking with these tree trunks.

After I had been working this job for two years around 1986 Jimmy got a bad back and had to stop. Joe and I would go to the jobs. I remember how we would psych each other up for work.

"We are going to hit the beach today."

Joe would say.

"Guadalcanal."

I would say.

"Anzio."

Joe would say.

"We were pinned down on the beach."

I would say.

"Chosin Reservoir. They are coming at us from all sides. The Chosen Frozen."

Joe would comment.

We would keep an undeviating face and be serious about this, because some of those trees were mighty big. I would stop by a store on the way home from church after my Carter's job on Friday and get roast beef for sandwiches on Saturdays. The roast beef wasn't very good but this would make sure I didn't get too high at lunch, because there was more work on Saturday afternoons. This became a good habit, which I started and I would regiment myself with being fecund. I would always tell Joe when getting into the truck, "Let's have a fruitful day."

"Storm the beaches of Normandy."

Joe would then say something like.

"Ya, we were pinned down on the beach taking shot after shot. But we got up."

"We were pinned down."

I said.

"Fix bayonet."

Joe said.

"The heroic bayonet charge."

This was a controlling learning job as we were joking around but serious. This actually seemed to help the work go by better.

I had gotten an apartment and this is why I had to work on Saturdays. I started a job of bringing a book cart around volunteering at the Veterans Hospital. This was an escape from a hectic week. I would have piece of mind here at the V.A. West Roxbury, Boston. I can remember the books, which went the best, were the Westerns. They went like hotcakes.

After a while of doing this I began to keep track of the floors, which would take the most books. I would check off how many magazines, hard covers, or paperbacks each floor would take. I came to the conclusion the people whom did the most reading got better more.

I went to my tenth high school reunion and this wasn't so great a night. At the end of the night I was a little nervous so I was thinking of leaving early. I saw the girl Denise, whom I told you I would see her, with her too become husband, at the semi-pro baseball games. Well when I was nervous, I thought a lot of people knew this. Then I heard this girl Denise say.

"That's Billy."

I knew I had done the physical and now when Denise said, that's Billy, this gave me faith I could also do the mental. I will always be grateful to Denise.

I would enjoy going to church at the 5:15 Mass each day. This also was an escape from a hectic day. I can recall saying the rosary while I would be driving anywhere. The Monsignor would always have finesse when saying the mass. I loved church, as this was a life savior for me up against the stigmas I was up against.

I can recall I was talking to the Monsignor one day.

"I pray I go to hell."

I said to him one day.

He smiled a bit and was caught off guard.

"Why do you do this?"

"I've done a lot of bad things."

I responded.

He was chuckling a little bit now.

"If there is any place worse, I think I could end up going there."

He said something like.

"He is a forgiven God. You can be forgiven."

After talking to him, I think I stopped praying this.

I met a girl named Patty at church. She was attractive and I felt good about where I met her, at church. I really didn't think this was too good to meet a girl at work, too easy. Well we would go out after church and get a bite to eat or coffee.

I was seeing her quite a bit and I felt comfortable being with her. I brought her to my apartment one night, and we talked a bit, but nothing much more then. I then began to think of furniture. I had an old couch and chair and this wasn't too cool.

I went to her apartment one night and I was devising this could be some night. We were sitting down on a small sofa and listening to the radio. I then put my arm around her shoulder. Everything was going smoothly. We *WERE* conferring comfortably.

She began to talk about people she had dated.

"I once dated this person whom turned out to be an engineer."

"Your not supposed to talk about people you have dated." I said.

"Well I am going to anyways."

Then I would get a quick kiss off of her. I would get some more quick kisses off of her, as we would exchange some good banter.

"I also dated this person whom turned out to be an alcoholic."

"I'm like an alcoholic. I take pills."

"What kind of pills?" She asked.

"Propanalol, this is a research medicine."

"I take vitamins, but I don't take any pills." She said rather forcefully.

I could tell now I was on the defensive, and I had to try and patch up the situation. I removed my arm from around her then.

"Ya, this is a research medicine. This is mostly used for heart patients."

I was trying to have her think I wasn't totally crazy. But I could tell the night had come to an end intimately. I was self-conscience about being on the propanalol never mind the psychiatric medicine. I thought I might become panicky, but a great calmness came over me and I stayed in control.

"Let's open our presents." She said.

This was right before Christmas. I got her a scarf, and she got me some scripture tea. I left after a short while and this was a sad night. I was self-conscience about being on the propanalol.

The next time I saw her she said.

"I want to hold off dating anyone right now, as this had been only a year since I had gotten divorced."

Now I really felt this. I didn't know what to do. I just sat down in my apartment and opined what to do next. She went out to California to visit her mother whom lived there. After this I began to look at girls at work. The girls Wendy and Randy attracted my attention. I would talk to these girls sometimes at lunch break.

I asked this girl named Trish out for a coffee one night. We just talked and nothing became of this. But she was a very good friend in the future. Whenever I would see her I would feel very good.

I was talking to the men one day at afternoon break and I was talking about how I was on the Math team in high school.

"I have a lot of math on my job."

Wayne said.

"Do you like the math?"

I asked him.

"Mediocre, I don't mind this once I get started. But it is just getting going at this which is difficult."

"I enjoyed math in high school when I was on the math team."

"You were on the math team."

Billy Star said.

"Ya, I was a backup. I didn't see any actual action, but I was ready."

I stated.

"Wow, did you have an injured brain?"

Billy Star asked.

"No, I was a reserve."

I said.

"Ha, Ha, Ha,"

Everyone was chuckling a little.

"Injured brain and didn't see any action."

Said Wayne.

"Ya, I didn't see any action. I was a back-up."

I repeated again.

I had also been talking about how I was captain of the football team a bit. As well as my math team comments, Harry said.

"You had to watch him when he carried the ball."

They didn't chuckle, as much because they must have known to be on the math team must have been a serious person.

I worked at Carters' practically six years, and on my final months there in like April 1987 I began to coach Babe Ruth baseball in Norwood again. Before this I had a vision in a dream. This vision came from above if I remember correctly. I have an on the spot analysis of the dream in my diary.

I called up the President of Babe Ruth baseball in Norwood. His name was George Hey.

"George, this is Bill Breen, is there any teams which need coaches?"

"Do you have any experience?"

Asked George.

"Ya, I coached right after high school and this was with the 13 years older. Then I was with Bill Tunning and the 13 and 15 years older."

"Well I'll see if a coach might need an assistant."

"Good thanks."

Well a couple of days later, George called me up and said.

"You can coach with the Indians. Frank Camp needs an assistant. His telephone # is 769-4460."

"Thanks George."

"Bill maybe you might want to coach in Walpole?"

This was the town I moved to.

"No."

I said when George asked me if I wanted to coach in Walpole. I had lived in Walpole for about 4 years. I knew the fields from coaching Babe Ruth in Norwood right after high school. I would really make quite good scenes as I coached then. I thought I would think about back then coaching to get me through the games and practices.

I called up Frank.

"Bill Breen, Frank, I got your number from George. He said you might be looking for a coach. Are you?"

"Ya, I graduated with your brother Bob."

"Really?"

"Ya."

"Bob Breen has been in Utah for quite a while now. He drove out there about 7 years ago on his motorcycle and hasn't been back since."

I said to Frank.

"All right Bill. We are going to have the draft for the baseball players. Mostly the thirteen years older, just starting out. This is on the 11ᵗʰ of April, at 10:00 AM at the Balch Field"

Frank said.

"I'll be there."

I said.

Well this was about 4 days later, and when this came I was quite contrived. I would go into the church before the games and practices to say some prayers. At the draft this was about 40 degrees out and my hands were freezing. I told Frank.

"We'll put 3 checks for really good players, 2 for a mediocre player, and 1 for not too good. Okay Frank?"

"This sounds all right."

Frank.

The children were batting, throwing, and fielding. I started to think about how the children were so enthralled about playing baseball. They had so innocent faces.

"3 for him, 2 for him, 2 for him and 1 for him."

I said to Frank.

"You think so Bill?"

"Ya, I think so."

I said.

I could tell Frank opinioned this was good to have me as coach, because my experience in playing baseball would trickle over to coaching. We would have practices at a field, at one of the Junior Highs in Norwood.

We went to the draft where we would draft the baseball players. I was a bit nervous, as I hadn't seen too many people from Norwood since I was living in Walpole. All the coaches showed up for the draft and we drafted all the players. I was thinking back to the vision I had seen and I believed in this very much so.

I went to one of the first practices and I would think about how to get all the boys arms and bodies into shape. I recall I met one of the boy's mothers.

"Hi, I'm Phil's mother Marian."

"Hi, I'm Bill Breen."

I could tell English was a second language for her. Her son had an under bite like how I had when I was younger. I kind of took a liking to her son because of this.

We had practices for a few weeks before the first scrimmage. I can recall I would use my left arm for throwing balls to the players. This took a little bit of courage as you had to be accurate or you would look foolish.

We had our first scrimmage at a field where I reminisced about when I was younger coaching. Back then I had given one of the coaches a forearm to the shoulder. This had been on the first base coaching side when I had done this. This seemed I had more confidence coaching when I would think back to when I had attention coaching, right after high school.

In this game we were winning but they came from behind to beat us 5-3 I believe. After the game I gave the team a speech. I was thinking of Knute Rockne whom had coached at Notre Dame. I said to the players.

"We had them on the ropes. We shouldn't have let them come from behind."

Well as I was leaving the field I began to get a bit anxious. The coach of the other team had parked his car near the field on an old road. I began to think when I was at UMass Amherst and I was running sprints while the UMass Team was practicing. There was a car parked in a parking lot, adjacent to the field. I thought then this person whom had the hood of his car opened and was doing something to his car. I thought then this person had been a heroin addict. And fixing his car was like fixing himself. I think heroin addicts needed, "fixes."

While I was running sprints back then I had thought before you could play for UMass Amherst you had to puke by running sprints to make the team. Then while I was running sprints I got something to come up from my throat. I thought somewhere along the way, the baseball players grouped together out in the fields while there was batting practices, were like "cows," while they would talk to each other out in the fields. They would be like grazing.

I walked away from the field as a Babe Ruth coach. I was a bit suspicious. I then went to my apartment and listened to some music. I also called my grandmother up.

"Grandma, I'm scared."

"What's the matter?"

"I don't know grandma. I'm just scared."

I would see grandma every Saturday night, after work at both jobs. I would look forward to seeing her and she I think looked forward to seeing me. I thought this was like after a man would have a hard week and then see his wife. As I got better my grandmother I think knew what to say to me over the years as I worked. She had come over from Lithuania in 1913. I always liked grams, not grams as in cocaine grams.

I was sitting down on the kitchen floor as I was talking to her. I can remember these days coaching, I might have been a father figure besides their coach to these players. There was a parent of one of the young boys whom would say while his son was pitching, "from the wrist." I wasn't sure what to make of this. I began to think of people whom cut their wrists. I tried not to get too concerned about this.

There also was the father whom had a cab company in Norwood. To this I would say to our team. "No towel Indians."

I was thinking of these young boys and the young children I would see when I assisted the physical therapists at the Mass Hospital School. The effort involved by healthy children couldn't compare with the efforts of cerebral palsy, muscular dystrophy, spinal bifida, etc . . .

One boy, whom was pitching in this game got up to bat as I was coaching first base. He got a hit and he began to run down the line to first base. He tripped about 5 yards before the base and fell. I thought this person had just about begun to run with finesse. Well he went to the ground and he had something wrong with his ankle. I hollered to the bench.

"Two Indians over here right now."

The name of the team was the Indians.

Two boys came over and they helped this boy to the bench. His mother brought him to the hospital to be x-rayed and this was just a sprain. I had earlier in the game had this person come out from pitching and I said to the fans in the stands.

"How about a round of applause for this young man?"

They all began to applaud after this. I was telling all the parents what to do.

We had a game and all the boys began to get out of control and I thought there might be a little scuffle. I took a deep breath and then hollered.

"All Indians on the bench right now."

The all moved like secret service agents guarding someone. I then said to them.

"I don't want any tom foolery here. You've come to play baseball and this is what you are going to do."

They were all on the bench silent as they were passed being in awe. They were now embarrassed a bit about the scene they had made.

I can recall one game when we didn't have a catcher, until one boy named Scott said he would catch. Well the game went on and he came over to the bench and said.

"Coach, I can't catch anymore."

He got on the bench and began to cry. His father came down from the stands and said.

"He threw-up."

I looked at the player and said.

"You were the only one on the team that wanted to catch tonight."

He began to sob more now. I knew how to hit these children's sensitive points. I could recall when I was at McLean Hospital and someone told me back then, if you make someone suffer, they will like you. Places where you suffer, you like the most.

The next game someone in the stands I heard say something like.

"Who is really Scott's father?"

Scott really began to like me after this. Scott became a real good hitter after the night, which he caught. I could tell he had prodigious new strength in his legs. I had him run backwards, to offset the range of his legs running forward. I told the whole team to run backwards so I didn't single out Scott. This person was the grandson of the house next to my old grandparents in Norwood.

I had been having a salary cut at work and I told them I wouldn't work with a salary cut. My boss Roger told me I wouldn't have my annual increase in pay, because I was being paid for lunch. I said.

"I thought this was where I stood with them."

"You don't get paid for lunch."

"Then why was I paid for this?"

I asked them.

"We made a mistake."

"I don't get paid for fixing Roger's mistakes."

Roger had told me his daughter was very ill once. He said she went down the local hospital. I told Roger maybe she was kidnapped. Roger said that his son whom was a psychologist thought she should get married as soon as possible.

They wouldn't pay me so I wouldn't work. I was supposed to get my yearly pay increase but they said I wouldn't because I was paid for lunch when I shouldn't have been paid.

Well anyways I stopped working here. I went to work with a local friend, whom had an arborist business full-time. This was Mike. I really enjoyed eating the sandwich at lunchtime, at the afternoon break. I can recall one of these days I had scrapped wallpaper off a wall with my left arm and I really thought I was working.

When we had a Babe Ruth game one of these days, I parked my car a street over from the field we had the game at. I was a bit nervous thinking I wasn't working quite steady as on my old job. So I told Frank, the other coach, I didn't feel too good and I was leaving. I got into my car and I began to drive to my apartment. Then while I was driving I thought I would go back to the game. I got courage to go back to the game.

Frank asked me.

"Where did you go?"

I told him.

"I went to move my car."

This was really feeling. I don't recall how we made out in the game.

The last game of the year arrived and I got a little wild. I started the theory of routing for the other team while their batters were getting up. I even let one player bat from the other side of the plate. When I would cheer for the other team some of the other players would also rout for them. I would tell them the other team was *ICE CREAM*. The other coach Frank was playing in some kind of softball league a field away.

I thought years later when the first Gulf War was going on President George Bush had like asked me in my mind what were we going to do when things didn't look good. I thought I mentioned in my mind we should hope the Iraqis win. I was thinking when I was watching the Boston Red Sox against the Chicago White Sox at Norwood Hospital in August 1975. I would usually cheer for the Red Sox, since I lived in the Boston area. But this time I began to wish for the other side. So I thought this strategy for the Iraqis War.

This last game our first and second baseman were throwing rocks at each other. At least this was what the umpire said. I was thinking last game of the season, have a little fun. I don't know if the two boys were bored or what. The umpire had declared the game called on account of the boys throwing rocks.

The president of Babe Ruth happened to be in the stands and he said he would umpire the game from behind the pitcher's mound. The game had ended and we had a vote for whom, would be the most valuable player. After the vote, I discovered this wasn't necessarily the best player. The person whom was chosen was the most respected by his peers, when they would be hanging around together as friends. Not school or sports but outside these perimeters.

In one game during the year one of the boys had been in a fight and there was this almost little riot. I had told him and everyone else to get on the bench. He was the only one to be in the fight. His father later said. "I'll take my son out of the game." Years later when I moved back to Norwood I began to think about these boys as their coach. I never wanted to lose their respect, as you and they are getting older. This person whom was in the fight was Paul. I thought about this person years later.

I was looking for employment after the salary cut here. I went to a Pearle Vision in the Dedham Mall. This was in the next town from Norwood. They had given me the job and I was an optician trainee.

I worked there my first day about two hours to get acquainted too. I was at my first day of work and I was talking to my supervisor.

"Hi Michele."

"Hi Bill."

"I called up your job references and they told me you were on medication, you wanted to be paid for lunch, and you left without a notice. Your boss Roger told me this. We have decided not to hire you."

"You already gave me the job."

I said.

"You'll get paid for the day you worked here, but I can't let you continue working here."

She said.

Well this job was short. I had been doing the tree work while I would be looking for employment. I was on call. This job cutting down trees was really working physically. Mike would call me when he needed help.

I decided I would let the Pearle Vision and Carters' situation pass. I applied for a job at the Stop & Shop warehouse in Hyde Park. I decided not to use Carters' as a reference. I succeeded in getting the job as a data entry. They had told me to call them a few days later. I decided I would by pass the call, and go there in person. I told this to them, when I went there in person after applying. And I did get the job.

In years later with the situation in Afghanistan looming in 2002 we were wondering how to combat against the Afghanistan situation. They would send a person by foot to deliver a message. These people didn't use a walkie-talkie, but a person whom would run to deliver messages. I came up with the idea also in mind that we, instead of using the walkie-talkies, we should drive the message by car or by jeep.

I was thinking I would give this job everything I had, as I would awake at 4:30 in the morning to be at work by 6:00, bright and early. This dawned on me. I would wake up so early I would see the sun rise. Also I would be having my 4:00 o'clock tea.

On the terminal at work, I would close out the day by saying.

"The Lord God Jehovah is All Powerful."

The two girls in the main board would also say this.

"The Lord God Jehovah is All Powerful."

I can recall when there was a lot of work to be done and we worked till 9:00 PM. There was roast beef for the men. I can recall I had come out from eating the roast beef, which had been shipped over from the Frozen foods section at about 5:00 PM. I had gone down early for the roast beef with the supervisors. As I was coming up the steps I can recall all the selectors say.

"How's the roast beef Yook?"

"Ya, Yook."

The selectors said.

"The Lord God Jehovah is All Powerful."

"Ha, ha, ha, ha etc . . .

They all began to laugh crazily. I felt at a new level of awareness and I began to have a different outlook about the selectors. The selectors were the men whom would use the power-jacks to pick up the pallets of the food for the tractor-trailer trucks.

The name I gave these Bostonians was Yook. The statement, The Lord God Jehovah is All Powerful, was a voice I heard in a dream one night. In the dream I recall there was a ray of light, which I thought went around the world. "Coming around again." Carly Simon.

As I said I would awake at about 4:30 every morning. This was a battle every morning. I would fight every morning to get up. I can recall one morning when I thought about when I had fought for my life at Norwood when my uncle Joe had given me the family prayer to me. I thought like I was being pulled up from above. But this time I was upright doing this. Like I had when I was the sophomore running sprints in basketball.

Stop & Shop had a Christmas Party at the old Chateaux D'Ville in Randolph. I went there and all the managers from all the Stop & Shops were there. I was a bit nervous when I got there but this descended after a short time. I recalled our senior prom was there and I had exemplary memories. I sat with some folks from another part of the warehouse. There was one girl whom was sitting next to me.

"What is your name?"

I asked her.

"Lorna. Yours?"

"Bill."

I replied.

"I work in the flower section of the warehouse."

"I work at the main board."

I stated.

"How long have you been working there?"
She asked me.
"Since July."
I said.

I had dinner and I danced a few dances with her. As I talked with her, I felt a little bit trepid, because she seemed to be in the driver's seat. When I would dance with her I would dance on my heels. I thought I could correlate this to my supposed physical and mental problems. I thought these people here like didn't think mental problems counted. That is if you had mental problems then you should fight instead of taking medicine. If you ended up in jail then this is this. I thought the people at Stop & Shop didn't think there was any real thing as mental problems.

I talked with this girl a little bit, but she didn't seem to be interested in me as much as earlier in the evening. I left the party and as I was driving home, I thought seriously about this night. I thought I might have had a drink this night. I went home and went directly to bed.

At work when I would go out back for the spice orders, I would point my index finger up in the air. One of the workers there would say. "Back to the front." As if a soldier was being sent back to the front in a war.

I would have about a half an hour ride in the mornings and I would listen to the radio in my car. I wouldn't default listening to the radio, when I would get out of my car to go into the warehouse. You could say. "I had the radio."

I can recall one day at break during work, I was talking to head of the department Eddie Dur.
"I have a B.A. from Boston College."
Eddie said.
"Ya, I have an associates from Mass Bay College."
Donna said.
"I have a MD from Harvard and a PHD from Yale, and a BLT from MacDonald'.
I said.
"Ha, ha, ha, ha, etc . . ."
Everyone except Eddy was laughing. Later Eddie commented.

"I almost went insane when I heard this."

I would still do the tree work on Saturdays and this was a very assiduous week. I tried to psych up the selectors with the strategy Joe and I would do on Saturdays. I began to talk to the selectors this way. These as I said, were the men whom would go around with the power-jacks to pick up the food orders for the tractor-trailers trucks.

"Guadalcanal Jimmy."

I said this to a selector and he smiled quite a bit.

"Anzio Fred."

"Ya, sure Yook."

Said Fred.

"Chosen Frozen Kevin."

I said.

"Ha, Ha, Ha,"

Kevin laughed.

"Pork Chop Hill, Mike."

"Pork Chop Hill Yook. You were there."

"Sure you are all there."

I responded.

"Storm the beaches of Normandy, Yook."

Dave said.

"Right you've got the right idea."

"Hamburg Hill Steve."

I said, as I would give them an order to do with their power-jacks.

"I don't know what he is talking about."

Said Donna.

Donna was a girl about my age whom worked there. She had grown-up in Hyde Park but moved to the suburbs. She had a nice figure and she was street smart. She was about 5'6" and such and such a weight. I had a little social contact with Donna. I guess Donna didn't like this way of motivating the selectors so I put a lid on this. I can also recall I had tried to cut back on the prolixin by 5 mgs, when I was talking to the selectors this way.

I remember one person whom worked here named GG. He was a World War 2 and Korean War veteran. He had worked at the warehouse

34 years. I can recall when I was sitting down with him and I thought of all he had done and I got up and said.

"I can't sit here with you."

One day he came into the Main Board and said.

"Do you have your pink papers?"

I had been talking about how I received possible acceptances from Harvard and Brown Universities. Here in a Boston City warehouse when someone would say, do you have your pink papers this would mean putting up a fray before going into a mental Institution. In a healthcare setting working pink papers would be considered bad, but in a Boston City Warehouse this would be considered normal.

I was going to church everyday after work and I really enjoyed this. The priests were very smart people. I can remember one night at church and the lights went out there. I blessed the monsignor when he was blessing us. I would use the blessing signals as a way of praying, when I would stretch. I had blessed one of the priests one night, in the chapel at Mass. I did this without even thinking.

One of the priests name was Fr. Water. He wouldn't do all of the proper gestures when he would absolve himself before reading the Gospel. I tried this once and there seemed to have something go wrong with me this day. If he blessed himself properly, he could feel good anytime.

One of the supervisors from South Boston would read my paper everyday. This got to the point if he didn't read this, then I would feel bad. I think you might call this taking. This was so normal of him reading the paper, if he didn't, I would feel bad. Just a little bit, of Southy.

I can recall one night when the monsignor was speaking, to try and get money. He was the best one speaking to get money from the congregation. He mentioned the word sustenance and this hit a spark with me. This means to give to the point of hurt, and you will be rewarded if you do this.

I was waking up at 4:30 every morning and there was always the question if I would be able to get up in the mornings. I also began to stand on my head in the mornings and nights. I was having Tt or Mt or Pt. I would call Mt mental therapy and Tt or or cross therapy. I would do this and this was quite painful. I can recall kicking my legs against the wall when I would really begin to hurt. This was a way of coming down so I would get tougher. I can also recall I would have my most fruitful writings when I would write forthwith following when I would get up in the mornings.

I remember at work when one of the supervisors named Ron said to me.

"You cross one of those selectors and they will slice your tires. I'm not kidding they will do a job on your tires."

Ron would read scripture at the local prisons. He knew what this was like to be a hell raising, when he was younger. H would be a good volunteer at the prison.

"So watch out what you say to those selectors."

On Saturdays I would sometimes volunteer at a Playhouse in Walpole where I now lived. I had auditioned for a play on the stage before this. This was just reading a part of a play. I had gone there and was sitting down quietly. Then the director came over to me and asked me.

"Do you want to audition?"

I said.

"Yes."

The director had seen me sitting there. I was haranguing to myself, why not have a productive night, while I was there. I got up on stage and I felt comfortable. There were two girls on stage also. They I recall had tights on. I felt a great calmness and I read the script perfectly.

Well I didn't get the part but I began to do volunteer work there sometimes on Saturdays. This was putting up the curtains and also doing a little carpentry work. I can recall one actress there whom was also getting the stage prepared and said something to the extent.

"He talks a lot."

Not in a affronting way but in a caring opinionated way. I was doing a lot of talking while I was working. The actors and actresses were very nice and this was their second occupation at nights and weekends.

My grandmother passed away in February. I can recall before she died, I began to think I was like her husband coming home to see his wife. My grandfather had died in 1959. My grandmother lived all these years after. When I got the Stop & Shop position she would tell me, "scare'm Billy." She knew the right word at the right time.

I saw an ad in the Boston paper for coaches for the Boston Park League. I called up.

"May I speak with Don?"

I asked over the phone.

"This is Don."

He said.

"I'm Bill Breen. I am inquiring on the coach's position in the paper."

"Ya, there is an opening. We have practices in the Prairie in Boston."

He also said.

"Where is the Prairie in Boston?"

"This is off of Mass Ave. in Roxbury."

"Where about off Mass Ave.?"

"Do you know where the Howard Johnson' is?"

"Ya, I do."

"Well take your left after Howard Johnson, then take your first left then straight. Then you can't miss the field."

"All right."

I ended with.

I went to the field and spoke with a Don Illen. I saw one of the players whom had just taken batting practice. He looked to be around 22 or 23 years old. He looked like he had a good time batting.

"You hit the ball good today."

Don said.

"Ya, you did look good."

I said.

The player then went out into the field.

"How do you think you can help the team?"

Don asked me.

"Well the pitchers I know of a technique in which to throw faster."

"That's good."

Don said.

I talked to Don for a while, and then got the time for the next practice. I returned for the next practice and the weather was a bit drizzly. I can recall I went there while I had a cup of coffee. Also I had an umbrella. I was up for a cup of coffee and an umbrella. The practice was called short because of the weather. I was thinking two things then. One, I thought I had a connection with Roger Clemens as I tried to be the skipper here. Two, I thought about Brooke Shields with the umbrella.

I got Don's telephone number. I got Don the next day.

"Is Don there?"

"This is Don."

"Bill Breen Don."

"Yes, what can I do for you?"

He said.

Right around then I coughed. I don't know why, but I did.

"I would like to know how much the coaching position pays?" I asked him.

"There is no pay for this, but I own a lumbar business which you might want to buy something there."

Don said.

"I thought this was a paying job?"

"Well if you are not interested now that's all right."

Don ended with.

"Ya, all right."

Then I hanged up.

This would be going into Boston three or four nights per week. This would be quite a bit of time also while working, averaging ten hours per day. I would have to get paid to make this a worthwhile adventure. I decided the desire not to coach without pay. I tried to be the skipper for a very short time.

At work one day I can remember there was a lull in the orders. The selectors were gathered together in bunches with their power-jacks. I would holler out to them things like.

"Spread out a hand grenade will take you all out." Or I would say.

"Keep moving. It is harder to hit a moving target."

They would all begin to chuckle.

When we would get the orders so they could go back to work, I would signal them with my left arm. They began to unwind a bit because they were averse about coming forward, but they did.

There was one day when I was talking to the Insurance person from personnel. I went to his office once and he wasn't there. So what I did was, to do a little detective work in his office. I looked over his records in the back of his office for about 20 seconds. This person was in charge of the insurance for the company.

I would come home from work after church at about 6:00. I would work my computer each night. But for some reason I was being detoured to work with the computer for about 5 days. Then all of a sudden I found a disk in my apartment. On this disk was my book with quite a few changes. I don't know where the disk came from. I think now with the name of my book, "By Bill," maybe there is some higher power, which made this disk appear.

Also I can recall one of these nights, which I was detoured to not use the computer. I thought the world was going to come to an end one night. I thought there was going to be a nuclear War and the whole world was to be destroyed. So this night I thought of going to Rhode Island, when I thought there was to be the end of the world. I drove to Rhode Island and I pulled up to a police car and asked the officer.

"Is there anything on tonight?"

He said.

"No, nothing I know of."

Then I went to the police station and asked them there if anything was happening. They didn't say anything though. So I called my own number up at my apartment. Then I drove home. I thought this was the end of the world. Right around this time I found a disk in my apartment. One of the statements, which was on this disk was, "A body in motion tends to stay in motion."

Chapter 8

New Testament

This is my journal from Monday July 25, 1988. Today work was up and down as usual. El came back from work and she is very pleasant. I had a better than average day today. When I got back I moved my bowels some, then I turned on the radio and went again. I'm thinking back when I saw the Chief at Mickey's funeral and he had a big chest. I think about what Joe said on Sat. pump. Then when I got real horny yesterday and I felt that my erection was pumping when I would look at the playboy book in segments. When I think of pump I think about when then people in the trenches in the First World War would pump out the water in the trench. I had a dream the other day about the people whom put me in bed at the Norwood Hospital and I felt like the crowbar out the stitches in my face all the time. That thick pounding pain. Then what Lev would say pound on them.

I have a thought that all the people that have suffered like the real Jesus Christ when then they would be past the sun and only people that are Jesus Christs' are alive. The dream had only few people living ax if.

I went over Casey and went out the window in front this was rather fast and quick. I said hello-e while I was in mid-air flying and then I saw and turned my head. I landed on the left side of my face. When I hit bottom I could picture a rather puzzle of a crack going around my head when I landed. I did this so quick that I felt no pain. I had earlier gone around Oldham and this got me ready. I raced into the house after and I was like running real quick. My right arm. I went into the bathroom after talking to jack. Then I went out the bedroom window downstairs. I crawled right out. I feel my head rather hard and strong. I had my talk with Jack-o. I yelled out Jack-o a couple of times. I went down the cellar then came back up. I took and this I had to wonder if it would work. I watched tv and then I felt better. I a quite tired now. I also took. I feel better now. Hello-e.

This all started when I turned on the radio and then I began to think of the night Aug. 1, 1975. I was very restless and I was thinking of sleeping on the floor. I thought about how I wasn't injured permanently the first time. I also thought of the dream I had with no sun. I recalled this dream and I did the same thing in reality, go out window then go into bathroom and go out first floor window. This dream was when I came into bathroom said. "I missed you Bill." I was going to go out right side of window then saw or someone coming down street in car. I came back out window and, "He might help you." I then said. Then a young boy took a right turn in his jeep.

Back to real. This night had the feeling I should do what I thought because this was like another command from God. I thought if I didn't do this then things would be worse. I drove over Casey and went upstairs and said a few words to Jack-o. I went into my old room and got in the place where I had gotten the command in 1975. I then got something in me, which meant to go out the front window. I opened the window and I felt I was real strong and I went out the window without any hesitation. As I was going down I said in a soft tone of voice, "hello-e." I was going to say e the third letter spelling out America this time but out of my mouth came "hello-e" I then had looked down as I opened the window but I don't remember as I was going down. I thought of turning my head to the right and I landed. I could picture a rather cracked star of white, and I felt for an instant like I had when I went out of bed at the Norwood Hospital. I did not feel any pain going down. No fear whatsoever. I then got up as quickly as I could and I raced into the house on the side choppily. I think sometimes I saw my uncle Henry whom had died, appear and he was walking up the steps. I then came back into my body and walked right through the doors of the house. My right side of my body felt like my left and left right. I can recall going up the steps like a person who just had arm and leg transplants. I could feel a rather line that separated my right side from my left. My legs were achy also. I can remember looking at the radiator after I walked through the doors. I went into the house and sat down in the dining room. Jack-o came down and told me to take what the doctors say to take when I get this way. I told him I take prolixin. "What do you do when you are like this?" Said Jack-o. "I'm supposed to take prolixin." I said. "Well take it." He said. My lip was swollen and bleeding from inside. And I had a shiner on my right cheekbone. I was looking at Jack-o as we talked and I felt he was a person whom only thought about making himself feeling the best he possibly could. I then drove back to my apartment. I had gotten the phone and I was thinking of calling dr. Eloc. I had even pressed the numbers on the phone, but then I decided not to call him.

Well a few days later I had been to work. There was a girl whom was working in the main board with me. I slid her a kiss. I gave her a wet one. I sometimes call this kiss a, "slider."

Then I said to Dave Too Tall in the Main board.

"Why are you giving him a bad order?"

I said to David.

David was person also whom, worked in the main board. He had given a bad order to a person on purpose. The selectors would have different sections of the warehouse to pick up the stock. They would be very bitter if they got a steel order or cans, which were very heavy to pick-up. When they got like paper towels these would be a jocund order, because this would be light to pick-up.

Well the boss David said to me after what I said to him.

"Just shut up and do your job."

"You can't talk to me like that."

"You want to bet. Just shut up and do your job."

I went out of the main board and told the selector what happened with the order. I went down the break room and spoke with the head supervisor Bruce. David came down after a few minutes.

"What happened?"

Bruce said.

"David gave a bad order to a selector on purpose."

I said.

"It's none of your business what I do."
David said.
"I'm the third person to complain about how David treats his help."
I said.
"I can treat my help anyway I like."
He said.
"It' isn't any of your business what he does to the selectors."
Bruce said.
"Well maybe, but I've heard that people with drinking problems like treating people badly."
I came back with.
"Drinking problem? I don't have a drinking problem."
He lashed out.
"He is a confirmed alcoholic."
I said.
"Confirmed alcoholic? I'm not an alcoholic."
He came out with again.
"You've said you were an alcoholic plenty of times at break."
I said.
"I was just kidding. You didn't take me serious."
He said.
"Well you do have alcohol on your breath sometimes after lunch, and you are always talking about drinking."
"I want an apology. I'm not going to work with him till I get an apology."
Dave said.
"I'm the third person to complain about how David treats his help. This must say something Bruce."
I said.
"You have to apologize to David before I let you work."
Bruce said.
"Well maybe I was wrong about the order incident, but I'm the third person to complain about how David treats his help."
"Take the rest of the day off."
Bruce said.
"All right."

I said.

One of the workers, whom brought the big orders to the office said one day.

"He has booze on his breath." about David.

A few days before this had taken place I had applied for a supervisor position. I was turned down though.

I took the next two days off of work and when I came in the third day I felt the wind movie stars are supposed to feel while walking. I could feel waves of wind as I walked into the warehouse. I walked in front of the main board and got a drink of water. When I came back to the break room Donna told me.

"You have to resign or I have to let you go."

"I can't resign Donna."

"Then I will have to let you go."

After this I asked her.

"Did I see you in a truck?"

She gave a smile and said.

"No."

I didn't realize this till later, but if I were fired then I would be eligible for the cobra insurance. If I resigned then I wouldn't be eligible. I should have looked into this better. The cobra insurance I think is good 1 and ½ years after being fired. They never had sent me the information about the Cobra Insurance, which I didn't know anything of then. This is the Law they have to send you information for if you want to continue with the Cobra Insurance. But they didn't.

From here I went to Electrolux in West Roxbury, Boston. This was the Roslindale branch of Electrolux Boston. When I got there I saw the woman Lorna.

"Hello, I'm looking for some bags."

"They are $19.95."

She said.

I then saw the manager whom said his name was Don Stroke.

"Does Faster still work with Electrolux?"

"Ya, he has a store down Plymouth."

"How about Sullivan?"

I asked.

"Ya, he has a shop in Framingham."

"And Koster?"

"He has a store in Wellesley."

He retorted.

"Ya, I worked with them when they had the store in Norwood years ago."

Before this I had gone to my aunt's place in Wareham. This was a good place to think. I had come back from there and I went to Electrolux. I had filled out an application at Electrolux. Don looked this over and after a day or two asked me.

"I couldn't find the telephone # of the Stop & Shop reference you gave me."

"That should be the right address in Hyde Park."

I said to Don.

I didn't use Stop & Shop to call up for reference. On the application with Electrolux they had a question. "Did you ever resign, or were you ever asked to resign from a position? I forget but I think I might have answered this no. I could recall when Donna had asked me, if you don't resign, I'll have to fire you. I had told Donna. Donna I can't resign. I thought there might have been some kind of connection with what Donna had asked me, and the question on the Electrolux application.

I was being trained by a very smart person my first day on the day soliciting on doors. The first house I knocked on I said.

"Hello-e, I'm Bill Breen. I work with Electrolux, We have invented a new vacuum cleaner called Discovery. Would you like to have a free demonstration?"

I asked this house dweller.

"I'm not interested in a demonstration, but I do need bags."

She responded with.

I then got the bags and came back to her house. As I was talking to her, she mentioned.

"My husband is a lawyer at the Dedham Court."

I gave her the bags and I felt I had made my first commission on the first house I had knocked on. I did the "door to door" first in Dedham.

The word hello-e, which I had made up when I had the secret flight I would use when I would knock on the doors.

Don had told me to call up homes from my apartment from the telephone directory for the local towns. I began to get interested in the secretary repair girl Lorna. She had very nice looking breasts. She had about a 36-24-36 figure with medium length black hair. She would wear corduroy pants and she looked gorgeous. I thought her nose was a bit opened too much. This was the Electrolux store for the Roslindale branch in Boston.

There was a Frenchman named Louis or something another. He had come up from New York to work in the Boston area. I heard him say one day. "I'll fix it myself." I thought he meant, he would get me better by himself.

I was talking to the salesmen one day and we were talking about pro-ball players. Don said something like.

"I would like to have their dough."

I said to him.

"It's so easy to play baseball. They can't appreciate their money."

"Are you serious?"

"Baseball is easy. Do you think this is difficult to run around?"

I responded.

I thought Don would look at baseball differently, after I had talked to him about baseball.

In a way this was like sex therapy by knocking on doors and talking to housewives. I can recall I was knocking on doors in Canton and a woman came to the door with just a negligee on. I began to really think about the position 69 after this. She really aroused my interest. I was drinking a lot of liquids during the day, because this was a side-affect of the medicine I was on.

I can recall I had my first demo in Foxboro. This girl worked at the local dry cleaners in my hometown. I had been drinking quite a bit of water. I went into the home with my vacuum cleaner equipment. Her vacuum cleaner had been broken and I had begun to put down dirt, which I had gotten from her unclean rug back on the carpet. I must have put 6 or 7 pockets of dirt on her rug.

I would say to her.

"My vacuum cleaner picked up this dirt."

I then showed her the demonstration with the metal balls.

"This vacuum cleaner has this much suction power, one ball, two balls, and three balls."

This person had a water heater and I was sweating quite a bit from all the liquids I drank. Also I was a little bit exigent about my first demo. I began to think about the lawyer I had seen at my uncle Joe Breen's retirement party. I had heard or thought about people whom would sweat in mental institutions. Then if they had sweat then this is the signal to shock them. This time I was sweating from demonstrating the vacuum cleaner.

While I was exhibiting the vacuum cleaner here, I wasn't making any headway. I thought I was over kill. Getting her past so much embarrassment about the dirt, she didn't rejoin. So I began to try and got up the stairs to the second floor. This was part of the strategy to go them into the bedroom thinking they might have some fun with a salesman, and then go in for the sale. When I began to go up the stairs she said.

"Oh no."

From her retort I knew my chances were doomed. So I packed up my gear and left.

I can recall I had been knocking on doors in Walpole Mass. And I came up with someone whom might be interested possibly. I talked to Don about this and he said.

"What was her name, Donna?"

I began to think Donna was a mother's name for someone to be a mother figure. So I thought Walpole which is in the rural area wouldn't have real mother like figures. So I asked this girl as I knocked on the door.

"Is your name Donna?"

Her eyes lit up and I knew I had got her.

The first vacuum cleaner I had sold was from someone I got the lead from over the phone. They said they would be interested in a demo. I went there and while I was with Don there he said.

"We agreed over the phone about how you would pay."

This was what I call closing the sale. I don't know if she had already made agreements but this was a way in which you didn't ask questions. You had to close sales, so the customer will feel comfortable.

I went into their kitchen and I called up to double check on her credit card. I was sitting in the kitchen doing the paperwork, and I felt I was up a level a bit. I received about $200 commission on the about $700 vacuum cleaner.

The name of the street, which the homeowner had bought the vacuum cleaner, was Beach Street. Around this time I saw my uncle Joe Breen wearing a beach hat while he was driving by. I thought a connection Beach Street and beach hat.

A person whom had her machine in for repair had called the office, and said she wanted her machine brought back immediately. I did my own computer printout for what was wrong with her machine. I had picked up her machine when I first brought this to the office.

This was right about now I came down with one of those spells. I was bringing her machine to her home when I put on my hat, and I felt a big calmness came over me. I thought to myself I had taken this demon or spell whatever this was. I was tougher than this. This was all in the mind. I began to think *REALLY* like the psychiatric more than the physical. This took about 8 years to conquer the demon. I was definitely tougher than this. Over 8 years of working I was working harder and harder, until finally, I was tougher than the spell or demon.

I can recall when I was driving to work one day, and a car swerved in front of me, then away. I turned really quick and I thought about possibly following him, but he was long gone. I tried to see his license plate in my rear view mirror, but he was long gone. I was thinking what the rat race was now.

When I would knock on doors I would say, "hello-e", the word I had made up.

When I would demonstrate the vacuum cleaner to some housewives during the day, I thought these housewives have more on their minds than just a vacuum cleaner demonstration.

I was with Don one day and we were demonstrating the vacuum cleaner in the house of a Dedham policeman. The housewife said.

"My husband works 100 hours per week."

I said to her.

"He must be sleeping standing up?"

As we were leaving after the sale, Don said to me.

"You're abrupt."

I began to think being sick mentally was like abrupt, instead of sick. Don had a real witty way about him. When Don was talking about attorneys one day he called them, "Wetbacks."

Another one was.

"If you are ever going to see a doctor, see a dentist."

I had started a position at the Veterans Hospital. I was going to try V.A. because my sales weren't too good. I called up my hometown doctor and told him I received a job at the V.A. When I told Jack Yado MD I got the job, he said.

"Get right on it."

When they had told me I had the job and I was to start initially the next day, I recalled what dr. Jack Yado said, to get right on it. So I went there this day. I went into the hospital and called up the person in personnel and they said.

"You are supposed to start tomorrow."

I said.

"I thought I would get right on this."

The next day I had the pre-employment papers to make out at the V.A. As I was writing the paperwork my legs began to shake. They would go up and down. They were like really quaking. I began to think big. I was a research clerk. I checked the whole hospital for the day. I could recall when I would see the doctors throughout the day. I began to think while I would see the doctors.

"Doctor."

"Doctor."

"Doctor."

"Doctor."

I was thinking I was at a higher discipline than a doctor, a "door to door" salesman. I was like thinking if I saw people really sick in bed, then I could help them. They could pull me down. The idea about how I could watch misery on television and this would pull me up.

There was another time when Don and I went to a home in Westwood Mass. to do a demo. This person said to Don when we were demonstrating the machine, about our store, "that little store." I was in a whole new world now. Material things really matter to people.

There was another time when I went to the house of the owner of the Westwood Lodge. I gave this person a service check. This was when I would service check their machine. I thought the owner, whose wife was there but not him, was like a bit upset. I thought he was like threatening me with shock treatments, but he really had no jurisdiction to any of my care now. This was because I serviced checked their machine.

Well when I would knock on doors I really felt people with mental problems were really good, because they fought. I could recall when I would succor people. I felt the feeling of a needle going in me, but in my mind. The people with mental problems would really help me.

This was as if I were doing the "door to door" sales right out of high school again. When I was at the Veteran's Hospital, I saw a person whom was paralyzed in the Korean War whom lived in the neighborhood I grew up in. When I saw him I felt so elevated he didn't even say anything to me.

I remember when I would see dr. Jack Yado at church years before and he would look down at his right arm. I would do this at the Veteran's Hospital when I would tour the hospital. I can recall the new building they were putting up, "the Oreo Building." I had picked up a rock from the sight and threw this. This was just a very little bit, but I did do this.

A girl whom started the same day as I did worked in the Gift shop, I was thinking of getting interested in. She was rather tall. I was probably at the highest level of social life in my life.

I tried to stay busy the whole day at the V.A. I thought I really was like a recreational therapist, by how I would have to find out what to do the whole day in the Hospital. The same thing the patients would have to find what to do the whole day.

At the end of the night of working there, I went to say good night to the patients in bed. While I was doing this, a nurse asked me what I was doing. I then told her how I had started the job this day. I was in contact with personnel and I was let go, because I went AWOL. Meaning I didn't report to the personnel at the end of the night.

I was given a pay stub for the day and was told to keep this on me at all times. I read all the criteria for V.A. personnel and I thought I was to report all doctors, whom would stand in the hallways in groups talking to each other. I'm not sure if this was written in the papers, but I was to report doctors talking in groups in hallways.

Around this time while I was a salesman, I saw a person named Russ, walking down Norwood center. I thought he perceived the kit I would use before going into houses to demonstrate. Russ was one of the first persons, to make me feel normal. Russ had been on Guadalcanal.

I remember I saw Joe and Marian whose daughter Paula I knew in my youth. When I dated their daughter she told me her dad was a salesman. I think she said he was a "door to door" salesman. So with me getting better, I felt a connection.

I can recall each night when I came back to my apartment I would put my head in between my legs. I would try to do this to calm myself down after the very stressful day of sales. This I thought later is what attorneys need. They need some kind of break, to their very difficult day. I thought they would call this 15, meaning a 15 minutes break. I felt like an attorney while I was a salesman.

I can recall I was soliciting in Milton one day. I saw the female letter carrier delivering mail. She was sitting on a wall smoking a cigarette. When I walked by her, I put the sole of my left foot on the ground as if I were putting out a lit cigarette. I also saw her later, and I would salute her, as I would click my heels. I was beginning to have masculine attributes. This is, I would score with girls. When I would act as if I were putting out a cigarette, I thought about how I lost the way to ejaculate on purpose.

I was calling up houses to try to get sales and I thought I called up my old PT Billy Kold's home. I'm not positive but I know at least the correct last name. I probably had knocked on his door in Dedham, as I must have knocked on 150 per day.

I would do "door to door in Roslindale. I can recall when I sold bags in Roslindale to a person named Johnson. She made out a check for this. I can recall the ploy of being quick. When I came back to the office with the sale, Don had me stamp the cards for the "Roslindale Branch."

I can remember I had knocked on this distinctive door and a dog came barking through the screen. When the house dweller came to the door, they were worse than the dog. I can recall one of the best responses I had heard was. "We have a sickness in the family."

You had to learn to be stoical with the people. If you were overzealous, then the customers would recognize this and decline. When I was talking to a person over the phone I felt I was a decipherer in wartime trying to decipher a code. You had to like lift weights with your mind. I really couldn't tell what words would come out of my head. I tried to be as persuasive as possible.

My sister Stephanie was supposed to move to Sweden and marry her boyfriend Lars. But at last second he declined and she was rather disappointed. I thought the reason why was because of me possibly being ill psychiatrically supposedly. I thought he declined because of the possibility of the hereditary of the illness. I would sometime have dreams of her crying, because her boyfriend didn't like her, because of the psychiatric problems I had. Now he stood her up and she was quite discouraged.

I would stop by each day at my folk's house and try to help her out by giving her the word of the day. Every day while knocking on doors there would be one word, which would stand out. I would say this word to Stephanie. I was working so hard I would be very slow. Stephanie took this not moving quite so fast from stress, as not being active.

Don my boss told me one day when I was knocking on doors.

"Well what do you want to do meet people, or sell vacuum cleaners?"

We put up a stand for Electrolux in the Dedham Mall. Don was about 26 years old and he would always be intimate with his blonde haired girlfriend right out in public. I had made a stand in the Dedham Mall. I felt tall. I would feel very positive about this stand years later.

You couldn't get excited about making a sale, because people would detect this and decline. I was worrying about how I thought I wasn't mainstream. Meaning "door to door" wasn't common anymore, as this was back in the sixties. I was on commission. I was berserk thinking all I had gained during the week was going to the pharmacy for pills. I was paying cash for my pills. This was about $150.00 each week for pills.

I can recall I was picking up a machine in Franklin. The person there said.

"I was a POW 44 months in Japan."

I asked him.

"Do you work?"

"I work shop."

He said.

I thought this person was a high school shop teacher. This person I thought was acting as if people would want to talk to him about his POW time. I felt this way when I wanted people to talk to me about being paralyzed. I thought people would be interested in hearing about what this was like. My uncle Henry whom lived in Franklin before he dieing Christmas morning 1965, was saying in my head, "Help him."

I could recall when I would be trying to remember something in particular, I would drive by the streets in which I knocked on the doors there, and what I was trying to recall would come straight to me. I thought about how I was a "door to door" salesman right out of high school. I recollected about a quote I had read, "Children Hunger for knowledge." I thought of all the boys and girls whom went off to college right after high school, with the hunger and thirst for knowledge.

When I had sold the bags in Roslindale I had gotten out the stamp to label the cards Roslindale Branch Electrolux. I remember when I was doing the stamping and Don said.

"Stamp them out in the backroom."

He was motioning to me to not do something menial in front of people coming into the office.

I would awake at about 7:30 each morning to be at work by 9:00. This felt like I was sleeping late, after having arose at 4:30 for the Stop & Shop warehouse. As I said this would like dawn on me, to get up before the sun, when I worked at the warehouse.

I could also recollect I would drive by the Dedham Courthouse each day before going to work. I felt a connection to all the court people I would see each day going and coming from court.

I recall I set up an appointment with my psychiatrist Jon Eloc MD. I thought of the song, which had the part, "Get here if you can."

I was thinking about what Don told me at Electrolux. If you are going to see a doctor see a dentist.

I drove to about 5 miles from the hospital and I was about 15 minutes late for my appointment, so I called him up and said.

"I am right around the Engineering Plant, do you want me to still come in there still 15 minutes late?"

He said.

"Don't come in."

When I would take my pills, I no longer wanted to be seen by the pharmacist to get the pills. All the hard work I had been doing was like being wasted buying the pills.

I recall I went to buy a new car at the Bock car dealership in Norwood. I was looking at cars. I said to them about a particular car.

"I'll offer you $3,000."

They said.

"We want $3,600."

Then they said.

"We will go down to $3,400."

I said.

"I'll go down to $2,800. You go down, I go down."

This was the famous Bock dealership on the Auto-mile in Norwood. I had been with a cousin of the Bocks Lisa Fraso, when I was younger. We had gone for a walk and when we came back around her home I said to her.

"Can I have a kiss?"

"He only asked for my love," Stevie Nicks.

I had heard Lisa had gone away with the bands after high school. She was my only link to a sane world, by the dreams I would have of her, every so often at night. If I had a dream with kissing her for 3 or 4 seconds, this was my medicine. Just three or four seconds of kissing her in a dream every three or four months would sustain me. She would believe in me. Maybe this was just myself listening to music each day. She was my link to a sane world. When I thought I didn't have a girlfriend I thought I had Lisa.

They asked me at the Car dealership if I wanted to be a salesman there.

I began to call up dr. Jack Yado every so often.

He asked me.

"What are you doing?"

"I went back to Electrolux. I had been with them right out of high school."

"Come on to Norwood Bill. Join the community."

I applied for a job at NVHS, which included the Norwood Hospital. I believe I spoke with a Russian girl whom was doing the interviewing. I can recall the months before, when I lived in Walpole, and my uncle Joe Breen told me I should move back to Norwood. My last day in my apartment was New Year's Eve. There was a girl either separated or divorced in the apartment next to mine. I believe I had some wine in my apartment. So I asked this girl if she wanted to have a drink with me on New Years Eve. She had a young child of hers and when I knocked on her door, she I don't know exactly what she said, but this was a kind polite, no.

I can recall the previous week or so when I had loaded up my station wagon and my belongings to move back to Norwood. I can recall the slow chug down the road back to Norwood. As I was driving I stopped by my uncle Joes'. I walked up the store to get some gelatin for my aunt Mary Joe. I then proceeded to drive to my folk's home and unloaded the car. I can recall what I had to do to get back in Norwood. You had to have "back." I had my own phone at this house.

I had had an interview with NVHS, which was the umbrella name, which included the old Norwood Hospital. The woman whom was interviewing me was Linda.

"Hello, I'm Linda M."

"Yes, I'm Bill Breen."

"Your references have been checked and you can start in February."

"*OH*, that sounds good. Thank you."

"You were a salesman?"

She asked me.

"Yes, the Roslindale Branch of Electrolux."

I had been taking some medication and I was a bit nervous. Her eyes lit up when I told her I was a salesman. I began to think like I had, when I was a "door to door" salesman right out of high school. All the goodies would be in rather awe of a salesman.

"Well your job would entail sterilizing the instruments, going to the different floors to check supplies, etc . . ."

"Sounds good."

"Alright, I'll see you February 7."

"Thank-you."

While I was talking to Linda, I thought she was the nurse whom I had seen when I went out of bed at Norwood in August 1975 with the busted back. The nurses then, I thought had crawled into the room like snails. I thought I was on her knee and she was stroking on my penis. I thought back then to the Revolutionary War. I also thought she was the nurse whom wanted to wash down my genitals, after I had the hand to hand combat with Billy D. I told the nurse not to wash down my genitals back then. I thought if you were happy, then God would think you weren't suffering, and wouldn't heal you. So I had this confidence about Linda because of these experiences.

While I was waiting to start this job in February I went down the Norwood Cinema and tried to be a film projectionist. I sent into the State Government for a film projectionist's License. The person there trained me to put in the film. I did this there. I met one of the boys I had coached in baseball. He worked at the counter there. I talked to him and he told me he was in accelerated courses, which he was taking in high school. Also the sports he was doing there at high school also.

After being this person's coach in Babe Ruth, I began to think about how you want these people to venerate you even though the sports are over. How the young boys would look up to me, when I would holler at them. I wanted these boys to look up at me, even though the sports were over or gone.

I was watching the screen this particular night I had put the film in. I was sitting in the front seat left of the upstairs screen. The upstairs and downstairs screens were on. My eyes felt a fearfulness of people. This seemed I had increased my own fear of people about me.

I can recall these days in which I had gone back home as trying to stay sane. I can recall I would look at the preseason articles about the Boston Red Sox. My daily routine was to go to a deli and get the paper every day. I would also park in front of the Cinema and just prodigy about things.

I can recall I would see another Babe Ruth player of mine. He worked at a gas station. I had heard the theory if you make someone suffer then they will like you. I can also recall an article with pictures about Germans and English in First World War. This was about how each of them had veered gifts during the Christmas, while they were in the trenches. I had looked into the eyes of these people and you could see a recondite ray, which would come from their eyes. I would look at the dirt in this World War 1 picture and I could recall pockets of holes of dirt, when I was younger and the grass roots, which would hold together clumps pf dirt.

I can recall one person seemed he was about 30 or 35 years old. I then recollected back then, they drafted aged people because they needed them for the front. They needed manpower from all ages, which they could procure. Our family was part Welsh, from the coalmines in Wales.

Well I started the job at the hospital and the first month was rather hectic. There were two girls in my department, Moe and Donna. I was pretty nervous there the first few weeks. I could recall going to the café for lunch and this was a rather a little of compulsion. All the operations done on people seemed to be in the air.

I was sitting down eating one day, when I overheard a person say, "pink papers."

This made me think how I had been pink papered. I then calmed myself by thinking when I worked at the Boston City Warehouse. The World War 2, and Korean War veteran there said, after I had been talking about Harvard. "Do you have your pink papers?"

In Boston City warehouse this is the other way for pink papers. Meaning did you put up a struggle before going into psychiatric Hospital. In the Norwood Hospital setting pink papers would be considered something wrong with you, but in a Boston City warehouse you better have your pink papers.

I would sit with Linda and some of the other workers there at break. I can recall there was a man whom worked in accounting whom would sit with Linda. I was talking about operative in the warehouse.

"We would work till we dropped and then get up and work some more."

I would have a rather callous tone of voice for this when I said this. This man began to guffaw and couldn't hold in his giggling. Linda looked at me a bit different, as she saw the man chuckling uncontrollably. I was gaining Linda's respect.

Mondays were probably the worst. I had to go around to the different floors, cardiac, pediatrics, psychiatric, Intensive Care, etc . . . I had a small computer which I would check supplies. You had to concentrate. I can recall the girl training me Moe. She was a pleasant woman.

I can recall the pre-examination physical I had. There was a nurse there named Jane N. She examined my lower tailbone when I had taken off my shirt. I would remember this. I didn't put down any mental condition on the application.

I can remember one of these days I was sitting with Linda and some other co-workers. I had said something to Linda and I thought this was kosher. I had actually thought Linda was the girl, whom had touched my penis, after going out of bed back in 1975. I thought I had caught Linda. After this time at lunch I thought of the idea of slowing down time. I could see Linda walking by me in the operating carts area. I thought time had slowed down. In the air this looked like miniature bluish black stars flickering in the air. Well in a little while Linda had me in the office and said to me.

"I want you to sign this piece of paper in which you were inappropriate to your supervisor."

I said to her.

"Can I make a phone call?"

"Do you have to call someone to make a decision?"

I thought very deeply and hastily said.

"What happens if I decline?"

"You will be terminated."

I thought about this and then I signed. Where would I go if I were terminated? I was thinking could she do this? She did say if I didn't sign, I would be expired. A little while later, the top boss Bob Nosp, I talked to, and he said to me.

"Linda was very upset about what happened out in the cafeteria. I was going to let you go but I decided to keep you on."

"Well thank-you."

"Do you know Moe is one of the best workers around? I got a call from the Faulknor Hospital, they wanted her to work there."

"She is good worker."

I responded.

Well the weeks were turning into months and I began to cutback on the medicine. I was feeling rather high. One of these days the top boss Bob Nosp bought me a cup of coffee. He had motioned to the cashier he would pay for the coffee.

I can recall when I had done some extra work for NACL solutions to one of the floors. I could recall one male nurse say or I interpreted. "He cleaned." I thought about how I had been a salesman instead of college after high school. I would clean homes.

I can recall this particular night when I had a glass of water at the end of the shift. I was talking to the night supervisor Brenda. I had gotten something off of my chest, as I drank a glass of water. I thought before I had gone to rugby practices and I was getting bread from reading the Bible. This glass of water really had quenched my mental thirst.

I could recall the girls whom worked on the psychiatric unit. These girls seemed to have a better smile on their faces than then regular nurses. Possibly to omission to the Intensive Care nurses. There was one MHW mental health worker, whom I liked a little bit. She would come down to the supply area where I worked. Only the psychiatric nurses would not wear nurse's whites.

I can recall when I would go on the psychiatric unit to check supplies. I can recall seeing some of the patients and I thought to myself they were saying in their heads to me, "you get to go home."

This was rather difficult doing this unit, as I would wear tinted glasses. I can recall when I was putting supplies into the supply closet, and I was worrying about the sharp things, like razor blades and the patients. One of the MHW was walking by and I thought she thought I shouldn't be too concerned about the patients. That maybe over concern would worry or aggravate the patients more. I was just learning to work on a psych unit.

I can recall all the workers on the psych unit would be all dressed up real neat like. I thought when I was seeing the psychiatrists, MHW, and nurses on this unit. Then I was really seeing them. There was one MHW there and she was the one whom would open the draws for me to put in the sharp razor blades for shaving. She I thought was really cool. I now think she was maybe projecting something in the back of her head. Week by week I was cutting back on all the meds.

Dr. Jack Yado called me up and I think he had said to bring all my bottles down to Ambulatory Care at the Hospital, to sign your-self in. I said something, fighting back with words, and he then said. "They have a hospital doctor for all employees.

I called up the nurse Jane N. whom had examined me at the pre-examination physical. I asked her.

"Could you tell me whom is the hospital doctor for the employees?" I called her up in the hospital.

She said.

"I'm sticking my neck out by telling you this."

I was thinking the hospital doctor was for minor problems, and all the meds I was on wasn't so minor.

I can recall when I was bringing the crash cart to the pharmacy one day. The pharmacist there was a pharmacist at a drug store, where I would get all my psychiatric meds like prolixin and also macrodantin, which was for a bladder infection. This was in the seventies. I was on Medicaid back then and my prognosis wasn't too good. I thought this person hadn't forgotten me back then, and the shape I was in. He would look at me and recall the old, and I would begin to think of myself back then, and I was ashamed of myself. His old pharmacy he worked at went out of business, and we gave him a job at the hospital pharmacy.

Well seeing this person I felt I wasn't welcome, if I were to get my meds here. I can remember this pharmacist in the cafeteria and I looked at him and while he was walking out of the café he like "Ccc," coughed. I was thinking I wasn't back in Norwood yet. This person thought he was someone whom could, "see me." I still had work to do, to be in. When I met this person's eyes, he projected I was a customer at his pharmacy, rather than another employee at the hospital.

He made me feel good thinking I was on the bladder infection medicine, when I had the repercussions from the spinal problems years ago. You had to fight. You had to meet people's eyes in which you knew you were in. You are in the Norwood Community. I was out of Walpole and I was trying to get back in the Norwood Community. This really is what mental illness is, in which you have to be back into your community. Some people call this mental illness but this is really just, "being home."

I can remember the social worker at the hospital and she was really tall and gorgeous. I thought she was giving me sex therapy a little bit. She had blonde hair and a very nice figure. I can recall once when I thought she wanted me to sit with her at break, and she was sitting all alone. I thought she was thinking sex, which is supposed to be the best thing on earth. Then she would give me a freebee. Meaning you didn't have to get paid for helping someone with sex problems. If you help them, then your reward is, you helped someone to have wonderful joy. She would help me as a fellow employee.

The girl in charge in the Central Supplies, which I worked in, would assist the doctors on operations by handing them their instruments, when they operated. She had dropped an instrument once when she was working. She came down with a problem with her neck. She couldn't work this job anymore, so she took a less amenable job. She took over the Central Supply department. She would say things like, "We got this critter." I thought she meant me, whom was paralyzed, had put Norwood Hospital on the big map, by having a paralyzed patient recover. She knew by working in the operation room the chances of paralyzed people recovering are very slim.

I even thought at times the hospital might have an idea of, "Certificate of Need." This would mean if the hospital needed someone to recover from paralysis, then they would sign a piece of paper stating to me, they needed this to happen again, to recover from paralysis. The odds of them recovering are very, very few. This girl would refer to me as a critter at times.

My uncle Joe Breen would tell me at times to "Pick their brains," meaning the doctor's brains. I can recall I did exactly this, when one of the doctors was calling down for stitches from the operating room. I called down on the mike something regards to silk stitches. There was some kind of connection with picking the doctor's brain and the stitches I sent up.

As I was coming off the meds I was getting very restless. I began to walk around the grammar school, which I went to when I was younger. I reminisced when I went by a place where I played square ball. I could recall I was playing square ball there in sixth grade. One of my friends was Ricky Deer then. He pushed me down when I was waiting to play square ball. He then said.

"I didn't do it."

I then grabbed him and through him down and said.

"I didn't do it."

I could remember my friend skip said then.

"He didn't do it."

While I was walking by this spot playing square ball I thought of trouble with your heart would be square, or Dedham Square. This is the town next to Norwood before you get into Boston. I thought this to help your heart.

I could recall also these days when I would walk around my old neighborhood. I can recall I had made a decision, I would really see one of my girlfriends in ninth grade. I was thinking about girls more as I was coming off the meds. I was becoming straight on no meds. This girl whom I was dating then, was named Paula. She was my first girlfriend. I wasn't sure if I wanted to descry one night, which I would go to her house on Friday nights. I like struggled through and really made an endeavor to go to her house. I began to think of all of these days now, as I was coming off the pills. My concentration wasn't too good on the pills either.

I would come home at about 4 or 5 o'clock each night. I would watch the Breen sportscaster on the sports channel. I was hardly sleeping much at night either. I was beginning to think about, after I had the salesman job, right out of high school. I was thinking like I had then this wasn't good to help people.

I was walking to hospital one day to pick up check and I thought about at the spot I saw an alcoholic, whom also was on D-Day. I was cogitating now as I walked by this house he was saying. "It stinks down there." Meaning the Normandy beach really stunk. I had heard the beach had stunk of the dead.

I was trying cough drops as I was coming off of the meds. But as I had the throat lozenges in my mouth, my chin began to have movement to this. I began to see what chemicals and compounds were in the medicines I was on. I found one of the chemicals in prolixin was gelatin. I also heard gelatin was in seaweed. I began to eat a lot of gelatin back then.

I could recall as I was coming off the propanalol, which was a heart medicine, but I was taking for the movement in my jaw. This was when my jaw would rock side to side. I was thinking of the Chief in the now World Renown Spinal Hospital in Boston. My heart was really beginning to pound as I was coming off the propanalol. I thought I could tell how someone had died in Emergency by how my heart felt.

I would have confidence over the male employees there. One doctor came to our department and I began to think style. I began to think writers have there own style of writing. I was still writing quite a bit. I thought doctors have their own style of operating.

I would go to the field where the high school baseball team would practice. There was a person whom was in the minor leagues, after he played for Norwood. I was playing catch with him lefty.

"I thought you were a right handed?"

He said,

"No, *I'm* a lefty now."

I responded.

I asked Pete, the coach, if I could pitch batting practice. He said okay. I began to pitch lefty and Pete said to me.

"Use your right arm."

"My right arm is sore."

I said.

I could recall when I first met Pete in tenth grade I called him Pete and he said to me to call him coach.

I began to pitch lefty and I recalled one of the coaches in high school, whom would pitch really in close, while he would pitch batting practices years ago.

"Come on the big-6."

I pitched to the first six batters and I would say things like the big-6.

I could espy Pete behind the backstop with one of his hands to his chin. The assistant coach Minty whom was on one Canadian crutch was the scorekeeper. He had spinal neck problem years before. He had been with Pete three years. I would say things to Minty like, God Speed." He would walk rather slowly with one crutch.

After I had pitched lefty, I thought this was the talk of the town. I thought, "flashback." Meaning all the flashbacks I would have about mental and physical problems that "Flash back," or me back home. I think people were a bit in awe, of how I could throw lefty all of a sudden. I felt I was back in the Norwood Community.

I can remember one of these nights I thought Chief was telling me, "Sleep on the floor." Well I went down on the floor one night and I had been drawn up by some kind of power up into the bed.

I would think of dr. Jon Eloc when I was coming off the pills as saying in my head, "You want pills?" I thought how he was an ex-Korean War psychiatrist and you want pills, as do you want bombs or shells, or these kind of pills. He had the power back then to send people back to the front during the Korean War.

I can recall I would eat honey nut crunch cereal with biscuits. I would have a nice piece of fish with melted butter and mashed Ritz crackers. At night sometimes, I would think of the girl Donna, whom couldn't work in the operating room. I would think of her like taking in air. I would think she felt vexed for me and this was why she hired me.

I can remember the girl nurse in Emergency. I had a dream with her and in the dream I said to her. "You know I'm sleeping."

She said something like in the dream.

"I stuck my neck out for you."

This may sound crazy, but my social life I would have in my dreams. I would kiss girls or have sex with them in my dreams.

I was thinking this was true. Don't help anyone. People only take credit for helping. No one wants to take the blame for hurting. There is no hurting chastisement for hurting-emotionally.

Linda my boss was a Lithuanian and French woman. She was about 38 years old and had a good figure. She must have had a 34" inch bust. She had a little long black hair. I liked her, even though she made me sign the piece of paper, I was such and such to her at the café. I thought she really admired me for overcoming this. I would give her the right hand to the head move. This meant to girls, right head or right color hair. This would make the blonde haired gals think right hair and black haired woman right hair. I thought for some reason the black hair would be connected with the Holy Mother, and blonde haired girls emphasized, maybe blondes have more fun theory is still on.

Well the weeks were turning into months and I was on no meds whatsoever. I also thought the Chief was saying in my head, "smoke cigarettes." Meaning me to smoke cigarettes with Linda at breaks which she smoked.

I was reverting to the side room addition of our home. I had helped put this up when I was about 14 years old. I would have my meals there. I think a lot of mental illness is poor. In meaning where else can you go? This would get to the point, I had to be in this room or I wouldn't feel good.

I was sending the Chief and dr. Jon Eloc pictures, which I would draw. As I was off the meds, I had more awareness of the circulation of blood to my head. This I would feel when I would be in public as in the hospital café. The idea of "straight flush," which you would have in self-conscience situation was coming back. I would rather have a self-conscience situation verses one of those spells. James Taylor song, "you can run but you can not hide," was so true.

I recall the girl whom I worked with Moe and they made me think they still thought about when I was there in 1975 when I laughed and cried. I thought when you cry when spinal problem, you do out of tears. When I tried to tear the paralysis right out of me, by trying to get right up.

I can recall Donna my forthwith boss, she said once. "This girl lost feeling in her arm." I began to think losing feeling could be rather quite serious. I would sit with Moe at break sometimes. At lunch, this was where the academics importance mattered of where you sit in the café. I was fresh from business as a "door to door" salesman. I would sit with the doctors sometimes. I could recall the doctors talking about their children going off to college.

"My daughter is doing fairly well at Syracuse."

One of the doctors said.

I was thinking when I graduated high school. I didn't opine this was too long ago. I thought my fellow employees at hospital were saying in my head "call a girl."

Well I ultimately acted upon this, and called my old girl friend Elizabeth. I called her at her parent's house in Norwood, where she would bring her children during the day from her home she abode in Foxboro.

"Hi, is Elizabeth there?"

"This is Elizabeth."

"Hi. This is Billy."

"Billy, how's is your family?"

"All right, How's is yours?"

"Good."

She I believe had three children. I could also remember her say something like, "It's uncle Billy."

I began to think we were so close years ago we couldn't stay together. Maybe like cousins.

"I saw your brother Neil wearing sunglasses even though there was no sun out."

"Ha, ha, ha, etc . . .

She chuckled.

"Where are you working?"

She asked me.

"I'm working at the Hospital. I had worked at Electrolux a while ago. I don't know why I did it. I hated it. I don't need it."

I remember she said something, which I didn't like so I said.

"Don't be talking back to me."

"My children are studying in school now. They are studying arithmetic."

I was thinking she was making do about learning arithmetic. She had married an engineer, lived in the suburbs, and had four children. All throughout high school I would think I wanted five children, be an engineer, and live in the suburbs, until I had the Electrolux position after high school.

I could remember after I got out of the Boston Hospital in 1976, Elizabeth had gotten a job at the hospital. I showed a picture of Elizabeth and I when we were at our senior prom to my aunt Jenny. Jennie was my great aunt whom worked at the hospital for 55 years. She was the head nurse. When she heard Elizabeth was getting married to an engineer around 1978 or so, I think Jennie had thought, she had used me to get the job at the hospital. I had showed Jenny a picture of us, and with her getting married to someone else, this seemed she had used me to get the job at hospital. When Jenny thought about this I think Elizabeth had lost her job at hospital.

I can recall these days when I would clean the instruments for the doctors I would be coughing up blood and debris. I thought this was from working with all the instruments I would clean and sterilize. I thought this was the profusion amount of blood and debris from all the operations on me.

I can remember I thought of dr. Jack Yado saying in my head, "the operation." This would mean to straighten out the operation, which I had on my spine by the Surgeon years ago. I began to think the Surgeon had put his finger under his nose, as if to stop from sneezing, when he was operating on me. This was why I had so many psychiatric problems after the operation. I had motioned this to Donna the ex-operating instrument girl.

I was seeing shows at the Norwood Cinema. I also was eating a lot of gelatin. When I was completely off all meds I was talking to my boss Linda in her office. I had gotten her a requisition for a date at the Norwood Cinema, the real professional way to go about to get a date. I was sitting alone with her in her office. Now Linda was a married woman. I had written on the requisition about a light year. The requisition was for a date at the Norwood Cinema.

She asked me.

"What is a light year?"

I told her.

"This is something like the speed of light."

She was smiling a bit, and I thought there might even possibly be a chance to score or kill time with her right there in her office.

She asked me.

"Are you on any medicines?"

I told her.

"No."

We talked for about 15 minutes and I felt very comfortable. She asked me.

"Were you ever in a hotel?"

I told her.

"Ya."

I can recall I walked to a restaurant one of these days. I met an old friend Tommy Lac. He was an attorney. We were talking and there were a lot of old people there also. There was a lot of World War 2 era aged people there, whom were around the counter. I began to talk to Tommy.

"Where are you working?"

He asked.

"The Hospital."

"What are you doing now?"

I asked him.

He said.

"I'm with a Law firm in Braintree. I'm an attorney there. My father just died a week ago."

He began to ramble on. I now thought, I was his outlet for him to talk to about his dad, whom died. I thought he had come to the restaurant to talk to the World War 2 aged folks there. But I was the one he dumped on. I said to him mentioning about a psychologist. He said after he unloaded on me.

"I don't need any psychologist."

We both had coffees and I was trying to pay for the bill. He got up and pulled up his pants from the ass a little, and we both paid for each other's coffees. This was a heavy yoke.

I would walk around some woods sometimes and I would think I was in the jungles of Nam. I would take leaks, and I would think which way the urine came out, and this was, which way I should go. You may laugh about this, being the jungles of Nam, but when you had been on haldold, which was the last resort for people, your mind is really changed. My mind felt this was going 100 miles an hour. This is why they use this as last resorts. I was barely sleeping at nights. Maybe two or three hours per night and I had to get up for work.

Back to after I talked to Linda, I thought of the girl whom was in charge of Emergency. I was filling out orders for different operation carts. I began to think of the girl in Emergency as if she was buck-toothed over and over again. I thought the hospital was rather big now. There had been a new addition back in the early eighties. This bucked-toothed drove me crazy.

I said something to Linda after this and I knew something was wrong. There was even a third girl in the picture. This was the nurse whom examined me at the employment physical. I saw her walking to hospital one day with a cigarette in mouth. She had the last name of a patient from Robby 7 in Boston, whom was a quadriplegic and never recovered.

Well I had parked my car behind the Norwood Cinema one of these days. I then walked to hospital. I was going to start a second job at night at the Norwood Cinema as an usher. I began to think this wasn't good to help people. When I got to work I began to think of Abraham in the Bible. I thought how he almost offered up his son Isaac. I began to think of the future now. I began to think if I were to have children, then one of my children might need an operation. This day I walked up the stairs to the surface area where they got the instruments from the elevator for the operations. I had been sending up all these instruments all these months, and I didn't know what was actually betiding them. I thought I would bypass the elevator and bring the instruments up personally. One of the operating technicians was walking down the stairs, as I proceeded carrying the instruments up. I can also recall I was on the operating floor and I thought I could become a brain surgeon.

Well when I got down from upstairs, the technician must have said something to Linda, about me not sending up the instruments by the elevator. Then Linda said to me.

"Go down Emergency and see nurse Jane N."

Jane was the girl whom had given me the physical. I really began to feel this would be perplexing being down Emergency as a patient. I thought the whole school would be seeing me. So I told Linda.

"I'll go see the doctor."

Chapter 9

The doctor was dr. John Yado. I was thinking if I were terminated then dr. Yado would come down the Hospital. I thought he could do quite a lot of trouble just by showing up. I was thinking he would come into the hospital just enough distance to get people in line. Dr. John Yado was called the doctor. A lot of doctors would get a kick out of being called doc, but dr. Yado was known as the doctor.

Our family had paid for this doctor's Medical School in the thirties. He went on to enlist in the Navy during World War 2. I think he had a tour of duties. Maybe where the doc tour would be justified.

Well I got into the locker room and got my clothes. I stayed in the hospital blues as I left the hospital. I was thinking I was carrying clothes out to my car and there was some kind of connection between firefighters and clothes at fires. I walked back to the Cinema where my car was. I got my clothes in a carrying bag, and headed for the fire department. I recall I was headed to the fire department and I thought of Audie Murphy was saying in my head, "your head is on."

I also began to think about when I had feeling restored. I had been swallowing my saliva. I thought this meant the Holy Spirit. I was thinking what is the Holy Spirit.

I began to think I would just begin to start operative at the Fire Department. I went there and I heard a firefighter say after I asked him.

"Where do you apply for the fire fighters position?"

Then I heard *A* fire fighter articulate.

"You have to get an application at the Town Hall and send this into Boston."

Then I heard a firefighter there say.

"He was in Boston."

I was thinking of walking straight up to the firefighter's quarters. I was thinking I would become a firefighter without filing application, like I had at the A&P in Norwood years ago.

I then headed for the Town Hall, where I got the application and sent this into Boston. I recall I went into some daily conferences the Town personnel were having at the Town Hall. I think these meetings were for the public also.

I filled out the application to send into Boston. After this I got in front of the Cinema and was trying to sell tickets there. I had bought a special offer for ten tickets at the Cinema. I had the day earlier got the okay to work at the Cinema the next week in two days.

I recall now before Linda sent me to Emergency, I had told Donna I was going to start work at the Cinema at night. After this Linda had told me to go down Emergency. I had given Linda a requisition for the show at 7:00. I now got in front of the Cinema and said things like. "Come on now get your tickets here." I would also say. "Hot chocolate, get your hot chocolate here."

I was here about ½ hour saying things like this. I then went into the Deli store next to the Cinema. I believe I got a submarine sandwich. As I was there two policemen were eating also. I can recall they would have the clearing of throats noise. I thought whom, had worked the hardest by the clearing of the throats noise.

Then the police officer Billy Curb came over to me and said.

"Have you been trying to sell tickets in front of the Cinema? There has been a complaint someone has been trying to sell tickets."

This policeman had a smile on his face as if I were controlling him. I thought this officer was saying in my head, "lifting the weights."

I thought he knew I had gotten an application for the fire department. Lifting weights meaning staying in shape for being a fire fighter. Now if I were to become a fire fighter lifting weights for your children whom you could help for lifting weights for sports. I said to the Italian person whom ran the deli.

"Japan is in third place."

After this I advanced to where my car was parked out back of the Cinema. I had begun to drink motor oil. I would take a chug straight down. I was thinking this was supposed to be the new fad in colleges. Years ago they would eat goldfish. Now was to drink motor oil. I also put my hat on the top of my car and began to tap this on the roof with my left hand. I even did some cleaning out back of the Cinema.

After a while here, I went home for dinner. As I was there dr. Flew whom was dr. Jon Eloc's understudy from McLean Hospital called and he said he thought I should come into the hospital. I thought maybe the Norwood Hospital had called them because I was acting bizarre. I was thinking I should go to get a pizza. There was a little fire we had at the house back in the sixties. Now with me applying for the fire fighter's position, I think everyone felt better about the fire, which was at this home. The fire department had come to the house to put out a small fire down the cellar. I think everyone felt better about the small fire now, with me applying for the fire fighter's job.

I was thinking dr. Jon Eloc MD whom was a German and I was fighting, as fighting fire. I left the house and went down and got a pizza. As I was eating the pizza, I began to look at cars driving by, as I was eating the pizza. I thought I could tell by what kind of car people drove to tell which nationality they were.

I parked in front of the Cinema and began to sip a cold drink, which I got with a straw. There were a lot of children hanging out at the park across from the Cinema. I began to think of a friend, whom I would pal around with when younger. He was a bartender about 100 yards from me, and the Cinema. I thought he was saying in my head, "I see you." This I began to recollect about when I was 13 or 14 years old.

The boy whom I coached in Babe Ruth was working in the Cinema with the counter help. I went into the Cinema and got a Charlestown Chew candy bar. I thought this person was saying to himself, "Charlestown Chew he eats." I also thought this person's father was saying all the time to him, "He quit, he quit the hospital, he quit." I thought I had lost this boy's respect.

I can recall earlier in the day, I went to a waitress at a restaurant across from the Cinema. I can remember I met this girl's eyes Carol, and I thought we had connected. I can recall I thought to myself, "faker," while I was in front of Cinema. Faker, meaning I was faking the mental illness, which I supposedly had. I then thought I should go to the restaurant and shake this girl's hand lefty. I went into the restaurant and shook this girl's hand lefty, and asked her to the show at the Cinema this night. I gave her a ticket to the show but she showed me her ring, which she was getting married. I didn't get a date from the girl at the hospital, and now the waitress said no, also. I shook Carol's hand lefty and I thought to myself, I was having the handoff from Rocky Blier. Rocky Blier was the pro-football player whom had some toes blown off in Nam, and then came back to play pro-football.

I then went back in front of the Cinema and I was saying to myself dr. Jon Eloc MD was saying in my head, "I'm paranoid." Then I thought to myself, "I'm blind."

I thought I might have had a cure for blindness by diving down and letting the breeze in the eyes drop. I had my eyes improve when I took the eye test after my first jump. Maybe the meaning for eye drops.

I then had the thought to drive to Franklin where my uncle Henry had lived before he died Christmas morning 1965. As I was driving I started to say to myself, "M & Ms." I drove and I thought my uncle Henry was guiding me up in the air at about 9:00 at night. I turned around in a building, and then came back home. I went to bed at about 11:30.

I awoke the next morning, and I had the urge to go up the woods, where I had gone to the Grammas school when I was younger. I went into the woods and took a leak. I began to think which way should I go, by which way the urine came out of my penis. I came back to my car and vacuumed this out.

This morning I was driving to my brother's Jackie house in Plymouth. I was saying to myself I wanted to sleep in his house there. I began to think he was saying in my head, "I'm under." I got lost driving there, so I called home and they said, "Come on home for some fish."

I then drove home and saw my sister Stephanie. She had been in Spain and now she was home. She did something and I then I felt I was very young. I began to think of the person whom I thought was a CIA agent when I was at UMass Amherst back in 1976. There was an article in the Boston paper front page, about the owner of the Stop & Shop, and about gallons of water, which was one of their products. I though the CIA man was saying in my head, "grub up." Meaning this Stop & Shop person was up, after being down for a while.

I was eating mushroom soup in the den which I had helped build. From here I went to the supermarket, and got a real nice piece of fish. I could recall when I was there and I saw one of the nurses from the hospital. I was a bit lean and she was also. I then went home and began to think about the night August 1, 1975. This night I had the fish and went out the window the first time. People looked as white as ghost. I was thinking of going down the Crisis Center.

I had a little bit earlier in the day had cleaned the cellar, as if I had a flamethrower as the vacuum cleaner. I was cleaning where we had the fire in the sixties. This night I drove to dr. John Yado's office out back. I was just parked there thinking about things. I began to think about my old psychiatrist I had at the Westwood Lodge. I cogitated about a Hall, which was in our town. What came over me now was "pot," marijuana. I thought about how I would smoke marijuana before I would see this psychiatrist. I thought back then he would like say to me in mind. "Get lost."

While I was at dr. Jack Yado's I was thinking about buying firecrackers, like I had when I was about 10 or 11 years old. The place where I bought the firecrackers was proximate the gas station of Bartuc's Car Wash, right before South Norwood, which was the poor section of town.

Well I contemplated of this person Donald Canyon. I thought he was saying in my head, "Pot." I took a dip as I thought about this word "pot." I left here and I went to a hotel on Route 1 in Norwood.

I gave the manger about $85.00.

"Here is $85.00 for the room."

I said.

The manager said.

"Here is your key for room 611."

"All right. Thank-you."

I responded.

I then proceeded to take the elevator to the sixth floor and I had my suitcase with me also, of clothes.

Well I put on glasses and went to the front desk and gave the clerk $5.00 for the Sunday paper.

"Here is $5.00 for the paper."

He didn't respond.

I thought he was rather in awe. I had on a pair of glasses when I went down for the paper. I think someone at the front desk was in control of the air conditioner. This began to get real cool in this room. I recall how I had on a yellow shirt, meaning I fought the Korean War. I believe there were two alternatives on the control panel on the wall. Either bed or drop. I pressed the one to drop. I called up the house service 763-4450. I had pressed the # of Linda's office at hospital. Just out of random for the number here in the hotel. But this was the hotel number.

"Yes, Can I help you?"

This was the answer on the house service.

"Yes, I would like a BJ."

"Do you mean Victory in Japan?"

She asked.

"Yes please with some water."

"All right."

This woman responded.

Well the room was quite cool, and I had done a sketch of a person while I was there. This was late Saturday night and I began to watch television. I can remember I had a little bit of artane. This was a pill for the side affects of the meds I was on. I thought dr. Jon Eloc MD said this could be good in a pinch. I didn't take this though. I think I had a diminutive amount of bread also.

I woke up in the morning and I was thinking what I was going to read in the Sunday paper? I went to the sport's section and I was hearing in my head the head clerk saying, "He's reading sports."

Then this other voice inside my head began to say as I was conceiving to go to the Hotel restaurant. "Are you coming out? Are you coming out?"

I thought I was real young and I was at my friend Michael Caroner's house and I was calling him to see if he would come out to play. I had been saying, "Michael, Michael, Michael, are you coming out? Are you coming out? I then heard one of the doors close on the hotel floor, and the sound of the door closing made me a bit trepid. I took a shower in the morning. In the morning I called up the house service again and said.

"Could you bring some water up to room 611?"

"Okay."

She replied with.

I began to think of my uncle Mickey whom had passed away two years ago. He would sit on the side of his bed at my grandmother's house. My uncle Mickey liked water a lot. This morning I put $10.00 inside the latch of the door for the girl coming up with the water. "Are you coming out? Are you coming out?" This voice kept on iterating in my head.

Ten dollars, I thought the girl, bringing up the water had said. I thought she would want at least $50.00.

Well, I was sitting on the side of the bed and was just waiting for the girl to come up with some water. I was just sitting on the bed and I really just wanted someone to talk to. I thought about the AIDS virus, and then I thought there wasn't too much chance of having sex, or a VJ, which this was called. At about 10:30 the next morning I decided to leave the hotel. I took the fire escape stairs.

I can recall I heard what I thought was a Cadillac car, which had muffler trouble and this sounded like a boat. Well I hearkened this car or what I thought in this hotel room a boat.

I went over to dr. Jack Yados' MD house. There was only his daughter there. I began to think of this doctor as giving the physicals at the High school. How feeling the scrotums would be like feeling breasts right out in public in broad daylight.

I asked her.

"Is the doctor here?"

"No, He went to church."

She said.

"Where is your bathroom?"

"Right over here."

She points to the door over by the side. I then went into the bathroom and brushed my teeth. Then the brother of the doctor whom was an ex-policeman Dorey came into the house and said.

"*JESUS CHRIST*, you can't come in here like this."

"I just brushed my teeth."

"You will have to leave."

Dorey lived in a house right next to the doctors'.

I then drove my car to my aunt Lucy's house. I went into the house and I asked her husband frank.

"Where's is Lucy?"

"She is going to the 12:00 Mass."

From here I went to church and parked my car across from the church. I then went into church and sat in the first row.

While I was there I began to think on a different level. When the priest would say please stand, I would be ahead of the priest and put my arms to my side and kind of levitate them to signal to the audience to stand. I even collected the money for the Mass in the wooden baskets. I had my luggage with my clothes in front of the first pew. I was one step ahead of the priest when he would say, please stand or please sit.

When the time came to receive the Holy Communion, I walked up to alter, in front of everybody and got my Eucharist. My hair was standing up straight on my head. After I received communion I motioned to the usher.

"Could you please get my bag?"

He said.

"All right."

He then picked up my bag and walked out of the church with them.

"This is as far as I can go."

He put the bag down at the walkway to the church. I can also remember quite clearly the choir would sing, "Fall to your knees, etc . . ."

I thought back then this was like the Walls of Jericho coming down. This seemed the choir was really hollering. I walked out of the church and got into my car across the street from the church. I began to think of the woman Eucharistic minister at the mass, I had known, was saying in my head, "Look at your self?" I began to get self-conscience. I thought my hair standing up didn't look good.

As I was in my car across the street, I began to look at people coming out of church. I thought to myself about people whom had crossed the street. After about a half hour I went down to the Norwood Cinema. I got out front and I began to sit down on the sidewalk, and I thought I was so low people coercing by in their cars, couldn't even notice me sitting there. I then got up and began to holler out things like.

"Your out."

I said as if I were an umpire. When I said this I thought I had come out of my body to the fireplug across the street.

"Hot chocolate, get your hot chocolate here."

When I would articulate this loudly I was thinking people in Boston whom would sell hot chocolate.

A police car came by and I gave the officer $5.00 for the policeman's Christmas fund. I was thinking of the movie "Slaughter House Five." This was when Billy Pilgrim gave the police officer money when his son had tipped over some of the graves.

One of the police officers said to me.

"Father Nunny would like to see you. He asked me to ask you if you would want to go to the rectory to talk to him?"

What came over me was I just didn't want to talk to him. As I said, when I was at Mass I was a bit out of order. This was one of the priests of the parish. He had asked one of the patrolmen to ask me, if I wanted to talk to him. I didn't say anything though.

The cleaners for the Cinema came by and they went into the Cinema. I was hired by the Cinema to start work on Monday the next night, as a ticket man or usher. I began to look into my reflection of myself on the door and I began to say to myself. "Do I look ample enough to come in?"

I began to try and look as good as I could. I was saying you had to discern before you can work there. I began to think about how could I bring business to the Cinema. I kept on saying things like, "your out, strike three." The patrolman Eddie came by and gave me the $5.00 back from when I had given this to another patrolman. There was a girl as well as a young man whom was cleaning the Cinema. Then there were these words, which I heard the voice from somewhere say.

"Sit down. Sit down, sit down."

I was very restless. Then I fancied the girl whom had gone into the Cinema to clean, I thought was telling me, "Put your foot through the door."

I was thinking, I didn't want to do this. I was thinking I wanted to take the easy way out and leave. I thought I wouldn't do this, and "run."

I had a feeling come over me if I didn't do this then things would be worse. I then got a piece of bumble gum on the ground and began to chew this. Then I turned to the left, and my hips began to sway, and I went towards the front door of the Cinema and I began to kick the door. The first couple of kicks and the door began to crack. Then I kept this up with 7 or 8 more kicks. Then the whole door shattered and I began to go into Cinema. My whole head and face felt like a cringe. I could only penetrate so far. This was like when I had pulled the catheter out of me, and there was blood and people could only penetrate so far, looking at the blood. Back then the blood was like, "Bled White."

The boy cleaner was with his vacuum cleaner and he looked at me with amazement. I then began to walk to my car about 250 yards away. I was walking. I tell you walking, really tall through the park. I felt I was big. I could remember when I was swaying my shoulders now, instead of hips when I went to the door at first. I had a memory lapse for about must have been 1 or 2 minutes. I later thought I walked like Christ on earth. I walked to my car and I had complete piece of mind while walking.

Then I was getting into my car and the boy cleaner followed me up there and I thought he had taken down my license plate #. Then my piece of mind began to race. "You are going to be convicted of a felony," I would hear in my head.

I then drove to my aunt's home. There I parked my car out back of the house. I began to put dirt and grass on my license plate, like camouflage. Then I thought my uncle Henry was telling me. "Eat dirt, eat dirt, and eat dirt."

I said to myself the Breen's had the Atlantic water, the Atlantic Ocean. So I kept on eating dirt. I went into the house and I talked to my aunt.

"Someone put their foot through the Norwood Cinema door."

"Who did this?"

"I don't know."

I stated.

"I have to go to the store."

She said.

"Eat dirt, eat dirt, and eat dirt."

I thought my uncle Henry was telling me inside my head. My aunt came back and I had gotten a plate full of dirt, which I was eating dirt from. I also picked up her backyard a little bit. My aunt then came back. Then a police officer, and a person from the light Department came to the house.

"Can I help you officers?"

My aunt inquired of the police officer.

"Billy Breen just kicked in the door of the Norwood Cinema."

"Did you do this Billy?"

I was sitting down eating dirt. Then all of a sudden I felt like I was being tickled. I began to get silly. The officer took in air from the side of his mouth to I believe to get me to stop being silly.

"You'll have to come down the station Billy."

"I'll go down tomorrow with Joe Breen."

"Joe Breen is retired."

The police officer said.

"I'll go down with Joe Breen."

I reiterated.

The police officer and the light Department person decided to leave. As they were leaving my aunt said something like.

"Would you want a cup of tea?"

My aunt I could tell was being quick, as they were leaving, and I could tell they wanted to get out as quick as possible. I then went into my aunt's shower, and I took a shower. As I was showering I began to holler out, "cheese, cheese, cheese," I thought the policeman was still in the house.

I then thought. "Get-t-up."

I don't know what came over me, but I thought I should go to Emergency at the Hospital. Before going down to Emergency I thought of calling the Veteran's Hospital in West Roxbury.

"326-7000."

"Hello, this is the Veteran's Hospital. What can I do for you? What department would you like?"

"Volunteer department please."

"Yes, can I help you?"

"This is Bill Breen. I'm coming over Monday."

Then hanged up.

I thought the people from Veteran's Hospital were saying in my head. "This is Emergency."

I was thinking this was so much emergency they were like saying this isn't too serious. I can recall the road driving there. This seemed like the idea of time was exaggerated. I went into Emergency and I looked at a doctor at the front desk smiling quite a bit. Three days previous I was working at the hospital. Now I am a patient. I was really, really embarrassed. I decided to walk right through the hospital. I went through a corridor and I also took a little bit of water from a bubbler.

I headed out of hospital, and I got on a wall, which separated the Post Office and hospital. I got up on the wall and began to walk on this. As I was walking on this my left foot sprang me up into the air and I headed for the hospital parking lot. As I was in the air I could feel I was entering hospital air space. I can remember my head go up and then head first onto tar. As I was in the air I could recall a boy kind of like say something like.

"Oh, oh."

I must have done a complete flip in the air. I did the flip and I was on the hospital parking lot. I was on the tar and just lying there on the ground. I thought later I was in spinal shock for the second time. I was just on the tar yelling something, which made me think Wichita. Like Witch-it-tar Kansas.

A couple of patrolman came there while I was yelling out. I was hearing a voice in my head saying, "Get up, get up, get up etc . . ."

I was brought back when I was on the wrestling team and the coach would constantly be saying to me, when I would be, tried to be pinned, "get-up, get-up, get, etc . . ."

If I had gotten up I would have been arrested for sure. I thought the police, if they could see I could move, I would have qualified for the jail cell. But I just kept on hollering. I think at first they had called an ambulance, but they declined to pick me up. I was thinking I wanted to be carried by stretcher about 75 yards into the hospital. But you won't believe this, but the only thing, which the police could pick me up in, was in a hearse. I can recall a patrolman put me on the stretcher and into the hearse. I remember going into the hearse and this seemed going from so much light, to darkness in the hearse.

The next thing I recall is I was in the Hospital Emergency. A person there identified himself as being Veteran's Hospital personnel and he was there to draw blood from me.

I could remember him saying.

"Charley is out again."

He drew blood on my left arm I believe. I must have bought about 15 minutes of time by jumping off the wall. This must have been just enough time, for the Veteran's Hospital staff to get to the Norwood Hospital about 15 minutes ride from Boston. I began to think in wartime they actually just shoot at each other right out in the open. So the police with guns can't really have the experience as shooting, without any cover.

I had a small laceration on my head when I landed on the tar after going off the wall.

"Should we give him an anesthetic?"

Said a nurse.

"No, I don't think he needs stitches."

I was so embarrassed here in Emergency when I worked here just 2 days earlier. A woman psychiatrist came to check me out. Someone here had said.

"He works at the Hospital here."

Then this lady doctor comes in to check me out. I thought she really felt bad she had heard I had worked at the Hospital, and she really took this out on me. They brought me to x-ray and when I was in x-ray, I sat up and said.

"Nothing is wrong."

I was thinking a girl whom I had dated, Janis A. whom had worked in x-ray as an x-ray technician. I had dated her when I was younger. She wasn't on this shift though. I felt she helped me here now by me being in x-rayed.

They took me back to Emergency and the psychiatrist ordered a shot of haldold. When I got the shot I sat up straight. I began to think about your soul when you get up in the mornings. This is your soul of sitting up before getting out of bed.

I was wheeled into an ambulance to Newton Wellesley Hospital. I can recall the security guard at Norwood, while I was wheeled out look at me, and projecting to me, "you are really sick."

I was brought to Newton-Wellesley Hospital and I don't recall too much there in the beginning. I can recall when someone there said.

"What were you trying to do?"

I don't know how I said this, but I was talking now controllably.

"I tried to cut my wrist."

I could recall back when I was at Norwood Hospital in August 1975. I was arching my back, back and someone asked me.

"What are you doing?"

I then said.

"I'm not dead yet."

I was thinking there was some higher power trying to kill me. When I said, I'm not dead yet, I was meaning to the higher power you haven't killed me yet. I thought about my uncle Mickey when he died, and his time was up, and he was being taken. I thought of him saying to the almighty. "Shoe." Meaning go away, to the higher power.

I recall whenever I feel as if I'm being brought down in any way, I sometimes say.

"OOO."

This is like a wolf howling. I thought when the almighty came down on the mountain to talk to Moses, this was the wolf's howling which made him go back up.

While I was on this unit there, I called up a doctor whom I had seen for ear problems. I called him and asked him about something or other. He left a message on this unit he would see me after I was off the unit.

I also called up the Marine Corps in Norwood and said to them.

"I'm looking for that medal."

They hadn't said anything this time. I had sent them some writings when I was a salesman, the antecedent year.

"I should get a medal."

The Marine there said.

"You don't get medals, you earn them."

Now I called them up and said, "I'm looking for this medal."

I was in a single room with a staff member outside my room, so none of the other regular patients there, could go into my room. I recall one of these days when I had some thread and I attached some paper and hooked this up to an air vent. I was thinking of the idea, "Go fly a kite." I had like a small kite hooked up to the ventilator.

I can recall I thought one of the girl MHWs wanted to perform fellatio with me. I can recall her controlling herself from smiling, by taking air through her nostrils and pulling up one cheek. I was being put on prolixin again and I began to get very tired. I was practically lying down in bed all day long. I was sedated quite a bit.

After about one week at Newton-Wellesley I was transferred to McLean Hospital. I was rather propitious I was going to McLean. When I got there, I was in an open room. Right around this time I began to think of dr. Jon Eloc as shaking a glass with ice-cubes and drink in his hand portraying the idea of rocks. He asked me one of the first days here.

"What did you do?"

"I put my foot through the Norwood Cinema door. I was supposed to start work there the next day."

"You were going to work at the Norwood Cinema?"

He asked me.

"Ya."

I said.

My doctor on this floor was dr. Nosl. I wanted to have dr. Eloc as my doctor.

Dr. Jon Eloc said.

"You can't have me. You have to have dr. Nosl."

Here at McLean I was being put on inderal as well as ativan. I wasn't getting along with dr. Nosl at all. I began to put furniture outside my room into my room.

Dr. Jon Eloc asked me one day, when he was stopping by very shortly.

"What is the staff trying to make you do?"

"They are trying to steer me into the television room."

I felt I was working 24 hours per day. I was being paid for an extended leave of absence from Norwood Hospital, which I had worked before I left. I was sedated a bit from the ativan. I was watching television and I was having a hard time keeping my eyes opened. I thought of the Marine quarterback from the New England Patriots. I said to one of the visitors there one day.

"He's is going to be a lefty quarterback. He is going to throw bombs."

There was an MHW whom spoke perfect English as a second language. When I said bombs lefty, his eyes lit up. I thought sometimes this guy was running the whole show there.

One day I walked right through the med area and into the staff room. There was a big cake there. I took a piece of cake and ate this. Dr. Jon Eloc was sitting there. One of the MHWs said.

"You can't come in here."

"Jonathan this is all right for me to come in here, isn't it?"

"It's not up to me."

I had proceeded to get a piece of cake just like one of the regular workers there. I was being paid for an absence of leave from the Norwood Hospital, which I had worked on the psych unit there. I would like experience the idea of eating cake for psychiatric work. I thought these people at McLean wanted to get back at me for eating the cake.

One night I couldn't get to sleep, and I wanted to take an ativan to get to sleep. I told the night nurse I wanted an ativan to get to sleep. She said.

"You can only have ativan for anxiety."

I decided not to take this then. This seemed like once you were just about asleep, they would come in every half hour to have a bed check with the flashlight, and this would awake you again.

One of these early mornings, when I felt like moving my bowels, but didn't, I thought of dr. Jack Yado as saying in my head.

"That was a bomb."

I asked to be taken off the ativan. I began to get anxiety from off the ativan. I was looking at one of the MHW there named Ken. I was projecting, as if I was a worker there and he was the patient. Now I was being paid by the Norwood Hospital, which I didn't know then. I was looking into Ken's eyes, as if I was giving the anxiety to him. I got the anxiety and then I took 5 mgs. prolixin PRN. This didn't seem to help any. I had equated this anxiety, as like being in a cold shower and not being able to get out.

I made a quick dash to the staff door where I got the cake, but I didn't get out. This was a locked unit. They stopped me and I went limp, as I had a little bit of thought of going crazy. But I knew this wouldn't change my state of mind, so I just did as they said. They brought me to a single room with just a mattress of the floor. I began to yell out this time.

"Jesus, Jesus, Jesus, etc . . ."

I began to call a certain doctor Red Satan. The MHWs outside the room were saying to themselves what is next? They seemed they were gloating over me. They were even chuckling a bit. I really didn't think they cared about me then. I then began to yell out another doctor was Lucifer. I had heard in the Bible Lucifer wanted to be God. The people outside my room began to say to themselves this wasn't Kosher or cool. They were saying, "ya sure". Now I think of this, they were really gloating over me. How do you fight back in this situation? A doctor and nurse came in and the doctor said.

"Lets' give him ativan."

I then opened my mouth to take the ativan orally, but they gave me a shot in the ass. He also gave me a shot of prolixin in the ass also. I was thinking this dr. Nosl whom was my doctor liked my idea of calling doctors Satan. So he could steal this way of fighting this way from me. So he pays me back, by giving me this shot of prolixin, which he and everyone there expected, this would be a shot for life on the needle each week.

Another idea which came to me was the idea of the movie coming out, "Born on the Fourth of July," was being made. The person in this movie Ron Kovic had accidentally killed a Marine named Nosl. This doctor here might have been a bit upset about this. Well my connection was I happened to be injured the same spot on the back as Ron Kovic T-6. So this dr. Nosl's way of getting back at Kovic, was to give me the shot, which he thought I would be on the needle the rest of my life once per week.

This doctor had written in my Medical Records, which I retrieved," thank-you" next to the medicine, which was given me for each week's records. Like really rubbing this in. He thought I would be on the needle for life. He also began to take me off the inderal which I was on. He called putting me on the shot as progress and taking me off the inderal as progress. I also thought this was his way of getting back at me for taking the cake.

I wondered why they hadn't put me in four points restraint? I later thought they had known I was being paid from Norwood Hospital, which had a psychiatric unit. I thought me being in restraint wouldn't be too good for them, with me getting paid at the same time.

They moved me to a quite room where you couldn't leave. I began to think of the dancer in Hollywood years ago Bobby Breen. I also began to run in place, which I thought about with the Breen sport's commentator on channel 6. I began to think of candy, "good and plenty," which my sister brought in for me.

This dr. Mark Nosl I think really liked my way of fighting back, by calling people Red Satan, so much he came in the room and gave me papers for shock treatments. I gave him a little kick with my foot and then ripped them up. They then began to take me off the inderal, which I didn't want to come off. I dressed up in my suit coat and attire and I would begin to supervise the girl whom would come in to vacuum each day the rug. I was recalling back when I was the "door to door" salesman. This dr. Mark Nosl would say to me.

"Are you sure you wouldn't want a little electricity?"

I would say to him.

"Keep on smiling."

One of these days I can recall a Cardinal bird was outside my window. Then after a couple of days as a cardinal, then came a robin. I was thinking of calling Mass Rehabilitation to help me with my insurance to help pay the bills. When I began to think of calling them I thought very bad thinking of, "He is asking us." So I declined.

I was going to see if I could get dr. Jon Eloc to sign a piece of paper stating I was of sound mind. When I asked him this, he kind of began to really think like, "Of sound mind, you have to be crazy."

I had been on a medical leave of absence from my job at the hospital. I called my supervisor Linda to see about my job. She said I needed a note from dr. Jon Eloc. I was at first thinking I didn't want to do this, but then I thought what was the alternative. Dr. Mark Nosl said I could go back to work. When I then called Linda, and told her I would get a note from dr. Jon Eloc. She then said she couldn't hold open my job. I was desperate. If I didn't have a place to go during the day then where would I go? I said to Linda.

"I'll take anything, even dishwasher."

I later thought the hospital personnel thought I would take a job, which didn't take any brains at all, a dishwasher. But I don't think they knew of the alternative. When I had no job to go too then dr. Mark Nosl said I could go to a halfway house in Walpole and be administered the shot and meds there. At the Norwood Hospital they said they couldn't keep open my job. The insurance I had with Norwood Hospital wasn't good for another three months. You had to have paid into the plan for nine months. I had another three or so months to go. I think people at McLean were quite content maybe my hospital stay at McLean, would be paid for by the Norwood Hospital.

I had worked at Norwood Hospital for just about 9 months, but I had paid into the system for around 6 months. I said to myself I didn't want Norwood Hospital to pay for my stay in a psychiatric Hospital. I thought I wanted to be part of the Norwood Hospital. This is why I didn't pay into the system right away from the start when I worked at Norwood.

I was transferred to the Arbour Hospital in Jamaica Plain, Boston. Before I left McLean I had made pen marks on the bureau for every day I was there. When I was making the marks I was thinking I was an oversea's spy and had to stay there so many days. I just wanted to lye down. I kept myself content by saying to myself, "hello-e, hello-e, hello-e, etc . . ."

I was at the Arbour about 4 months. There was a young violent adult patient there. He would try to intimidate people there. I said to him.

"Get in your cage and eat your meat."

I could recall when I was about 11 or 12 years old and a neighbor of mine was in Vietnam. I heard he had guarded prisoners as a Marine in the war. His younger brother would say back around this time, "get in your cage and eat your meat." I thought his brother would say this to the prisoners in Nam.

There was a girl nurse there named Julie. She I think was pregnant also then. She came by my room one day and I think she knew I was in McLean before coming there. Supposedly, a better cut of people, were from McLean. When I had gotten in McLean for the first time, this was supposed to be the Hospital for the rich and famous. I didn't even want to go to McLean at the beginning, but what other alternative was there. This was the worst of all evils. Well this girl Julie came outside my room one day and like took in air with her nostrils. She I thought wanted some of my McLean air.

This was a terrible situation. I didn't even want to go to McLean Hospital in the beginning. Then when you have the condition then this place is the best of all evils. I called folks there, Biblical name diagnosis. They give me their diagnosis. I give them my diagnosis. They can have some of there own medicine.

I really don't know how I got the strength to endure this hospitalization. The ears, nose and throat doctor whom I saw for ear problems I thought about. He had worked on my ear once. He called the feeling I created in my ear once as.

"Primitive."

This is the type of feeling you have when you have your ear vibrate. I think this would be like you are trying to move your ear. I would do this all throughout the day here. The feelings I were fighting I can only explain by I worked on a psychiatric unit one week and the next I am a patient. This seemed I was someone healthy, and like had to go the other way to be down to the level with the patients on the psych unit.

I called up the owner of the Norwood Cinema and spoke with the owner.

"John Igrams?"

I said.

"Yes, this is John Igrams."

"This is Bill Breen. I noticed a new ad you had in the paper. I had cleaned up some trash in the back of the Cinema. I hope putting my foot through the door will bring in more business."

"Bill, Do you understand what you did?"

He asked me.

When he said this, I crouched down and said.

"Yes."

There was now a bigger ad in the paper for the shows at the Cinema. I thought the attention I had with my foot in the door had brought notoriety to the Cinema. I made out a check for $200 for the door which they wanted $175.

Around this time here I thought dr. Jon Eloc had said in my head like, "join the herd."

Dr. Jon Eloc MD had worked at Boston City Hospital as a psychiatrist before he came to McLean. He had worked with all the wild people of Boston. He thought I would be going to a hearing, for when I put my foot through the door as a criminal. He probably had like a lot of wild guys whom would assault policemen, or got into trouble, and he had to tell the courts there was really something wrong with them.

I called up my uncle Joe Breen whom had retired now from the Courthouse. This seemed I would be going to a hearing for after I put my foot through the door. After I called him up he said to me.

"Everything is all set."

He had the great calmness he had when he said the family prayer to me when I was dieing at Norwood Hospital years earlier. Everything will be all set. This is what I heard when after I had fought for my life at Norwood and also when I first went to be interviewed at McLean.

Here at the Arbour there was one girl in particular whom I thought had projected in my head, "he's a monkey."

When the staff heard, the proceedings had been stopped by my uncle, their eyes lit up. My uncle Joe must have talked to his pals the judges at the Courthouse to get this thrown out of Court. During and after my uncle had straightened everything out, I had been thinking of the concept foil. This is 9+7, or 8+8 or 9x7 to 8x8. One is 63 the other 64. I had thought I could prove this theorem wrong. I had remembered studying this in tenth grade and questioning this. There was an occupational therapist there and she asked me out at the Arbour Hospital. I declined though. She would go to a bar about 75 yards away from the Norwood Cinema. We would talk about what was going on in Norwood. I don't know what town she lived in though.

I would try to stay out in front of the front desk. Some of the workers would say.

"You can't be standing in front of the front desk."

I think maybe I would be overhearing them talking about news to each other.

A psychologist, whom I would sometimes talk too, had some kind of problem holding down food. After I talked to her once I felt like throwing up or I did.

Well the rowdy young adult boy got down on his knees in back of me at about 2:00 one day in front of everyone. This person must have realized what I had done. Some of the staff there said things like, "Get off the floor." I began to think we will call the Arbour, now Glenny, after this boy on his knees. This person was transferred to another Hospital. I think they didn't want another spectacle like this from him in front of me, so they transfer him out.

We would have community meetings in the mornings and I would say at these meetings.

"If you have any kind of problem whatsoever, all you have to do use your other hand, left vs. right."

There was one MHW boy there whom would constantly harangue things like.

"You'll have to leave the meeting if you continue to say things like this."

The MHW boy' name was Arnold. You could tell that Boston didn't want anyone to infringe on the care in Boston.

I can recall the custodian whom would wash the floors each day. I began to think again, psychiatric problems were positive in Boston. There wasn't anything to be ashamed about in a Boston Hospital. This custodian was from Roslindale, and he would even converse with all the patients there.

My sister brought me in a Reader's Digest magazine one day. Rocky Blier had written an article about Art Model the owner of the Pittsburgh Steelers. He had passed away. Rocky Blier was the Vietnam Veteran whom had some toes blown off, by a hand grenade and played pro-ball after this. His article was about being regimented. I recalled back when I had the dream, with the regimented chromosomes in my brain fighting the unregimented chromosomes in the brain on the other side. Schizophrenics supposedly have unregimented chromosomes in the brain. I was working with Electrolux then. Rocky then said after Pro-ball, he was like back in the jungles of Nam. I thought of all of my statistics playing baseball and Rocky's statistics playing football.

I can recall one of these days I began to eat water as soup with my left hand. I was being put back on the inderal here. I said to myself with the soup, "Jesus will still help me."

I wrote a letter to Jean Yawkey on this unit. I told her about everything I thought about sports. I really consolidated, when I used an envelope. This envelope was the hospitals envelope, which was for a sharp object of mine. This sharp object was a sewing needle. I would use thread from the bed when I would use this needle. I crossed off sewing needle, and used the envelope for the letter to Jean Yawkey.

Around this time Jean Yawkey had an award for Kitty Dukakis. Something like woman of the year or something another. This was when Kitty Dukakis drank the rubbing alcohol. She was the wife of Gov. Dukakis.

There was a patient there whom had been a colonel in the Army. He was in his late fifties. He said to me one day.

"When I was younger about 15, I was abused by a person. I've held this in all these years. This is why I have these problems after all these years."

I said to him.

"Sure, sure."

I could tell he had to admit this to someone. My answer with sure, was like agreeing with him as well as a little bit farcical. I began to think sure or now I connected this with shore, which would be in wartime to hit the beach. This was to be my combat word whenever I would feel a phony about having mental problems. The colonel would say things like.

"Grapefruit juice."

I would begin to think of the grapefruit league. I could recall when I was dieing at Norwood in August in 1975, I thought when fighting for my life to eat grapefruits skins and all. The colonel would ask the patients what brought them into the hospital?

"Eleanor said her son had died an she couldn't cope. Mary said she got divorced and she got depressed. You see real things happen to people to make them need hospital."

He would also say things when people would need physical restraint as.

"They are shackling them down."

Around this time I was transfer to an unlock unit. I was with a lot of alcoholics. There was a man named Mike Ke. whom got depressed because of back problems. He walked with a cane. He had worked on a trash truck for 5 years and was out on disability. I would say to Mike.

"They are shackling them down upstairs."

I said this jokingly, but Mike's voice would tremble a bit when I would say.

"They shackle them down upstairs."

I would call my family Physician Jack Yado MD whom just worked on Tuesdays in his retirement. Some of his statements were like.

"Do as they say."

He said this in the beginning when I was here. I was thinking of possibly having a very hard time with the staff here. But when Jack said do as they say, I thought best to do as they say.

Around a couple of months here jack said to me.

"I know where you are Bill."

This would mean he knew I was in a hospital. He had probably had admitted tens of thousands.

Another one was like.

"Gorbachev and Reagon would feel things out."

When I thought this I brought to mind how Jack would give the students at the high school physicals, when he would examine them, as the high school doctor. Now feel things out was he would feel the student's scrotums.

This unit at Glenny was a fear unit. Most of the time there would be orders from the staff there. I would have probably never had done as they said, if dr. Jack Yado hadn't told me to do as they say. He knew if I went overboard by doing as they said, then this would be less on me. They at one point wanted to give me shock treatments there. I think I stopped this by saying I want shock treatments. If you want them, then you don't get them.

When I was here I began to on purpose move my jaw side to side. My jaw would uncontrollably do this when I was officially put on the inderal 10 years earlier. When the people here saw this, they began to study me, by having tape recording studies of me by one of the doctors there.

I told the psychiatrist there I wanted to march in the veteran's day Parade. I thought when I was on a pass in Norwood plenty of people were downtown Norwood to give me a welcoming home parade. I thought many people were in Norwood Center to see I was back. The air felt a bit like moving fog, Billy's back.

I had thought if you died in Texas, then you would go to hell. My brother Jack had been there for a year in 1987. I was saying to myself, "put the fire out." This was Texas. I thought I was having therapy from Audie Murphy. The idea of, put the fire out, was coming over me. I later heard Audie Murphy had died of a plane crash in 1971. He had been wounded five times in World War 2. This would be the 6th time down with the plane crash, which he died in.

I can recall one of these days I had to get staff to help me. I had been talking about rugby with one of the staff members whom played rugby himself. I told another patient there when I knew this staff person was listening.

"When the men were in the trenches in the First World War, they would play rugby in the trenches before they went, "over the top."

Well this rugby staff worker I don't recall actually what he did, but I do remember he said or did something, which helped me.

There was this one patient there whom I was conferring with and he said about the marines in the Second World War.

"When the marines were hitting the beach, they would roll a coke machine onto the beach. The marines were, "hitting the beach."

This person had whiplash in his neck. He also said once.

"This always works."

There was a man named Howard whom was in WW 2 and also the Korean War. He labored for the Post Office. His wife had a bad back and was in hospital. I guess she wasn't too serious to be on a regular medical unit, but she was on a psychiatric. I can remember this person Howard put his left hand leaning on his right shoulder. I can recall I did this one night and I bridled myself to go to sleep.

I can recall when I was on pass with my brother Jack. We had gone to a restaurant in Braintree Mass. I could recall my pants were tight because I had put on a few pounds. We were in this restaurant and my lower back was showing as the pants were to tight. I thought this idea of your lower back and part of ass showing, was from Boston Mass. This was a pristine idea, which came out of Boston.

There was a nurse there whom I thought she told me her last name was Burns. I would call her nurse Burns all the time. I found out a while later her name wasn't Burns. She I think thought I meant nurse Burns as in burning. I never really realized why she gave me a hard time. I was calling her the wrong name.

I also went on a pass and I saw my pal Jimmy Sivad, whom I would work on the truck cutting down trees with. I met my friend Henry S. there also. If you remember correctly I would pal around with him right after high school. Henry was sent to the Marine Corps with the Courts. Henry said.

"I had my fourth baby,"

"I deliver babies."

I said to Henry, as I would bring all the supplies to the maternity unit when I worked at the Hospital.

"We kick."

I also said.

"Fourth down Henry."

"We punt."

Henry said.

Then Jimmy was chuckling a bit, and said.

"Fourth Down."

I was thinking Jimmy was reckoning like a sperm, which went down a vagina of a woman and down would mean down to fertilize and egg in a woman's ovaries. I was also bringing to mind this was the fourth sperm down. Sperm swim like people swim when they would be, "hitting the beach." As I was leaving Henry said to me.

"I wanted to talk to you."

But I had been going to my car and left.

Well I got discharged from Glenny in February 1990. I was put on Social Security in February 1990 also. When I was at Glenny, I applied for a volunteer job there. I had insurance from the Hospital, which I had worked the previous year also. I devise I was paying over $300 each month for the premiums.

I had gone to Norwood Mental Health Center when I was at Glenny in regards to, I had some place to go when I left hospital. When I was discharged I just couldn't get myself to go there. I had worked on a psychiatric unit the previous months and now I was a patient.

I had left a note on the door of the Center about how I think I needed a face transplant. One of the doctors there said maybe he is not ready to come out of the hospital yet. He thought I would have to go there to get the prescriptions. They didn't know I had an ace up my sleeve with dr. Jack Yado whom wasn't a psychiatrist but was a doctor, and he wrote my prescriptions. A lot of the shrinks I think were a bit perturbed about this.

I think Jack understood this, so he had me see the shrinks in my town. The first one I saw was dr. Jimmy. Jack had recommended him for me. I went to see him the first day. I went into his office and began to glance at his paintings.

"Nice pictures you have here."

I kept looking at his pictures. Then I said.

"You have a tough job on the psychiatric unit at Norwood Hospital."

He was smiling a little bit.

"I need prescriptions."

He gave me prescriptions and I began to go.

"You don't have to go now."

He said.

"Well I think I'll get going."

I responded.

"I can see you each week."

He said.

"My insurance doesn't cover this much."

I said.

"I'll accept Medicaid."
He said.
"No, I don't have Medicaid."
I replied.
Well I got my prescriptions and went on my way. Jim's office was right next to the Marine Corps recruitment office. I also began to do a little tree work with my old pal Joe mostly in Brookline again. I just worked a few times. I had been calling up dr. Jack Yado on Tuesdays and I told him.
"I'm tired Jack."
"Tell the psychiatrist this you are tired."

One day I just start painting.
I began to paint then. I began to paint about a half an hour each day then, which I have ever since. My uncle on my mother's sister side, was a very established painter. He did President Jimmy Carter wife's portrait as well as Chief Justice Burger. His name was George Augusta. He studied after World War 2 under the GI Bill.
I had my pills in cups on a book shelve on the wall. I had begun to stretch also. One of these times I stretched and banged my body against the pills on the shelf and a lot of the pills got wet. I then had to call up dr. Jimmy to get more pills.
"Jim, I need another prescription"
"I gave all you need."
He said.
"I need more."
I said.
"No."
He was just about to hang up when I said to him.
"Wait."
I said to him.
He then listened.
"I got some of them wet."
I said.
"I'll call up the pharmacy."

He said.

This doctor was someone in which reminded me of the guys I would chum with in school, which went on to the Ivy Leagues. I talked to him as if he were a student friend.

I had also begun to do a diminutive amount of coaching with the high school football team. I told dr. Jack Yado.

"I'm doing a little coaching at the high school."

"I examined those people, Bill."

He would give the high school physicals.

Well this was just preseason and I would try to psych up the football players now. I would say things like.

"Look alive, step alive."

Joe Charles had been head coach for five years now.

Dr. Jack told me.

"Joe Charles was the only person to thank me for examining the students. John Fudd never did."

I told this to the head coach and he felt a bit better after I told him this. I would throw the football with my other arm. Our football quarterback would also throw the ball with his other arm.

I was reminiscing when I played football in high school and this seemed more organized back then. The first scrimmage Joe thought I would help the team most by being in the booth which would video the game, and also head phones to call down different strategies. The first scrimmage was against Weymouth I believe. I saw one of the running backs and I said to him at half time.

"Spin once you get hit. You look good. Try spinning."

"All right, do you think this will help?"

"Ya."

I said to him.

I had been studying him up in the press box with the filming.

We played Natick under the lights in Natick. I thought to mind then Eketron. I followed some coaches in my car over there. I was up in the press box and they had both side's cameras there. Drum was the other coach whom had the headphones. I was taking inderal throughout the night. I remember I saw a woman whom was on the camera there.

She seemed she was interested in me. I thought my social life was gone on the shot of prolixin I had to have very week. Well we weren't doing too well in the game. I told Drum.

"Try them up the middle"

This was where I could detect they weren't too strong there. We went into the locker room at half time. I kept on saying to the players.

"Step alive out there."

Joe Charles the head coach was trying to psych up the players. I was thinking he really knew how to start the ball with the players. The only thing I could think of was coaching football was not like coaching baseball. This was like football was harder than baseball to play and also to coach.

I begun to recollect when we played Natick in football in high school and we lost 9-8. I had heard one of the players on Natick whom was really the whole team, had been on speed the whole game. I began to think if we won this game we would have been league champs. I thought about when we played Braintree in baseball, I had been speeding in this game. If Braintree had won, they would have been league champs. I thought if we could have traded the baseball champs for the football champs, then this would be good.

Now, we lost this game against Natick. I went down to the field to shake hands with the coaches. I shook hands lefty with the Natick coach. I saw the sport's writer Frank Curb there. He looked at me and I thought he was going to say something to me, but he went over and interviewed the Natick coach. I saw my old semi-pro baseball coach Red there. When I would be walking on the field I would look down towards the left.

Dr. Jim the psychiatrist said over the phone.

"I'm not going to be your psychiatrist anymore."

"Are you quitting?"

I asked him.

"Ya."

He said.

"Well you will have to refer me to another doctor."

He said.

"No, go see Thom."

I had seen Thom in February once. Back then I had called up dr. Thom for an appointment. He wanted me to go to his home. He gave me the directions. I tried to get there, but I got lost. I called him up and he said.

"Do you have proper directions?"

I said.

"I'll see you in your Norwood office."

"You don't want to come to my home office?"

"The Norwood office should be all right."

I said to him.

I could detect their was some reason why he wanted to see me in his home office. I went in to his Norwood office and he was sitting down in a chair. I didn't think anything wrong. He didn't get up when I shook his hand in a greeting gesture. He then said to me.

"Do you have your Blue Cross card?"

"No, I don't."

I said, but I really did.

I said to him.

"One night I had a dream the regimented chromosomes, were fighting the unregimented ones on one side of my brain."

He said.

"Did you have brain damage?"

"No."

I defensively said.

Well after about ten minutes, he got up from his chair and got into another one at his desk. I could tell then he had problems with his legs. He was hobbling along.

I said to him.

"I'll be getting along now."

He said.

"You still have thirty minutes."

"That's all right. I'll be getting along now."

Then this hit me. He wanted to see me at his home because he felt much more secure than his office. I thought about seeing him as a psychiatrist, but I should be the person whom should be getting paid.

I had to pay 20 % for the deductible for the insurance. This was about ten dollars. Well I paid dr. Thom this. He then got a collection agency after me. They kept on calling me up and hounding me for money. I would keep on saying to them.

"Listen, the bill had been paid."

After about 5 times with this, the collection agency would keep on saying they needed this in documentation. I knew something was wrong. Well I said to them at about the fifth time.

"You can tell Thom if he keeps on hounding me, I will send him a bill."

I never heard from them again. Dr. Thom had the big get even problem. He had to always try to just stay even with people because of his physical handicaps. This was Thom the cripple whom really wanted something which could help his legs.

Dr. Jack Yado told me later Thom had asked him if he could write his name for an anti-depressant for Thom. I might have had credit problems with the Thom situation and the collection agency. I think Jack told me this about the anti-depressant because of Thom getting the collection agency after me.

I would get my pills in the Guild Building. The girl cashier there said to me when I was coaching football, "Mental Block." I was put threw a loop by this. Everyone is really against you when mental problems arise. I could recall when I worked at the hospital. I was in the Hospital store and a mental patient was in the store getting out of the psych unit, and even a doctor there didn't want him to do good.

The third game was against Braintree. We were really doing them in. I thought the Braintree parents were thinking this swamping by Norwood, will be good for the Braintree players, to make characters of them. I then got down on the field and did the left down left maneuver. This was the look my uncle Henry looked like when I had gone out the window in secret when I made up the word hello-e when I actually flied one night.

This also was the time the Iraqis were invading Kuwait, and the troops were being deployed in Saudi Arabia. I was hearing a voice in my head, which was saying, "Soldier sir, Soldier sir, Soldier Sir, etc . . . ."I would say this to myself. I thought these boy football players, may some day be in the USA Military. I had also begun to do volunteer work at the Veteran's Hospital.

When dr. Jack Yado heard about my football coaching he said.

"That is something really good, Bill."

I began to think of how James Taylor had done so much for mental stigmas. I thought I might be able to speak at the fall sport's banquet as a coach. I didn't have the confidence to capture an audience. I really didn't think I made sense, to be obeisance, respected.

I met the athletic director at the Press Box in Braintree.

"Arthur."

"Billy."

He said as we shook hands. I had come a long ways. I had recollected when I was in 11th grade and I had been suspended from high school for being drunk at the junior Prom. Arthur had given me a gruesome look after this. He seemed not to be interested in me after this. He was the dad of the arborist I worked with cutting down trees for a little while. I had worked with arborist full time before I got the Stop & Shop position. Now when I shook hands with Arthur everything seemed altogether.

The next game was against Wellesley at Wellesley. When I was there I helped set up the film projector. I then went down to the field. For some reason I didn't tie my shoe lacings. I was talking to the coach of Wellesley. I thought the Wellesley coach had said to me under his breath, "Get lost."

I was with our team doing exercises. I saw the boy whom I had coached in Babe Ruth baseball and also he worked as an attendant at the Cinema. Now this was the third time I was seeing him. I wanted his respect. We were down on the field and I thought this person was trying to understand me as coach with the footballers. He looked at me and his eyes like cringed.

I had a feeling come over me I really had emotional problems. Something when people were laughing at you, they are really laughing at you. As if I were a fool. I looked at some of the students in the stands and I thought they think I'm something like a mascot.

The doctor whom I was seeing before I went out the window on May 21, 1979 was from Wellesley. When I had no job and was home for the summer from UMass Boston the previous year he like mentioned to me to, "get lost." Meaning go get really sick and comeback into the hospital, where I can see you every day and I will collect from your insurance every day.

Here in Wellesley this day the head coach Joe Charley gave me $5 for to get some water. I walked away with the $5 and told some students to get some water for the team. I then drove home. I was really steamed after this, me being like a mascot.

From here I called up my Congressman's office and spoke with Roger Ken. I had been for about 20 years been getting signatures for the re-nomination of the congressman.

"Roger, I'm looking for the medal from the Marine Corps."

He asked me.

"What are you doing now?"

"I'm coaching football."

I said.

"Roger, what do you have to do to get a medal?"

"I coached the congressman's baseball team years ago."

"Ya, I coached semi-pro baseball in the Prarrie in town."

"Ya, there is a team on every corner."

I was beginning to think about where you lived and if you were overseas in Vietnam actually in combat fighting. This wouldn't be just like coaching in Boston. This would be on the front lines in Nam. I blew off a lot of steam with Roger. I began to think what a medal would mean for me to procure. You would have to withstand the publicity of getting a medal. I told Roger about the letter I got from Tip O'Neil and Roger said.

"Tip O'Neil is eighty years old."

As I said, I began to do volunteer work at the Veteran's Hospital in Boston. I went over there with my coat and also filled out an application for employment. There were about 5 or 6 World War 2 veterans there whom would volunteer in their retirement. A couple of them were from Roslindale. There were Italians, Jewish, Lithuanians, and English veterans of World War 2 whom were volunteering there.

One of the Italians there said of Jeffrey Dahmer the serial killer.

"He had the heart for dessert."

The Italians would say to the Jewish.

"Your anti-semitic."

"How can I be anti-semitic when I'm Jewish?"

Everyone would chuckle.

I would watch the daily mass in the morning before going to hospital. I would tell the people, which city the priest whom said the Mass was from this day. This was the town the priest whom would say the Mass came from each morning, on the Catholic television Station. I would bring the book cart around to the different floors and also work in the library. I had this voice, which said in my head around this time, which was, "Stay."

I thought this word stay, was something which dr. Jack Yado had heard after his stint in the service in World War 2 as a doctor. This word stay was he should stay in the service. Now I was hearing this word stay, maybe for me to stay at the Veteran' Hospital.

I was writing down quotes of all what the veteran's would say to me about their stints in the service. I have these quotes possibly hundreds of them. Every veteran would have his statement about his time in the service. I would walk downtown Norwood Center and ask the middle aged men.

"Were you in World war 2?"

If they would say they were either Korean War Veterans or WW 2 veterans I would then say.

"Let me shake that hand."

Maybe shake their hands lefty. I would call up dr. Jack Yado on Tuesdays and this was what would symmetry me.

I saw my third Norwood psychiatrist dr. Pres. The first day I saw her she wanted me to sign a piece of paper, which would enable her to look at my Medical records. The shrinks really like looking at records. I would imagine this gives them something to do. I was in her office and I began to talk about our Norwood Psychiatric unit. She had two rocking chairs away from her desk chair. I said to her.

"How is everything at the Norwood psychiatric unit?"

I was trying to talk to build up the Norwood Hospital. She asked me.

"Why don't you go to McLean?"

"Dr. Jack Yado thinks this is too far to travel."

The psychiatrist, ask for your history the first time you see them. This would entail all the hospitals you had been in over the years.

She said something to me when I was talking about the Norwood Unit. She possibly worked there also. She got me angry, so I said to her.

"Your like the rest of the psychiatrist, you like to get people angry. You have chips on your shoulders, you like to get people angry."

"I'm not like this."

She persisted.

Well the session was over and I said to her.

"I need prescriptions."

"Our time is up."

She insisted.

"I need prescriptions."

I said again. I was very angry. I came very close to giving her a kick with my leg. She said again.

"Our time is up, you have to go now."

She finally gave in and wrote the scripts. She said she would call the pharmacy on the first floor for the scripts. She only wrote this for 10 of one of the meds, when you had to pay $10 even if you had a 100 of them. I had to pay the flat rate no mater how many I received.

I was wondering why she was putting up such a beef. I thought later she wanted to see me without writing prescriptions, so for her psychic she was seeing someone, just to talk too. This would be good for her mental health when seeing people. She could project folks pay just to talk to her.

I saw her three times before she told me she only sees someone twice before she decides to take folks on. I sent her a check for $15 money order for the 20% deductible, which I had to pay. I thought she just kept the $15 money order and people would think I gave her a check like a professional hooker. I would worry about this, years later in which people would think I paid her a check.

After the game against Wellesley I went up the high school one day and as the boys were running, one of them said.

"How are you coach?"

I thought being called coach would keep the coaches going. I was being called a football coach. This felt very satisfactory.

The next game was against Brookline. I could recall I had cut down a lot of trees in Brookline as the second job. I even had the computer printout for all the vacuum cleaners in Brookline. When I had the computer printout for vacuum cleaners, I thought the folks in Brookline were saying, he is knocking on doors here. Now I had been coaching football here at Norwood High. I decided not to coach anymore. Thinking I was like a mascot, was a little bit much.

I was going down Ambulatory Care each week for the injection of prolixin. I really hated this. The secretary there would always treat me bad. She had the same last name of an amputee I had known. I even had to pay for this shot. All the folks I had worked with there, now I was getting an injection there.

The Norwood Hospital was having financial trouble. This was my hometown hospital. I even worked there. I wasn't hesitant about the premium I paid each month for the cobra insurance. When I would pay the premium each month I would count off to the cashier there, 100, 200, 300, 400 dollars. I worked in the hospital, so why wouldn't I try to help, as much as I could.

These days I would go down to Memorial Hall at the Norwood Town Hall. This was a room where all the military folks in Norwood had their names on plagues. WW 1, WW 2, Korean War. Vietnam War, Civil War and even War of 1812. Years earlier I had been having dreams about this room. I thought I was like in a confessional in the dreams. Well now I would come here just to unwind.

In this room I would stretch a little bit, like arch my back, back. This particular day I left the room and as I was leaving, I saw a policeman whom was walking into the Building. I thought later someone at the Town Hall had called the police up, for when I would be stretching. I thought the patrolman was there to bring me down to the Mental Health Center, which I would call the Boston Red Sox clubhouse. 15 or 20 seconds more and I could have been gone, gone. I thought one of the girls whom smoked cigarettes there might have complained.

One of these days I was pulled over by a regular patrolman, right around the point of when I would hang out with the corner folks. I thought folks were upset about how my uncle had pulled strings to get me off the Cinema time. I just didn't argue with them. This was right where I would hang out with the street gang. I thought they would make me think I hanged around on a street corner and I got off the Cinema time. I just let them go through the procedure. Nothing became of this.

I would go out for coffees every other week or so, with my uncle. We would go out to a fast food restaurant. I asked my uncle whom, was the court psychiatrist? He gave me his name and I tried him also. When I saw this shrink he asked me.

"Why don't you go to McLean?"

I told him this was too far to travel. I talked to him about how we could build up the Norwood Psych unit, because I did work on this. He had his office at his home. When I left his house I had to take a mean leak. I drove out back of a church and let this go. When I got back home I had a little anxiety. I had told this shrink I would tell him of my decision.

I had gotten an apartment from the Norwood Housing Authority. I was still going to the Veteran's Hospital. I used to go both ways in football. This time I didn't want to go to the V.A. or comeback from the V.A. either. I think they call this in the military, "going the V.A."

I applied for a job at a Mobil Gas station as a cashier. They had run out of applications, so I wrote on a piece of paper my name William Breen Edward. I thought you were supposed to put your last name second and middle name first. I put down football coach, and the Veteran's Hospital volunteer. When I put down the football coach, I think this was the deciding factor in me getting this position. The girl manager there said to me.

"You were a football coach?"

"Yes, at Norwood High."

"All right, you can start right after Christmas on Tuesdays and Saturdays. Since you are just starting you don't have to work Christmas."

"That's sounds all right."

I said.

I was working Tuesday 3-11 and Saturdays 3-11. Since I had used a plain piece of paper for the application, I had my last name second and middle name third. They had my name there, William Breen Edward. This I think of using as my pen name. They even gave me my checks with last name Edward.

Tuesdays weren't too bad as I enjoyed this job. I would see all the people getting gas from Norwood, I had known in my youth. On Saturday nights you would get all the children whom would party on the no school night. These nights were a little hectic.

I had a little trouble working the cash register and about ten gas buttons for the pumps. This was during the winter. I can recall when the register wasn't working befittingly, and there was a line of about ten people waiting, to either get gas or pay for gas. I was really serious here. Them waiting in line to see me. This winter I went outside, when some of the pumps I think had frozen, and I like shivered like with a chill. I thought this shiver is why some folks can call other folks, "dinks." Also I thought the food people would eat. I thought the saying, you look like what you eat was so true.

I met all kinds of people as being back in Norwood. I saw some of the Babe Ruth baseball players. I saw old friends I hadn't seen in years. I even saw my old boss here, the girl Linda whom I had asked for a date at the Cinema. I had used a requisition to get a date with her. This was like a buzz to see all the folks from Norwood again.

I would at the end of the shift calculate up the totals Gas, oil, liquids, concessions, etc . . . I would use my calculator for this. When I slept at night these nights, I can recall I would sleep on my back. I began to think people whom have mental problems repose on their stomachs.

I began to think of Mobil Corp. was thinking with me, "tired." When I would blow this up, I thought Mobil Corp. as being with the Federal Government to do something about, tired, or Tie heard. I had written about the Vietnam War in the beginning of my book. Mobil Corp. had stations over in Vietnam. At first I wrote about the Vietnam War was a tie, at the beginning of my book, before Saigon fell.

I was also thinking Mobil Corp. as having a "head." This was someone whom would be the leader of all their employees, to motivate them. I thought of the Mobil Corp. president as someone whom would have a knife pointing down the throat. I thought back then this was to motivate the employees, to get the spark to do something.

There was the supervisor of the area named Sherman. I thought of Gen. Sherman as telling his troops in the Civil War time to yell or holler. This was to scare the southerners back. Then I thought of "fool." This word' "fool," I correlated with people in Boston, when I went out the window and I didn't tell anyone, back when I said the word "hello-e," while I flied. I thought fool was something of Boston. Now I thought of the saying, "kid." I thought' "kid," was something of New York.

While I was working here I would see the boys and girls whom would smoke marijuana and come into the store for gas. I thought the dr. Jimmy whom I saw a little while ago would say in my head, "crackpot." Then I thought of my great uncle Bill Breen as saying, "cracktop," or backwards of crackpot. This meant Jesus or the top crack up or crack top.

One time when I was under a lot of stress I hollered at some 15 or 16 years old boys, and I gave my bad feelings to them. I can recall I thought my head was three feet higher when I blasted the boys. I began to think this was what in prisons the inmates would do, to intimidate others to have this bad feelings transferred to others.

There was a mental patient whom came into the store one day. I had the people in the line waiting, because I was having trouble with the register. I said to the people in line.

"Could you please leave the station, the register isn't working now."

"Your not a manager."

Said the mental patient.

"Please leave the store."

I said to him again.

He left the store. I felt rather relieved and good about telling a mental patient what to do. I felt like a worker on a psych unit again. I believe mental patients have this negative to them that this makes this seem they can never win a verbal fight.

When I went outside in the winter I would as I told you get a chill. When I would tell the folks to leave the station because of the register, I thought this was what they call in the oil business as, "losing water." Gasoline was like selling water to the oil giants.

I had been stretching throughout the days. When I would sell a lot of cigarettes at the station I began to not stretch. I think my sister Judy whom smoked cigarettes had stopped smoking them then. I thought the executives at Mobil Corp. were affected by my not stretching. This stretching was like I was enjoying myself.

I went down to a supermarket in my hometown and I had cutback on the prolixin by 5 mgs. I saw the girl supervisor at this supermarket sitting out front, and I thought to myself, "too high." I began to think of the feeling when you are doing better. So good this is detectable and people would be thinking you are doing too good. You have to be able to do some real keen introspection.

Dr. Jack Yado was writing my prescriptions now. Around this time was the deployment of troops to the Persian Gulf. I was still doing the volunteer work at the Veteran's Hospital. Over the V.A. this was very serious business. I can recall one day when I was getting off the elevator and a person said.

"They kill the scout."

I thought I was like the scout.

I was thinking I was the scout for this Iraqi War. I had dropped off my writings to the Marine Corp. recruitment two years previous now. As I said I had gone out the window on August 1, and the Iraqis invaded Kuwait on August 2. So this was my connection. I even thought the President of the USA was having trouble what to do, so they were like asking me in my mind, in a particular situation in the war. The strategy was to hope the Iraqis to win which I said in my mind.

I could recall back when I was in the visitor's room with my sister Judy at Norwood Hospital, in August 1975. I was watching a game between the Chicago White Sox and the Boston Red Sox. Myself being from Boston, but I began to route for the White Sox. Another words I was cheering for the other side. So now I gave this strategy in my mind for the strategy for the Gulf War in 1991.

One of these nights I worked for Mobil I had a dream with my old social worker Nancy. I thought of all the boys and girls out at night using foreplay. This was another fringe benefit of the job. I thought Nancy was happy I was doing well.

I would walk about ½ mile back to my apartment at about 12:00 at night, after work. I would walk by this bar. I recollected when I was in high school and I would walk by this bar when I would come home at night. The patrons would urinate out in public. This was another rush of being back home.

I was getting my checks to William Edward. I was having a second name. I thought as I told you earlier of using this name as my pen name. I would cash my check at a bank where the tellers knew me. So with the name William Edward instead of William Breen they cashed the checks. I thought later this was proof I had done enough work in a lifetime for two people. This was the name proof.

I had worked there for about 3 months and then the supervisor cut me back to just working on Saturday nights. I told her I didn't care too much for Saturdays. I said to her.

"I didn't say I didn't want to work on Tuesdays."

"I thought you said you didn't want to work then?"

She said.

I then was scheduled to work only on Saturday nights. I went to the station to pick up my check one day and I noticed I wasn't scheduled to work any days. I didn't know what to make of this. Well I few days later she calls up and says.

"You are not working here anymore."

"Why."

I asked her.

"You didn't use a credit card properly."

I was thinking of telling her the line, this was the grocery money for me. I recalled back when I worked right out of high school with Electrolux and I would say to people.

"I can win a micro-wave oven if I get one more sale."

The idea of making them feel sorry for you then you go in for the kill. Now this happened at Mobil. I didn't though say, this was the grocery money, which I was thinking of saying.

I called up an attorney friend of mine whom had dumped on me when his father had died. He was living in Quincy. I thought he owed me. I called him up and asked him.

"Tom I just got let go from my job. I don't know if this is discrimination or not."

"What did she say to you?"

Tommy asked.

"She said I thought I didn't want to work on Tuesdays."

Then Tommy picked up on this immediately and said.

"I thought, thought, She said thought. Well I do mostly divorce law, but she said, I thought, though a ha."

"I really liked this job, Tom."

"Ideal, the job was ideal."

When he said ideal, I thought this job was like as if I were playing cards and I was dealing. At this job I was dealing the cards. Tom told me the meaning of the word contingency.

"Ya, this is when the attorney doesn't get anything unless you win."

Then we shot some little bull.

"Tom did you hear about how they got on Oil Can Boyd in New York. They supposedly began to yell out, Oil Can, Oil Can, Oil Can etc . . . In Boston the sport's writer said they were razzing Oil Can when they should have been giving this to Clemens. Clemens was talking about having someone bring in his suitcases. They should be giving the flack to Roger Clemens"

"Ya, I heard a little about this."

"Okay Tom I'll be seeing you."

"Ya goodnight."

Tom worked for a Law Firm on the South Shore. After talking to Tommy I began to think of the Secretary of State. I began to go to the V.A. more after this. I was thinking of doing something legally with Mobil but no dice.

I began to think about my job I had with the Norwood Hospital. This was really taunting me after they didn't let me work there after I was in hospital. This was badgering me. The idea I worked on a psych unit one week, and the next I am a patient. Inside my head was complete shame. There I was no job. If I didn't have dr. Jack Yado and the V.A. these days I might have died of shame.

Going through my mind was they wouldn't give me the disability insurance money at hospital. They would have me sign all the papers to have them get all my records at different hospitals. Then they would tell me I wasn't eligible for the disability insurance, even without the records. They would just want something to do for the day, by looking at records. I tell you this is a jungle out there. This was what my uncle Mick would say, "it's a jungle out there."

I began to think about when I was first hired at Mobil Corp. I thought an executive in some high building, and he would be feeling so, so good during the days. I thought he thought about the Boston Red Sox like really. He I thought contemplated being in an office on a high floor in a building. Why would someone think about jumping out a top floor? I thought of the sun rising and setting. This executive began to think really Boston Red Sox. This might be really good in city like Boston. I thought the idea of this was very emotional feeling for this person, which he felt. I thought this was one reason why I was hired in the first place with Mobil.

I was let go from this job in February 1991. I would see dr. Jack Yado every few weeks and I really liked sitting in his waiting room. There was a station from the 70's on the radio. During the 70s was probably the best time of my life when I was in high school in the 70s. I could recall the smell of alcohol in his office. I could recollect when I would read books about people with Medical problems and I could smell Jack's office with the alcohol while reading. Jack's radio he must have had since the forties when he opened up shop. A great calmness would come over me when I would be there. Jack would have statements like.

"Everybody needs help."

I thought of him being an ex-WW 2 surgeon, he would cater to Hitler's care. I thought Adolph Hitler was in my head as, "foolish." This was what could be called catching Adolph Hitler as if he were Jack's patient. Meaning what Hitler did was foolish.

I asked Jack one day.

"Jack, have you ever heard of a super sensitive psychosis?"

"No, what is this?"

He asked.

"I heard the Russians in Siberia would give prisoners thorazine, prolixin, etc . . . as punishment. Then when they got out after 20 years or so they became to need these chemicals even though they didn't need them in the first place."

Jack would say.

"Those people in Siberia are just plain tough."

I had begun to decrease the injection of prolixin, which I was administrating to myself now. I received a prescription for the needles from a doctor. I would usually give the injection in my thigh. I can recall when the pitcher Dravecky I think his name was. He had his arm amputated. I was thinking of really cutting back on the amount I would inject myself with a lot, when I heard the baseball pitcher Dravecky had lost his arm.

When I would go out for coffees with my uncle, he said to me about when I said something about lying, as.

"A fib."

When we would drive to the coffee place my uncle would always wave to the patrolman. I think this best to stay on the side of the law verses against. I would wave to the patrolmen myself. My uncle had lost his voice box to cancer. I would think of the patrolmen as thinking like on their walkie-talkies, as I began to walk and my uncle began to talk again. I said to Joe one day.

"Your new voice is rather cool."

He said.

"I smoked Kools."

His last 8 years at the Courthouse I heard he was taking care of everyone. His nickname was Sam. I would call him "Friday." One Dedham patrolman said one day.

"Uncle Sam takes care of everyone."

Joe was Chief Probation Officer before he retired. I think he was head for all of Norfolk County and even would help the Judges.

I would go to the Veteran's Hospital a few times per week. I would really like the fish on Fridays. This was a little motivating to look forward to the fish dinner on Fridays. Volunteers would have free food. I was collecting Social Security Disability and when I worked there, I thought of all the folks whom worked there, as paying Social Security taxes.

I would bring around the book cart to the different floors. I would also work in the library as getting articles copied out of journals, for the doctors for when they would operate. I began to think all the patients here would have to struggle through operations to go back to work. I thought I would help myself, if ever I got tired, and didn't feel as if I could go on anymore. To make sure I kept on working, after maybe being let go from jobs. So when these folks here would keep on going after operations, I helped the doctors with, I would be helping myself. I thought of the woman named Mary in the library. When I would see her each day I would call her *M*, which was short for Mary.

The Gulf War was happening and I once asked one of the World War 2 veterans about the Gulf War and Nick said.

"Ya, George Bush is still over the golf."

Meaning there wasn't a real lot of combat in the Gulf War.

I can recall one WW 2 veteran whom was in the Battle of the Bulge said one day.

"Ya, I was in my fox hole and I kept on saying where is the f'n air cover."

This was in the Bulge when there was bad weather and the airplanes couldn't fly then. He also said about a soldier in a foxhole, next to him as.

"The bastard had pneumonia."

Well in about July I was watching a documentary about the Civil War. The commentator said.

"There was this Union soldier whom was going through the woods one night and he heard. "OOO," an owl. He the soldier then said. "It's me sergeant Ahearn your friend."

I would think of this when one of my old neighbors Fran, would always say, "OOO," to everything. Fran had been a cook in the Second World War for five years. He lived a few houses away from where I would live.

Chapter 10

I was watching the Red Sox on television one night and I began to think about the eyes of the players. I thought I could see right through to the eyes of the players on the television set. I began to think you could be sucked right through the set by the people's eyes. This got a little trepid. The name for our Red Sox was, "the ball club."

I walked to the Mobil gas station one night and got a pack of crackers. When I was coming up the steps to my apartment I had the urge to unlock the downstairs door. I was a bit trepid. I got up to the kitchen window. I then took a belt of rum I think and some of my pills. Then in my head I heard this voice say, "The coast is clear." I then went out the kitchen window feet first this time from the second floor.

I was going to say "r" this time. Which would be the fourth letter in spelling out America. The first time I went out I had said, "AAA". The second time out I said, "M." The third time out came out of my mouth was hello-e. This time I was to say, "R." But I thought I would bite my tongue. So this time while going down I just clenched my teeth and went down.

When I hit the ground I landed on my bottom and out of my mouth as I hit the grass was, "u." I thought I saw a helicopter up in the tree outside my apartment building. I was sitting down on my rump when I began to think about when I was on my dieing bed and I put my hands to my side when I fought for my life. I can remember looking down to my right hand on the grass. Then in one motion I got up and went up the unlocked doors to my second floor apartment. I had a premonition to unlock the door.

When I hit the ground I thought I heard a boy child around the neighborhood say something like.

"Oh, look at that."

I went into my apartment and I began to think this boy might call the authorities. I began to pray like there was no tomorrow. I mean really praying. I looked at the window in my bedroom and I was thinking of possibly going out this window. I was then thinking about like a head on a windowsill. As if there was a pumpkin on the windowsill. I claimed the saying, if you pray hard enough you won't be denied.

I looked at these spells, which was the side affects of the medicine as like a fighter pilot's mission. People never really figured mental problems were serious. Now looking at this in the likes of a plane mission puts new life into what some of these mental problems are equal too. A lot of people make fun of people with mental problems, but look at this in the limelight as a air mission puts a whole new light on this.

My uncle Joe would say to me at times.

"I don't have any get-up and go."

After this flight I enjoyed moving around more, as well as bladder and bowels. This seemed I had new feeling. When I saw Jack Yado before this he would say to me, I should see a psychiatrist because of the word, land. Jack was a WW 2 amphibious landings doctor, during the big War and he saw a lot of amphibious landings. Everyone didn't make this. Now he thought because of this I should see a psychiatrist. After he had said this, I had gone out the window and I was really taking a chance.

The real scary part about this was I didn't have any insurance. My Medicare wasn't good for another two months I believe. Also my hospital insurance had run out. I took pictures of the bruises on my arms and legs after this. I took pictures of them for proof I did this. I took two pictures.

My pal Brian was in the 82nd Airborne and he was also in the Green Berets. I had read the last time someone went out of an airplane before the real thing, they would say, "geronimo." He didn't know this.

I went down to the Social Security Office a little while after this and I saw my caseworker there. I saw her at the front desk. I thought this might be possible to ask her out and make time with her. She had a wonderful smile. I thought she might have liked me then. I had gone there for something or other.

I began to think years later I was an Englander. I had gone out a window other than at one home. The little bit of Welsh in me I thought I like landed into France after the First one was over. I was an Englander. England-land-deer.

A short while after this I began to go up Norwood Center to the old Guild theatre. My great, great uncle Bill Breen stood there in the 20is and 30is for the Guild theatre, which he owned. I began to stand there also. He would take the tickets to the shows back then. He also had built the Norwood theatre in 1927.

I applied for a job at a local cab company. I went into the office of the owner Bob Dog. Bob mentioned, "Still remember him." Bob also said, "that was MCI Walpole." I thought when I put my foot through the door of the Cinema I could have gone to MCI Walpole Prison. I thought the call to the Veteran's Hospital was what saved me.

When I was talking to Bob to get briefed about the cab duties Bob said.

"It's hot in here."

I was beginning to think he didn't really want to hire me, but since I was a Norwood man he would try to help me out. I started the job and this was in the summer. I can recall I thought the Secretary of State as saying in my head, "he's printing." I would write down the different cab fares with my left hand.

I had started my second day on the job. I got my gas at the Mobil Gas station where I had worked there. I was putting on my tie while driving when I was bringing a person to a destination. I can remember the passenger saying something like.

"What are you doing?"

"I'm putting on my tie."

I stated.

I dropped him off at the Norwood Country Club. He had given me a five-dollar tip. I began to think how people could be abused. When I had looked at him he looked as white as a ghost. He said after he had gotten out of the cab.

"He went through two red lights and a stop sign."

I didn't recall this. I went over my uncle Joes' and told him I went through two red lights and a stop sign. He got kind of mad and said.

"Your flying."

I didn't have any insurance and he kept on saying I should stay with the cab company.

"You should see a doctor."

He also said.

I told him I had an appointment with Jack on Tuesday. When I was talking with Joe he seemed to be on a new level as anger came out of him. I wasn't sure of how I would do if I stayed on with the cab job. I had a hard time sleeping when I worked at the cab company. After seeing Jack I thought best not to stay with the cab company.

As I said I would go to Memorial Hall in the Town Hall in Norwood. This was where all the names of all the veterans from all the wars names were on plagues. I would have dreams about this place, which I never correlated with till now. I would go in there and have a little confession with a really big picture there. The Town Hall is right across the street from the church. I would have a rather piece of mind here each week. There was a false fireplace with the big picture named after a reverend from 1917. The big painting was of the daughters of the sons of the Civil War.

I would go to my spot at the old Guild theatre. If I had anxiety I would say to myself things like, "back-up." This would mean to take a step backwards. When I would talk to myself I felt I was talking a different language in a foreign country. I correlated the rush, which foreigners get from speaking a new language. I was talking to myself as if I were planning what to do, to comeback from the dead.

"Drink a little water, say a prayer, take a leak now, etc . . ."

Then if I had anxiety I would say to myself, "your tougher than it. Or even, go soak your head."

One day when I had gotten back from the V.A. I said to myself the word, "proceeded." I thought this word had broken through the barrier of anxiety. I could recall I thought of the words, "good thinking," when I would work the tree work. I thought these were words, which also broke through the anxiety barriers. I thought of all the State Reps in

Boston as saying, "living will." I thought this would mean me Bill or me as Will as living it up.

When this spell from the side affects would come about one each week, I would usually take more prolixin. I began to think of John Silbur from B.U. as guiding me through one of these spells. I thought he might have experienced this with his one arm. Also my friend I knew in high school Mary whom happened to be a Rhodes Scholar, I also thought she helped me through one of these spells. Thank you both.

I would count the trains outside my apartment. I thought I had to get out of this spell by 5 or 6 trains, which had to go by. I think I could have started to drink, to lesson this spell, but I thought I would just wait for the prolixin to kick in.

I thought about prolixin, which was invented in France in 1950. I would think of my uncle Henry whom received a bronze medal for directing traffic from June 6-10 1944 without sleep. This would gradually calm me down. I would also eat as much popcorn as I could.

I would say to myself, "stay low," as if I were in a war shooting a gun. Stay low I would say to myself constantly. You're tougher than it, I would also say. I thought about how I had conquered the demon when I put my hat on and brought the vacuum machine to the woman's house. I think this was coming from the side affects from the prolixin.

I went to the library and I got a book by Stanley Breen on business. I read this book and I saw a picture of a person making a circle over his head like a halo. I also got a book on the "Called ones." I thought of my uncle Henry as being one of the first Americans into Hitler's Wolfe's Lair, the Berchtesgaden in the Bavarian Alps. This book was about how Gen. Eisenhower had 175 Americans, which the Russians allowed to Berlin, to represent the Americans. I thought of my uncle Henry as standing up in a jeep while someone was driving.

"Drink water," I would also say to myself. I would pray the rosary quite a bit also. I began to think of the expression, "beady eyes." I didn't do much writing, because I always feared I might die.

I would watch the talk shows on Sunday mornings. I thought of one person on these shows as saying, "He's driving it." I thought about when I would be in one of these side affects from the medicine, and I would go to a gas station and say to the attendant.

"Put in five dollars."

I would try to give orders. I would comeback from the V.A. and I would think of all the business people driving on route 1. I would think of Gen. Norman pointing one finger up into the air as if to go onwards. I thought of Gen. Norman as when he had to go to the PX to get a flu shot. He came down with the flu during the Gulf War. A doctor must have administered the shot.

I went over my folk's home and I went down the cellar. This was a little while after the Persian Gulf had ended. I was saying to myself, "watch out for mines." I would walk in the dark cellar using a stick as if I didn't hit a mine.

I thought Norman was quite upset about having to go to the Medical tent. I thought of Jack Yado as a World War 2 doctor. I would think of the word, "fish," when Norman had to get the flu shot or anti-biotic. I thought a military doctor like gave him the shot.

I was walking back to my apartment and I went by the St. Catherine's church. The pain was coming from my eyes. I thought the pastor there was saying, "your eyes hurt you, you need eye drops." The next day I went to the pharmacy and purchased eye drops. I had a little faith this might help, but this didn't though.

One time when the side-affects were so bad two words came to me. I thought my uncle George Augusta said, "touch him." I thought of all the times I would have my blood pressure taken and the all nurses would take this. This was for the inderal I was on for research at McLean. Then I thought of my maternal dad as saying in my head once, "left hamburg." These two words calmed me for a short while.

I would watch an artist on television and paint along with him. I would say to myself in these spells what you would call. "Take the bull by the horns."

What I would do was think of whom to give this spell to. I began to think of, to call certain doctors Red Satan. I would begin to threaten them, as if to start saying this, right out loud in public. If this spell isn't lifted then I will call you Red Satan right out loud in public, then I thought "prove it." I would begin to threaten doctors in my mind I will call them satan if this spell isn't lifted.

I began to think this spell was really all the shrinks I had seen, that they were like jumping me in my mind. All of them would converge on my mind all at once. Then I would feel the fear of possibly being jumped when younger.

I would most of the time be saying to myself.

"You're tougher then it."

Meaning I was tougher than this demon or spell.

I thought one of the WW 2 volunteer at the V.A. made me think, "Dial." This meant to me, die yell. The reason why I had been hollering so much was because I had died.

I got a book by Christine Breen and Nail Williams. I was reading this book while I was waiting in line for a battery at a Garage. I was waiting on purpose for the mechanic to come out to my car and motion me to move into the garage. This was at a Sears in Dedham. I was just concentrating ignoring things while I looked down reading. Then the mechanic came out to tell me to go into the garage. I would then be in the driver's seat.

I drove my car in and I began to get a bit tempered because they were taking their time or whatever. I began to get tempered and I began to order the mechanics around. I thought to myself I was a grown-up and I have my own apartment and what I do is justified.

I had gotten my old battery instead of trading this in for the trade in. I got the re-imbursement as well as battery. While I was driving home, I began to say to myself, there is no doubt I am going to go to hell for eternity, while I passed under this bridge. I later thought this was a Sear Sucker.

I would tilt my hat back and I thought this meant coming very close to losing it. If you ever see policemen sometimes they do this. Their hat pushed back. One time I recall I parked my car out in front of my apartment and I crouched down and put my hat down over my forehead. For some reason, I don't know why but I felt furtherance. Maybe this is really what the media sees you as.

I was seeing Jack Yado about every two weeks. When I left his office once I went to my apartment and took my pills. I was thinking to myself, some people over dose, and kill, themselves. Some people start drinking also. But I was just tapping the prescription bottle to let some of the pills come out. I then went to Braintree and to a Mobil gas station.

I would think of a psychologist at the V.A. when I would be in this spell and she seemed to be able to help. I had met her in the café at the V.A. one day.

"May I join you?"

I asked her.

"Sure sit down."

She said.

"Hi, I'm Bill Breen."

"Hi, I'm Maura Hogan."

"What department do you work in?"

I asked her.

"Spinal cord. I am a psychologist."

She said with rather inborn conviction.

"Where do you work?"

She asked me.

"I work in the library."

I said with not too much confidence, because I was just volunteering. I didn't say I was a volunteer, as she had a PHD and I was just a volunteer. I then told her about my saying.

"I have a B.A. from Harvard, a PHD from Yale, and a BLT from McDonalds."

She began to chuckle a bit.

"I worked at the V.A. in the Bronx. I just came up from New York. Do you know of any apartments in the area?"

I said.

"No."

I was going to tell her about my apartment, but I began to get self-conscience about where I lived. At this time in my life, I looked down at New York. I should have realized the woman she could become after working in Boston for a while. This seemed the doctors with the PHDs were the only doctors whom really understood me. She also told me she worked in psychiatric in the Bronx V.A.

I thought a little bit she was hired by the V.A. because of her name Hogan, as in Col. Hogan on Hogan's Heroes. I told her about the different mental Health clinics of the Norwood Hospital wings. I would see her the next couple of weeks and she knew I did work in library but volunteer. I felt I had sunk. No chance whatsoever of scoring with her.

The next week I brought her in some M&Ms. She had told me she had gone to Simmons College in Boston years before. I thought about my uncle Henry when he was on his journey to Hitler's Wolfe's Lair, Berchtesgaden, he ate M&Ms on the way. I gave her some M&Ms. When I gave her some she then put some in my hand and said.

"Do you want some?"

She would smile at me and I felt she actually understood.

When I would say to myself, "stay low," I also began to say, "Tow one."

I thought my great, great uncle whom paid for dr. Jack Yado's Medical School and died in 1941 was saying, "tow one." Dr. Jack Yado enlisted in the Navy in I think 1941 or 1942. I think he gave Jack money for everything he needed for Medical School.

I began to think, could a material thing like a telephone, help when in one of these side-affect spells. Sometimes I would get help by talking over the phone.

My uncle Joe Breen whom had beaten cancer I would think about visiting while in this side affect reaction. But I thought he understood also. In which dieing with the sun up in the sky is rather scary. He wouldn't like to come out when this was raining out. I myself liked the rain.

I thought of drinking while in this side affect reaction, but I stayed away from the booze. With Booze you lose, with dope there is hope. This would take about ½ hour for the pills to kick in, so I would just wait.

I would read the Bible and then I would look at my hands and they seemed so pale. They seemed a bit sweaty and as I say looked pale. I would read passages and I thought the words seemed to have a great look as they were in print. All the words seemed then as if they were in italics but they weren't really.

Probably the august thing was, "stay low." This would mean for me to get on the floor.

I would think of all the doctors and psychiatrists I had seen over the years. As I explained earlier I felt I was being jumped by all of them. In that these people were like equal to the fear when you are possibly being jumped by a group of people when younger. This time all the psychiatrist would jump me mentally. I would be seeing all these people and be surrounded by them in my mind. I began to cry.

Then I thought I could get help from dr. Jon Eloc whom said in my mind, "He's crying." He would then pull me out of this spell or side affect with the right words in my head. Years later I thought my sister Judy's husband, I thought he would think to try and act like you are crying, and someone will help you. He kind of squinted his eyes a little bit. Crying was a sign you were really hurting. This isn't an emotional cry though. So to get help, act as if you are crying.

I joined the choir at the St. Catherine's church. I would recall when before I had put my foot through the door at the Norwood Cinema I went to church this day. I could recall when I heard the choir then, I thought this was like the Walls of Jericho coming down. This had so much power back then.

I would go to the choir practices on Monday nights. I would sing at the 9:30 Mass on Sunday. I can recall one of the elder choir singers there said to me one day the Norwood expression, "wing it." I thought this was a Norwood saying, because we had our own airport in Norwood. I would listen to the religious station on the radio and I really could listen differently, when I would get in one of these spells, and listen to the religious music. I began to think there was a connection between the religious music and the side affects of the prolixin.

I had begun to gradually lesson the injection of the prolixin I gave myself, until I wasn't on any injection at all. I would think about listening to the music just on the prolixin pills. I would give the injection into my leg as I told you. I thought about when I thought my legs were in heaven when I went out of bed at Norwood Hospital back in August 1975. I thought my legs went to heaven. This was when I would pray instead of, on earth, I would pray, in boeland. This was my land, which I thought my legs went to. So now I felt very confident about giving the injection into my legs. I would slowly decrease the injection each time, till I was no longer on any injection at all.

I had also been coming off the inderal, and my equilibrium was much better, because this is a side affect of the inderal. I think I was just on about 20 mgs. prolixin and also on artane and klonopin. I was just on pills.

I went to a party once for everyone in the choir. This was at the director's apartment. I thought back when I went to the party at UMass Amherst. There were one or two girls there whom weren't too bad, but I just was getting out. I thought back then with my experience at the UMass Amherst party. This felt good going to a party.

When I first went to the choir there was one person whom would sing real loud and was really stealing the show, by singing quite loud. Now with me arriving on the scene without a steady job, I think this person left the choir over fear of associating with me. I thought the choir director knew this person wouldn't get too strong an influence. So he brings me in, and this person leaves, and the director nips this in the butt, with this person and his strong influence singing real loud.

I can recall I really enjoyed watching television and the actors on televisions. I thought about how the actors would act, act on the show or movie. This would be like if they had a part on the show, which was a play, then they would be acting, acting. This would be depth acting.

I can remember watching Humphrey Bogart in Sierra Madre I think this movie was called. He was up in a mountain in the end, and they were trying to, "flush him out," off the mountain. In the end he got shot. I think I would watch Charley Chan the Chinese detective on Saturday mornings. I just had one little television set.

When I would watch the news I saw the criminals whom were on the news. If they had a physical ailment, the police wouldn't think anything of this. They would keep them moving. The authorities didn't think physical injuries needed catering too for criminals.

I would paint everyday and I also liked watching the show, "The Judge." This was a show about people going to court with all kinds of problems. To tell you the truth I think this show just might have appeared on television for me. This was a private court television and I learned all techniques for all types of cases. I really knew if you were in court, then you should try to talk to the Judge a little bit out of session.

There was one girl whom was on medication sometimes off, and sometimes on. While she was on meds she thought she was, "Candy Watts." She was really a knockout as she walked on the television. She had walked up to the stand and I mean walked. Some ass. She got up on the stand and said.

"You have to pay for thinking below the belt."

The Judge told her to take her meds. She took them and her head began to rock, side to side. She sometimes didn't know who she was on these meds. She would wake up in a hotel room and wonder how she got there. When she was on the meds people liked her because she was so sexy.

I began to see mental patients on this show. I began to see how mental patients, are treated by the law. I knew what best to do if you were ever in a court of Law. This Judge had really come very far himself. His name was Judge Franklin. Really, I don't know if this show was on television or this show Judge Franklin appeared for me. I really liked the woman attorneys. I felt they understood me.

After about 4 years painting I finally had a painting hanging up. I think my brother Jack put the painting up above his fireplace. After I painted I would clean my brushes and my puddy knife in the kitchen sink. I began to think one of my brushes was a fork and another one my knife and spoon. This would justify me eating with these utensils. And even years later I thought my artist name "Utensils." I had even written Washington about grants for the Arts. They sent me back something about how most of the money for the Arts is being sent to Art Societies.

I went to be a juror at the Quincy Court. When I went there, I thought, "head in jury," or head injury. I thought of my uncle at the Dedham Court when he worked there. My uncle would be telling me to pick the brains of the doctors. I began to think of all the people my uncle had sent to jail.

I can recall the girl whom had guided me through one of these side affect spells. She was Mary and she went to Dartmouth University. She was going to study Pre-Med but decided not to. She had been captain of the cheerleaders in high school. But she went much further than this. She was a Rhodes scholar at Dartmouth.

Her mother had seen my mother one day, before I was in McLean. Her mother had said to my mother.

"He got one of the loudest applauses."

When I heard this I think she thought my life was over. I began to sink into a very deep abyss. I was feeling negative or minus almost all the time back then. The only thing, which kept me going then, was the First Hospitalization was so baleful. I would think, "your alive."

Also I had applied for a job at Polaroid Corp. before I received the job at Stop & Shop and her Mary's mother did the interviewing then. She had me get a physical for this job, because of my broken back.

There were a few people in my high school class whom were going to be doctors, but changed their minds. Mary was one of them. Larry the star athlete whom went on to go to Harvard, and Dave R. the person I was to room with at UMass, all decided not to be doctors. I'm not sure if Hal whom I saw at the Thanksgiving game, when I was on crutches, became a doctor. Hal also went to Harvard.

A person whom was in a hospital and also a Vietnam Veteran told me whenever a Vietnam Veteran came into a hospital, he automatically saw a psychiatrist. This particular person was in for a knee operation. When the psychiatrist came in to see him he said.

"I've been in worst places than this, start off with one month in the Artic Circle."

This person would also tell me.

"If I ever wanted to get high, I would go to the highest pint of the earth, the Artic Circle."

Dr. Jack Yado set me up with an evaluation at McLean. I think he did his job of getting me off of the injection. I spoke with a woman psychiatrist named dr. Anne Marie Nagidam. I went to see her and she asked me.

"What do you do now?"

"I work as a volunteer at the Veteran's Hospital in Boston." I stated.

"How did you get here?"

"I drove." I responded.

"You can drive?"

"Ya."

We talked for a while and I told her about the Book JFK wrote, "Why England Slept." He wrote this in his fourth year at Harvard. We began to talk about my work history. She said to me.

"You worked at the William Carter Co. for six years?"

"Yes."

I replied.

This reminded me of when I would be checked by the spinal doctors, after I had recovered from paralysis. They would check the muscles in my legs and say things like then, "you can move this much." Now I was having another flashback about how the doctors were amazed at my mental progress. They were in awe of me physically and now mentally. I craved the expressions on the faces of the doctors on their faces. I was brought back 15 years when I would see the spinal doctors.

I began to think of Sen. Bob Dole one day in about April 1993. I was thinking Bob Dole was like one of the German Generals whom would advise Hitler. I was thinking about the situation in Bosnia. I was thinking Bill Clinton was like Hitler and Bob Dole was one of the German Generals. There was word Bob Dole was too old. But then he had done what they call a metamorphosis. He had advised Clinton to make a stand in Bosnia.

This was when I thought he was like a German General telling Hitler what to do in Eastern Europe. I don't think Clinton liked the idea of becoming what Hitler ended up. This particular day Clinton began to think about Hitler and Dole these days, and he supposedly flew straight down to New Orleans. I began to think of the pilot of this plane. I thought Pilot like Pontius Pilate, whom ordered Christ to be crucified.

While I was in the choir I had been cutting back on the inderal. I wouldn't tell anyone in the choir about this because this was rather personal. There was a girl in the choir whom had started taking inderal. She was a girl in the front row, about 45 years old and blonde hair. I thought she knew what this was to fight and she didn't complain. I thought the milieu your in, everyone is affected by one.

Around this time the Waco situation in Waco Texas was on the television every night. This was the David Koresh situation. When I was watching this one night, I thought my old girlfriend Elizabeth was like telling me to eat chicken. I had cooked up a roaster. I was watching television when the whole place in Waco Texas was burning up. I recall I could only stay so close to the television set.

In our community there was word going around about spousal violence. I thought about the love tap I had given Elizabeth right after high school. I was coming back into the community.

This particular Sunday I put the Eucharist into my pocket instead of consuming this in the church after I sang there. With the Clinton situation I began to think of his wife Hillary on her knees. This was very pungent Sunday afternoon and I even did a painting of a cabin in the sun. I drove to my aunt Lucy's house. I could remember Lucy say something about someone on television set as, "They will be doing hand stands." I thought about driving to my aunt Libs' in Franklin. She was the wife of my uncle Henry whom had died on Christmas morning 1965.

I remember driving to Franklin and listening to the radio. I recall pulling into the Franklin DPW and I thought of Audie Murphy taking a shit. I thought as I backed up Audie would have taken a shit there. I was listening to a Russian radio station. I thought this was guiding me. I hadn't been to my uncle Henry's home since he died in 1965.

I went into a convenient store and I met a man there about 65 years old. I knew my aunt Lib lived on Milk St. but I didn't know where this was. I hadn't been to this house as I said since my uncle died in 1965. I asked this man.

"Hey charley, where is Milk St?"

"Take a right at the lights, then go down two sets of lights, and this is down two miles."

He told me.

"*BYE.*"

I said.

I was thinking about Clinton and how he flew straight down to New Orleans. I was thinking of the pilot and co-pilot of the jet he was on. I was thinking of Bob Dole and how he was like a German General whom would send Clinton to hell. Like how the Nazi Generals did to Hitler. Clinton went straight down to New Orleans.

When I was driving I thought of a friend of mine whom was a teacher in Franklin. I thought about the air when I drove to Franklin. I remember taking a breath. I drove around looking for Milk St. but I couldn't find this from the directions the person at the convenient store gave me. I met two girls at the convenient store when I came back to the store. I asked them.

"Do you know where Milk St. is?"

"Take a right, then left through two sets of lights and Milk St. is on your left."

They said.

I then used a payphone and called Lib, but there was no answer. I thought they gave me amiss directions. So I went into he bar where the person I called Charley was and said again.

"Where is Milk St. Charley?"

I asked Charley as he played cards there.

"Didn't you follow my f'n direction?"

He said.

I looked at him and I could tell he was curious.

"I went those directions and still couldn't find this."

I said to chuck.

"Take a right then take two sets of lights then down two miles."

He said as he had a pretzel in his mouth.

I didn't know this person's name but I just call him one American Charley.

I then proceeded to drive these directions. I drove there and came upon Milk St. I then drove to the house Lib lived in and my cousin charley lived in the house next to Lib. I drove my car up to the driveway and parked my car there. I looked around and I left my car running as I knocked on the door. No one was home. I knew Lib lived in the house next to my cousin Charleys'. So I went through a little bit of woods and asked a neighbor there.

"Where does Elizabeth Breen live?"

"The house on the corner."

"Thanks."

I said.

I proceeded to go to the house on the corner and I knocked on the door and also rang the bell. No one came to the door. I had to take a leak as I was pacing on the porch. I thought I saw someone in the door looking through. I kept on ringing the bell, and knocking to no avail. I can remember looking at the trees and I thought I had made headway. The trees began to shudder and foil. I thought of all the trees I had cut down when I worked with the arborist. I took a leak and then stayed on the porch.

I thought of my maternal dad, knocking on the door years ago, when we would visit my uncle Henry when I was younger. This was when my uncle Henry was alive. I was saying to myself what I would say if the police came. I then thought of Clinton flying down, straight down to New Orleans. I had all kinds of thoughts go through my mind. I thought about the different chieftains throughout history.

Then I put my fist through the glass door and opened the door from the inside. My left knuckle was bleeding profusely. I then went into the house looking for my aunt Lib. I walked around the home and I heard the parrot talking. My left hand was bleeding prodigally. Blood was pouring out of my left fist. I looked everywhere for Lib. I tried the phone and I also thought Lib's sister whom lived with Lib might be hiding. I then called out.

"Charley."

Out loud to Charley's house.

I sat down on the kitchen floor and I saw all the blood on the floor. I thought about the show Mash and when the doctor whom had seen enormous amounts of blood from being a doctor from the Chosin Reservoir, and Pusan Perimeter and so on. He was what Colonel Potter said, "he just drifted in here." He was on the floor after he said to Colonel Potter he just couldn't go on. Colonel Potter had said then. "It's out of our ballpark now."

Lib came home and I heard her say something like to charley.

"Someone broke in."

Lib then came to the door and I saw her.

"It' me Lib."

I was thinking if the police came I would say my name and United States Marine Corps. I thought the situation in Bosnia was this serious. Well Lib came in and I said.

"Lib, it's me Billy."

"Billy what happened?"

She asked me.

"I heard someone in the house."

I said.

"What happened to your hand?"

She asked me.

"This should be all right."

I came back with.

Charley came into the house and he looked astonished.

"I called the police. I thought someone had broken into the house."

Charley said.

"No, this is just Billy."

Lib said.

"I'm all right Charley."

"Let's clean up this blood."

Lib retorted.

I was thinking about how I was just sitting on he floor and just sitting there. The police arrived and Lib said to them.

"This is my nephew officer. He thought he heard someone in the house."

The two officers said to each other.

"This is all right John. This is their nephew."

1st officer said to second.

"Okay Peter, this should be all right."

Lib was bending down cleaning up the blood with me. We were running the water as we rinsed off the blood.

"Billy, let's put some peroxide on this gash."

"This isn't going to stop bleeding."

She said.

A neighbor came by and was inquiring about the glass, which was on the floor and the blood. Lib said to him.

"We are all set now Frank."

There were two girls about 16 and 17 years old at the backdoor viewing. I sat down with Lib and we watched and listened to the parrot.

"That's marshmallow."

Lib said about the parrot.

I was listening to the parrot and I was calmed. I just sat down and I talked to Lib. I remember the hot day and the sun up in the sky. The temperature was about 90 degrees and this was a hot day. I remember looking at the window again and I saw the trees. The trees seemed to be vibrating and they looked shallow.

"How long have you had the parrot?"

I asked Lib.

"I've had marshmallow three years now."

She said.

Charley came in and said.

"What are we supposed to think, smashing the glass door?"

"Did you turn my car off Charley?"

I asked him.

"Ya, I turned this off. Are you okay to drive?"

He asked me.

"I'm all right to drive."

I told him.

Charley came by with his car and he drove me to his house, and I got into my car. Charley seemed a bit perturbed. I got into my car and started the long drive home. I thought I was my uncle Henry whom died Christmas morning 1965 and went from Norwood to Franklin in an ambulance with a head injury. I was saying to myself while I drove.

"Nice and slow, just cruising, we are going home now."

I was saying to myself.

"There is Walpole State Prison, they are all doing time there. Don't worry about a thing, you are going home."

We passed Walpole State Prison and I was saying to myself.

"There all gone there, don't worry about a thing."

I would keep on saying to myself. I drove by Walpole State Prison and I said these things to myself. I drove by my old apartment, and I had heard weeks earlier a young boy 15 years old had gotten into an accident, and was paralyzed for life. I felt bad about this. I thought the Walpole Police had said in my head, "Red Sox."

I thought this was what the town of Walpole had said, when they let me move into their town in the apartment there, which I had years earlier. They would let me because of my connection with the Red Sox.

Now I was driving by MCI Walpole. I no longer felt guilty about this boy whom was crippled. When I had the cab job earlier the manager of the cab company said to me in my head. "That was MCI Walpole." Now I was saying to myself, I could have gone to MCI Walpole, so why should I feel guilty about this boy whom was crippled.

I drove into Norwood and I thought of the friend of mine whom was the teacher in Franklin kind of like say in my head. "No one say anything," about my escapades earlier in Franklin. My left hand was bleeding. I went into my apartment and I was racing a bit. I cooked a piece of veal, and I took a tub bath while I ate the veal. My hand and water in the tub were bloody. I thought for a short time I might bleed to death. I began to think the Billy Breen whom worked for the Feds was in Dutch. I thought he might have been taking a bath and he had been shot and there was blood in his bath.

I can recall about a week earlier I had taken my pills and flushed them down the toilet. I called my sister Judy and she went to the get me more pills. I had gone about one day without medicine, and this day I went to get a haircut. I can recall this day without medicine and going out to get a haircut. There was a special way I controlled myself with these pills and I thought I could definitely help folks to stop smoking cigarettes.

I can recall I would do a lot of fishing every now and then. I would throw popcorn up to the seagulls at the lake as I fished. There was a girl at the V.A. whom had cut her wrists before she worked at the V.A. I thought I could help her by motioning to my left arm when I would go to the V.A. as a gesture. When I tried to help her there, the nurses there some way in return hurt me. I really thought if you help someone, you get paid back, by with them hurting you, here in Boston.

Here I was in the tub eating veal as I was bleeding. I then put a hanky with pressure and the bleeding stopped. I think I even used my mind to get this to stop bleeding. I also had fallen asleep. A few days earlier I had been thinking of Hitler and this lonesomeness came over me.

I can recall when I would go to the V.A. I would see all sorts of people. I think the V.A. might have been a place where the spies would come sometimes. I would bump into them every now and then. There was one day I was sitting down in the V.A. corridor and I felt a Russian Spy had like dared me to do something. I thought the undercover spies would be thinking what I was doing, being at the V.A. and not being paid job. I thought about the Russian person whom had killed the Cosby boy I think from California. This person happened to be Russian himself, when he killed the Cosby person.

Chapter 11

I awoke the next morning and I was still racing somewhat but under control. I went out to the News box and got a paper. While I got to the news box I put my left arm inside my tweed coat. I thought this was what Napoleon did when he would put his arm inside his coat way back.

When I got the paper there was a man parked on the side, next to the paper box. We exchanged words somewhat. The next thing I knew we were arguing. Then I said to him, as I would motion with my arm in my coat, as if I had a pistol.

"I'll kill you."

This person then pulled out with his truck. I thought he was going to report me to the Police Station. I then after a short while of scaring someone, began to race again.

From here I got into my car and drove to Jim K's Bait and tackle Shop. This was in South Norwood. Jim was a neighbor when, I grew up in. I thought a few days earlier, we wanted Jim at the Veteran's Hospital to be seen there. He was a big WW2 veteran. But Jim was now being seen at the Norwood Hospital as a patient there. When I would think of Jim I thought of the idea of peel, as peeling fruit oranges, grapefruit, etc . . . Well I went in to see Jim.

"How are you Jim?"

"Oh I just got out of hospital. They just operated on my jugular vein," as he points to the scar on his neck. I then began to think he just got out of the Norwood Hospital, and I was just checking up on him. I didn't know he was in Hospital. He showed me the scar on his neck. I began to recall way back the theory, which person has the most scars. So I said to him.

"Ya, I have this cut on my hand."

As I showed him the scar on my hand from when I put my fist through my aunt's glass door the day before.

"How did this happen?"

He asked interestingly.

I don't know what I said, but I left the store and I could tell someone's number was up in Norwood. I shook hands with Jim left-handed from my car this time. I then headed up in respect to Norwood Center. While I drove, I saw a retarded person waiting for a bus at a bus stop. I put the passenger door window down and yelled out.

"*SHELLY* you're a Faker."

He was in this natural person's awe and didn't say a word. I thought later this retarded person would say to other retarded folks, "We can't fool them anymore." Meaning the retarded folks can't fool normal people by doing nothing anymore and thinking nothing was right.

I then drove up the Norwood Cinema. I parked my car disgruntled in the live parking spot in front of Cinema. I was saying to myself I would rather go to jail than into a mental Hospital. I then recalled a dream I had with my great uncle Bill Breen walking out through the Cinema door. This was Bill whom built the Cinema in "27." I remember I went up to the door and began to urinate on the door. I then began to kick the door a couple of times. Then when I thought I would shatter the glass door, the door jolted open, without glass breaking into pieces. I thought I would go to jail and I could get off the pills. But the door somehow jolted open.

I was saying to myself I didn't want to kick the door, but this was another one of these times in which I thought, if I chickened out then things would be worse. Or do this so later, you won't think this was something, which you have rather have wished you had done.

When the door opened I saw something like a crossbow, which had been locking the door, and had come loose. I later thought amputees should use cross bows like bows and arrows, to help themselves.

The alarm went off in the Cinema. I went into the Cinema and began to run around. I was thinking of trying to get up to the Movie

Loft, the second floor screen. Then if the police came, then I would tell them come and get me. You will have to flush me out.

The doors were locked to the upstairs screen. I went onto the stage area in front of the first floor screen. I just sat on the stage with my knees up. I tried to climb up to the like Lincoln balcony, but I couldn't pull myself up. I thought of the movie charley and all of the scientists asking him questions, when he was on the stage. I got the fire extinguisher and squirted water on the picture screen.

After about 15 0r 20 minutes of running around the Cinema the workers came in. I believe they had called the police because of the alarm. I came up to them and said.

"I saw the door opened and I thought the cleaners were here and I was going to apply for a job cleaning."

They didn't say much. I then went into the office there and began to make out an application for a cleaner. Three policemen came in and one of them Officer Hastings was out in the lobby. The other two officers came into the main office, while I was sitting in a chair, making out an application. Officer Hastings said to someone he was going to call some one up. This infuriated me inside and I didn't want to let the police officers know I was enraged. So I would get back at them in a silent way. I then said to the two officers.

"Get Detective Murphy on this break in."

One of the younger officers went out of the office after I said this.

"*HELLO-E*, What is your name?"

I asked the other officer.

"Officer French."

He said.

"Ya, I thought the cleaners were here and I was going to make out an application for a job."

I then wrote down this officer's name on the application.

"French, right?"

I then began to call the Norwood Hospital after one of the officer there said.

"You should have your hand looked at, at the hospital."

"Get off the phone Billy."

Officer Hasting said to me on the other phone.

"Get Officer detective Murphy. We have to know if there were any clues to find out on the breaking and entering."

"Get off the phone Billy."

Officer Hastings kept on saying.

The other two officers were standing in front of my desk there. The young officer was really reacting to the word, "where," which I thought police would react to. I thought I was like the chief of police here now.

I years later would listen to Ollie North's talk show, and I thought about how he liked then, the singing group, Fleetwood Mac." Ollie had said Clinton thought about the song, "Tell me lies." By Stevie Nicks.

"Let's go down to the Hospital and have this cut looked at."

Officer French said to me.

'FANTASTIC."

I was thinking of telling the officer I would drive down in my own car. I thought if I told them I would drive down in my own car, and they said no. So I decided I would play this safe and don't say anything.

The young officer then escorted me to the police cruiser. When I got to the car, I made a mad dash down the street. I ran about 40 yards when I got a "charley horse" and fell down. I later thought of the very long lines in 40's, 50's and 60's at the Cinema. In which one person with a "charley horse" walked out of one of these lines.

The young police officer then walked me back to the cruiser and into the back seat. I thought I had paid town taxes and I was entitled to a ride. I had on my tie and an old suit, but this was a nice jacket just the same. We drove to the hospital and while we were driving there I said.

"Turn the radio off."

"You don't like the music?"

He stated.

He left this on just the same.

We drove to the hospital and with this officer holding my arm I limped in with a charley horse. I got into one room there and a doctor looked and checked my hamstring, which is the Charley horse muscle.

"This should be all right in a few days your quadriceps is swollen."

As I was there I saw the nurse whom had given me the examination physical for when I worked at Hospital years earlier.

"Nurse Jane, how are you doing?"

"I'm busy right now."

She retorted.

There was a person outside my room whom was watching me. I overheard Officer French say.

"He got him."

One of the nurses then came in and asked.

"Do you know where you are?"

"Breen Ming Control."

This was what I had written in my diary in Boston. Two things were on my mind. The first was, when the officer said we got him, I thought this person outside my room had given like the old Master's try, and like pulled something out of the air.

The second thing was the complete uselessness I felt when the person came in and asked do you know where you are. I had worked at hospital for nine months previously. Now I was a mental patient. I think I was feeling so much embarrassment that I didn't get any respect from the people I worked with years before. So I got a little aggressive and I asked Nurse Jane.

"Can I have a blow job?"

This was a little bit out in left field, but I think I had help from someone in the future. Gloria Estephan had a song, which a part was, "Did I make you feel ashamed."

Nurse Jane N. looked at me and was a bit startled as the people there overheard me. I was getting pain in my eyes, so I started the only thing I only know, of helping me in these situations. I began to holler out things.

"Whom is his doctor?"

"Dr. Yado."

Someone replied.

"What medications do you take?"

They asked me.

"Klonopin."

I said.

I forget what I was yelling out. I can remember I lifted my voice and said something. The psychiatrists knew they couldn't abuse me this time. Because I would have scared them away by how I would call them Red Satan. So this time there wasn't any shrinks. The regular workers then began to tie me down. I then said to them.

"I've got AIDS."

I really had thought about how when there was a gay parade in Boston, the gays began to spit at the Boston Police and the Boston Police began to run away.

"There is blood on my hand, "as my left hand was bleeding.

A girl whom I had grown-up with in my old neighborhood happened to be a nurse there, at the Hospital on this shift. Her name was Patty and she came in and took care of me. I said to her.

"I had sex with Pammy."

Pamela was her younger sister. I recalled back when the window I went out of in August 1975, I had a dream later about having sex with Pamela up in the air where I had gone out the window. I was thinking this was like, "breaking and entering." Breaking when I broke my back, and entering when I had sex with Pamela. There brother skip had been caught with Armed Robbery years earlier. He served 1 and ½ years in Norfolk State Prison.

I had said to Nurse Jane.

"I took care of Walter."

Walter was from a town far away, and he was on the spinal cord unit when I was on this, years ago. He had the same last name as Jane. Jane I was supposed to see, when I walked out of the hospital after I was told to go to Emergency to see her when I worked there.

Well Pamela had a child from a person out of wedlock. This person denied this was his child. Her child must have grown-up around my old neighborhood. He must have climbed the same trees and all the places around the area. I don't remember him because I no longer lived there.

I can recall I had asked to get some *DELICIOUS* food at a McDonalds while I was here. I wanted something to eat here. I said if they could get me some food at the local McDonalds. I thought they reached out here to me.

Patty gave me some medicine and also took a urine specimen. I thought what you do in the community denotes what type of care you get at hospital. I had been a singer in the choir. I really thought of the bonds, which I talked about with the people you grow up with. These bonds can't be broken. Patty was my neighbor whom I grew up with.

I would have been way out in left field if patty hadn't been on this shift. I don't know what kind of care I would have gotten, if this weren't for her. She knew how to treat me. She probably saw me when I was 4 or 5 years old growing up. Thank you Patty.

I asked a nurse for a urine cup. They wouldn't give me one. So I took a piss on the floor. A person came in to clean up the urine. I said real loud.

"Get the f-out of here."

I thought this statement get the F' out of here, was what we used when we were going into Kuwait and liberating Kuwait. We were saying to the then Iraqis in Kuwait, "Get the F' out of here," as we were walking in. The Marines were walking in, not running.

I called the person outside the room.

"He's a monkey."

I thought spinal cord patients are really sick, in which they have heads like monkeys. Their heads are like smaller than normal people's heads. This is because of all the traction they were in. When I began to kick the Norwood Cinema door I thought my head was like growing.

Well now here, I had to do something, which would turn the whole thing around. So I stated.

"I'm an agent. I'm a Norwood Hospital Agent. I get paid from up in Maine."

I had gotten a check one day from Maine. I didn't know whom this was from. I thought this was pay as a Norwood Hospital Agent.

They must have contacted someone in a higher authority. A person about 50 came outside my door. This person would help me when I would begin to say something not proper. Then the tide was turned when I preached.

"There are going to make a movie about me. Whom do you want to play your part?"

Then I recalled the girl whom ran Emergency department. She was the girl whom did the bucked tooth move, before I was let go from being an employee at the Hospital. This time I fought back and said.

"How is Marylyn Monroe doing?"

We had hired her at the Hospital back in 1988 I believe to head Emergency. Everyone knew whom I meant by Marylyn Monroe. She had blonde hair.

I showed them my insurance card and I was able to go to McLean.

I would also yell out.

"Brockton, Brockton, Brockton, etc . . ."

I later heard the Neurosurgeon, whom would hand the instruments to the surgeon on my back operation, had now gone to a Brockton hospital. This guy would drive me up a tree. He was like a leach. He would take a bit from me. This is the hospital. They were like leaches. I holler out Brockton and this guy now feels this is all right to change positions to Brockton. They are grubs like in leaches.

At this hospital, I was going to have a meeting with a doctor and about 4 other patients. One of the patients knew karate'. I was thinking mainly with the karate' person to get some of the steel utensils and begin to have a "Coup de Hospital." I thought the karate' person would back me when I thought we would get some knives and to begin to demand to bring the cameras in. Have a "Coup de Hospital." The karate' person was transferred out because I don't think he had good insurance. So I didn't think of Coup de Hospital anymore.

I was in McLean about 30 days. I would *SIT DOWN* most of the day. While I would *SIT DOWN* I would talk to folks. I really would just *SIT DOWN*. I was thinking I got 30 days, as the Hollywood actors would get when they got into trouble. My sister Maura picked me up at the hospital. I came back to my apartment where I shaved off my beard. I had gone for a walk at the corner store and I saw one of my barbers and he said to me.

"How are you Chief?"

"*TERIFFIC.*"

I thought I was the chief of police, when I would give orders at the Cinema, to the officers. When I thought I would feel bad about being in a psychiatric hospital, and then hear these words from a person, I felt I wasn't in too bad of shape. This was what you needed. Someone whom would make you think the situation isn't too bad. This barber happened to be in WW 2.

I had a prescription for ativan, which was a cousin of valium. I wanted to be independent of doctors except for dr. Yado. On Tuesday I was supposed to see Jack Yado for an appointment. He only worked on Tuesdays in his retirement. But for this particular time I was being detoured by some higher power. On Tuesday night Jack Yado calls me up.

"*HELLO-E-U*"

I asked.

"How are you Bill?"

"All right doctor. I'm supposed to see a social worker on wed."

"You don't need a social worker."

Then Jack said something like.

"Nuts."

I began to think of the people in the Battle of the Bulge, when the American General had said, "Nuts," when they were trapped in Bastogne. The people whom fought in the Bulge were now equal to their last gasps.

"Jack, I'm supposed to be on ativan."

"You don't need ativan."

Jack came back immediately with.

I thought this Tuesday when Jack opened up for business he would have taken anyone in from the street. He was to the point of not charging anyone. Just walk right in. I thought the Chief at the World Renown Spinal Cord unit in Boston, was almost to the point of helping for free. The Chief was also in the Battle of the Bulge.

As I was driving one day, I saw a person whom was in the Bulge. I saw him with a cigarette on his left hand by side. I began to think left cigarette down. This meant to me on D-Day there were no cigarettes. Where there is no fellatio or cigarettes. I had tried to get fellatio at Norwood Hospital. You had to go up, which the Bulge was upwards. North would be towards Boston to me in Norwood.

I was in my apartment and I was thinking of going to the Norwood Hospital café. I thought the older person whom was watching me in Emergency was saying in my head, "Like a shot in the arm, like a booster shot." I had gotten a shot of ativan at Emergency. I was thinking of going to the Norwood Hospital café. I was also thinking Jack Yado was saying in my head, "we need back." Meaning at the Norwood Hospital, where Jack had his practice for about 50 years, that we needed back workers. This would mean people whom could help with a back capacity.

I saw a nurse walking near my apartment flat. I was saying to myself when I said, "get the f-out of here," I was meaning for the hospital personnel to get out of the security of the Hospital. They should try to get out and drum up more patients. Get out looking for business. Jack Yado had really built the Norwood Hospital after he got out of WW 2.

I did a little work with my computer. I saw some elderly woman outside sitting in chairs from their apartments. I began to think they were getting out. I began to write. I began to think of the President of the USA, the Mobil Corp. head, and also the head counselor for the Knights of Columbus. I was thinking of going to the Norwood Hospital café. I also thought about going to the V.A. I decided to go to the V.A.

I got into my car parked on the side and I saw the old folks sitting outside. I went down Hill Street and then onto the road under the bridge. The sun was very hot under the sky. I saw some people doing manual labor. I went under the bridge and I thought of when I came back from Sears. I drove by the Dedham Court. I saw a police officer directing traffic.

I was beginning to plan, what I would do once I got to the V.A. I was thinking I might go to outpatient and just collapse on the floor. Then when someone would come to see me, I would say, "I'm acting." I thought this would be rather comical.

I was going over the Charles River bridge from Dedham into West Roxbury, Boston, where the V.A. was. As I was going out of Dedham into West Roxbury, I thought about when I was caught from behind on a 70 yard run in football. This was the Norwood-Dedham Thanksgiving Day game. Chris of Dedham tackled me from behind. Now as I was going through Dedham into Boston I no longer felt bad about this run.

As I pulled into the V.A. grounds I thought of, "Coast," when the marines were surrounded in the Chosin Reservoir. I thought about just, "coast in." I parked my car in the Engineering space. I walked in the back door and to the volunteer office. I just sat at the desk. I began to feel bad about all the employees whom would project they were paid workers. I was having another flashback when I walked into the V.A. I was thinking about the wind which Hollywood actors are supposed to have before they become stars. I had thought this at the Stop & Shop when I was walking into the Stop & Shop after being fired. Now when I walked into the V.A. I was feeling these winds.

A doctor came into the office and began to use the phone. I was just sitting there, when I decided to make a move. I got up and I was about 10 feet away from this person using the phone. I then collapsed backwards onto the floor. The doctor got on the phone and said something like.

"Code blue, Code Blue, second floor volunteer room."

A few workers came down and began to unbutton my shirt. They thought I might have had a heart attack. I began to think I would rather have head problems than heart. I had been acting a heart attack. I then got up and said.

"I'm acting."

I went behind the desk and began to button my shirt up. One person stated.

"Who is this person?"

Then the volunteer head responded.

"He's is Bill Breen, a volunteer here."

This was Betty whom was in charge of the volunteers here. I thought she was selling me out. She knew I worked at the V.A. as an employee years ago. I knew from experience I was making news for the patients whom were really hurting, for them to talk about. I saw all the personnel whom responded to the Code Blue order outside the office. I saw all the woman personnel fondling their hands around their stomach. I began to leave the office and go out. This particular doctor there like said to himself. "Not so easy."

I tried to get by. I then took a quick shot at him around the chest and chin. He then stuck out is chest and another person there backed me into a corner. I was over by a few chairs, and I began to turn from left to right. The doctor then said.

"Bill's strong." Or "He's strong."

I was not swinging crazy. I was just about over by some chairs and I recall my volunteer badge fell off.

Well security came down and they put me onto a gurney. I told one of the security officers to get a piece of paper in my wallet. This was a pay stub when I worked at V.A. three years previously. He stated.

"This is a pay stub from the V.A."

Then someone replied.

"He was just discharged from McLean Hospital."

I began to think about before I was initially in McLean and I thought this was bad to be in McLean. Now I got the same vibes from the staff at V.A.

Then I would say my name and United States Marine Corps.

Not yelling out, but just a little loud.

"Who is his doctor?"

"First Lieutenant dr. John Yado United States Navy."

I said loudly but not loud.

Then someone said.

"He's a Marine."

They got a prescription from Jack Yado which I had in my wallet. I told him his telephone.

"769-2222."

They called this # and got the answering machine from Jack. Then I heard someone say.

"Have you ever used cocaine?"

"No."

They were asking me this because of how I acted a heart attack.

"Do you drink?"

Then asked me this question.

"No."

I repeated.

They had gotten a prescription from dr. Yado for syringes.

I would say constantly my name and United States Marine Corps. Then one of the woman doctors said something, which lingered on inside me.

"He needs someone to help him."

Then another doctor said.

"Should we put him on 4 North?"

"Let's bring him down Emergency."

Another doctor said.

The doctor, whom I had the physical confrontation with then, said something with his head held up high like.

"I'm going to write him up."

Meaning me as an employee, he was going to write me up for this incident.

They wheeled me down to Emergency and one of the doctors there said.

"He'll be looked at by everyone being wheeled to Emergency."

Emergency was about 100 yards over to the new Oreo Building. When I was in Emergency the first thing a doctor asked me was.

"Do you know where you are?"

I stated.

"Veteran's Hospital, West Roxbury."

"What day is this?"

I felt some higher power working in me. This was rather difficult to think here. I thought of my uncle Henry and how he directed traffic June6-10 1944 during D-Day. So I said like guessing.

"June 10, 1993."

The personnel here must have called McLean Hospital to find out what meds I was on. I would say my name then.

"United States Marine Corps."

I also heard one of the doctors there say.

"He's a marine."

My left hand I can recall had an ivy line going into the palm of my left hand. My right leg was over the side of the bed. Then a male nurse there says.

"Here is some ativan. You should feel better after this."

He put the cup of meds to my lips and also some water. Then after a short while he gave me 5 mgs. prolixin the same way. I was thinking I was like an animal here. Really like crazy in mind. I thought of all the veterans whom were treated through these walls. I thought of all the veterans here if anybody could get better, the best chances were from here.

I can remember looking at the ceiling and I thought after I got the meds I had felt much better. I could denote the idea of a, "glass ceiling." One person there asks me.

"Did anything that affected you have anything to do with the Weymouth Air Show?"

There was an air show in the town of Weymouth this day. I said.

"I don't think so."

Then someone else says.

"Are you allergic to any medicines? Are you allergic to penicillin?"

I stated.

"No, I'm allergic to ammoxicillin."

This was the cousin of penicillin.

"Take your medicine."

They all would constantly tell me here, in a truly caring way. Then as I was getting better with the meds being dissolved in my system I said.

"There are going to make a movie about me. Whom would you like to play your part?"

"What is the name of your movie?"

"*Coming Back*". A combination of the movies *Fighting Back* and *Coming Home*."

"How is Officer Cach?"

This was the security guard whom I knew from Norwood. I tried to let them know I knew one of the security guards. He wasn't on duty this day though.

"How about Robert Redford to play your part?"

I asked one of the workers there.

Well I knew I was helped here. I was in sane mind now. So I said.

"The Chinese, they are coming through the lines. They are coming in hordes of 1000."

I was really acting. I thought this would be interesting to hear. Then I said this statement.

"Code 60123, Code 60123, Code 60 123, etc . . ."

A doctor came in and asked me.

"What is Code 60123?"

I wanted to keep him interested, so I said.

"This is the code for the copy machine in the Oreo Building."

When I would copy articles for the doctors, I would go to the Oreo Building and use the copy machine which you needed the code to start the copier. The Oreo Building was the Research Building.

"Tell Officer Cach, I'll call him up."

"All right."

Someone said.

My name then I would say after this.

"United States Marine Corps."

Then I heard a person there say with quite a lot of feeling.

"He's is a Marine."

There was my own personal security guard outside my door. I asked him if he was in Vietnam. He said.

"Ya."

I told him.

"I walk right through doors."

He walks right into the room and said.

"I walked right through these doors."

I began to think of the guys in Nam whom would go in the villages and huts there. Maybe after they killed someone maybe they could walk right through doors. I heard years later from a Vietnam Veteran about walking through doors as. "You can't do steel doors."

At the end of my stay here, I began to blow out air out of my mouth and throat. Like blow out the air. "Stand at attention."

The male nurse then came in and took my blood pressure. I began to think of people taking your blood pressure in a totally new way now. I knew these folks here were Vietnam Veterans. They had the security of the hospital here. This male nurse was a Vietnam Veteran. I had on my tie with a coat. I would also say.

"I remember Nam when this was a tie. I have a tie on."

Well I finished off my stay here with.

"I pay back people for helping me. If you ever have any trouble breathing, eat grapefruits skins and all. There is something in the skins, which make you breath better."

I recalled back when I fought for my life and I thought of eating grapefruits skins and all. I thought maybe the grapefruit league in baseball I had a connection with.

I was Section 8 to McLean.

I was transferred to McLean again. I can recall the docks where the ambulances would pick up patients. I was having a flashback with this and the docks at the Stop & Shop. This is where the tractor trailers, would pick up the food. This ambulance was from Norwood. They never charged me for this ambulance ride. I was thinking the idea of, get that one too. Meaning get the one war and the second war too. I think Norwood was thinking with me being an agent they wouldn't charge me. They would be paid back, by having V.A. patients.

Years later when I got my Medical records from McLean, I read the V.A. had transferred my records right up to McLean this day. I began to think at the V.A. they are so sensitive, even paper they think this seriously about. My records from the V.A. were sent to McLean.

Well this time at McLean I didn't want to take any meds. I was eating a lot of *MARSHMELLOW* though. I would just take the ativan and 5 mgs. prolixin, which the V.A. told me to take. I told them I would only take 5 mgs. prolixin. They like fibbed and would tell me they don't have 5 mg. pills. I began to think at V.A. they said to, "take 5." Five mgs. prolixin. I thought someone really thought about where the prolixin was invented, which was France in 1950. Now with take 5, I thought America had done equal to the First World War. Meaning take 5 years of fighting equal to 5 years in World War 1. World War 1 for us, World War 2 for us, Korean War for us, Vietnam for us, and Persian Gulf for us. Now we could take the prolixin. Take.

I was to have a hearing, which a Federal Judge from Waltham Mass was to preside. This hearing was to be at held at the McLean Hospital grounds. I had a court appointed attorney. My attorney Henry Lebra. He would come in to prepare me for the hearing. I would begin to paint and when I would mix colors I would think the attorney would begin to worry, he really was on a psychiatric unit, mixing in with mental patients. Also a psychologist I would see would begin to worry about when I would mix colors also.

The time for the hearing came. I showed Henry the actual diary I had about when I had the secret flight when I worked at the Stop & Shop. This was when I said the word, "hello-e," when I actually flied. He read this and said.

"You should be doing the representing."

I also had the two pictures of my second secret flight when I landed and said this time, "u". The pictures were for the bruises I had gotten from the secret flight. Plus I had a tape, which I had. Henry said.

"The Judge won't look at a tape, but will look at pictures."

The Judge was from Waltham. When the Judge entered the room I said.

"How is Freddy Smerlas doing from Waltham?"

Everyone knew who Fred was. He was the pro-football commentator for the New England patriots. I had played against Fred when I was younger and hit him head on and he went down for about a 20 seconds count.

The Judge looked at me and I knew from watching Judge Franklin on television the Judges will help you. I knew this is a smart move to talk to the Judge outside the sanctity of the Hearing.

The judge looked at me and I knew this was a commitment hearing for me, for 6 months if I lost. If I won I would go scot-free. I thought everyone was really against me. But I could recall watching Judge Franklin from the television, that the judges will help you if you get in with them. The judge said to my question about Fred Smerlas I think something like.

"All right."

In a rather, not out to get me as much judge. My attorney Henry tried to not get me to talk to the Judge. But I knew the Judge would help me if you get on their right side. I was a little bit more cordial with the Judge now, but not 100%.

"This meeting will be recorded. Will there be any objections?" Said Miss *QUILLIAM* the secretary.

Then Henry said.

"This is fine with us."

There was the shrink I was seeing from McLean, and also the prosecuting attorney. There was a girl whom was monitoring the hearing. She also worked the tape recorder.

"The honorable Judge. Please all rise."

Everyone stood up.

The prosecuting Attorney W. first started the questioning to his first witness dr. Reyam MD.

"Dr. Reyam, which school did you go to?"

"I went to Harvard undergraduate as well as Harvard Medical School."

"What is Mr. Breen's diagnosis?"

"Mr. Breen suffers from a condition which is referred as schizo-affective."

"You went to Harvard Medical School dr. Reyam?"

"Yes, I did. I graduated in 1980, and did my residency at McLean. We have all these records from Mr. Breen here at McLean."

He puts all my about 5 notebooks of records on the table. The Judge then said.

"We can't take permissible Mr. Breen's psychiatric records."

I felt a relief, as I knew I wasn't like doctor crazy. Straight from the book would be all his knowledge. Then he went on.

"Mr. Breen had broken into the Norwood Cinema and also broke into his aunt's house where he tried to cut his wrist".

The cutting the wrist part was way off, as I knew I didn't have to say anything about this. I had cut my knuckles at my aunt's home. I thought he was really trying to get me to react.

I was sitting like I would see my uncle Joe Breen would when I would visit him. He was ex-chief of probation at the court in Dedham. I put my hands on the table like a praying mantis. I would see my uncle do this. I would occasionally take down notes with my left hand. I thought this meant left hand up and right hand up money.

Henry said something to the extent about the job I got at the Mobil Gas Station.

"Mr. Breen worked at the Mobil Gas Station as well as a research volunteer at the V.A. Medical center."

I thought about then how we could make amends in Vietnam. This would be like D-Day all over again. I also thought how we thought we would take 1,000,000 casualties if we had to invade Japan. This was before we dropped the bomb.

In this hearing Attorney W. said.

"Mr. Breen has been on a heart medication of 80 mgs. inderal."

I was taking this for the inderal research from Washington I was on. I retorted to the judge.

"A heart medication Judge."

Right here was the turning point for me. I thought having a medicine for the heart would be all right. This wasn't a psychiatric medicine. Then the attorney for the prosecution began to mention what medicine I would be on in hospital. My attorney Henry motioned for me to be quiet about the heart medicine.

I then thought the Judge didn't want to have anything to do with a heart medicine. The Judge knew psychiatric problems were all right, but to have anything to do with heart problems wasn't good. This Judge had to watch out, because the Judge whom was middle-aged didn't want to have anything connected with heart problems.

Dr. Reyam also said to the Judge.

"Mr. Breen had been on an injection of prolixin the last few years.

He also had been advised to take electric shock but declined."

My attorney then gestured to me, which made me think about how I worked at Mobil Corp. at the gas station. Their international headquarters was in Dallas Texas. I thought they might help me. I also thought about how I worked at the William Carter Co. they might help me also. Then my attorney said.

"My client has quite a lot to lose if he were to lose."

I thought of the chief of staff at the spinal unit, how he was Jewish as was my attorney. That if I were to lose then to some extent the chief would lose a leg. I then put my pen in my mouth like I had at the V.A. when I worked there once. When I did this, the Judge said.

"Has Mr. Breen ever been on Lithium?"

I learned so much here. I thought lithium was for people whom had trouble with overseas problems. I was at the V.A. where all the veterans from the Pacific and Atlantic were from. I now knew Lithium was for people whom had bad connections with water.

I began to think about this room where this hearing was taking place. This room must have been 200 years old. All old paintings were on these walls. I knew my uncle Henry's ghost was here, but also he was fighting against a lot of other ghosts. He tried to persuade the outcome. I thought if I were to go free then the song, "Ba, ba, ba, ba, ba, ba, little drummer boy." This was if I were to leave straight out.

"Mr. Breen took a swing at a doctor at the Veteran's Hospital." Judge asked.

"Huntington Avenue Veteran's Hospital?"

"No, the Veteran's Hospital in West Roxbury." Dr. Reyam said.

"Mr. Breen had been treated by a dr. John Yado. He isn't a psychiatrist. He is supposed to be a friend of the family."

I then stood up and said.

"Medical Examiner Judge."

I thought I had fought back when I told the Judge about the heart medication. A medical examiner treats you after you are dead. So I thought who could help the judge the most would win. I really thought the Judge was here to help me, even though this was a commitment hearing. I still thought the Judge would help me, whatever way this went. Another time I stood up and said.

"Heresy Judge."

The Judge then went to dr. Reyam and said.

"Are you familiar with Mr. Breen's religious beliefs?"

"I am a little bit."

He seemed reluctant to say this. I knew then the Judge was on my side. This day I was watching the show The Judge on television. The person in this show was a little slow, but he inherited quite a lot of money and didn't have to have help from anyone. I thought about how I had social security, which I was collecting, but this was barely enough to pay the bills. My attorney Henry then asked for a recess. He said to me.

"If I let you talk you will screw yourself."

We came back in and the prosecuting attorney was saying something and I said.

"I can't hear you."

He spoke up louder and said the same thing over again. I was thinking you could get people aggravated by saying you don't hear them, but you really do. I was writing down things with my left hand and I thought the more I used my left hand the Judge would be more against me. When I switched over to the right hand I knew the Judge knew I was a bit trepid.

When they were talking about the prolixin, I had been on I thought the judge was a bit a compassionate when she said.

"The prolixin is a muscle relaxant."

The Judge said.

"Mr. Breen we have had great success with clozaril. This might help you with your arm movements."

I thought of all the years I was on the prolixin. When me with the muscle problems, when I had the spinal problems, these shrinks were putting me on prolixin. My erections were way off. The muscles for bowel movements were way off also. I wanted them to think I had forgotten the spinal problems. But I think the truth was there wasn't anything else they could give me. I thought the doctors were only really interested in the money. I was on the stelazine but when the shrink heard I wasn't taking this, I was put on the injection of prolixin.

The doctor thought I was taking this because he was seeing the reaction from my other arm I was using. So when he found out I wasn't taking this he puts me on the injection of prolixin route. Now the Judge was asking me to try the clozaril. I said.

"Well Judge, I'll try this."

We left the hearing and the recorder was turned off. I came back in and asked the Judge.

"Have you ever heard of Judge Franklin?"

"No."

The judge said.

I was thinking when I had heard the words GET-UP, GET-UP, GET-UP, and how close I came to being arrested, when the police were going to arrest me, when I went off the wall at Norwood Hospital. I was saying this maybe good to be in contact with these folks from McLean. I was thinking the Feds in country might have been upset if I went scot-free.

I was always watching the show The Judge each day. To tell you the truth I don't know if this show was in this world. The lady whom was working the recorder I thought was saying to herself when I came back in, am I going against the sanctity of this hearing. I left the hearing with my baseball friend CHARLEY Buckner a name of the Red Sox legend. I was committed for 6 months. This was around July 10 or 11. I heard this was the hottest day in Boston since the 1880's.

I was put on clozaril. I began to talk to other people there about the Breen Maneuver. This is to use your other hand to help yourself with any problem. There was a girl whom was really depressed. She had been in the hospital for nine months really depressed. Now I was supposed to be committed for 6 months. I think this girl had no other options. She had tried to use her other hand the Breen Maneuver. I began to look at her and I was like seeing her as an employee at the Norwood Psychiatric unit. I served about 1 and ½ months and then I was let go. My opinion was I was seeing patients there, like an employee and McLean didn't like this. So I was let go.

I had about 300 dollars of cafeteria receipts, which I paid for my food there in the café. These pay receipts were stolen, as well as some clothes. Maybe this was the reason why I wasn't stayed committed. I think the workers there would be upset, I would claim the receipts for something.

I can recall one time when my shrink had come in with his children into the hospital. I began to talk as if I were a father figure. I would say the two words I made up on the two secret flights, hello-e and hello-e-u. This shrink didn't care too much for this so he tried to talk to me in his office. I went into his office and I didn't know this, but I dropped some playing cards. I must have lost about 60 dollars to this shrink in his office. He was a hell of a card player. We didn't really play cards, but if you look at money he gets, for seeing you, you can try to make this look like, you lost money playing cards with him.

I was let go after about 1 and ½ months. I came back to my apartment and I thought two letters I had Social Security and a letter from Mobil Corp. in Dallas Texas were missing from my apartment. I thought when the Housing Authority found out I was really treated at the V.A., they came in and fished around. I can't prove it but I was missing these two letters.

I had been home, and a while later, I marched in the Fourth of July Parade in Norwood. I would pass out candy. Before I got ready to march I thought mental problems are even more difficult than like a politician getting ready to march. We started in the South Norwood section of Norwood. As I was marching I heard the people of the folks whom had a bit too many whiskeys. You could hear the whiskeys in their voices.

We were going out of South Norwood to uptown Norwood and I could see the different type of people. These people were the people with more money, than South Norwood. South Norwood was where all the immigrants came at the beginning of the century. My grandmother came from Lithuania in 1913 and lived in South Norwood.

As we were heading towards uptown I heard someone say. "We are on level ground." This was right around where there was, the old tennis courts. When I would pass out candy, I had cutback on the pills, which I was taking, by 25 mgs. The days following, when I had cutback, I would think of all the candy I had passed out. When I would feel a bit nervous, I would think of all the candy all the time. I didn't tell anyone I had cutback till about 5 months later. I didn't want to let anyone know about the cutback. This was successful. I was home. *OH NO.*

ws out of tourney